Like Embers in the Night

by

Andrew Goliszek

The Wild Rose Press, Inc.
PO Box 708
Adams Basin, NY 14410-0708
Visit us at www.thewildrosepress.com

Publishing History
First Edition, 2024
Trade Paperback ISBN 978-1-5092-5929-8
Digital ISBN 978-1-5092-5930-4

Published in the United States of America

Dedication

To my sister Sophie, who survived the horrors of war
and Soviet labor camps and whose stories and
memories inspired this book

Author's Note

If history reveals nothing else, it is this: that throughout millennia, as inexorably as the seas rise and fall, the seasons appear and reappear, and the ceaseless onslaught of fire and ice consume and continually reshape the land, a veil of evil descends like a scourge upon the earth and finds its way inside the hearts of men. At times such as these, unlikely heroes are born and rise up, shining light where there is darkness; and, like embers in the night, glow brilliantly in mankind's blackest hours, forever changing the course of humanity, then vanishing as memories fade and the world once more forgets what ordinary men and women had done when hope was gone and all seemed lost. And so it was that in September 1939 a new and unspeakable horror pervaded mankind when the most brutal of men laid siege to Poland and brought hell, in all its fury, to every corner of the globe.

Chapter 1

Slumped almost lifelessly against the tufts of her chair, Wanda stared out an open window overlooking a lovely garden. Warm August rains had colored the grounds with a sea of vibrant flowers, their scent filling her room like a bouquet, though she barely noticed. Occasionally, even the most insignificant events would trigger memories from a time long gone: a soft whisper, a faint smell, the delicate warmth of a child's breath against her face, the soothing melody of a Mozart sonata. It was at those moments that Wanda would waken from her darkness and, with a look of fear spreading across her face, remember her family in Radom, who had no idea that a hundred miles south, the skies rained gray with the ashes of a thousand souls. On most days, they hardly detected the grainy soot around them, or even witnessed an evening sunset because the five incinerators in Auschwitz burned bodies day and night. Before long, everyone in Radom simply got used to it—a lingering grit that filled the air and settled upon the smallest things: a blade of grass, a delicate flower, a pat of butter spread on toast, a tongue that flicked unconsciously to rid itself of a strange and fleshy taste that hours earlier had been someone's husband or wife.

Wanda's memories these days came in and out, bubbling to the surface, then vanishing as if someone had reached in and wiped them away. On especially bad days, her world was a blank slate. No parents or grandparents to remember. No children or grandchildren to bring joy into her life. Not even a husband to keep her warm at night as she slept. The good sisters of Saint Francis who ran the Catholic nursing home tried as best they could to ease the bouts of anger and depression that overcame her. It didn't help that Wanda, afflicted with worsening dementia, had, on some days, reverted to speaking Polish to everyone around her.

That particular day in early August started out as a good one. Perked up and searching the room for anything familiar, her eyes sparkled as she caught glimpses of happier days, but suddenly turned despondent when she remembered the day she'd seen her beloved Janek for the last time. He was eighty-six years old when she walked into his hospital room in Pensacola, Florida—a gentle shadow of a man with a Polish accent, a kind but stoic face, and such remarkable stories of love and suffering and war that they'd forever changed the way his children and grandchildren looked at life. The few friends he had knew him as John, but he preferred Janek, one of the few reminders he had of his beloved Poland. His hazel eyes, so animated they seemed to dance, would glisten with tears whenever he spoke of what his wife and daughter had endured in the brutal labor camps of Siberia; and it was at those moments when Janek's eyes would harden and expose the very depths of his soul.

Wanda remembered that morning like it was yesterday, picturing the ventilator tube snaked down his throat, his frail chest rising and falling to the rhythm of oxygen that kept his heart from stopping until his family could all gather and say goodbye for the last time, staring at his ashen face as she thought back to a life that most people would find unimaginable. Her bony fingers clenched as if holding onto something precious, she looked at a small painting of the Virgin Mary, then glanced around the stark room. Something familiar pervaded the silence. She felt alone, as she did on most days, though she rarely knew it or even cared, until her memory suddenly returned and she would whisper, "Janek. Where are you, my love?"

For the entire minute she was lucid, Wanda remembered pressing Janek's cold hand into hers, thinking that he had no business being alive; that his children and grandchildren should not have been born; that whosever's life he'd ever touched or changed, made better or worse because of his existence on earth, would be as different as night and day. And that whatever he'd done in his next forty-six years, whatever contributions he'd made, significant or not, would have vanished like dust in the wind were it not for the fateful day he'd risked his life and walked to freedom while twenty-five thousand other Polish soldiers marched in lockstep to Stalin's execution order and on to their graves in the Katyn Forest.

Over the years, Wanda had heard the tragic story of Stalin's Katyn Massacre and the Polish soldiers executed and thrown into mass graves where they lay buried and forgotten for decades. Though she'd never spoken of it herself, and it pained her to listen to Janek's heart-wrenching tales of war, she'd accepted that, for him, it was cathartic. But as she grew older, and because she'd experienced more pain in seven years than most women would suffer in a lifetime, she prohibited even a mention of anything Russian, especially when Janek would describe a time in history when hell, in all its fury, had made its home on earth.

Wanda's Poland, with a population of only thirty-five million, was the only Allied nation that fought in World War II from the opening salvos of Nazi occupation and Russia's invasion in 1939 until Germany's surrender a week after Adolf Hitler had committed suicide in 1945. For its size, no other nation on earth had given as much or had suffered more than Poland: millions sent to gulags or deported to labor camps in Kazakhstan and the frigid regions of Siberia; millions more exterminated in concentration camps dotted across the Polish landscape; countless men, women, and children starved, tortured, murdered, and worked to death simply because they were Poles. By the time the war ended, its population had been reduced by at least ten million.

To survive six years of the two most brutal regimes in modern history was not only unlikely, it was truly a miracle. But amongst the ashes and smoldering ruins, broken lives and unspeakable horrors of war, miracles did happen; survivors who'd lived to tell their children of war and gulags, of victors and unlikely heroes, trying in vain to forget the shocking cruelty of a world that had taken everything they had from them, living their lives in the shadows as if no one else in the world cared. It's said that these heroes are like embers in the night, glowing brilliantly in the darkest moments of history, forever changing the course of humanity, and then, just as suddenly, vanishing as distant memories fade and the world forgets what ordinary men and women did when hope was gone and all seemed lost.

Wanda and Janek were two of those seemingly ordinary people, and on that day and at that moment in Sandusky, Ohio, Wanda remembered.

"How are we doing this morning?" one of the sisters asked as she walked into Wanda's room and pulled the curtains apart to let the morning sunlight in. She never expected a reply, but she'd ask anyway, just in case. Wanda squinted when the brightness hit her eyes, and her gaze drifted from the Virgin Mary to the window.

Sister Regina, who had taken her vows less than a year ago, was a young, plump nun with a roundish face and rosy cheeks. Rarely were her lips not turned into an infectious smile and not once did she enter Wanda's room without a song or a kind word. On Wanda's darkest days, the good sister was a godsend, though Wanda would see only a pretty but unfamiliar face and hear neither song nor kind word.

"You look nice this morning," Sister Regina said. She pulled the blanket over Wanda's lap and gently brushed the hair from her eyes. "Did you sleep well?"

"*Tak, zrobilem,*" Wanda said. "Yes, I did."

"What are you looking at?"

"I see Janek," Wanda said, her finger reaching outward, a broad smile crossing her face. "He's in the garden, picking those beautiful flowers for me. Do you see him?"

Sister Regina's face beamed with delight because she knew that, for a moment at least, Wanda's memory had returned. "Yes, I do," Sister Regina said happily. "I see him smiling at us."

"Isn't he handsome?" Wanda asked her.

"He is," Sister Regina said. "Very handsome."

Wanda then closed her eyes tightly. Her lips turned downward, and she began shaking. "He's gone," she said. "Janek's gone. The earth is moving, and the sky is so dark. Why are they doing this to us?"

"Wanda?" Sister Regina adjusted the blanket and saw the void that had suddenly come over her. "You rest now," she said, looking dolefully at Wanda's face and seeing the emptiness of someone who'd just descended back into her darkness.

Chapter 2

Wanda sat trembling as she rocked back and forth, clutching six-year-old Sophie to her chest so tightly her hands grew numb. The electricity in the city had been out for days. Water was scarce. What little food she had left would run out in a week. Through a small broken window, she could see and hear the nonstop barrage of artillery fire off in the distance. Fingers of thick black smoke rose columnlike along the horizon and swirled eastward in the cold wind. For days, the pungent stench of death and decay had descended upon the city of Lwow like a shroud.

Next to her home, a row of small houses sat empty, abandoned for weeks as news of Germany's march through central Poland had finally become a harsh reality. In the back of one, tattered, mud-stained clothes flapped in the wind on pieces of clothesline; behind another, toys lay scattered like trash beneath a broken swing. Stray dogs, bones visible through ragged fur, roamed and sniffed the streets in search of edible scraps. A perpetual haze from smoldering buildings and bridges lingered in the air, and no amount of water could wash the sting from Wanda's eyes. It seemed, from what little she could see, that many of her neighbors had fled their homes and sought refuge as far from Lwow as their legs would carry them. She wondered now why she'd not done the same.

Wanda suddenly flinched and tightened her grip on Sophie as a bomb whistled through the air, followed a second later by a thunderous explosion that rocked the ground and sent plates crashing. An eerie silence followed. She could hear her own heart beating as though it would leap from her chest. A minute later, she could breathe again, waiting and listening.

Sophie's face, buried against Wanda's breast, was wet from tears. Her lips quivered as she fought to catch her breath. "When will they stop?" she pleaded. "It's so loud."

Wanda wrapped an arm around Sophie's head, trying to ease the pain in her ears. "It'll be over soon, my love," she said, hoping to soothe her daughter as best she could. But as she rocked Sophie in her arms, a dread came over her that one of those bombs would drift from the sky and snuff out their lives at any moment.

Paralyzed with fear, Wanda huddled like a child herself, too frightened to move. She'd grown frail, her small, thin-boned frame reduced to a shadow of what it had been from constant worry that Nazis would flood their land and that her home would be bombed at any moment. Her beloved husband, Janek, an officer with the Second Polish Artillery Unit, had been gone for months, preparing for and then fighting off a swift and brutal Nazi invasion of western Poland that began the morning of September 1, 1939.

"*Nie płacz*. Don't cry," Wanda whispered into Sophie's little ear, tears streaming down her own face as she watched the sky above Lwow grow black, then cocked her head and listened to the sickening rumble of distant tanks that threatened to end the world as she had known it.

"Please, dear Lord, make the world a better place for my child. Make this all be over soon."

For a few moments, the shelling stopped, and only then did she think of Janek and the last night they'd slept together, embraced in each other's arms, promising that no matter what happened, they would always be there for each other. Her breathing quickened as she pictured his lean, muscular body pressing against hers and his strong but gentle hands caressing her so tenderly it took her breath away.

"Don't move," Wanda had told him. "I want to remember you this way, inside me, a part of me forever."

"I love you so much it hurts to know I'm leaving tomorrow," Janek had told her, then kissed her so passionately she felt every inch of her body quiver.

Even after Janek had fallen asleep, Wanda was content just to run her fingers across the hair on his chest, to watch him breathe and to gaze upon his handsome face and naked body. As she fell into a deep sleep herself, she dreamed of walking the fields together, holding hands, kissing, teasing, talking for hours about life and children and all the things that lovers say when life is good and nothing else in the world matters except the moment they hold each other in their arms.

Long before her world was set ablaze, Wanda, born to a wealthy family in Radom, just south of Warsaw, had given up everything—land, a villa, servants—when she met Janek, who'd grown up on a small farm a few miles from her home, near Lodz. When he left the farm for technical school in Radom, he'd sung on weekends with a local church choir; and it was there that Wanda had first noticed a handsome young student with masculine concave cheeks, wavy brown hair, and broad shoulders, who'd locked eyes with her and couldn't take them away. She flushed as she stared back, wondering what he must have looked like beneath his clothes, imagining being with him, kissing him, stroking him, and being stroked back. At the end of the evening, a mutual friend introduced them to each other. Soon after, they fell madly in love.

But as young Wanda would soon learn, in a world where people were often judged less on character than on social status, love was not enough. To their misfortune, Janek, born into a family of poor farmers, had nothing to offer but himself, and Wanda's noble parents could never approve of such class interactions. "You must end this now," her strict father had insisted. "If you don't give up this foolishness, we'll disown you."

But love, such as it was, had tossed those warnings aside. The lovers met each night in secret. Their passion grew. Wanda became pregnant. Her parents, incensed at her defiance, had carried out their threat; so Wanda and Janek married in a small private ceremony, knowing they would never see her family again.

A year went by. Wanda had given birth to a beautiful little girl they named Sophie. Janek graduated from technical school, secured a government job with the Polish national railroad, and the happy couple moved to Lwow where they settled into a new life with no one else in the world but each other.

"What's happening, Mama?" Sophie clutched a small ragdoll to her face, covering her eyes and pressing ever closer to Wanda's breast, startling her back into reality. "Why are they doing this?"

Wanda had no words for her daughter, a beautiful little girl with a soft round face and deep brown eyes who only weeks earlier had played with friends and run through fields of lavender, but who suddenly was too terrified to even open her eyelids. Poor little Sophie had not smiled for weeks, which broke Wanda's heart, since her daughter's wide smile would bring such joy and laughter to her parents. The two had become inseparable since Janek left for the western front. And all Wanda could do was try to comfort her daughter because she knew that together they would either survive the onslaught or die embraced in each other's arms.

"When is Daddy coming home?" Sophie asked. "Is he coming home?"

Wanda suddenly felt wetness as Sophie soiled herself on her mother's lap. "*Tak, moja kochana.* Yes, my love," Wanda answered, her voice quivering. "Soon." She knew it wasn't true. She wasn't even sure if Janek was still alive. All she knew was that his reserve unit had been called up when intelligence learned of German forces mobilizing along the Polish border for what Hitler hoped would be a final and overwhelming attack designed to crush Poland's defenses.

As Wanda closed her eyes and tried rocking little Sophie to sleep in her arms, she remembered the summer of 1939 as a happy and peaceful time. Even after German boots first hit the ground in the west, those first days in eastern Poland—far removed from the front lines where Polish troops were already fighting and lay dying—had felt so serene and distant from the reality of war that children still laughed and played as though life stood still. But despite a pact by France and Great Britain that guaranteed the sovereignty of Poland's borders, Wanda's hopes had vanished when she heard on short wave radio that two million Germans had begun a war of racial and ethnic annihilation. Word spread of shocking brutality, entire villages obliterated, refugees shot while fleeing their homes and left to rot where they lay. In Warsaw, only 250 miles from Lwow, the invasion and occupation were especially merciless since Hitler saw the city as the very heart and soul of Poland.

Wanda, whose estranged family lived just outside Warsaw, prayed that the horrors descending upon her homeland could not possibly be true. But despite her prayers, Lwow was thrust into complete darkness. Shells from a thousand artillery units fell like rain from the sky. Relentless swarms of Luftwaffe planes dipped and crisscrossed beneath the clouds and dropped incendiary bombs that filled the air with fire and smoke. The ground shook nonstop, as if hit by a series of earthquakes. Homes that only weeks ago had entertained birthdays, baptisms, parties, and weddings were lifted off their foundations. Dishes, cups, and family heirlooms Wanda had brought with her to Lwow crashed onto the floor and in an instant became a million pieces of debris. Sophie clung to her mother and screamed as they both ran from the room and desperately sought cover.

We're both going to die, Wanda thought. My beautiful little girl, only six years old, will never see her seventh birthday. But maybe a quick death was better, she figured, than being tortured by Nazis, burned alive, disfigured beyond recognition, or lying in a bed with no arms or legs for the rest of their lives. She covered Sophie's ears so her daughter couldn't hear the screams of agony as mortar and machine-gun fire ripped through the chaos and sliced bodies apart. For what seemed like an eternity, Wanda and Sophie cowered in a dark hallway, waiting for the ceaseless shelling to end. Not even the mice that normally scurried through their home in the middle of the night were brave enough to venture from cracks and crevices in search of food.

It was like that for the next five days, with German forces repeatedly breaking into the city only to be repelled by local volunteers who fought to the death in long and bloody skirmishes. Wanda had nearly gone out of her mind with terror as the invading forces began summary executions, destroyed businesses, scorched homes, stabbed defiant women and innocent children with bayonets or burned them alive in their homes. Nearly every hour, she heard the ringing of gunshots outside her window, and whenever she dared look out, she could see Polish soldiers lined up and shot. She thought, Is that what is happening all over Poland? Is that what's happening to Janek?

Within a week, food and water had become so scarce that survivors crawled from their homes after dark and scavenged streets and alleyways on their hands and knees for anything they could find. Electricity was nonexistent. Dust and ash from ceaseless explosions and fires hung in the air like a gray mist, covering everything it touched. The Luftwaffe continued to pound churches, hospitals, and water and power plants in a last-ditch effort to bring Lwow and its citizens to its knees. Even in the dead of night, batteries of 150mm guns waited silently to shred whatever was moving or left standing.

And then, on September 17th, with shocked Poles reeling from atrocities that German troops had inflicted on innocent civilians, a new monster, with its own thirst for Polish blood, laid siege from the east and set out to devour the remains of what only weeks earlier had been one of the most beautiful cities in all of Europe. The Soviet Union, emboldened by the Nazi invasion, had declared that the Polish state no longer existed and ordered the Red Army to link up with the German army in its own march toward the city.

As Wanda soon realized, her beautiful city of Lwow had become the beating heart that would soon be ripped from Poland by two ruthless enemies. Almost 600 miles from Poland's western border, it had been completely encircled by the Germans only weeks after their massive assault. But just when it seemed as though the city itself would be wiped from the face of the earth, a miracle: Adolf Hitler, not yet ready to confront the Soviets, had capitulated and ordered his bloodthirsty troops to leave the city, and Lwow, after reluctantly surrendering to the Red Army, was swallowed up into what would become known as Liv Oblast, a province of western Ukraine.

Every minute she could, Wanda listened in rapt disbelief to news on her shortwave radio, so she knew that within twenty-six days of Germany's invasion, despite a valiant effort by her countrymen to defend their homeland, Warsaw had surrendered. One hundred forty thousand Polish troops had been taken prisoner. The Polish government had fled into exile, leaving behind a nation conquered and divided, with Wanda and Sophie living under Soviet occupation with little hope and no way out.

At first it seemed that Lwow would be far better off with the Russians than the Germans. After all, everyone knew what the cruelty of Nazi occupation meant. News of bloody massacres throughout Poland had been on everyone's lips. Nazi soldiers, Wanda had heard, had their own favorite way of killing. Some were callous and efficient, lining up and mowing innocent victims down as they stood naked along trenches they'd been forced to dig, sometimes with their bare hands. Others preferred victims kneel before shooting them one by one in the back of the head. Still others enjoyed making them run while shooting them. The sadistic ones used babies as target practice by having fellow soldiers throw them over a trench as they picked them off in midair and watched the bodies drop lifelessly into the pit. Innocent children picking potatoes in the fields outside Warsaw were killed by mortars and machine-gun fire. The more Wanda heard of these atrocities, the more she believed that God in His infinite goodness had finally intervened.

But even after the German army left her city, most people weren't aware of the Nazi-Soviet pact in which Poland was to be divided between Germany and the Soviet Union. Things changed almost immediately, and Wanda learned quickly that her life would never be the same. Within days, the Soviet government broke the terms of surrender and began deporting countless Poles to the far reaches of the Soviet Union. Jews, 110,000 of them, were taken either to newly created ghettos or to concentration camps. Whoever remained was either arrested, murdered, or left to work as slave labor in what was left of the city.

To Wanda, the Soviet soldiers, with a stench that clung to their tattered uniforms like rancid sweat and urine, were nothing less than filthy barbarians who'd marched into a paradise they never knew existed. She was certain that nothing they'd ever seen in Russia compared to Lwow, which was why they sacked and looted everything they could get their hands on until every store shelf lay empty. Life turned into a daily struggle for survival. If she didn't steal, she and Sophie would surely starve; if she got caught stealing, she'd be imprisoned or killed; if she were imprisoned, she would probably die anyway, so she stole and prayed to God that He make her a good or a lucky thief.

But for Wanda and Sophie, that's when the horror began in earnest. Not two months after the Red Army had crossed the border and laid waste to eastern Poland, Moscow's thirst for blood was exceeded only by its unquenchable thirst for power. No darkness they'd ever seen or despair they'd ever felt compared to what they were seeing and feeling at that moment. The Soviets, ruling over Lwow like it was part of Mother Russia, thought less of their captives than of the stray dogs hunting streets and alleys for scraps of food. From the first day of their occupation, Poles were transformed from human beings—living comfortable lives in nice homes, tending lovely gardens—to little more than animals. Money was worthless. Fuel and food had become so scarce that Wanda would sneak into fields and forests in the dead of night, collecting dung she'd burn to keep from freezing to death, and digging up with her bare hands whatever she could to keep her and Sophie alive. The only thing she had was hope that their nightmare would soon end, and even that was quickly slipping away.

One night, Wanda heard Sophie whimpering, begging for food in her sleep. "Why are we treated worse than farm animals?" she whispered beneath her breath, crying and stroking her daughter's head to comfort her, but then realized, as she watched her daughter's face twist in pain, that neither of them meant anything in this new world they found themselves in. What right did she ever have to complain about a missed meal, a broken nail, a room too hot or too cold, when she had heard the screams of mothers as they watch their innocent children slaughtered? Wanda suddenly felt shame that what she'd considered suffering was nothing more than inconvenience that paled when compared to the sufferings of a child pleading for a crust of bread or for her life.

By the winter of 1939, life in Lwow had become unbearable. The NKVD, Stalin's secret police and precursor to the KGB, had taken over everything in Poland, including executions, deportations, and administering the gulag system. No one was immune from arrest: peasants, farmers, members of trade unions, town councilors, civil servants, government officials, members of the police force, skilled workers, teachers, volunteers at hospitals and organizations. Fear swept over the city: fear of being woken in the middle of the night by cars screeching to a halt; and fear of hearing ugly voices of Russian soldiers pounding on doors, which meant that the cars with Russian men had come to take away whoever was sleeping peacefully. So great was the fear and so sickening the anticipation of arrest that some had become relieved when it was finally over, and they no longer had to endure the trauma of wondering every second of their lives if they would be next.

It seemed to Wanda, who prayed to God daily and always found peace in her faith, that she was no longer living in a world that a merciful God created. As she learned soon enough, the Russians preferred killing slowly, by cold and starvation, instead of by summary execution like the Nazis. So, she and Sophie simply existed as best they could while the Soviets began to erase all influences of Polish culture. Street names were changed, libraries burned, ringing of church bells banned. Schools were taken over by Russian authorities. Children were forbidden to study Polish literature or speak their native language, forced to learn Russian. Religious beliefs were ridiculed. Children were taught that Poland no longer existed and there was no God. All day, their heads were filled with the glory of communism and the love of Joseph Stalin.

As the Soviets began to remold Lwow into their likeness, Wanda and Sophie were barely surviving. There was never enough food. Neighbors were thrown from their homes, arrested, never heard from again. Wealthy businessmen were branded enemies of the state and lost everything they had. Security officers routinely stormed through locked doors in the dead of night, flashlights and guns pointing, even at young children, to check papers, ask questions, sometimes for hours, and search for weapons or anything else that could be used against the state. The visits typically came at night to strike fear into everyone's hearts. Within a few months of the invasion, not a single family was left unscathed, with a husband, son, or brother either killed, imprisoned, or deported to gulags, where many would work with little food until they fell and died where they lay.

By the late winter of 1940, just when Wanda thought life could not get any worse, Soviet officials began a series of mass deportations to the interior of Russia. As the number of trains coming into Lwow increased, Wanda had become suspicious, terrified of hearing a knock at her door, which meant they would be next to go. She'd heard rumors that women and children were being sent out of Poland to God knows where, the men to prisons or labor camps from which many would never return. Her instincts proved right, as she would later discover. Of the two million Poles deported to arctic Russia, Siberia, and Kazakhstan, at least half would be dead within a year of their arrest.

Wanda's day-to-day existence was nothing more than that. What little food she scraped together was never enough. She took whatever work she could find while Sophie stayed behind with neighbors and friends and waited for her mother to bring home scraps of meat and an occasional can of milk. Rationing had become a way of life to keep from starving. With the worst of winter coming, Wanda hunted for extra blankets and clothes that would save them from freezing when their electricity went out. And every night, as she tucked Sophie into bed and kissed her goodnight, she waited for word that Janek was alive and that somehow they would all survive and soon be reunited.

"Sleep, my love," Wanda pleaded, trying to soothe her daughter's constant hunger pains. "Daddy will be home soon, and everything will be better." She gave Sophie water with a little sugar to ease her discomfort. Sophie closed her eyes and fell asleep. Wanda left her daughter's bedside, then sat alone for hours, crying and wondering if Janek had been captured and imprisoned or if he was even alive.

"Open!" A loud voice suddenly boomed through the night air. "Open now!"

The rapid banging sent a chill through Wanda's entire body. Her heart was racing. Her breathing nearly stopped. Jumping up from her chair, she rushed to the door, and as she opened it, her worst fear was realized when soldiers, revolvers drawn, shouted to her that she had ten minutes to gather only what she could carry.

"I have a small child," Wanda pleaded but saw no compassion from the guards who'd burst in and started ransacking the room.

"Get on with it," one of the guards said, ignoring her pleas and pushing her away.

Sophie awakened and called out to Wanda from her bed. "Mama, what's happening?" She ran to her mother, trembling and screaming, her little face distorted with fear. "Mama!"

"Stay beside me," Wanda told her daughter. "Get dressed quickly and put on your warmest coat."

Wanda raced through the house, packing a few clothes, two small blankets, and a bit of food as two brutish soldiers looked on. Not knowing what would happen next, she couldn't believe that a mother and six-year-old child were being arrested. Was it something I did, she wondered? Was it because my Janek is a Polish officer? Who would have told the secret police? Why would anyone do this to us?

"Move, you filthy pig," the younger soldier yelled, no doubt angry that his sleep had been disturbed in the middle of a cold night. "Hurry or you won't bring anything!"

With Sophie latched tightly onto her mother's hand, one of the brutes pushed them both out the door. A neighbor, sobbing uncontrollably, stood alongside her in the bitter cold, holding two small children. That was all the poor woman could carry, nothing more. Wanda looked out at the darkened homes along her street and noticed that one of them had a curtain drawn with a shadowed face peering out. Could it be, she wondered? That someone she thought was a friend had sought favor with Soviet officials and reported her as the wife of a Polish officer? As inconceivable as that seemed, Wanda knew that, in this new world, even selling your soul and watching your friends and neighbors sent to their deaths was possible.

For the next two hours, streams of people, beaten, poked, and pushed by angry soldiers wielding rifles, joined others already waiting. When the order was given, a collective wave of humanity turned and began to move. Leaving their home, their life, and all their possessions behind, Wanda and Sophie took one final look back, then marched from the city to a line of waiting trains. The night air was especially frigid. The wind howled and bit into their exposed flesh like needles. A full moon shone on the grim faces of as many as a thousand men, women, and children who were prodded and crammed into cattle cars not meant for human beings.

Inside the car, Wanda and Sophie huddled in a corner, shivering. "Where are they taking us?" Sophie wailed, tears streaming down her face. "Where are we going? I want to go back home."

"I don't know," Wanda answered. She wrapped the blanket they'd taken from home around Sophie and watched fifty more people, some with nothing more than a suitcase and the clothes on their backs, pushed through the door. "We'll be back home soon, my love. Stay close to me and try to keep warm."

Within an hour, the train, its engine straining, the white steam from the large smokestack billowing up into a thick cloud, lurched forward and slowly began its eastward trek across the Polish border.

"Where are you taking us!" an old woman screamed in vain as the train rocked side to side and built up speed.

They were not told where they were going or how long they'd be gone. And as Wanda and Sophie embraced, shocked to their core at being taken from their home, all they could think about was Poland disappearing behind them and the frozen steppes of Russia ahead.

Chapter 3

Poland's Eastern Front
Early October 1939

A month had passed since German aircraft rained hell on the town of Wielun, killing twelve hundred civilians, and the battleship *Schleswig-Holstein* launched an all-out assault on Danzig in the opening salvos of World War II. By October 1939, all of Poland had been swallowed up in Hitler's quest for world domination. The attacks had lasted until Warsaw fell to its knees on September 27th. A week later, on October 6th, the last of the Polish forces that fought against Russians invaders had surrendered as well, giving full control of Poland to the most brutal of all men on earth.

Janek, who'd miraculously escaped a few weeks earlier, and then fought valiantly against the Soviet invasion from the east, was captured again, his unit gathered up and marched fifty miles across the border to waiting trains that would take them to prisons in western Russia. After having battled day and night against superior forces, the arduous trek had left many exhausted and too weak to go on. Some of the men, their arms and legs numb, their spirits broken, had dropped to the ground and were left to die. Others were executed after pleading with guards to end their suffering. The Russian soldiers, who hated Poles anyway, were more than willing to comply and simply tossed their prisoners to the side and shot them where they lay.

Janek, a farmer before he'd become a soldier, was strong, surviving the fifty miles and arriving relatively unscathed at a train depot near a small town along the Ukrainian border. Whenever the wind blew and the pungent scent of grass filled the air, visions of his walks with Wanda in the fields near Lwow filled his mind, and he prayed to God that his precious wife and daughter had survived the onslaught that destroyed their city.

As the men lined up in front of waiting trains, some weeping for the families they'd left behind, convinced they'd never see them again, a tall Soviet officer took two steps forward to the edge of a wooden platform and looked down his nose at the prisoners. Everything about him screamed NKVD, the Peoples Commissariat for Internal Affairs. His khaki shirt, pulled tight against his waist with a brown belt and a strap that ran diagonally across his chest, bore the telltale insignia of the agency: a hammer and sickle covering a dagger, and beneath it the letters НКВД woven in yellow against a crimson background. A blue hat with a red band and bronze star in the middle of it covered his head. His blue pants, meticulously creased as if painted onto his legs, ended at a pair of black knee-high boots that glistened in the sun. Holstered at his side was a black pistol the men before him were certain had been used many times.

Janek stood beside his men, looking up with disgust at a man looking down at them with equal disgust. Goddam soulless pig, Janek was thinking. If they killed my wife and child, I'll die trying to kill as many of you.

The NKVD officer raised a bullhorn to his lips and began to speak. "You are being taken to Smolensk, where you will await your final orders." He stared condescendingly over the ragged heap of men who could not allow their eyes to even look at him. He couldn't care less if they looked up at him or not. They were defeated Poles; and defeated Poles, as far as he was concerned, were nothing more than animals awaiting slaughter. "Poland no longer exists," he continued in a harsh tone, "but if you cooperate, you will live another day and you will return home."

His emphasis that Poland no longer existed tore into Janek's heart like a dagger. And though he and his men stood shoulder to shoulder like brave soldiers who fought till the end to defend their homeland, every last one of them shed tears at the thought that Poland as a nation had been wiped from the earth.

The Poles, who trusted the Soviets as much as they trusted the devil, did not believe the officer's words for a second, but they took heart in knowing that at least they'd survived the long march and could soon sit down with a piece of bread and rest their weary bones. All Janek could think about at that moment was kissing Wanda goodbye and promising that he'd come back to her no matter what. Everything else was a blur: men screaming and falling dead next to him, his unit's surrender to a Red Army that overwhelmed them ten to one, their march east away from the Polish border, and now the sight of a contemptible Soviet officer spitting orders at them as if *they* were the ones who'd started the war. I *will* come back to you, my love, he thought. I *will* survive this.

The commanding officer continued. "The train ride will last a few days. When you arrive, you will be questioned and given further orders." And with that, the officer turned and climbed down from his platform while guards with machine guns directed the prisoners to board the train.

****

A week had passed since Janek and his men were captured inside Polish territory, forced onto waiting trains, and taken to one of the many prison complexes dotting the Russian border. Once there and unloaded, the exhausted men were separated into smaller groups and marched to individual prison buildings.

Most of the prisoners, including Janek, were thrown into crowded holding cells too small for even one man to sit on the floor. So many had been arrested throughout Poland that the prison teemed with new arrivals. The stench of a thousand men, soiled and unwashed, sick and dying, hung like an asphyxiating cloud in the dank air. As the mass of bodies grew day after day, men turned violent, fighting for every precious inch of space. The lucky ones found themselves pressed tightly against a wall and could at least ease their misery by relaxing their legs and allowing themselves to be pinned upright by the prisoners next to them.

One morning, Janek watched as the cell door opened and a new arrival set eyes on his new home. A look of shock and disbelief overcame the young man; and it saddened Janek to think he'd turn old before his time. How can it be, Janek asked himself, that such hell could exist on earth? And that was just one such place. When the regular prisons had been filled to the brim, offices, hospitals, schools, basements of government buildings, railroad depots, and stores were taken over and transformed into makeshift detention centers. Any space, big or small, that could house the massive influx of detainees was conscripted and used as an improvised jail.

When the men were finally taken to larger, more permanent cells, they could at least sit and sleep with their legs drawn up to their chests. No concession was made for men who fell sick. Even prisoners at death's door were ignored, the thought being that one less prisoner meant a little more room for the others.

The stench of filth and human waste so overpowered new arrivals that even the hardiest of men would double over and vomit, adding to the slime that covered the floor. A single bucket, used for a toilet, would overflow in less than an hour. There was no such thing as food without maggots; and though practically inedible, every morsel was gobbled down by men too hungry to be picky eaters. As Janek soon learned, one of the ways that Soviet guards broke down prisoners psychologically was to keep their cells so filthy and hot that lice would flourish. And because delousing procedures were not at all efficient, the lice thrived and reproduced in a frenzy, crawling over and biting the men in a furious attempt to feed on their flesh and blood.

By week's end, the rancid smell of unwashed men with dirty teeth and festering wounds that oozed blood and pus had so dulled Janek's senses that he thought no more of it than he did the scent of his own sweat. Rarely was there enough soap to wash the layers of dirt that clung to their bodies, so it simply became part of their skin. On days when he fell into a stupor, numbed by hunger and pain and the screams of men in cells next to his, Janek considered himself lucky because at least his mind could shut itself down and give him a moment of peace.

Interrogations went on day and night. Men were

sometimes beaten before interrogation, but usually only after they'd failed to confess to crimes they didn't commit or to give up information they didn't have. Howling and cursing from rooms adjacent to the cells pierced the stagnant air and seemed to linger in everyone's ears before fading away. No one knew when or if they'd be beaten, even if they answered questions truthfully. Some, especially those foolish enough to put up resistance, were locked in special cells shaped like chimneys and designed so that even a single person could not sit down. After many hours, an exhausted prisoner would collapse, his knees buckled painfully against the wall of the cell, forcing him to stand up again. Eventually the pain no longer mattered; and sometimes the prisoner, hopelessly begging forgiveness and agreeing to cooperate, would die wedged inside the cell and had to be fished out and discarded.

Janek feared for his men, but more so for himself because as a valuable Polish officer he was expected to know more and would be tortured in return for information the NKVD assumed he was withholding. He was right to fear, because no sooner had the Polish officers been separated from the enlisted men, Janek was bound and taken to a small windowless interrogation room. In the middle, below a single light bulb, stood a metal desk and wooden chair, nothing else. The walls and floor were cement; and as Janek stood waiting, he could see blood stains in the dim light in one corner of the room. He braced himself for his face-to-face encounter with an NKVD agent who had the absolute power to charge anyone with crimes against the state.

An interrogator, along with two large guards, entered the room from a back door. A large man with sunken cheeks and jet black hair, he sat down at the desk and lit a cigarette, inhaled deeply, then put his pen to a sheet of paper in front of him. As a good and loyal NKVD agent, he'd been trained to view anyone before him as an enemy of the people, a counterrevolutionary working against Soviet power. Scribbling a few notes, he looked up at the man trembling before him. After another long drag, he filled the room with a thick layer of smoke.

"Name and rank," he demanded.

"Janek Gorowski. Captain."

"Unit served when captured?"

"Ninth Artillery Regiment."

"Hometown?"

"Lwow."

"Ah, Lwow," the interrogator repeated. He watched Janek's eyes with interest. "It fell in ten days, you know." There was obvious glee in his tone. "So many dead. Such a pity. Anyone there that you left behind?"

Janek looked back at his interrogator's crooked teeth and a set of thick lips that stretched into a sardonic grin, and for a second considered lunging at the man's throat. "No," he lied, afraid to say anything that would endanger Wanda and Sophie, should they have survived the relentless bombing. And at that moment he swore to himself that he'd sooner die a million times over than give up his wife and daughter.

"No?" the interrogator asked again skeptically. "No wife? No children?"

"No one," Janek answered. "I was told they died when Germany invaded."

He knew the NKVD had descended on Poland like a swarm of locusts and no doubt were hunting for anyone with ties to Polish soldiers, especially officers. Janek's entire life, the details of his birth, his family, his education and marriage, travels abroad, his job with the railroad, any friends and associates he had or actions he'd taken, were no longer his but belonged to the state. Everything, innocent or otherwise, aroused suspicion. Since October 1917, the U.S.S.R. considered one either with it or against it, either part of the revolution or a counterrevolutionary because, as they saw it, the Soviets were not conquerors but liberators, saviors of the weak and the oppressed in a world that needed to shed the evils of capitalism and fully embrace communism. To form a totalitarian society, information was not only vital, it was at the heart of the Soviet system. Without cooperation from citizens like Janek and Wanda, it was doomed to failure.

Dispatched throughout Poland, the NKVD had infiltrated the very fabric of the nation to ensure that nothing stood in the way of that dream. And so, in Stalin's utopia, there were only three classes of people: those who'd been in prison, those who were currently in prison, and those who would be in prison for not accepting completely and devotedly that they were no longer Poles but willing subjects of Soviet rule. Cooperation with the NKVD had soon become an odious routine; wives of prisoners testified against neighbors; workers who feared for their jobs betrayed colleagues and friends; mothers turned a blind eye to the horrors around them so their children could have milk and bread. To Janek, hometowns such as Lwow had been transformed into hateful and detestable places where monstrous beings ruled, and innocent people were subjected to the most vile existence.

"I see here that you have a diploma from

Polytechnical School. Were you an activist there?"

"No," Janek answered. "I studied civil engineering."

"Really? What else did you study? Religion? Anti-Soviet history?"

"Of course not," Janek said. "Just engineering."

"You think us fools?" The interrogator pounded on his desk, seemingly agitated that he had to continue this charade. "Are we to believe you never participated in counterrevolutionary activities?"

"Never. Not once."

"You're a filthy lying Polish pig and you'll spend the next ten years in a gulag unless you cooperate and confess everything."

"I can't confess to what I've not done or to what I don't know." Janek hoped he was convincing enough to avoid a shattered jaw, or a cigarette burn to his face or genitals. He'd seen other prisoners returned to their cells with broken fingers, missing teeth, and bodies so bruised, bloodied, and swollen they looked as if they'd been pummeled and left for dead. "Believe me, if I knew anything I would tell you, but I don't, I swear."

"We have irrefutable evidence that you are an enemy of the people," the interrogator then stated matter-of-factly, raising his cigarette and inhaling deeply. "You must sign a confession beginning with a statement that you repent your anti-Soviet activities and promise to reform and provide further testimony should it be necessary." He stared up at Janek, hoping that his change of tone and his lie about evidence was convincing. If not, there would be many more days and nights of questioning, of breaking Janek down until he saw the misguided error of his ways and accepted his place as one of a million new and brainwashed Soviet allies.

"I'm innocent of everything," Janek said. "I'm a soldier with the Polish army and have no enemies but the devil."

Ignoring Janek's denial, the interrogator demanded: "Give me names of anyone you know in Lwow who is resisting Soviet authority…anyone who might be acting against the State."

"I know of no one like that. I've been gone for months, even before the invasion." How many times must I say it, Janek was thinking. How stupid are these people?

"What about your men?"

"I don't know anything about their wives or children. We fought together for only a short time, so I have no knowledge of their families."

"You're lying!" the interrogator shouted in an attempt to startle his demoralized and exhausted victim into a confession. "Confess! Confess that you know!" He stood up and walked around the desk until he was eye to eye with Janek, his cigarette inches from Janek's face. "Confess!" he shouted again, the spit from his lips dribbling down his chin.

Janek tensed his muscles and readied himself for a beating, or worse. In the next second, his face burned, and he saw a flash of stars as the back of his interrogator's hand smashed the side of his head.

"You know, don't you? Confess and you can go back to your cell."

"I have no information," Janek pleaded, his ear bleeding from the blow. "I have nothing to confess. My men and I were following orders…"

Before he could finish, Janek dropped to his knees. Another blow, this one to his midsection, knocked the air from his lungs. Still another to his head left him almost unconscious. The interrogator waved his arm toward the door. Doubled over on the floor, Janek struggled to breathe, gasping for life, grimacing in pain as the two guards lifted him by his arms and dragged him away.

The interrogator sat back down, hurriedly drafted a preliminary report of his actions, and slid the paper into a file folder marked prisoner number 9478. "Bring me the next prisoner," he ordered, satisfied that he'd made Janek think twice about lying to him because the next time he'd not be so kind.

Back in his cell, Janek was finally able to breathe. He couldn't hear in one ear and his ribs felt as if they'd been shattered.

"What did they want to know?" one of the men asked, his eyes wide with fright.

"They want you to report on anyone you know back home. Names and addresses of people who won't accept Soviet authority or who may be part of the resistance."

"And if we don't know…or refuse to say?"

"They'll beat you whether you know or not. That bastard will assume you're lying, so prepare yourself."

The men surrounding Janek grew somber, paralyzed by fear, knowing they'd have to survive that hellhole until questioning was completed, sentences meted out, and transportation made ready for the convicted to be transported to the far reaches of Siberia. Who among them would be next, they wondered, or have the strength and courage to resist? How many would die unless they confessed something? And how much longer could they endure the hell they'd found themselves in?

Every so often, Janek would notice that a few of the men seemed healthier and better fed, and he assumed the traitors were rewarded with a good meal and more sleep in exchange for information or a false confession. It wasn't surprising that an extra piece of bread and two hours of uninterrupted sleep would encourage even the most hardened and intransigent prisoner to break his resistance. Besides, who could blame a poor soul who'd been told that unless he signed his name to a confession his wife and children would be arrested and tortured. Some men, knowing this, had committed suicide rather than expose and risk the lives of their families.

Janek had discovered that just thinking of Wanda and Sophie would make his ordeal more bearable. So that's what he would do: picture their faces, visualize life with them after the war, imagine the joy he'd feel when they were finally reunited. He drifted into and out of consciousness, barely able to force open his eyes, wondering at times if it was all part of a dream. His prison didn't seem real. Human beings, after all, would not do what was being done to fellow human beings. From his initial strip search upon arrival to the horrific images of hungry and emaciated men with ragged beards, blank eyes, and grim faces battered and misshapen from constant beatings, aged ten years in less than a month, it was as if he'd traveled back five centuries to the Middle Ages.

"Jesus, give us strength and hope," Janek prayed, then slumped against a cold wall and fell asleep in the arms of his beloved Wanda.

Chapter 4

February 10, 1940

For Wanda, whose frail bones ached from the bitter cold, the beautiful world she'd known had crumbled around her. As the Polish border disappeared, the profound dread that everyone she loved and everything she knew had suddenly vanished was now a reality. She tightened her hold on Sophie, whose shivering and whimpering broke Wanda's heart. Huddled masses pressed against them, a hundred eyes that once gleamed with joy filled with tears, faces that laughed and told stories and kissed other faces now twisted in agony. For everyone on that train, it was as if they'd just crossed into an unknown abyss, and the fear of that made even grown men collapse and cry for days.

"Who are these strange brutes?" Wanda had asked herself those first few days of the Soviet invasion, seeing them outfitted in rags, rifles attached to their stooped shoulders by pieces of string, some riding on tired horses that limped beneath nothing more than skin and bone. "How could such miserable wretches now be masters of Poland?"

She was confused and confounded, but no more than the Russian soldiers who were told they were being sent to liberate their oppressed brothers and sisters and instead found well-fed horses and cattle, peasants dressed in fine clothing, more food than they'd seen in their lifetime, and store shelves overflowing with goods that made their eyes well up with tears. So great was their disillusionment with the Soviet lie that some deserted. The majority, however, dismissed the lie, intoxicated by what they were seeing around them, filled with hatred at the thought that while they'd been living in squalor and denial back in Russia, these filthy Poles had been living such beautiful lives.

When the arrests first happened, even the hardiest of men and women lapsed into shock and disbelief, crying, screaming, falling into a stupor at the idea that it wasn't a dream. Wanda and Sophie had been crammed together with fifty other people, the train car outfitted with a few thin slats for air, four buckets for bathroom use, and a small hole in the floor in case one could not get to a bucket quickly enough. There were no seats, only makeshift shelves that a few lucky souls could lie on while everyone else leaned against one another like blocks of dead wood. Men, women, and children of all ages were thrown together, shocked and embarrassed at the thought of relieving themselves in the midst of others. Some of the men defecated into their hands and threw their waste out the open-air vents rather than take down their pants and sit on a bucket in front of women. For the women it was worse, especially if they were menstruating.

Only after it had crossed the Polish border did the train occasionally stop, and everyone was allowed to rush out at once to relieve themselves as brutish soldiers stood guard with rifles at their sides, ogling and laughing at the women. But mostly the train pushed north as days and nights blended together, rocking and swaying in a seemingly endless march toward hell. By the second week, Wanda was lying in puddles of urine and wet feces, sleeping where others had relieved themselves, too cold, hungry, and exhausted to even care.

Forty boxcars per train was not unusual; forty to fifty people in each was common. Over a thousand deportees had left the train station, not knowing where they were going and believing they might not be coming back. No one was immune. University professors defecated next to shop owners who vomited between mothers and screaming children. The only relief from the suffocating confines came during an occasional stop when everyone was allowed out for a breath of air, given some black bread and foul-tasting water, and ordered to a shower while the boxcars, filled with sewage, lice, and maggots, were hosed out. In an hour, the misery began anew, the boxcars sealed shut, and the battle for survival continued until the next stop, perhaps two, maybe four days later. Wanda and Sophie were lucky to be assigned to a train that at least stopped. A train leaving Poland a few days after their arrest had run into trouble and didn't stop for twenty-five days. When it finally did, every Pole who'd arrived—almost two thousand—had frozen to death, their bodies stacked together like mounds of human icicles.

The moving hell lasted for three miserable weeks. From the little she could spot through the wooden slats, Wanda saw nothing but endless, naked steppe moving past the narrow window, frozen wilderness, lifeless and sterile. It was like nothing she'd ever seen: a uniform bleakness that seemed too harsh and alien to be real. Every so often, the train rumbled past farms or small villages in the middle of a wasteland where native people would stop and stare as though watching a circus train go by. Day after day, the steppe grew harsher and bleaker, with no end in sight. A lone factory popped up here and there, spewing fumes so noxious it seemed as if birds would drop mid-flight from asphyxiation.

Wanda had only heard stories and myths of this brutal land, a vast swath of gulags and mental hospitals constructed in the 1930s by Joseph Stalin during the Great Purge. After Lenin was laid to rest in 1924, Stalin viewed anyone with ties to the Bolshevik party as a threat, so he began a campaign of terror, killing or imprisoning everyone he suspected. On his orders, the secret police held mock trials, found most people guilty, and either executed them or sent them to gulags where over a million people were killed between 1936 and 1938 alone. Those who survived starvation and disease said they would rather have ended their misery with a quick bullet to the head than endure the horrors of Stalin's labor camps.

"I'm hungry," Sophie whimpered, too tired and weak from shivering to move from her mother's arms. "When are we going to eat?"

Wanda quietly broke off a small piece of bread she'd hidden inside her coat and slipped it into Sophie's mouth before anyone noticed and tried to steal from her what little she'd saved for her daughter; not that it mattered, since many on the train had already gone into shock and had frozen to death. An older neighbor she'd known since moving to Lwow sat motionless against her husband; her eyes, Wanda noticed, had not blinked in hours. A few children younger than Sophie had died in their mothers' arms, the tiny corpses held tightly as if that would somehow bring them back to life. When the train stopped and was searched, the lifeless children were ripped away, tossed from the cars like garbage, the parents watching and screaming as the doors closed and the train once again continued its journey while small bodies lay scattered like black dots in the snow.

Wanda attempted to comfort one of the women with little success. "I'm so sorry," she said, reaching for the woman's trembling hand. "God is with your baby." The woman sat paralyzed as if she had died along with her child.

Sophie began to cry uncontrollably, imagining herself tossed into the snow. She pushed herself hard against Wanda's breast. "Am I going to die like the other children?" she asked. "Are we all going to die?"

"Don't cry, my love," Wanda said. "We'll be okay." She then pulled the blanket over her daughter's head and tried as best she could to keep her warm.

Another two days went by. Another stop, this one in a remote area two hundred miles north of their last. Wanda had finished her last morsel of dried crust twelve hours ago, so it was a relief when the guards distributed one bucket of water and a bucket of thin soup per boxcar, along with a small piece of bread for each person still alive. When the water was gone, some reached out and gathered snow to quench their thirst. Wanda didn't move from her corner of the car for fear of losing whatever warmth she had, heartbroken as she listened to children around them wail like animals from cold and hunger. The old just whimpered and begged God for a quick death to end their suffering. In some cases, their prayers were answered, and the dead would travel alongside the living for hours, sometimes days, until they arrived at a station and were thrown from the train like blocks of ice.

The train, lightened from countless bodies having been tossed each day along the route, had taken the living and the new dead to a small village in Kazakhstan and deposited in a strange country where brutal Siberian winters would freeze a person's limbs in minutes. Because Russia desperately needed farm workers to supply their citizens and their army, Wanda and her neighbors had been selected to work in faraway settlements as slave labor.

After three weeks, the passengers were finally told where they'd arrived. Their final destination, Kazakhstan, the largest landlocked country in the world, stretched more than four-thousand miles along the Russian border. A third of the country was Kazakh steppe, a massive stretch of grassland and cold desert that Joseph Stalin found perfect for the notorious system of forced labor camps where people were literally worked to death. Considering their three-week journey through one of the harshest regions on Earth, Wanda and Sophie were fortunate to have made it there alive with their limbs intact. Winter temperatures throughout the country, especially north where they found themselves, reached forty below zero, with frigid winds that swept across the barren landscape and pierced even the heaviest winter coat. Many deportees who arrived hadn't been able to bring enough to warm their skin and quickly froze to death.

"Everyone out!" a guard shouted. The doors slid open as a cold wind battered the remaining deportees. "Move out!"

"I'm cold," Sophie cried, icicles hanging from her coat, the words forming a thick cloud on her face.

Wanda held her daughter as tightly against her as

she could. She would have sacrificed her own life if she thought it would comfort Sophie and protect her from the bitter cold, but she also knew that if she died, Sophie would not last another two days. "Put your hands inside my coat," Wanda said, "and keep you face close to me. That'll help keep us both warmer."

Sophie snuggled into Wanda's arms, so weak from the cold that even her whimpering faded and eventually stopped as if frozen along with everything else. "When can we eat again," she pleaded, not even the cold pain of winter diminishing the pangs of hunger that constantly gnawed at her.

Wanda pulled out a few remaining crumbs of bread and put them against Sophie's lips. "Don't chew too fast," she said. "There's no more until we get to where we're going."

Like a baby bird, Sophie opened her mouth and took in what seemed like a feast, barely swallowing the tiny morsels. When she finished, she closed her eyes and fell against the comfort of her mother's chest, a small blessing that for a moment freed her from a cold she'd never experienced before.

Wanda knew little about Kazakhstan, but what she did know was that it extended into the southern reaches of Siberia, which historically had been part of modern Russia since the sixteenth century and was one of the most sparsely populated regions on Earth. What she didn't know was that by the spring of 1940, fifty-three gulags and over four hundred slave labor colonies lay scattered across Kazakhstan, Siberia, and the Soviet Union. The camps were unimaginably brutal. Workers would spend up to twelve hours in open steppes with nothing in every direction. Escape was impossible, if not suicidal. Each day, workers collapsed and died and then were taken by other workers to unmarked graves, where their bodies would lie forever. If laborers refused to work or were not cooperative, the Soviet party line was that it was better to kill too many than too few. The threat of painful starvation was often enough to induce even the most intransigent worker to pick up a shovel from morning till night.

"Let's go, let's go," the guards barked, prodding Wanda in the back with their clubs.

"Where are they taking us?" Sophie asked her mother, her little legs trying to keep up. Bitterly cold winds howled from every direction, battering them so hard it was difficult to walk, much less move as fast as the guards wanted them to.

"Somewhere warmer," Wanda hoped, then tightened her grip on Sophie as they took one small step after another in swirling drifts of snow.

People were separated into groups depending on where they were being taken, some transferred to other trains that travelled south and farther east. Wanda and Sophie had been selected for work at a labor camp in northern Kazakhstan where not even trains could travel, which meant three more days and nights exposed to bitter cold and Siberian winds. In some places, the snow was waist deep. Wanda's only thought was how she could protect Sophie from whatever lay ahead of them. If Janek was there with them, he'd surely try to save them, she thought. But where could he be? Was he fighting somewhere? Was he still alive?

She remembered sitting with Janek at their kitchen table when he confided to her about Germany's plans to attack Poland and why he would have to be mobilized with other reservists to a special artillery unit along the western front. "How do you know this?" Wanda had asked, tears streaming from her eyes. "Are you sure?"

Janek had nodded, and they both sat and cried and felt helpless because they knew that their beautiful world was vanishing before their eyes.

Wanda's thoughts of Janek were suddenly interrupted by a booming voice that pierced the night air. "Move faster!" the Russian guard ordered.

Wanda and Sophie plodded along a narrow road as fast as they could manage until they came to a line of waiting ox carts. No one dared ask why they were being transferred from the train to ox carts, but it seemed the only way to get to where the labor camps were located. Besides, after three weeks in the brutal conditions of a boxcar, with so many dead left behind, not one among the group thought it could get any worse.

As Wanda climbed aboard one of the carts with Sophie, she again thought of her beloved Janek and wondered where he was at that moment. What she couldn't have known was that five months earlier, as Janek fought valiantly against the Nazi invasion, Polish forces had lost several thousand men and were forced to retreat to Poland's eastern border, which was poorly defended because no one suspected the Soviets had similar intentions. So, on September 17, 1939, when the Red Army broke through Poland's defenses, they slaughtered 7,000 brave soldiers and destroyed whatever they could on their march toward Lwow. Janek, lucky to have made it through the battle alive, was taken prisoner along with thousands of others and began a long trek through Poland to the Russian border.

There was nothing any of his soldiers could do but

surrender, Janek had convinced himself, then wondered if he'd ever be able to look into his children's eyes for fear they'd catch a glimpse of something he was ashamed of. A painful secret. A darkness buried deep in his heart that only survivors who knew what it was like could share.

Once the Soviet Army had surrounded his unit, the choice was obvious: die or save his men. He chose the latter. The Soviets rounded up the survivors and began a relentless march east toward a prison in western Ukraine. In Janek's group, two thousand prisoners, many of them Polish officers, walked towards the Russian border. One morning, when they stopped to rest in a small Polish village, Janek thought of Wanda and Sophie waiting for him in Lwow and decided at that moment that he would rather try to escape and risk dying in that village than be executed wherever it was they were taking him.

As luck would have it, because Janek had been mobilized so quickly, he'd kept a few civilian clothes with him. Before his surrender, he'd thrown them on, figuring the Soviets would assume he was a civilian working with the military and treat him better than an enemy combatant. So, as the prisoners sat and rested in the small village, the guards all busy eating and relieving themselves, Janek recited a quick prayer and then stood up, making sure the guards were preoccupied, took a few steps away from the formation, and began walking in the opposite direction alongside some villagers who looked on and seemed shocked by what this man had just done. His only thought was to look straight ahead, hoping that someone wouldn't scream for a guard to toss him back into formation or more likely shoot him in the head. Instead, he found himself walking for what felt like an eternity.

Not daring to turn until he no longer heard the shuffling of boots, Janek cocked his head and listened. A few feet away, just past the outskirts of the village, a flock of birds whistled and sang as a cold wind swept through a line of trees in front of him. It was as if nature was telling him it was finally safe to stop and look. Still shaking with fear, only when the wind died down and fell silent did he turn his head. Nothing. Everyone had disappeared. Not even the dust from a thousand boots filled the air. Finally able to breathe, Janek dropped to his knees, looked up to heaven, and cried at what he'd just done.

At that moment, it seemed to Janek that he was given back his life and nothing else in the world mattered. Why, amongst the several thousand other soldiers, he asked himself, was he chosen to be the one to walk away, to feel the wind against his face and listen to birds sing instead of hearing the sickening crack of a final gunshot? For Janek, it was like being reborn, given another chance to make right whatever wrongs he'd done, to become a better man.

And then, when the reality of what he'd done finally hit him, Janek whispered, "My God, what have I done? I abandoned my men. They'll probably all die…every one of them…and I'm going to live." He then pictured his men's faces, watching him walk away, not uttering a word, looking on with lifeless eyes, some nodding as if to say "Goodbye, my friend," as he walked to freedom while they marched to their deaths. "May God forgive me," he prayed.

The men that Janek had abandoned were ultimately taken to Kozelsk and Starobielsk in western Ukraine, which already held mainly Polish officers. Other groups of soldiers were transported to prison camps scattered throughout Russia. For months they were interrogated by the secret police, who often charmed them into thinking they'd soon be released but in reality were selecting who would live and who would die. When nothing more could be uncovered about their families or their activities, Joseph Stalin signed a death order condemning all the prisoners to what the secret police called the supreme penalty: shooting. The Polish prisoners, more than twenty thousand, were moved from the internment camps to several execution sites, including the Katyn Forest.

Within a few days of his daring escape, Janek had joined another unit of the Polish Army stationed along the eastern border. For the months that followed, he lived with the pain of knowing that friends who'd laughed and eaten and drunk with him, shared stories of family, and slept beside him as war raged on, may have all been slaughtered and left to rot where they lay while he walked away to live a full and beautiful life. But then, with some consolation, he rationalized that if he'd not chosen to walk away that fateful day, if he *were* one of those bodies that were probably buried in mass graves, the precious children and grandchildren he and Wanda had planned to have would never be born, his legacy nothing more than a cold statistic etched in a moment of time. And as much as he tried to forget the past, he knew he would hold those brave men in his heart till the day he died.

What Janek could not have known was that his premonition of Polish executions was right; that every one of the soldiers he'd marched with would be shot and buried in mass graves in the Katyn Forest; that once Germany was defeated, the Katyn lie would become official history for the next half century to perpetuate the myth that Nazis were the murderers while Soviet soldiers were gallant liberators. Even President Roosevelt dismissed Nazi claims of finding mass graves in 1943, despite overwhelming evidence of Soviet complicity, because at the time everyone thought it was simply German propaganda used to discredit the Soviet Union. And Russia, desperate to hide its vile crime from humanity, had happily allowed Germany to take the blame, knowing from the outset it was Joseph Stalin who committed one of the bloodiest acts in Soviet history.

But the real untold story of the massacre was the Soviet attempt to exterminate Poland's intellectual leadership. Because most Polish officers like Janek were reservists—doctors, lawyers, engineers—they needed to be eliminated for fear they'd return home and undermine Stalin's utopian socialist dream. Miraculously, Janek had managed to escape what the Soviets would not admit they'd done, not until April 13, 1990, forty-one years after the head of the KGB released the details in a secret memo to Nikita Khrushchev. The final total: 21,857 killed, including the Polish officers Janek had left behind and would think about every remaining day of his life.

"I'm freezing." Sophie trembled beneath her blanket and pressed closer to Wanda. She felt a warm trickle of urine run down her leg and relieve her suffering for a few seconds until it turned cold against her skin.

"Come closer to me," Wanda said, wrapping both her arms around her child. "Try to sleep."

By the time the train had reached its final destination some days earlier, it was nothing more than a row of putrid cages with the stench of urine, vomit, and dried feces caking every square inch. So, despite the freezing temperatures, everyone thanked God they now had air to breathe and trees to look at. Even the snow was lovely to see. When the order was given, the line of ox carts loaded with straw and human cargo nudged forward. Wanda held Sophie on her lap and they both pressed their faces against one another to keep warm.

Again Sophie asked, "Where are they taking us?" And again Wanda said, "Somewhere warm, my love," hoping it was true, even a little.

In the bitter cold, even the blazing sun could not take the chill from her thin bones. The snow was an alabaster white, pristine, free of the ash and dust and debris from artillery shells and fallen shards of brick. It seemed almost serene and hauntingly beautiful were it not for the sickening crunch it made beneath the wheels of the ox cart that formed two lines of ruts in the road and reminded her that she was being taken far away from the warmth of their home. Sometimes, when moonlight broke through the clouds, illuminating the snow and casting ghostly shadows along the banks, a tranquility permeated the air; but then, especially at dusk, Wanda could hear the faint cry of wolves in the distance. Were they following, she wondered? Would they be bold enough to sneak up to her and Sophie in the dead of night? What would she do? What *could* she do other than sleep with her precious daughter in her arms and hope the smell of humans would keep the creatures at bay.

But other than ravenous wolves and freezing to death, the biggest fear Wanda had, as their ox cart moved ever faster through the snowdrifts and headed north, was not knowing how Polish women would be treated, especially by Russians, in this new and strange land. Like all Polish women, who considered themselves the caretakers of the Polish state and the heart and soul of Poland, Wanda had a deep sense of national pride and self-worth. Men were the soldiers and breadwinners, but in a deeply Catholic and familial country, women bore the special burden of ensuring that Poland, as a nation, remained pure. And for that reason, whatever atrocities that would occur in Kazakhstan to any of the women would be kept secret, hidden in their hearts forever.

Matka Polka, the holy mother of Poland, had symbolized the view of women in Polish society for centuries. Just as Mary cared for Jesus, and watched over the Polish nation, the women of Poland sacrificed their lives and inherited the responsibility of caring for families and ensuring Christian values. Few other nations revered mothers as much as the Poles, and no nation had placed such a premium on the woman's role as nurturer, steward, and soul of the family. Every last woman taken to Kazakhstan, Wanda included, was convinced they would no doubt return to their homeland not feeling worthy to be a piece of that soul.

"We're here!" a guard cried out. "Everyone off!"

Wanda and Sophie climbed down and saw nothing that looked even remotely like home.

"Where are we?" Sophie asked.

"A farm, somewhere in Kazakhstan," Wanda replied.

What is that?" Sophie gazed up at her mother with a puzzled look. "What's Kaz..." The word stuck in her mouth.

"Move on," a guard ordered. "That way." He pointed a gun toward a winding road.

49

As daylight faded, snowflakes drifted from the sky like shimmering diamonds, dancing and weaving and sticking to their faces and coats and blankets as they pushed forward into a vast and desolate labor camp. A few large barnlike structures sat off in the distance, leaning precariously to one side as if battered by constant winds, surrounded by enormous fields that seemed to stretch for miles to the horizon. Some of the women fell on their knees and cried bitterly. Others stared ahead lifelessly, having given up any hope they would live another week.

Wanda stiffened with pain from three weeks of sitting on wooden boards. "Don't be afraid, my love," she told Sophie as bravely as she could. "I'll protect you." She pulled her daughter closer, then cried at the thought of not knowing when or if Janek would see his child again.

Sophie reached up with her tiny fingers and slid them into her mother's hand. "I'm frightened," she cried. "I want to go home."

"We will, sweetheart," Wanda said, trying as best she could to comfort Sophie. "We'll go home soon." She tightened her grip and marched through the falling snow, praying to God that they would soon be given a little food and a bed to sleep on.

Chapter 5

Sandusky, Ohio
August 8, 2004

On Sunday morning, the little chapel at Wanda's nursing home was smattered with a few residents who still remembered where they were or felt well enough to rise from their beds and attend mass. A stained-glass window of Saint Francis, birds perched on his arms, filled one of the side walls and allowed the sun to break through and light up the wooden pews. A simple altar covered in white linen faced the cross of San Damiano, a replica of the large Romanesque crucifix before which a young Saint Francis of Assisi had been praying when he claimed to have heard the voice of God commanding him to rebuild His Church.

Wanda, whose mind that morning was lifted from its void, had insisted that Sister Regina take her to mass. "Over there," she said, pointing to her favorite spot in the back right pew where she'd gaze at the intricate piece of colored glass and, for the next hour at least, would be at peace.

"Is this all right?" Sister Regina asked, positioning the wheelchair Wanda sat in next to the pew.

"Yes, thank you," Wanda said, then closed her eyes, rosary beads wrapped around her fingers.

"I'll be back for you after mass." Sister Regina

stroked Wanda's head before heading out the door.

Wanda began reciting the rosary, which had always been a comfort to her during the darkest hours of her life. "Our Father who art in heaven…" Wanda's lips stopped when she heard herself say, "As we forgive those who trespass against us." It was difficult for Wanda to hear those words, especially on mornings when she was told "to love your enemies and pray for those who persecute you," but particularly on mornings when she was lucid enough to remember the years she'd spent being persecuted herself by an enemy that had nearly killed her entire family.

"Father," she whispered as she looked up at Saint Francis's face. The stained-glass image reminded her so much of her own father that she imagined herself sitting on his lap, listening to tales of Poland and its rich history.

"Tell me more, Father," she remembered pleading. "Tell me about Poland." Wanda's mind suddenly drifted from Sandusky to Radom, her birthplace, where she would beg her father to retell stories of her homeland, and from the back row of her pew, she became oblivious to the sound of prayers and chimes and hymns and instead imagined listening to her father and watching history unfold in her mind.

Poland, she remembered her father saying, was at the crossroads of northwestern Europe and the fertile plains of Eurasia, where waves of migrants, nomads, settlers, and invaders had shaped and molded the land into a diverse patchwork of Slavs, Germans, Huns, Mongols, Celts, and Samaritans. With so much interaction between people of varied cultures, languages, and religions, Poland's population had become as diverse as any in Western Europe.

Wanda knew that until World War II, Poland was noted for its ethnic diversity and richness, with Germans living in the southwest, Ukrainians in the southeast, Yiddish-speaking Jews in towns and cities, and mixed populations stretching into Lithuania and Belarus. But by 1945, the war had radically eliminated much of the minority population, so much so that Poland had become one of the most ethnically homogenous nations in the world.

"How did Poland start?" Wanda remembered asking her father, an innocent question posed by an innocent child who knew nothing about the land in which she lived.

Wanda's father had thought about it for a minute and then recounted the tale that Poles had been telling their children for a hundred years: that the medieval legend of Piast the Wheelwright was the supposed story behind the very birth of Poland.

As legend had it, he explained, a young man named Piast Kolodziej was paid an unexpected visit by two strangers who repaid his kindness and hospitality by casting a spell that kept Piast's cellar filled with food. Seeing the miracle, his countrymen declared him a prince and the first ruler of Poland, whose name came from the Polan tribe, descendants of the Piast dynasty, and literally means people of the fields. It wasn't until the tenth century, when the first ruling dynasty was formed under Duke Mieszko, that the country emerged as a Polish state. The marriage of Mieszko to Princess Doubravka of Bohemia had become known as the "baptism of Poland," arguably the most momentous event in Poland's history because Catholicism had henceforth become the most important aspect of Polish culture. A series of rulers converted their nation to Christianity and created the Kingdom of Poland, which only then was integrated into the culture of Europe. What followed were centuries of brutal military expansion, war, and economic prosperity that ultimately led to the reign of kings and monarchs that took their place among the nations of Europe.

In the meantime, Poland endured wave after wave of invasions by Prussian tribes that sought conquest and territory. The Mongols then marched through the heart of Poland, destroying everything in their path. This "Period of Fragmentation" tore the nation into provinces that left its people divided and influenced by their conquerors. Along came Casimir the Great, whose reign lasted thirty-seven years, and who once again strengthened the kingdom by a renewed expansion of territory taken from Poland during the previous two centuries. It was also Casimir who, in 1334, had allowed Jews who left their homelands to settle Poland in greater numbers than ever before, which accounted for the large Jewish population present in Poland at the start of the twentieth century.

By the sixteenth century, because it had emerged as a beacon of hope and tolerance, Poland had become a sanctuary and refuge for those fleeing persecution and religious strife. The Renaissance of Poland followed. Culture and science grew deep roots during this golden age, evidenced by the famed astronomer Nicolaus Copernicus, who discovered that the earth revolved around the sun, thus revolutionizing how man viewed his place in the universe. Poets, writers, architects, inventors, and painters all added to Poland's reputation as a place where the arts and sciences had few equals.

Wanda had asked her father about that once, to which he replied sadly, "If history teaches us anything, it's that nothing is permanent; that empires come and go; and that nations succeed, rise, and fall in what seems like a fleeting moment in time."

So, despite its strength as the largest state in Europe, and its rise to prominence as the continent's most powerful nation, Poland had virtually disappeared less than three hundred years later. Known as the Partitions of Poland, it was continually divided among the empires of Russia, Prussia, and Austria for the next one hundred fifty years, sending thousands fleeing abroad, including some of the world's greatest literary and artistic minds. But even then, Poland flourished. Revolutions sprang up, and Polish artists, patriots, and musicians shed light on what the world saw as one of the best examples of a nation rebuilding its history.

One of those artists, Frederick Chopin, Janek's and Wanda's favorite composer, had learned of his nation's crushing defeat while traveling to Paris. Because he knew that he'd never again set eyes on his homeland, Chopin requested that, upon his death, his sister remove his heart and smuggle it back to Poland because he was certain the French government would never allow his body to leave Paris. A small monument at the Holy Cross church in Warsaw bears the simple inscription: *Here rests the heart of Frederic Chopin.* With that final gruesome act, Chopin, his body buried in Paris, had ensured that his heart would forever remain in his beloved Poland.

Wanda remembered listening to Chopin's music filling their home and Janek saying, "Nothing brings me back to Poland like a Chopin etude. When I listen to his music, I can almost see the Polish mountains in my mind." He would finish listening, then wipe tears from his eyes.

Throughout the centuries, Poland's destiny ebbed and flowed. Dynasties came and went. Independence and expansion gave way to invasions from east and west until finally, by 1918, the Second Polish Republic was born and continued to exist in peace and harmony with its neighbors.

That is, until 1939, Wanda thought, the image of sitting on her father's lap suddenly fading into apparitions of Adolf Hitler and Joseph Stalin and sending her back to a time when Nazi Germany and the Soviet Union had once again destroyed the Polish State. She knew that history all too well, and she began reliving it in her mind:

Furious that the British and French had entered an alliance with Poland, Hitler had abrogated the German-Polish Non-Aggression Pact and launched the invasion that started World War II. Looking to the West for help was futile, since the western powers were not yet able to defend their Polish brethren, who realized from the outset that they clearly had no chance against the powerful German army. To say that England and France had stabbed their ally in the back would be kind, for in not honoring their pact, they had ensured the death of a nation and the slaughter of innocent millions.

The final death blow was struck when Germany and the Soviet Union hurriedly signed the Molotov-Ribbentrop Pact in Moscow, which secretly called for the dismemberment of Poland into Nazi and Soviet territories. Seventeen days after Germany marched eastward along Poland's 1,750-mile border, the Soviet invasion of Poland from the east had begun. Resistance proved futile, despite fierce battles that killed tens of thousands of civilians and soldiers. Both Hitler and Stalin understood that Poland's allies had neither the planes nor the ships to stage a counterattack. Some one and a half million German infantry, Luftwaffe bombers, and German warships attacked from the ground, the air, and in the Baltic Sea. The military strategy known as the blitzkrieg, or "lightning war," had quickly destroyed the Polish armed forces and left in its wake a country shocked and isolated. Without help from its allies, Poland was no match for the superior Wehrmacht, which immediately began a campaign of mass murder throughout the occupied territory.

Meanwhile, to the east, as Polish soldiers fought and lay dying in battles with the Nazis, the Red Army rushed in, overwhelming and savaging villages and cities. In little more than two weeks, German troops had fought their way as far east as Lwow, where they handed over their Polish prisoners of war and left behind thirteen million Poles to the fate of rule by the Soviet Union. All hope was lost. And once again, as history would have it, the Poles had found themselves without a nation.

The question Wanda had asked herself a thousand times since cowering in her home during the siege of Lwow was why Germany invaded Poland to begin with. The answer was simple: for Hitler, conquest meant that his people would have living space while he enslaved what he considered a subhuman population, first setting out to eradicate Polish culture and national identity, then massacring Jews he blamed for Germany's defeat in World War I. And because he considered Jews nothing more than thieves that controlled most of the world's financial institutions, Hitler placed the economic downfall of Germany squarely on the shoulders of people he believed so inferior that he saw them as nothing more than a human subspecies.

German concentration camps, established in 1933 as a place to imprison anti-Nazi sympathizers, at first had nothing to do with Jews. Within a few years, though, thousands of ghettos, used to segregate the Jewish population, began to pop up throughout Poland. As the war dragged on, the ghettos gradually disappeared, along with their inhabitants, who were shipped in boxcars to places like Auschwitz and Treblinka where their ashes turned beautiful Polish skies from blue into a perpetually gray haze.

For non-Jews, it wasn't much better. Once Poland was invaded and occupied, evictions of entire villages began in order to create fresh new colonies for German settlers. Poles were either executed or deported to concentration camps, leaving parts of the country devoid of any population. Children that Nazis deemed healthy and fit were kidnapped, adopted by German families and Germanized, many never to return to their families, even after the war had ended.

Historians say that to understand Russia's justification for invading Poland, one must understand Russia from a historic and ideological perspective. Prior to 1917, large swaths of eastern Poland, as Josef Stalin saw it, had been part of Tsarist Russia. What better way to take back its lost territory than to join with Nazi Germany and divide the spoils of war? In the process, he saw Poland as a buffer against future and inevitable German aggression, which everyone suspected would happen sooner rather than later. To say that the Soviet

Union was partly responsible for setting off World War II would be a gross understatement, since Hitler would never have risked a unilateral attack unless he knew full well that his ally would also be attacking Poland along its western border.

Ideologically, the Soviet Union had sought desperately to export communism across the globe, even if that meant world revolution. Stalin, after all, had been a devoted communist who believed that a system of government espoused by Karl Marx would free the world through the ideals of collective property and a classless society. If that meant sealing a pact with a devil like Hitler, so be it. So, in a very real way, stirring up conflicts throughout the continent was Stalin's way of weakening and fragmenting Europe, thus making it an easy target for a communist takeover. His words and ideas had indeed spread like poison; and by 1985, one-third of the world's population was barely surviving under a ruthless communist system of government.

Poland, however, was a special case, since its long and turbulent history with Russia had opened the door to an alliance between two countries that sought nothing less than the complete eradication of Polish sovereignty. Even more reason for Russia to invade and subjugate the Poles was the Marxist idea that, because Poland's aristocracy was exploiting the working class, it had become the natural enemy of communism. In Marx's own words, "Let the ruling class tremble at a communist revolution. The proletarians have nothing to lose but their classes. They have a world to win. Working men of all countries, unite."

Hatred for Poland was nothing new, Wanda's father had once told her. In a speech he'd given in 1848, Karl

Marx condemned Poland as a constitutional monarchy, which to him meant class distinctions, ruling elites, and unequal rights for its citizens. Nobility and aristocracy, according to Marx, were cancers that needed to be excised for a society to be truly free and equal. While the fabric of Polish society was based on marriage and family, Marx had an almost pathologic contempt for the institution of marriage and sought to transform society and human nature by eliminating what Poles held most dear: God and family.

An avowed atheist, Marx spewed hatred for Poland's adherence to Catholicism. In his world view, religion had no place. In fact, he considered religion the "opium of the people" and the "impotence of the human mind to deal with occurrences it cannot understand." To Marx, it was inconceivable that a nation's destiny and very foundation were so inextricably tied to family and its belief in God. There was no family but the state; and nineteenth-century Russia, with an explosion of industry that relegated workers to little more than slaves of the rich, was ripe for revolution.

And then came Vladimir Lenin, who toppled Nicholas II and the Tsars that ruled the country for three centuries and led Soviet Russia and then the Soviet Union from 1917 to 1924. He was equally intolerant of Poland's large Catholic population. Like Marx, Lenin immediately targeted religion, marriage, and family. Freedom in Lenin's Russia meant freedom *from* religion, freedom *from* marriage, and freedom of Russian women to have so many abortions that in 1936, his successor, Josef Stalin, fearing the population of communist Russia was on the verge of collapse, put an end to the practice.

As much as his Bolshevik followers thought of him

as a giant, Lenin was a smallish and ordinary-looking man with a bald head made more obvious by a large forehead and the Van Dyke beard, popularized in seventeenth-century Europe, he sported throughout his life. To an ordinary man on the street, Lenin appeared deceptively simple, until he stood opposite him, his slanted eyes, almost black, piercing the air as they glared his opponent into submission. "That stare, that awful, powerful stare," one of his fellow countrymen had described, "would reach out and grab you by the throat."

Though he'd grown up a privileged child in a well-to-do family, Lenin preferred the company of working folk. He distrusted intellectuals, though he needed them to build his new and improved political system. As Lenin grew fearful that the masses would reject his nascent revolution, something had to be done. And so, the "Red Terror" began, an unspeakable period of death and destruction during which hundreds of thousands—men, along with their families—were forced from their homes, killed with a bullet to the head. Those were the lucky ones. The less fortunate, found guilty of imaginary crimes, were tortured beyond belief: burned or flayed alive, drowned in boiling water, or crucified. Lenin stopped at nothing to make the system work because, in his words, "As an ultimate objective, peace simply means communist world control."

Historians had questioned why Lenin found it necessary to be so cruel, torturing and murdering his own people. But Lenin despised anyone who disagreed with him. If one didn't believe in the revolution, one did not belong in Russia or anywhere else. Even after the mass murder of his fellow countrymen, Lenin knew it was still not enough. Certain freedoms had to be cut away like rotting flesh for him to succeed. "Why should freedom of speech and freedom of the press be allowed?" Lenin wrote. "Why should a government which is doing what it believes to be right allow itself to be criticized? It would not allow opposition by illegal weapons. Ideas are much more fatal than guns."

Believing to the point of blindness that his was the only way to achieve greatness, Lenin had claimed that "Germany will militarize itself out of existence, England will expand itself out of existence, and America will spend itself out of existence." And so, under his iron-fisted dictatorship, Mother Russia had been transformed before the eyes of the world from a Czarist empire, ruled by old aristocrats who'd sat on their thrones like fat Roman emperors, to the Union of Soviet Socialist Republics.

Only twelve years prior to Lenin and the Bolshevik's overthrow of Tsarist Russia, the Vatican had signed an Edict of Toleration, which had allowed the organization of the Catholic Church and the free and open practice of the faith. But now that Lenin had taken absolute control of Russia, it had become the first state to have as its ideological objective the elimination of all religion. Thus, religion was replaced with atheism, church funds and property seized, religious books and histories destroyed, and all religious teaching in schools banned. Poland, a nation born in Christianity and mostly Catholic at the time of Lenin's revolution, had suddenly been threatened with a next-door neighbor that looked west and saw a chance to spread its hateful ideology into Europe.

But the world Wanda's father knew back then had witnessed an especially brutal chapter in the communist playbook when Josef Stalin took the reins and ignited the fuse that would burn through the very heart of Poland. For Stalin, ideology was overshadowed by a ruthless lust for power and a paranoia so great that he'd murdered or imprisoned vast numbers of government and army officials in what had become known as the "Great Purge." No one—not even the most innocent—escaped his wrath. Anyone viewed as a threat was tortured, executed, or exiled to a system of gulags that were often worse than death. The best and brightest minds—scientists, engineers, writers, philosophers—were also extinguished for failing to produce what Stalin had demanded of his obedient citizens.

Born in a peasant village in Gori, Georgia, 1200 miles south of Moscow, Josef, a frail and sickly child, had contracted smallpox at age seven, leaving his face scarred and pockmarked. Some years later, an accident had left his left arm withered and shorter than his right. Children in the village treated him like an outcast and pariah. As a result, Josef, only five feet four inches tall, grew up seeking respect and superiority and developed a sadistic personality that would make him one of the most brutal dictators in history. His trademark thick hair and mustache belied his cruel personality and had inspired the nickname "Uncle Joe" by the American press. What the world didn't know was that anyone who crossed or even criticized the man who adopted the name "Stalin," meaning steel in Russian, met a quick and often deadly fate. In fact, by the time Uncle Joe had been honored with *Time Magazine*'s 1942 "Man of the Year Award," he had directly or indirectly murdered some twenty million fellow Russians.

In his early years, Stalin had raised money for

Lenin's revolution by robbing banks, kidnapping, and extortion. His reward: position as General Secretary of the Communist Party, where he controlled party member appointments, a move that enabled him to build his future base gradually and irreversibly. By the time Lenin died in 1924, Stalin had gained total control over the Communist Party.

At the beginning, Stalin had simply removed opponents by reshufflings, firings, and exile; but his fear and paranoia soon took a sadistic turn. In the Great Purge, so-called enemies of the state were arrested in the dead of night, put on trial, convicted on false or no evidence, and summarily executed or sent to gulags. Until his invasion of Poland in the summer of 1939, Stalin's regime proved far worse than anything Nazi Germany had done, with ten to twenty millions of his own citizens victims in a brutal campaign of mass genocide. Countless others had suffered at the hands of a monster who colluded with Hitler to destroy the Polish State, divide the land, and enslave its people. Religion was especially targeted. Within two years of Stalin's grip on power, the Catholic Church had no bishops left in the Soviet Union, and by 1941 only two of the 1,200 churches that existed in 1917 at the start of the Bolshevik revolution were still active. In one fell swoop, Stalin had succeeded in purging not only his nation of religion and clergy, but his neighbor to the west of its freedom, its identity, its religion, and its rich, nine-hundred-year history.

Once, when Wanda had asked Janek what he knew about Stalin, he turned to her with a scowl on his face and said, "In his perverted system, anyone who reported inefficiency was branded a counterrevolutionary, but not reporting it would be treason. And so, workers spent twelve-hour days fearing everything and doing nothing that would rock the boat. That's why no one in Russia had an incentive to do or say anything."

As historians explain, both Germany and the Soviets sought to destroy every vestige of Polish culture, to the point of forbidding the use of the word "Poland" in any of the divided territories. From 1939 to 1949, Poland suffered through an occupation in which it lost at least six million of its citizens. Of those, roughly three million were Catholics, including many priests and other religious persons, in a quest to destroy the very roots of Christianity. The Soviets were no less brutal in their persecution than were the Nazis, and sometimes more so. Even today, the forty-five years of occupation by the Soviet Union is remembered as the "red plague," a time when Poland was relegated to a non-state by the USSR.

Wanda sat up in her wheelchair and turned from the image of Saint Francis, her mind beginning to wander, the pews in front of her and the beautiful stained-glass window becoming less familiar.

"The Lord be with you," she heard the priest celebrating mass announce.

"And with your spirit," she answered reflexively along with the few others at mass.

"May almighty God bless you, the Father, the Son, and the Holy Spirit," the priest concluded as he blessed the tiny congregation before him. "Go in peace to serve the Lord and one another."

Wanda wasn't sure why on that day she had relived all that Polish history, only to be reminded so bitterly that, after the war, she and Janek could never again set foot on Polish soil, walk the fairytale-like mountains, lush valleys, and picturesque villages. After leaving Poland, only in their dreams would they see the colorful fields of poppies and saffron, cities with large open squares, and bustling marketplaces they had so loved visiting. Tears would always form in her eyes, as they did now, whenever she thought of not being able to return to her beloved Poland as long as it remained a communist nation. The anguish of that tore at her heart more than sixty years later. What made the pain even worse was that by the time her homeland broke free of its Soviet yoke, Janek had become too ill to travel and could only in his mind visit the Poland he loved so much.

"God forgive me for hating," Wanda prayed, her eyes cast downward, her bony fingers interlaced and pressed against her breast. "Forgive me for cursing the men who took everything from me. Forgive me for wishing them dead, for wanting them to burn in hell for all eternity. Forgive me for not loving those who did such evil things to me that my soul is emptied and my heart forever hardened."

Wanda then made the sign of the cross and fell silent, her thoughts and memories gradually floating away as if a mist had swept into her mind and taken them to another place.

Chapter 6

Northern Kazakhstan
March 1940

Wanda's three-week journey from her home in eastern Poland through Ukraine and into Siberian Kazakhstan was just the beginning. By the end of it, many who'd been arrested, especially babies and the very old, had perished. Others simply gave up, refusing to eat, thinking it better to die on a filthy train and get it over with than spend whatever time they had left slowly dying of starvation. But most willed themselves to go on rather than be left to rot beneath Ukrainian and Kazakh soil, where no official graves were dug and no markers placed where the frozen bodies lay. Sometimes the earth was chopped up and shoveled away, the bodies tossed in and covered by a thin layer of cold dirt. But mostly the corpses were gathered, stripped of whatever clothing was worth keeping, and burned like trash.

Shock and despair swept through the mostly women and a few older men as they approached their final destination, looked past a rotted wooden sign that read Village Number 8, and caught their first glimpse of what looked like nothing they'd ever seen.

"What is this vile place?" a woman screamed.

A guard slapped the woman, who barely flinched and then screamed again. "Where are the homes? The water? The trees?"

The new arrivals were funneled past equipment sheds and into one of several large wooden gray buildings. As they shuffled in, they were visually examined by Dimitri Popovich, overseer of Village Number 8, a large, well-fed man with closely cropped hair that receded into a sharp point above his brows. His black eyes darted from one deportee to another, looking for the sick and the weak who'd survived the journey but who probably wouldn't make it to sunrise. Each time he pointed, a guard would rush over and whisk the poor soul away, never to be seen again.

"You are here for one reason and one reason only," Popovich announced without a trace of emotion in his deep voice. He clasped his hands behind him. "To work. If you work hard, you will eat and you will live. If not, you'll starve and be fed to the wolves that prowl these woods every night. If you try to escape, you'll be shot. If you *do* escape, you'll freeze to death before you can walk ten minutes. If you don't freeze, the wolves will make sure you're never seen again."

Wanda stood in the middle of the damp room, too numb to cry and too tired, cold, and hungry to even think of not doing exactly what she was told. She wrapped her arm around Sophie's shoulder. My baby, she thought. How will I protect her from these savages? The words coming from Popovich's mouth made her want to scream, but she thought better of it with Sophie at her side and Popovich more than eager to throw any troublemaker into an early grave.

Popovich continued: "Before the spring thaw, you will learn survival skills to keep from freezing to death. You will learn how to fashion mud bricks into earthen homes and how to burn dung for fuel. From this day forward, all cultural traditions are forbidden. Expressions of faith are illegal and will be punished. Speaking of Poland will get you sent to a cell without food and water for an entire day. For the next two months, you will clean, take care of animals, repair buildings, work in the forest, build your homes, and prepare the farm for the spring planting season. Winter does not mean you will sit idle. Children will remain with parents."

One woman screamed, "How do we care for our children when we work all day?"

"That's no concern of mine," Popovich shouted back. "Take them with you or leave them behind to fend for themselves. Either way."

Several of the women next to Wanda wept bitterly. Their children would not have to bear such pain and suffering because their frozen bodies had been left behind. Wanda pulled Sophie closer and thanked God her daughter was still alive.

Popovich paused to see that everyone had understood the rules, then walked from the room as a small army of guards prodded the group into an adjoining barrack lined with wooden sleeping pallets, two stoves, and a single toilet and shower on each end. The air was heavy with the smell of people who'd not bathed in weeks and wore clothes caked in human waste. Wanda looked around and wondered if this was not some humiliating and purposeful attempt at making all Poles suffer.

"Is this our home?" Sophie asked, her lips quivering, her eyes darting around the room in search of other children. She then buried her face in Wanda's coat and began to cry.

"For now, my love," Wanda said. "Tonight, let's find a pallet to sleep on and try to regain our strength. Tomorrow we'll get clean and find some food."

Wanda spent the night wondering what was so special about Kazakhstan; why send people there in the first place. Most of the deportees, Wanda included, were not aware that Joseph Stalin had created five republics, including Kazakhstan, as a strategy to keep them from being an Islamic threat to the Soviet Union. Ethnic groups were divided, grouped together regardless of religion, language, and culture, and moved into the republics. It was akin to creating American states that would never be independent. Those who Stalin thought untrustworthy were arrested and deported there. During the war, Kazakhstan, the largest republic, was used to replace depleted fuel and food sources in Europe.

For Wanda and the others, it was like nothing they'd ever seen or experienced, with few trees, not many people, and vast open plains with endless stretches of grassland and plateaus. Kazakhstan's fertile soil, even that far north, was an ideal place in which to establish farm labor camps to feed the Red Army. But since it was still winter and blistering cold, with nighttime temperatures reaching twenty below zero, the first order of business was to keep from freezing to death.

Together with a small group of women, Wanda dug blocks of frozen earth, then shaped and piled them one atop the other until they formed an earthen hut. Once the crude shelter was finished, the women tried as best they could to make it a home. They took turns searching the fields for wood and for dung they'd mix with clay and mold into bricks to burn. Some of the women contracted brucellosis when the dung bonded to their cracked skin and seeped into open wounds. In the middle of the mud floor, everyone huddled tightly around a fire they'd start to keep ice from forming on the inside walls. At first the smoke choked their lungs and made breathing difficult. But after a few days, the smell and the burning in their eyes had become a mere nuisance, and they considered themselves lucky to be alive, to have something they could use to keep warm, especially when a snowstorm blew in from the north and completely covered the hut in several feet of snow.

Day after monotonous day, the women fought off boredom by telling stories and reminiscing about Poland, and it was at those times, in the dimness of the fire, that Wanda's mind would drift back to her childhood in Radom and think how laughable her definition of suffering had been. Just thinking of Janek, though, would make the nights more bearable. She would slip from her coat a photo of her and Janek she'd taken with her the night of their arrest and hold it against her chest, whispering, "I love you so much, my love."

Wanda slept each night with Sophie drawn up into a little ball next to her side. After twelve long hours in the field, worn down by backbreaking work that left even strong men exhausted, it would take her no more than a few seconds to fall into a deep slumber. But at least once a week, when the night winds blew and battered the hut with twigs and debris, her body would convulse, and she'd relive the nightmare that began in the middle of the night on February 10, 1940.

"What's happening?" Sophie asked one night, startled when her mother jarred her from a deep sleep.

"Nothing, my love," Wanda whispered then pulled

Sophie closer. "Go back to sleep."

As Sophie dozed off, Wanda lay with her eyes open, remembering what an older woman living there for months had told her the day they'd arrived: "You'll be here till the day you die... You'll never return to Poland... If you don't get used to it, you'll drop dead in the fields and never be heard from again." And as she thought that, she inched closer to her precious daughter and cried herself to sleep.

So, like caged animals with nowhere to go and nothing to do but wait out each storm and look forward to sunlight and warmth, Wanda, Sophie, and eight other women hoped and prayed they'd survive in their earthen hut through the winter until the arrival of the spring planting season. Each day brought new arrivals to replace those who'd perished, and Wanda would question them anxiously, asking where they'd come from, who they knew, how they were arrested, hoping to hear anything good. Instead, she heard nothing of the outside world, terrifying rumors of Poland's destruction, and tales of how miserably life had changed for Poles in every walk of life.

March in Kazakhstan was no better than February. During blizzards that swept across the vast steppe, Wanda saw women drop and freeze to death simply walking to work. Every second, hunger tore at her innards, and on most days, she was tortured by the fear that she'd not last the few hours until she ate again and that she'd leave Sophie an orphan who couldn't survive without her mother's care. It was bad enough she had to leave Sophie alone in the hut while she worked; it was worse thinking of what would become of her. The bitter cold of winter was no excuse for not working. Women as small and fragile as Wanda cleared fields and forests, felled trees while standing in waist-deep snow, gathered and hauled wood, sawed branches, and tended livestock. When temperatures dipped to minus twenty, women, desperate to keep from freezing, splashed water on their coats, which froze in seconds and formed an icy layer of protection. Within weeks of arrival, half the workers were no longer fit to work, their strength and endurance diminished so much by lack of food and exhaustion they could barely lift themselves from bed each morning.

The work was numbing and brutal. By the end of the workday, even the hair on Wanda's head seemed to hurt. A growing and constant pain had settled deep in her bones from spending half her waking hours in the cold. When she walked back to camp, she limped. A stick she'd fashioned from a fallen tree branch helped ease the burning in her legs, and the only thing that drove her to plow forward through the snow were thoughts of Sophie sitting in their earthen hut and waiting for her to return. From morning till night, it consumed her. Was my baby hungry? Was she cold? Lonely? Did she go outside and freeze? Did someone take her away? The sight of their hut in the distance would make her heart race and her legs stiffen, and she walked ever faster against the wind.

To Wanda, it seemed like miles before she reached the hut. When she stepped inside what felt like heaven on earth, Wanda didn't know whether to stretch out her arms with joy at seeing her daughter or to cry at the look in Sophie's pitiful little eyes.

"Momma!" Sophie cried, then leapt to her feet and embraced her mother.

"I missed you, my love," Wanda said and couldn't hug and kiss her daughter enough. "What did you do while I was gone?"

Sophie raised her little ragdoll up to her mother. "We played and took naps and waited for you," she said. "Are you staying with us?"

"Yes, I'm staying," Wanda said, then almost cried thinking that in another twelve hours she'd be leaving Sophie once again.

By April, the winter storms had mercifully disappeared. The cruelty of freezing temperatures and violent winds were followed by the warmth of glowing sunlight and light rain. The constant gloom of ominous gray clouds and brown vegetation gave way to fresh blue skies and the lovely green of new life. But as the snow melted, the earthen huts had turned into a brown sludge and literally washed away; and Wanda, together with the other women, were forced to reconstruct their earthen hut before they were homeless once more.

Lack of food in that godforsaken part of the world was often worse than the bitter cold. Not a single day went by that Wanda and Sophie didn't cry from the constant pain of hunger. Food rations were typically a few portions of bread and some watery soup, if they were lucky. On some days, when the guards were too drunk to make their way to the food lines, women would faint from weakness. Food was all anyone could think about. It consumed them. The entire day, from morning till night, was spent working in the fields and daydreaming of food. Wanda had begun to think of herself as an animal, tortured by hunger and working her fingers to the bone so that she and Sophie could be rewarded with a stale piece of bread. In the spring, she would scour fields near the farm for wild mushrooms, berries, or anything else they could eat to stay alive. One of the women in

Wanda's group had become especially good at trapping mice and rats she shared with the others.

But though the long, brutal winter had thankfully come to an end and brought with it a welcomed sense of relief, Kazakhstan had yet another merciless surprise in store for the deportees. As frozen ponds thawed, and the blistering sun baked the land to a crisp, Wanda struggled to fend off newly hatched swarms of bloodthirsty and relentless mosquitoes that attacked every living creature they could find. The tiny predators, unyielding in their ferocity, had only a few weeks to feed; and feed they did, covering from head to toe every man, woman, and child working in the fields until their faces swelled and were no longer recognizable. Skies, nearly blackened with the little monsters, made everyone long for the abysmal cold of winter. In that brutal land, there was no respite: not from work, not from hunger and disease, not even from the lowly insects that launched their attacks in a human feeding frenzy from the moment they hatched till the day they died.

As the weather warmed, Wanda took Sophie with her to the fields. She could no longer bear to leave her daughter alone to lie on a blanket and stare vapidly at mud walls. "I saw other children that looked your age," she told her as she tilled the earth. "Do you think you'd like to meet them sometime?"

Sophie hesitated, then asked, "Are they Polish?" Her eyes seemed to brighten a little.

Wanda was saddened that her little girl's first reaction was not joy at having new friends but concern that the children she'd play with were not Polish.

But for Sophie, the fear was not unfounded. As the train that had carried them made stops along the way, it picked up women and children who spoke in strange tongues, looked different, had clothing she didn't recognize and faces more hardened than any she'd seen before. Nothing in her young six-year-old life made sense. For the past five months, she'd witnessed death and destruction, bombings, executions, arrests, deportations, rape, and murder; and the safe and happy world she thought would last a lifetime had vanished before her eyes, replaced by the horrors and atrocities of a war she couldn't understand.

"Yes, I'm sure they're Polish," Wanda assured her. "Most of them travelled with us on the train from Lwow."

Sophie thought for a second and nodded. "Okay," she agreed, then ran over and hugged her mother. A hint of a smile crossed her face.

Wanda's eyes teared up. My poor baby, she thought. No child should ever live like this. "I'm glad," she said. "I'm sure you'll find nice friends."

On some mornings, Wanda would notice a space in the field where someone had been working the evening before. Instinctually, her head would shake as she whispered a short prayer for the poor soul who'd probably died in her sleep. It was common for the weakest and the elderly among them to wither away and die from starvation or from diseases like dysentery and typhus, but many simply died from exhaustion, worked to death by cruel men who'd told the new arrivals in no uncertain terms that those who work will eat and those who do not will die. The next day, Wanda would see a new face grimacing in the field. Poor soul, she'd think to herself, I pray she makes it.

"You're not meeting your quota, Wanda," a voice

bellowed from behind her. "Pick up the pace and dig faster or you won't get your usual ration tonight."

"I'm working as quickly as I can," Wanda said. She looked up at the huge guard and saw nothing in his eyes but contempt. "My legs are hurting. Something's wrong. Is there a doctor?"

The guard sneered. "Doctor? Don't be ridiculous. Get back to work."

Wanda turned and continued tilling despite the pain in her legs and the blood on her hands from new blisters. She'd seen what happened to women who didn't work fast enough or who broke the rules. Just the other day, one of the women in the hut next to theirs was forced to move piles of dung from one area to another for no other reason than to humiliate and exhaust her.

What have I done to deserve this? Wanda asked herself. Am I a criminal? Have I been sentenced for something I did? In some ways it was worse than being a prisoner, she figured. At least those sent to Soviet prisons were fed—if you could call it that—and had shelter. They didn't have to worry about freezing to death working in a swirling snowstorm or dropping dead from exhaustion in the fields when the temperature in a few months would reach 110 degrees. But there, on the forgotten steppe of Kazakhstan, the world couldn't see the tears of anguish and suffering or hear the wailing from the pain of frostbite and hunger.

"Why are you crying?" Sophie asked with a frown.

Wanda, who cried often since arriving in Kazakhstan, didn't feel the wetness on her cheeks as tears but unconsciously thought them beads of sweat. "I have a little pain, that's all," she lied. "It's nothing."

Sophie suddenly dropped to her knees at the sight of

a caterpillar crawling along the turned-up earth. She lifted it, put it to her lips, and kissed it gently. "Look, Momma," she squealed, smiling when its soft hairs brushed against her finger.

"It's beautiful," Wanda said. "Be careful with it, my love. In a few weeks, it'll turn into a beautiful butterfly."

Wanda turned from her daughter and wiped the tears from her face. She looked up at the blue sky and pictured Sophie's little caterpillar hatching and spreading its wings, free of its cocoon, its prison, flying along the westerly winds to a place where it could live and feed and mate for the remainder of its short life. And at that moment, how she wished that she and Sophie could likewise be swept up by those winds and float two thousand miles all the way back to Lwow.

The one thing that had kept Wanda from giving up was Sophie. Like a fierce animal that protects its young, she fought through the pain inflicted on her body and thought of nothing but the sacrifices she had to endure each day and night for her daughter. When things got bad, she stole; and although the punishment for stealing was severe, she'd become so desperate it no longer mattered. Everyone in camp, regardless of their role, was given an impossible quota. Wanda's job was to till the soil and to plant and dig potatoes. If she met her daily quota, she was given a full ration, but being small and frail, no matter how hard she worked Wanda could never meet that quota, and the hunger would drive her to the verge of madness. Sometimes she'd lie in bed and wait until nightfall, then sneak into the fields on her hands and knees to dig up a few potatoes, because listening to Sophie beg for scraps of food had made her brave enough to risk anything.

As weeks went by, Wanda noticed more men arriving at the camp, figuring that because the war in Poland had come to an end, there were more of them available for slave labor. She also noticed, to her dismay, that the Soviets made no distinction between men and women when it came to work. It never occurred to her that one of the first things communists did was to establish a system where men and women were treated exactly the same. To be liberated, women had to become more like men in every way, including physical labor. Thus, all distinctions between sexes had been erased. Pregnancy and motherhood were no excuse for missing work. According to Marxism, women could never be free unless they rid themselves from the yoke of family, and so government, in its attempt to replace mother and father, became family.

Seeing the equal roles that men and women had at the camp was alien to Wanda, whose Polish culture dictated that men and women, though equal in many ways, were still different and had different roles in society. In Russia, women dressed like and worked alongside men, digging ditches, felling trees, and carrying heavy loads, so they became used to hard, physical labor. Polish women were not. Some had never worked back home in Poland, and now had become nothing more than draft animals, treated worse than the livestock they cared for. Within a few months, they grew so weak they could do only half of what was expected of them. The less they produced, the less they ate, and the weaker they'd become, until they were no longer fit to work at all. Some became skeletons and dropped dead in the fields.

As more men arrived, some from Poland but others

from Ukraine and Belarus, something new and sinister had permeated the usual routine of Wanda's labor camp. Something that didn't add up: women arriving in Kazakhstan on the verge of death yet surviving backbreaking work and starvation while so many others were dying of far less. How was it *they* had beaten the odds when others had not? Wanda began to think the worst. What were these women doing? What would a mother do? What would *I* do if I watched my only child suffer or starve to death? Beg? Steal? Kill? Have sex with strange men for an extra piece of bread?

And then thoughts of Janek ran through her head. Would he forgive me for trying to save myself and our daughter? Would I have the heart to tell him things I'd done? If I *did* tell him, would he understand? Wanda thought of it a million times, and each time she did, she told herself she'd do anything to save her daughter. She closed her eyes and tried not to think about it, haunted by the idea that she'd give herself up and keep secret from Janek whatever happened in Kazakhstan. Once it's done, she told herself, let the past be forgotten so the two of them and Sophie could erase the years of horror and live their lives as though back in their beautiful city of Lwow.

Chapter 7

Smolensk, Russia
June 1940

Eight months had passed since Janek was thrown into a filthy prison where men lying next to him had withered away to flesh and bone from disease and starvation. Every week, newly arriving prisoners brought with them horrific tales of torture and executions in towns and villages where the NKVD had established detention centers in which they could kill at their own leisure. The stories were often hard to believe, exaggerations by insane prisoners who conjured up lies in their demented minds; stories of victims scalded with boiling water; noses, fingers, and breasts cut off; eyes gouged out; faces burned with acid; prisoners fastened together with barbed wire, unable to move lest they shred flesh from their bones. But with every new arrival, similar stories were told, so before long everyone feared those left behind were truly at the mercy of evil men whose only purpose in life was to torture and kill as many Poles as humanly possible.

Though an exceptionally brutal winter had ravaged Smolensk and turned its prisons to ice, summer brought with it a new torture. The prison cells became sweltering ovens that slowly cooked the men throughout the day. Desperate to keep from dying of heatstroke, they'd remove their clothes and lie naked on the hard cement, which at least brought them some relief. But mostly, all they could manage to keep from going mad was to close their eyes and wait for nightfall.

"How much longer can they keep us like this?" Janek wondered aloud. "We've told them nothing. Do they even care?"

"I think they hope we all die so they could be rid of us," one of the prisoners said.

"Don't worry," a third man chimed in. "We'll be sentenced any day so they can make room for more prisoners. They need workers, not people lying around doing nothing. If they can't break us, they might as well send us away."

"Maybe we're breaking *them* down," Janek joked. "Maybe we're pissing them off because this is the last place they want to be, just like us."

The men around Janek laughed. What else could they do? For more than half a year, Janek and his fellow soldiers had endured unspeakable cruelty by NKVD agents whose only purpose was to extract information before sentencing prisoners they despised to certain death in the gulags of Siberia. "Polish dogs," they'd call them repeatedly until the slur no longer meant anything. "Not fit to live with pigs," they'd say. "Sleep and eat where you shit for all we care," they'd chide as they threw spoiled food onto the cell floor and watch ravenous men lunge for crumbs that would scatter across wet slime.

For the past two days, the men in Janek's cell were being punished by the NKVD for being defiant. Their sentence: a cup of water and two pieces of bread to share among the men in the cell. If they cooperated, they could eat the same as the others.

At six o'clock, the cell door opened. Two Soviet guards waved pieces of bread in their hands, taunting the prisoners, hoping to see them fight like dogs over scraps.

"You're a cruel son-of-a-bitch," Janek said to one of the guards, who laughed hysterically at dying men begging for food.

The guards tossed the stale bread into the cell and slammed the door closed. Janek ripped one of the pieces apart and shared it with two others. In an instant, the food had disappeared. And like birds hunting and pecking for seeds, the men gathered any remaining crumbs and licked them from their fingers as if it were their last meal. It would be another twenty-four hours until they could eat again.

Another month went by before army officials and the NKVD decided there was nothing more they could extract from the Polish soldiers, so orders were given to deport whatever remained of Janek's unit to Siberia. At first, the men thanked God to still be alive and leaving that hell, but then wondered what kind of hell they'd be taken to next.

"Line up!" a Red Army officer commanded the ragtag mob of prisoners, who could barely stand upright on thin legs. The NKVD, satisfied that nothing more could be achieved by keeping the prisoners there and deciding they would be more useful elsewhere, had relinquished its authority to the Red Army.

"You've been sentenced to ten years for crimes against the state." He looked over at the condition of the men and knew that many would not see the next spring. Ten years may as well have been a death sentence. "You'll spend the next few days in holding barracks, then board the train to your final destination. There you will be given your work assignments."

Janek and his unit were marched across the vast prison compound to a separate area surrounded by barbed wire fencing and wooden guard towers spaced fifty feet apart. Atop each tower stood two soldiers holding machine guns. Giant searchlights ensured that every square inch of the area could be illuminated in the hunt for anything that moved. In the event of a rare escape, what the searchlights found would be targeted instantly by a rapid line of fifty-caliber bullets or a German Shepherd trained to rip human flesh from its bones. Only the most foolhardy, suicidal, or insane prisoner would think of attempting such a thing.

"Hell, this is far better than where we've been the last eight months," a prisoner said as the group entered a long barracks lined with sleeping pallets. "Am I dreaming?"

"Don't be fooled," Janek said. "They want us to regain our strength before sending us on our way. Nobody wants a trainload of dead bodies arriving at a work camp."

Of course, the men all knew that. Up until their sentences were announced, there were a thousand ways to die. Work was not one of them. By next week, it might be.

Janek dropped like a stone onto a sleeping pallet and shut his eyes. It was almost like heaven not feeling the frigid cold of a cement floor in winter against the open wounds on his skin or inhaling the hot air of summer that became trapped in his cell and nearly suffocated him to death. He could actually breathe, purge his lungs of filth, shift his arms and legs without hitting anyone, stretch out and move his weary bones, and thank God that for the next two days, at least, he'd feel like a human being.

"Everyone up!" a loud voice ordered. "Into the delousing room."

Another guard pointed to a door at the far end of the barracks. "Remove all your clothing and hang them on the metal hooks in the adjoining room. They'll be cleaned while you're washing. You can pick them up when you're finished."

In unison, the prisoners stood, formed two lines, and moved in lockstep to the delousing showers. Before entering, each man's head and pubic area were shorn down to the skin, and each was handed a small piece of gray soap. Inside the room, a line of lead pipes hung down from the ceiling with large shower heads attached. When the water was turned on, Janek scrubbed his body then drip-dried while the lice on his clothes in the adjoining room were exterminated by temperatures hot enough to kill anything that crawled. For the next few hours, his skin burned and turned red, no doubt from whatever poison had been put in the soap to make certain no lice could survive the washing.

After the treatment they'd received from the NKVD, Janek and his men thought they had entered paradise. They were fed three times a day, given water, allowed to rest, and were not beaten to within an inch of their lives. *What is going on?* Janek wondered. *What have we done to deserve such pity?* But the more he thought about it, the more he became convinced that the older guards who ran that section of the prison were more humane and compassionate because they'd seen enough evil and heartless cruelty and no doubt knew the fate he and his men would face when they left Smolensk. The younger guards and the indoctrinated NKVD agents, idealistic communists who believed in their Soviet system like brainwashed zealots, saw the world and the people in it through hateful and perverted eyes.

That evening, Janek sat with his fellow soldiers, trying to predict where they'd be taken in a few days. "No matter where we go," he said, "don't give up. Think of your families back home and live for them. If not for you, for your wives and children."

The men nodded. Some wept. They looked at one another and knew that many of them would not be going back. Outside, a network of shiny railroad tracks crisscrossed each other, stretching alongside the barracks, coming into and out of the prison compound either depositing or removing trainloads of human cargo in what seemed like an endless wave of suffering. The sheer number of tracks, Janek concluded, was a sure sign there were other places that prisoners were taken, places deep inside Russian territory where the broken bodies of men like his lay buried and forgotten. Later, when the men had all gone to bed, Janek could hear some of them praying, some crying. He began to cry himself, not so much for himself but for the friends he knew would perish in the gulag and never be heard from again.

"Jesus, give me the strength to go on," Janek prayed. "Give comfort to the men who'll suffer and die. Help them face their mortality and hold them in your arms at the moment they take their last breath." He made the sign of the cross, and for the next hour he stared at the faces of brave and innocent soldiers whose only crime was to love and protect their families and their homeland.

Three days and three nights had passed. The food was not much better than the men had been getting, but at least they were getting more of it. Janek was eating fairly well and regained lost strength. On the fourth morning, a familiar rumble jarred him from a deep sleep—a line of boxcars clambered into the compound and screeched to a halt. He bolted upright and rubbed his eyes. Sunlight that broke through the horizon just moments earlier seemed to weep as it trickled onto the walls and washed across Janek's face. His stomach churned, followed by the taste of vomit that seeped up and into his mouth.

"God help me," Janek whispered. "Is this it?" A gloom like no other he'd ever felt suddenly overcame him, a palpable fear that the rumble and the screech that woke him had come like death itself to take them away.

Janek was right, for just when he was about to lay his head back down to gather his thoughts and recite a quick prayer, a guard entered the barracks and ordered everyone to take some bread and line up outside.

The men did as they were told. They dressed, stuffed a few pieces of bread into their shirts, and left the relative comfort of their barracks to wait in the warmth of the bright sun. An older guard looked on; and if Janek didn't know any better, thought he saw a hint of sadness in the man's eyes. *Why would he be sad for us? Why would he care? Does he know where it is we're going?*

"Everyone line up and get onto the train!" a younger, less caring guard shouted. His eyes, unlike those of the guard they were leaving behind, were filled with hate. He waved his machine gun in a menacing fashion, and the men were sure he was anxious to use it in the blink of an eye. "Move your filthy asses! We don't have all day!" He hit one of the men in the back with the butt of his gun. The other guards, all seemingly chiseled from the same stone, had broad shoulders and ugly, expressionless faces that only moved when shouting obscenities or barking orders.

"Where are they taking us?" a prisoner asked, though he knew it probably didn't matter. Anywhere inside Russia would be no better than anywhere else.

"Shut your mouth!" a guard next to him yelled. "You go where we tell you to go!"

The men fell silent, shuffling forward as if about to enter some gruesome chamber of death. As quickly as he could, Janek climbed up into one of the boxcars. The air was damp and stagnant and smelled of its last cargo. These were not the usual train cars used to transport prisoners between compounds. He saw that, the second he entered and sat on the wooden floor. They were more like cattle cars with no slop buckets, a few narrow openings in one of the walls, and a single wooden trough to hold human waste.

Within minutes, every last man had piled like caught fish into the vile containers, packed shoulder to shoulder with just enough room to move to the waste trough if they needed to. The door slid closed. A heavy metal latch crashed down and locked it shut. Janek looked up to heaven and tried to breathe whatever clean air was left.

"Has God abandoned us?" one of the prisoners asked. "Can this really be the end?"

"Men die, but many survive," Janek said, trying to lift the young man's spirits. "Sometimes they die because they lose hope…they lose faith…and without hope and faith, there's no longer a will to live. Don't abandon your faith, and never give up hope. We'll make it."

"You think your wife and child are still alive?"

another prisoner asked cynically.

Janek nodded. "I have faith that I'll see them again."

"Where? In heaven?"

"I have faith that I'll see them after the war. You should likewise. It'll get you through whatever happens."

The train buckled forward and slowly gained speed. Janek could see through the few slits that it had left the compound and was moving at a steady pace through a dense forest of pine and spruce. He couldn't remember the last time he'd seen trees and flowers or walked beneath blue skies a free man. It seemed absurd to be sitting where he was. Only a year ago, he was running and playing with Sophie, lying in grass fields with Wanda, enjoying the life he'd dreamed of when they both moved to Lwow. Now, as he smelled the putrid air and felt boards shifting beneath him whenever the train veered and swayed on its tracks, he thought for the first time since his capture that God, who was supposed to be watching over the faithful, had closed His eyes and turned away.

"How can you allow this?" Janek asked himself. "Why would you let men do such evil?" And then he came to his senses and realized it wasn't God who allows such things—God, after all, had given even the most vile of men free will to do whatever they wanted to do—it was they and they alone who'd chosen to inflict their horrors on a beautiful world.

Days passed. The hypnotic monotony of the train ride had lulled Janek and the men into a daze they found almost comforting. But at least it had allowed their weary minds to wander, to be transported back to a time when everything seemed perfect instead of forward to a grim and uncertain fate.

On one morning, Janek forced open his eyes and tried to stand, weak from hunger and exhausted from squatting in a cramped corner of the cattle car, so he could catch a glimpse of the sun as it bathed the greens and mottled browns of tundra grasses one minute, then spread its rays across a barren landscape that seemed to reach into nowhere. *Am I dreaming all this? Is the barrenness passing us by like some abstract painting really part of the Siberian wasteland that will soon be my home?* As he wiped the blur from his eyes and caught sight of thin-boned women bent forward in fields of cabbage, their faces as brown and cracked as the soil beneath them, he knew at once that it was.

The endless uniform stretch of tundra was occasionally broken by uneven rows of stone and wooden houses that leaned on crumbling foundations as though on the verge of collapse. Children—expressionless, when Janek even saw any—stopped to watch the train of prisoners go by, their faces black from carbon swept down from factory smokestacks by cold Siberian winds and deposited on their flesh like a second skin. In this place, at least, there were no thoughts of cleanliness, nor rules to govern even the most basic rights of health and well-being; only men, women, and children who spent each day sacrificing their lungs and their lives for a piece of meat and an occasional pint of contaminated milk.

As soon as a farm or village faded from sight, Janek's train passed neglected graveyards dotted with wooden markers; sticks with no names, just weathered numbers and dates of burial scratched into gray fibers. Many of the markers had long since rotted into stumps or fallen over and disappeared in a tangle of weeds. The few trees remaining looked to have died long ago, also, kept upright by hardened roots and what locals believed were souls of men who tended the grounds before themselves becoming a part of it.

More than a thousand miles into Russia's vast interior, Janek couldn't imagine where he was being taken and how much more he could endure. Compared to the foul stench and the filth of his boxcar, the prison barracks back in Smolensk had been a comfort. Each day only added to his misery. July in a sealed container with little water and barely any clean air to breathe had sucked the energy from his body, so mostly he slept and tried to keep from using up what little strength he had left. But no amount of sleep or rest or thinking good thoughts or even praying to God could ease the struggle of living each day like a caged animal.

The boxcar that housed Janek and forty other men had soon become a moving sewer. The waste trough, typically filled by day's end, did not flush. On especially hot days, the wretched smell would make Janek cringe, so he tucked his face into the crook of his arm and fought for what little air he could sniff. As the train swayed on irregular tracks, it wasn't possible to keep everything in the trough, and before long the entire floor was painted in a brown slime that everyone would sleep on. Water was scarce, even when the air became hot and stifling. Many dehydrated. Some came down with dysentery. When the train stopped, guards would slide open the door and throw food rations onto the floor. The first time they did, Janek refused to eat for fear that he'd not be able to hold it down. But as hunger overcame him and the pain of starvation made even the smallest bones in his body ache, he'd grab whatever food he could, wipe it clean of sewage, and devour it in seconds.

Where the eastward rails ended and the train could no longer move north into the Siberian wilderness, Janek and the men were boarded onto a caravan of closed trucks. Another three days of relentless heat battered the men who found it so hard to breathe that some perished from heat exhaustion. Sometimes the men would be forced to disembark and walk through knee-deep swamps and bogs so the trucks could lighten their load and drive through. Nightfall was a godsend, a time when Janek and the men could rest their weary bones and at least gaze at the stars in the sky.

Days passed. And just when Janek thought he could not survive another day, he felt the truck slow and grind to a stop alongside a wooden fortress guarded by menacing towers ringed by a pair of ten-foot fences topped with razor wire. The fields surrounding the camp, as far as the eye could see, were pocked by broad-leafed grasses and an occasional stand of vegetation, stunted and twisted by the frigid winds into a sort of arctic driftwood. Pools of coffee-brown water bubbled here and there, so polluted that not even a wilted plant could be spotted around its shoreline. "So this is what has become of the great nation of Russia," Janek said to himself, looking out at a place where the constant stench of death stung one's nostrils and men were taken to spend the last days of their wretched lives.

It had taken more than two weeks and three thousand miles before Janek and his men arrived in a gulag complex somewhere in northern Siberia. Up until then, the only thing that had kept him from going mad was dreaming of someday going back to Poland. He'd tried to keep sane by reminiscing with friends about life in his hometown, sharing family stories, crying when he thought of Wanda and Sophie, even laughing a little before the reality hit him that he was as far from home as he'd ever been. From what some of the men had gathered during their last stop, they had arrived in an area of Siberia known as the Sakha Republic.

"Can this be it?" Janek asked.

"Maybe," another prisoner said. "I heard one of the guards yesterday say we'd be arriving today."

"We're in the middle of nowhere," Janek said. "What could we be doing all the way out here?"

As the truck door opened, Janek looked out at something he could never have imagined. How far he'd fallen from his life as a farmer on the outskirts of Lodz, he thought, surrounded by green fields and snow-capped mountains, skiing and hiking when not tilling the soil, or spending hours just walking through meadows and forests that stretched as far as the eye could see.

Janek had only heard rumors about Soviet gulags, a system of prison complexes that began as a way to control the population and to have a supply of workers rather than punish criminals. That was the main difference between Nazi concentration camps and the gulags. Not many left Nazi camps alive, which were built specifically for extermination. At least in the gulags, prisoners had a slim chance—if they survived punishments, accidents, disease, and starvation—of leaving one day. The other difference was that mostly Jews and Catholics were sent to Nazi death camps, while gulags were populated with all ethnic groups, nationalities, and religions because Soviets did not discriminate in their brutality.

By the start of World War II, Stalin's gulag system, spread across the vast expanse of Russia's eleven time zones and consisting of more than 400 labor colonies, had grown into an economic empire that supplied the Soviet Union with everything from gold to food and timber. That demanded a need for labor, and lots of it. No crime was too small to avoid conviction, and a ten-year sentence to a gulag for stealing a bottle of milk so that a child could live another week was common.

"Everyone stand at attention alongside the receiving depot," a guard ordered, then waited with several other well-armed guards for the men to disembark.

Janek and twenty other men who'd survived the two-week trip climbed down from the truck and waited at attention.

"Move this way," the guard said, pointing in the direction of a large camp surrounded by a ten-foot-high wooden fence and an inner barrier ten feet inside that one. Guard towers stood twenty feet high at the corners of the camp.

"Move along the road and directly into the camp," the guard said. "Do not deviate. See that area?" He pointed to the death zone where guards were permitted to shoot without warning anyone who set foot in it. "Anyone caught between the fence and the barrier will be shot at once."

Janek and the men walked shoulder to shoulder for fear of stepping a foot outside the danger line. The only exits out of the camp had guard stations manned by armed soldiers and snarling dogs. In the center stood a large bathhouse, two disinfestation rooms, utility buildings, and five prisoner barracks.

"These are your living quarters," the guard

announced as he stopped in front of barracks number four. "You'll be sharing it with other prisoners already here. Go in and choose where you will sleep. Tomorrow you begin work."

Janek entered a large, cavernous room lined with bare plank sleeping bunks stacked three high and set into the walls. Each of the windows was covered with heavy metal bars. The entire room was lit by four hanging light bulbs that flickered as though they'd go out any minute. Tables and benches sat in the middle of a mud floor. Janek selected an empty sleeping shelf and sat, already beginning to sweat from the heat and humidity of the damp enclosure. Who had this bed before me, he wondered? How did he suffer and meet his fate? He looked around the dim room, picturing dying men staggering back from the fields, slumped on benches and tables until the next morning, too weak and exhausted from hard labor to even climb onto their beds. "Please, God, give me the strength to go on," he prayed.

That night, when veteran prisoners returned to the barracks, they were eager to share their experiences and tell the new arrivals what they could expect. Janek's first thought, as he listened to gaunt men with missing teeth and limbs like twigs, was how he'd survive such hell. An older prisoner with a scarred face and twisted nose came over and sat on the sleeping shelf alongside Janek. He stretched out his calloused hand and shook Janek's. It felt like sandpaper.

"I'm Tomasz," he said.

"Janek."

"We Poles have to stick together. There are things you need to know to survive."

"I'm listening."

"Don't ever look a guard in the eye," Tomasz warned. "They hate that. We're nothing more than pigs to them, so just look down or look away and do what you're told." What he didn't say, because Janek would learn soon enough, was that some guards, enraged that they'd been conscripted, torn from their lives and families and sent to the far reaches of Siberia alongside the lowliest Polish prisoners, had become wicked and bloodthirsty sadists.

"What are we here to do?"

"Work ourselves to death."

"I mean your job."

"Clearing brush all day," Tomasz said. "I guess they figure I'm too old and useless to chop trees or haul wood. The younger men have it worse, and there's more of them. You'll get your work assignment tomorrow."

"Which is?"

Tomasz looked into Janek's frightened eyes and let out a chuckle. "You, my friend, are part of Stalin's great plan to transform the wilderness of Siberia. If you're lucky, you might live long enough to see it."

"What about food? Is there enough in this damn place?"

Tomasz smirked. "Never, but you'll get used to it. If you see something out there you can eat, grab it. Insects, mice, frogs, whatever you can get down quickly without the guards seeing might just save your life."

"And if they catch you?"

"One of the men got caught last month eating a grasshopper. They stripped him naked and tied his hands to a tree for hours. Mosquitos covered him head to foot in a feeding frenzy…nearly drove him insane…but starvation is worse, so he did it again, more carefully next time. You'll learn."

Tomasz patted Janek on the knee, then dug into his hair, pulling out two lice from his scalp. "I hate these little bastards," he said, watching them squirm between his fingers before he crushed them to death.

"Are lice a problem?" Janek asked. "I hate them as well."

"Usually not, unless the bathhouse and disinfestation buildings are down, which lately has been every few months. When that happens, we all get infested because we can't wash or change our underwear. Anyway, if you watch yourself, do what you're supposed to do, you'll eat enough to live and work another day."

The next morning, Janek was assigned the backbreaking work of road construction and rail repair through a vast and uninhabited section of Siberia. That meant cutting down sections of forest, breaking rock, and moving wood and earth. He'd learned from Tomasz that many assigned that job either died from accidents, infections resulting from accidents, or from exhaustion. Some had killed themselves rather than go on. Janek was determined he would not be one of them.

Within a week, Janek had adjusted to his routine: he was woken at four a.m. for a pitiful breakfast—a small piece of bread and a little soup or fish—then lined up for inspection, where work orders were given. Outside, vicious dogs, constrained by large guards, snarled and barked, a warning to anyone within earshot that escape would cost them at least a pound of their flesh. And every day, he'd hear the same order from the same ugly guard as the men were escorted out to work: "Move quickly! One step out of line and you'll be shot like a filthy dog."

Most of the time, Janek walked in a daze, oblivious to his pain, weakened from hunger and exhaustion and already thinking about the little food he'd be getting in eight hours.

How was anyone expected to work like this, Janek asked himself, but also understood that it was of no consequence whether someone took his last breath or not, that no one gave a second thought to how human beings were treated because there was always a steady supply of prisoners. One died; another would arrive the next day. When Janek's team came close to achieving their quota, it was immediately raised, so rarely was it ever possible to earn a full ration of food. It was a perfect way for camp guards to control prisoners because it encouraged them to work even harder. But the harder they worked, the weaker they became until no amount of food was enough to make up for it. Soon, Janek and his men learned to pace themselves, even if they knew they wouldn't eat as much, just to keep from working to death.

The workday stretched from sunrise to sunset. Janek and his men toiled nonstop until lunchtime, at which time they were allowed to rest and given a small portion of soup. After lunch, they worked until dark and then marched back to camp, half starving and on the verge of collapse. Before supper, they were forced to stand at roll call for an hour to make sure all prisoners were accounted for. Only then did the men get their ration of food, and that depended on the amount of work they had completed that day, which was determined by guards who set a quota impossibly high and depended on the job. If it was clearing forest, the quota was the number of trees cut and piled in pieces to be taken away. That particular work was called "the green execution" because prisoners only lasted a short time before dying of exhaustion.

Prisoners lined up before supper and formed two rows. Those who filled their quota received an extra slice of bread and a piece of spoiled fish, twice the amount of food as the others. The poor wretches on the other line glared at the lucky ones next to them with hate in their eyes.

Janek was fortunate he'd arrived in better physical condition than others, because after only a few months, some of the men could no longer be recognized and had at most a few more weeks of life. For the next five months, Janek and many of his men managed to survive that first summer and fall. But it was winter he feared most because the brutal conditions of northern Siberia, worse than anyone could even imagine, would kill off even the hardiest of men.

Chapter 8

Sandusky, Ohio
August 14, 2004

"A blessed day to you, Wanda," Sister Regina sang out on a bright Saturday morning. "Do you know what day it is?"

Wanda looked up at the good sister's smiling face, her own drawn into a puzzled expression. She understood the question and shook her head no.

"Why it's the feast of Saint Maximillian Kolbe, of course."

Wanda squirmed in her chair the second she heard the name. It sounded familiar, and then she whispered, "Of course...Maximillian Kolbe...Auschwitz."

"You remember!" Sister Regina exclaimed. In her hand she held a piece of paper with two photographs of Kolbe. She handed it to Wanda. "There's a special feast day mass for him this evening. Would you like me to take you?"

Wanda nodded. The name had stirred something inside of her, a faint memory that trickled to the surface at the very name of Maximillian Kolbe. She perked up, her face twitching, her usually pink complexion turning a ghostly pale. "The Saint of Auschwitz," she mouthed, then sat transfixed as she remembered hearing the story told in every school and every church across the nation of Poland since World War II.

"How much do you remember?" Sister Regina asked. "Did you know anyone who went to Auschwitz?"

"I know too much," Wanda said. "You're so young…so innocent…and you've not lived with such evil. You can't even comprehend."

Sister Regina's smile disappeared. "Tell me," she said, not sure if she was doing the right thing by asking, but also thinking it would be good for Wanda's mind to work and to remember things about her past. "Do you want to talk about it?"

Wanda stared at one of the photos of a thin, serious-looking Franciscan priest sporting a long beard and round spectacles, and then the other of the same but balding and clean-shaven man dressed head to toe in striped prisoner clothes as prisoner 16670 in Auschwitz block number eleven.

"What most people don't realize is that the only way Poland survived the war was because of its faith," Wanda said, her demeanor growing darker. "They claim it was patriotism or nationalism, but it was really because Poland was such a strong Catholic nation. That's how we survived, you know. It made the difference between life and death."

Sister Regina leaned over and looked more closely at the photo of a small Polish priest with nerdy spectacles across his nose and understood why people who first saw him could not imagine that he'd be such a threat to the Nazis' regime. As a Franciscan nun, she knew his story well but wanted to hear it from someone who'd lived through it, who knew what it was like.

"Tell me what you know about Maximillian Kolbe…about Auschwitz."

Wanda began: "My Janek was fighting Germans in western Poland at the same time Kolbe was hiding Polish refugees and Jews at his monastery in Niepokalanow, a small town a few miles from Warsaw. He was later arrested for anti-Nazi activities and ended up in Auschwitz, a place you only want to visit once in your life. Even today, if you walk through those iron gates, you can sense the evil around you…hear the screams, the agony, the torment. You can almost feel death in the air…imagine the ashes…smell the burnt flesh. No photograph can capture walking past buildings that seem alive with the ghosts of their victims. When Poland was fighting Germany early on, none of us knew or could imagine what was happening there."

"What happened to Kolbe?" Sister Regina asked.

"It wasn't only Jews arrested and taken to death camps like Auschwitz. You know that, don't you? Catholic priests, political prisoners, Jehovah Witnesses, even homosexuals were targeted by the Nazis for extermination. When prisoners arrived by train, most women, children, and older men were sent to the left, which meant the gas chambers. Those sent to the right were mostly young men fit enough for forced labor. Kolbe was one of those, so he was sent to block eleven…where they had special punishment bunkers."

"Never heard about that," Sister Regina said.

"Prisoners who broke one of the rules were put in a standing cell three feet by three feet with a small opening covered by a metal grill. You could still see it on a tour Auschwitz. Four men would be forced to stand in the cell all night before being let out to work a twelve-hour shift. Sitting or sleeping was impossible, the men soiled themselves, and sometimes one of them died from exhaustion and the body would lean against the three others the entire night. Outside the block, in the courtyard, prisoners were often punished by tying their hands behind their backs and hanging them from hooks on ten-foot poles until their joints dislocated and their tendons ripped apart. Some died from the pain and shock; the survivors usually couldn't move or work, so they were either sent to the gas chamber or moved across to block ten for human experimentation."

"Is that what happened to Kolbe?"

"Two months after he arrived in Auschwitz, a prisoner had disappeared from the barracks. The rule was that whenever a prisoner escaped, ten prisoners would be selected at random to die in a starvation bunker to serve as a lesson to the others. So the prisoners were lined up and the condemned men chosen one by one. When one of the men cried out for his wife and children, Maximillian Kolbe stepped out of formation and said, 'I'm a Catholic priest and an old man, good for nothing. I want to die in the place of the man who has a wife and children.'"

"And then?"

"The camp secretary crossed out 5659 and wrote down 16670. Maximillian Kolbe and nine other condemned men were immediately taken to die a slow and excruciating death. While in the bunker, Kolbe provided spiritual aid and comfort to the other men as they died of starvation one by one. After fourteen days, he was the only one alive when the guards came in to clean out the cell. When they did, he raised his arm as one of the guards injected him with carbolic acid. There's a plaque on the side of block eleven in Auschwitz to mark the spot where Kolbe stood when he offered his life for another."

"What happened to the prisoner he saved?"

"The man's name was Francis Gajowniczek, a Polish army sergeant who lived for several more years in death camps until they were liberated. He spent the rest of his life telling the world about the act of love and sacrifice shown by Maximillian Kolbe. When he finally died, he was buried in Niepokalanow, one of only three non-clergy buried in the cemetery near Kolbe's monastery."

"You know anyone who died at Auschwitz?" Sister Regina asked.

Wanda paused and nodded, thinking of friends and neighbors who'd been forced from their homes and disappeared. It was impossible for her to speak of it to Sister Regina, who'd triggered painful memories of a time when Poland had become the center of evil in the world. And as much as she tried to rid those thoughts from her mind, she remembered it like it happened yesterday.

Auschwitz, two hundred miles from her home in Lwow, was little known at the time, and people simply assumed it was a POW camp. Wanda had later learned from survivors what no one could have imagined: rather than a POW camp, Auschwitz had been constructed as an extermination center. Whoever was not gassed upon arrival was assigned backbreaking work. Food rations were meted out in such a way that prisoners would stay alive for no more than a few months. If someone lived longer, the guards knew that he or she was stealing bread.

From the moment the death trains rolled through the gate and ground to a halt, newly arrived prisoners could smell the crematoriums, their smokestacks billowing flames and smoke that filled the air with soot and a sickening layer of human ash. The smell was nauseating as the unsuspecting passengers filed out and stood before a row of armed guards and snarling dogs. The selection process commenced the moment everyone got off the trains. Whatever belongings they'd brought were confiscated and thrown into a large pile. The strongest-looking prisoners were chosen for work and another few months of life. The weak, sick, elderly, disabled, and most women and children were marched to what they were told was a disinfecting room that contained false shower heads to give the appearance of a large communal bathhouse. On the chamber wall was a sign that read: *Put shoes into the cubbyholes and tie them together so you will not lose them. After the shower, you will receive hot coffee.*

As many as seven hundred men, women, and children would be ordered to undress and enter the chamber until they stood crammed like sardines, shoulder to shoulder. The doors were locked, and gas pellets immediately dropped from small openings in the ceiling. Within seconds, when the poor wretches realized what was happening, panic ensued. Outside the airtight doors, guards stood with no emotion as they listened to screams of agony when gas drifted upward to the victim's faces and began filling their lungs. Infants who didn't make it into the chamber were grabbed by their legs, smashed against a wall, and thrown into a row of burning trenches.

It took no more than twenty minutes before the final whimpers stopped. When the doors were unlocked, twisted bodies lay piled one on top of another as if the strongest had tried to prolong their lives a few more seconds by knocking down the weakest and using them to reach the gas-free layer of air near the ceiling. Urine, excrement, and vomit were everywhere: on the floor, the walls, and the corpses, which were dragged from the room with special hook-tipped poles. Even today, scratch marks could be seen on the gas chamber walls where victims tried clawing their way away from the gas before it burst their lungs.

By 1941, the Nazis had become adept at exterminating large numbers of victims. Corpses were sorted by size, weight, and how combustible they were to more efficiently utilize the amount of fuel required to burn them. Doctors conducted experiments to determine which body types could be cremated together most economically. An emaciated woman together with a child, for example, would be cremated together because once they caught fire, their bodies would continue to burn without the need for additional fuel.

But the horrors of the gas chamber or a single bullet to the head were at least somewhat merciful. The true horror was watching a black car drive slowly by the line of prisoners and stop to disgorge Dr. Josef Mengele, the Angel of Death, as many in the camp called him. Dr. Mengele, the medical commandant in charge of Nazi medical research, would make his selections and send them to block ten, where the most gruesome human experiments were conducted.

By all accounts, Mengele had made it a habit to stalk catlike in his crisply pressed uniform as he walked, his pristine, smooth hands clasped behind his back, an air of glee and superiority on his face upon seeing fresh new arrivals. If one didn't know the thirty-three-year-old, or had never stepped foot inside his chamber of horrors, one would not think twice about sharing a meal with this charming and soft-spoken fellow. Beneath the cap, dark thick hair matched a set of heavy eyebrows and even darker eyes that appeared stern and serious until they'd catch sight of a pair of twins; and it was then that he would come alive and flash a smile that made the children feel as though they were something special.

A scientist at heart, Dr. Mengele had a penchant for scribbling down the most minute details of his experiments. Survivors claimed that the man was capable of brief and intermittent bouts of compassion and kindness, one minute bringing children candy and other treats, the next injecting them with chloroform and sending them to the crematorium. Sometimes he had no need for the crematorium, thinking it wasteful and inefficient for disposing of such small bodies. On one occasion, he ordered hundreds of children and infants he no longer needed thrown into open fire pits and burned alive. Those who tried to claw their way out would be kicked back in, their screams silenced as flames engulfed their tiny bodies until nothing was left but what looked like pieces of charred and twisted wood.

"Those two children look perfect," Dr. Mengele would say gleefully as he pointed them out. "And that one will do as well." Twins, dwarfs, and those with unique physical traits were always chosen first. After years of obscurity, Mengele had found the perfect environment for his human laboratory, becoming fanatical in the selection process and insisting on being involved personally in choosing who was sent to work, who would die in gas chambers, and who would live to serve as human guinea pigs.

To the twins, it must have seemed strange to have

such attention heaped upon them, believing that somehow God had spared them from the horrors they saw happening to everyone else around them. For while the crematoriums were operating day and night, there they were, pampered and fawned over, eating better than anyone else, sitting in clean laboratories, having every square inch of their bodies examined and measured as if they were somehow special. How extraordinarily odd, they must have thought, that someone would be so interested in the color of their eyes, the texture of their hair, the size and roundness of their heads, the shape of their noses, the distance between their eyes and ears, the length of their penises, the number of hairs between the joints on their knuckles, and the number of freckles on their faces.

Unfortunately, after comprehensive family histories had been taken and exhaustive physical examinations done, it was time to get down to more serious business. The twins quickly learned that, although their uniqueness brought with it better food and a little more time, it had, in fact, sealed their fate. A series of torturous experiments followed that made the twins wish they'd been culled for the gas chambers instead. One of Mengele's favorite experiments included testing various dyes he injected into unanesthetized eyes, causing excruciating pain and sometimes blindness. In other experiments, he sewed children together to simulate conjoined twins, injected typhoid or tuberculosis to see how individuals of various races reacted to disease, and killed sets of healthy individuals spontaneously because he wanted to do autopsies on twins who died at precisely the same moment.

But as bad as the twins' experiments were, others

were far worse. Nazi doctors had welcomed the opportunity to use human subjects rather than laboratory animals. Painful freezing and thawing experiments were done to test hypothermia. Some prisoners were infected with bacteria, allowed to develop gangrene, and had limbs amputated. Other victims had tubes forced through their noses and into their lungs for collection of fluids. If the lungs didn't tear or collapse, the victims were given a few days to recover, administered enemas, strapped to a bench table and, without anesthesia, had their rectums distended for an intense and painful gastric examination. Once samples were taken, subjects were wheeled to the dissection room, killed with a single injection of phenol or chloroform to the heart, and dissected for study of internal organs.

"Wanda?" Sister Regina saw that Wanda's face had contorted, her hands clenched. "Are you okay?"

At that point, Wanda had enough of Auschwitz and answered, "Yes. Sometimes when I think about it, I feel like I'm going into shock."

"I'm sorry," Sister Regina said, then changed the subject. "Did Janek ever make it back to Lwow before the Soviets invaded?"

"If he had, he would have been arrested and shot. We got word that captured soldiers were being murdered, along with their wives and children, so he joined up with an Army unit in eastern Poland."

"How did you manage in Lwow?"

"Not an hour went by that I didn't think of him," Wanda said, her voice trembling. "Each day, I thought, would bring us closer to the end, but instead the Germans advanced through Poland, occupying cities, executing civilians, burning villages to the ground. The Soviets did

109

much the same, murdering and deporting people to gulags across Russia. It only got worse that winter. February 1940. I remember it like it was yesterday. That's when I was arrested and sent to Kazakhstan."

Wanda fell silent, her mind drifting from Lwow to Auschwitz to Kazakhstan and back to Lwow. And then she thought of Janek's years in prison and how much he suffered and fought to survive so that one day he could return to them. *How could my Janek have gone through so much?* Tears rolled down her cheeks as she reflected on the love Janek had for her and Sophie to do what he did. *What would I have done in his place? Give up and march to my death like so many others? Or walk away, risking death for the chance to see my family again?*

"I'd like to sleep," Wanda told Sister Regina.

"I'll come back this evening and we can go to mass." Sister Regina stroked Wanda's head and helped her into bed. "Sweet dreams."

Wanda closed her eyes and hoped her dreams would be of Janek. She smiled when she saw his face and reached her hand up to touch him.

"Janek, my love. Please don't leave me."

Wanda drifted toward sleep and thought about how people talk of love as some sort of lovely or noble trait, but she wondered how many would be willing to lose everything, even their lives, for a chance at that love. She knew her beloved Janek had, and as the room around her fell dark and silent, she began dreaming of a young girl in Radom swept up into the arms of a man who loved her in a way most people could never imagine.

Chapter 9

Yakutsk, Siberia
January 1941

Three hundred miles south of the Arctic Circle, Yakutsk lies in the Sakha Republic, which stretches 1,200 miles eastward from the Laptev and Siberian Seas of the Arctic Ocean, the most frigid and iciest of all waters in the Northern Hemisphere. Taking over the sparsely populated area in 1940, the NKVD built no less than 105 gulag camps where winter temperatures are the coldest on earth and continuous permafrost makes digging even a few feet down nearly impossible.

Janek, though weakened by little food and punishing work, had survived. Many of his fellow prisoners had died before the start of winter, replaced by new arrivals from Poland, Ukraine, Lithuania, Estonia, Czechoslovakia, and the Soviet Union itself. The men formed brigades of thirty to forty prisoners and worked under the watchful eyes of armed guards at all times. Janek, who always sought out new Poles, had become a gulag mentor, advising frightened young arrivals on how to survive, much like Tomasz had done before he died in the fields a month earlier.

At thirty years old, Janek seemed old compared to new arrivals he'd gather around him, some of whom looked decades younger. "I'm Janek," he said. "I've been here since last July, so I know a few things." He watched the men lean forward, eager to listen. "If you want to live more than a few months, you can't let them get into your head."

"What does that mean?" a prisoner asked.

"It means you do your work, and you don't allow what these bastards do or say to affect you. We work as a team, and a team is stronger than any one man."

Janek knew all too well that the biggest difference between German and Soviet camps was how they killed. In Nazi camps, a senior guard might throw a prisoner who broke the rules to the ground and kill him with a bullet to the head, no questions asked, no time for pleading, no emotion. In Soviet camps, sadistic guards would work and starve a prisoner until he could no longer move; and only then, after weeks of agony, shoot him like a wounded animal. Stalin himself, though never visiting any of the gulags under his rule, had admonished some of them for not being harsh enough.

A vicious despot by any stretch, Joseph Stalin had often tested the loyalty of subordinates by arresting their family members. State, for the dictator, came before family, and whoever didn't acknowledge that was doomed. While Lenin tried to convince and educate the population into accepting Marxism-Leninism, Stalin demanded absolute submission through repression and murder. There was no persuasion or patience, only terror and punishment. To the misfortune of every nation around him, he was not satisfied with killing only his own people if also killing others meant a new world order would replace the old and instill his communist ideals in everyone within reach.

Stalin first spread his evil ideology to a much

weaker next-door neighbor, invading Poland because he genuinely believed it was part of the lost Tsarist Empire. More pragmatically, though, he thought of Poland as the heart of Europe, and how Poland went so followed the rest of the continent. So, he forcibly imposed a tyrannical and alien Soviet-style system on Poland despite knowing how difficult it would be and admitting that it was 'like fitting a cow with a saddle.' But for him, it was worth every dead Russian soldier because the ultimate dream was to establish a classless society under complete Soviet domination. Patriots and soldiers who threatened that dream found themselves in mass graves or in Siberian gulags.

"What are the guards like?" a young man with the face of a teenager asked.

"Most of them are all the same," Janek answered. "Brutal thugs. Hatred in their eyes. They never smile, probably because they're miserable themselves, being stuck in this hell with the rest of us. I suspect that some were criminals, forced to join the Soviet Army rather than serve a prison sentence for what they did."

"So we have criminals watching over us?"

Janek nodded. "That's what makes them so effective. Even the worst prisoners can't intimidate them...and there's no one here to restrain them."

"Are any worse than the others?"

"There's one...Ivan...a big-boned, stocky brute with a large scar across his forehead and a crooked nose like it was hit with something. You'll see him soon enough. He won't think twice about beating you for the smallest infraction. Hates Poles. Every time he talks to us, he calls us pigs, sometimes spits on us."

"Have you ever been beaten?"

Janek sneered as if looking defiantly into Ivan's cold eyes. "Once, for talking back to him like a fool. I learned to keep my mouth shut, do my work, eat whatever I could get, and live to work another day. We all fantasize how we could kill the son-of-a-bitch."

Janek went on to describe how bad a day for a gulag prisoner could be, with desperate men clenching their teeth on a stick as they chopped a finger off with an axe, or drank kerosene, burned their hands on a stove, or froze their toes to get into the hospital for a few days of rest. The worst labor was any outdoor job, where men were exposed to some of the most brutal elements on earth and most died shortly after arriving.

In the Yakutsk camp, where prisoners toiled from sunrise to sunset building roads, hunger, exhaustion, unsanitary conditions, infection, and injuries led to starvation and painfully slow death. The quicker the men lost their strength, the less they were able to work and the fewer rations they received for their labor. In a matter of months, long sections of road were being laid on top of permafrost by skeletons that fell to their knees and died, their skin and bones laid beneath or next to the road or carried to unmarked pits and covered with cold earth.

A young soldier asked, "How difficult is the work?"

"Difficult. But if you work extra hard, thinking it will get you better treatment or more bread, it won't. They'll expect you to work even harder next time."

"So what's to be done? Get punished for less work?"

"You learn to work just hard enough to get your job done but not so hard that your body wears down. Don't make the mistake of thinking you're too young or too strong. Sometimes it's better to miss your quota and get a little less food than to expend your energy and work yourself to death. Remember that."

"How do you will yourself to go on?" another young man asked.

"I have something to live for," Janek said. "My family...my wife and child. Without that, nothing matters."

"You must think about them all the time."

"I do, and it seems like only yesterday I was with them." A tear fell onto the floor from Janek's cheek as he looked down and thought how quickly time had gone by.

"Are you okay?"

Janek shook his head. "It's funny. When you're a child, you don't even think about it. As a teenager, you want time to speed up so you can do adult things. When you get old, you wonder where all that time went, and there you are, reliving a life that seems to have come and gone in the blink of an eye. And then I think there was someone who lived and died, maybe right here in Siberia, a million years ago; and that's when you realize that time means nothing, that your life in the overall scheme of history is a millisecond and the things you do will be as insignificant as what that prehistoric man went through a million years ago."

The young man next to Janek said, "If everyone thought of time that way, they'd realize how precious little we have of it. Maybe we'd treat each other better."

Janek's face twisted into a scowl. "No, we wouldn't. We think we have all the time in the world, so when we're doing horrible things to fellow human beings, time stands still. Only when we're about to run out of it do we feel guilt or remorse. And then it's too late. We die and we leave all that suffering behind."

The men around Janek could see the sadness in his weary eyes, and they all knew it was time to leave him to himself. When they scattered to their bunks, Janek fell back onto his and tried hard not to think about the hunger pangs that would waken him throughout the night.

As the weeks went by, the young men that formed Janek's work brigade suffered more than they'd ever suffered in their lifetimes, but they also became numbed by the brutal conditions of a winter that seemed to worsen by the day. The winter gear issued was a small relief: thick woolen coats and hats, gloves, several pair of work pants, tall boots, and socks that were as precious as gold. Janek tried as best he could to get them through each workday, though he felt himself growing weaker and less able to keep up with the younger men. Sometimes he ate snow to stop the stomach pains. From morning till night, all he could think about was food and making his quota so he'd get an extra scrap of bread when he got back to camp. The work had become increasingly backbreaking, especially in the dead of winter when he was forced to dig through snow and frozen layers of soil to remove roots and tree stumps before preparing the ground for roads. Temperatures thirty degrees below zero were not uncommon and were never a reason to stop work. When snowdrifts reached waist level, it was impossible to fulfill even half the work quota, which meant less food that evening and less energy the next day.

This went on day after day, men dying where they worked while new prisoners took their place, some crying like babies because they'd never experienced anything like it in their lives. But eventually even the softest prisoners hardened to the reality that this was now their life, so they worked to eat and hoped it was enough to survive the horror they found themselves in. In many cases, it was not, and the body was simply added to the pile of unnamed and forgotten corpses that still lie beneath the long stretch of road that crosses the immense Siberian tundra.

What many of the prisoners in Yakutsk didn't know was that almost 6,000 miles west of where they were being worked and starved to death, the gulag system had been established first by Lenin as a place where people who opposed his ideology were to be rehabilitated and redeemed through hard labor. It was later that Stalin and his bloodthirsty police used it to transform millions of prisoners into mindless slaves that thought of little else but surviving the misery of torture, hunger, and cold. From its inception as a single political prison—the former Solovetsky Monastery in northern Russia—the gulag grew into dozens of major labor colonies with thousands of individual camps.

It was at Solovetsky that Soviet authorities had laid the groundwork for gruesome methods of torture and execution. To the casual observer who passed its beautiful structure, the ethereal beauty of tranquil lakes and pristine forest belied the nature of what had gone on behind those monastery walls: savage punishments and brutality so vile it shocked the most staunch and idealistic Soviet official. One such punishment, known as Ascension Skete, involved tying a prisoner to a log and hurling him down a 294-step wooden staircase. Today, at the foot of that staircase stands a cross memorializing those who'd died that agonizing death.

But long before the Solovetsky Monastery turned Lenin's utopian dream into a place of horror, its former inhabitants were no less innocent of crimes against humanity, and perhaps that's why it was chosen as the forerunner of the Soviet gulag. The grim history of Solovetsky cried out to Lenin, who looked at its past and saw in it the potential for Russia's future: workers disciplined and united through the efforts of hard labor. The monastery, for all its beauty and splendor, had for centuries kept secrets that made it the perfect model for what would become the most shameful chapter in Russian history.

From the sixteenth century on, Solovetsky monks, faithful to both God and the Czar, ultimately chose the Czar—perhaps in an attempt at self-preservation—and incarcerated political enemies of the State, including priests, who rebelled against it. Centuries later, even before Lenin's order to transform the monastery into a gulag, the islands surrounding it were considered an ideal location for a work camp. Thus, prisoners who began arriving as early as the summer of 1920 were the first of countless souls that would spend the remainder of their lives as part of Lenin's re-education program. By 1939, Stalin and his henchmen issued specific and detailed orders dictating life in the gulags, principle among them the strict control of behavior and productivity through food and living conditions. For Stalin, every aspect of gulag life was designed for one purpose and one purpose only: to transform the Soviet Union from a peasant society into an industrialized world superpower.

While the gulag was never profitable, the great camp complexes across Siberia acted as mechanisms of forced colonization in order to open up the Soviet Union's frozen north and its vast, empty steppes. No one was spared. In fact, forced labor of elite scientists in prison laboratories produced an array of technological innovations and weapons. Sergei Korelev, father of the Soviet space program, was the most famous of the prison scientists. Once gulag prisoners were released, many continued working as forced laborers on much the same work they'd done as prisoners.

Figures released by Soviet historians have shown that as many as ten million people were sent to hundreds of gulags between 1937 and 1947. The true estimate, however, is upwards of fifty million, with death rates of as much as ten percent a year. By all accounts, the system of Stalin's labor camps was the most heinous reign of death in history, exceeding even the Holocaust in its scope. Mortality was inconsequential since dead prisoners were constantly replaced by new ones. Many of the victims, innocent of any crime, were arrested nonetheless to fill the labor needs of Stalin's empire. The largest camps, located in the most extreme climatic regions, from the Arctic north to the Asian south, became lifeless, soulless places where men worked all day then waited for others to die so they could strip off a sock or pry a crust of bread from their cold fingers. The victims, it seemed, had become easy prey for once-civilized men relegated to being nothing more than vultures sniffing out death.

Today, the fortified sixteenth-century monastery still sits on the beautiful Solovetsky islands as the prototype for the camps of the gulag system. Like a lone sentry overlooking the barren taiga of northern Russia, the entire stone structure, thirty feet high in places, is connected by roofed and arched passages, surrounded by multiple buildings and living quarters where the smell of death once permeated every inch of its massive fifteen-foot-thick walls.

Janek had learned to use his wits and his survival skills in the middle of a brutal winter that saw a number of the men die. He began to have doubts about surviving himself. At night, as men around him groaned and wept from hunger and pain, he would think of escape, but as he pictured the frozen bogs and the vast expanse of open tundra as far as the eye could see, he resigned himself to the fact that this was now his life. All he had left was his faith and all he could do was pray, which at least gave him comfort when nothing else did. And so he prayed, not for himself but that Wanda and Sophie had somehow found themselves in a better place.

From the second Janek opened his eyes at four a.m. to the moment barracks lights went out, camp guards controlled every aspect of his life—how much he ate, what he ate, the clothes he wore, where and when he slept. But the merciless guards weren't the only ones who determined life or death. Criminal gangs in adjoining barracks often terrorized the other prisoners and were often worse than the guards themselves, fighting and sometimes killing one another over a morsel of food or a pair of shoes. What did they have to lose, after all? A few more weeks of life? The guards knew that the worst of them couldn't care less if they lived or died, so they turned their backs and let the predators do as they pleased.

But more than anything else, the hunger was constant. Even those who worked harder than they'd ever worked in their lives got barely enough food to survive. And when they did, a minute after they swallowed their last morsel of thin soup or spoiled fish, their stomachs once again gnawed at them in pain because it was never enough. The weakest among them, the underperformers, or the injured, lasted perhaps two months before losing whatever semblance they had to human beings and starved to death. Goners, as they were called, grew so emaciated they became a constant reminder to Janek of what would happen to him should he not fulfill his daily work quota. It didn't take long for him to realize that Soviet punishment, instead of beatings, torture, or solitary confinement, was a slow and painful death by starvation, especially in the dead of winter when he and his fellow prisoners would pick lice or maggots and devour them rather than become goners themselves.

Zygmund, a prisoner who'd arrived a few months ago, sat across from Janek at one of the tables and said, "If we could make it a few more months, we'll see spring."

"At least we could eat what little we find," Janek said. "You have to be careful, but I'll show you."

Zygmund nodded. "I'm counting on it."

Janek leaned forward and whispered, "I'm going to warn you, though. I've learned not to trust some of the newer men here, especially the ones who aren't soldiers. They're desperate; and they'll do what they can to gain favor with the guards."

"You mean they'll report on fellow prisoners?"

"Yes," Janek answered. "So watch yourself. Most of the men in my brigade are okay—at least the soldiers are—but I suspect a few may not be."

Zygmund patted Janek's arm and said, "Thanks. I'll be careful."

As the two sat and rested from an exhausting twelve

hours in the field, Janek couldn't help thinking that he and everyone around him had become nothing more than expendable cogs in the great socialist machine of Stalin's march toward communism, without any value and worthy of life only as much as they could contribute to the State. And contribute they did. As Laverty Beria, chief of Stalin's secret police once told him, "Show me the man, I'll show you the crime." And so, Janek now found himself in the middle of a cultural Soviet upheaval, a Polish cog in Stalin's brutal attempt to transform Russia into the world's great superpower. He knew as well that the length of time he remained a prisoner would determine whether he lived to tell the world his story or joined the millions of Poles who would labor and die without a trace on Russia's bloody soil.

Janek hardly slept that night, despite his exhaustion, because his will to sleep was overpowered by nightmares of what the day would be like when he opened his eyes and realized where he was. So he lay still in the darkness, listening to men around him groan in pain from wounds and injuries, wondering which of them would stop breathing that night and mercifully end their suffering. The stench of dirty and mildewed clothes overpowered his senses, making breathing harder than it already was. When he finally *did* close his eyes—not because he wanted to but because his tired and battered body simply shut down—sleep came as quickly as the nightmares that raged through the night until he was startled from his bed by a banging that sounded like guns being fired around him.

"Everyone up! Everyone up!"

Janek leapt from his bunk to see three large camp guards, sticks in hand, walking up and down the rows of bunks, waking everyone up for an earlier-than-usual roll call.

"Move your lazy asses!" one of the guards shouted at the men, spitting through his teeth and threatening to beat anyone who didn't jump to attention. "Line up outside!"

Though Janek expected this kind of surprise inspection at any given moment, it never became routine, no matter how many times he'd been through it. So, like a dog who'd been conditioned to respond on command, he turned toward the door and marched straight into the frigid darkness. He stood at attention, clenching his fists and shivering beneath the falling snow. The guards, like ugly monsters wrapped head to boot in large gray overcoats and fur hats, laughed at the suffering they'd inflicted, while Janek and the other prisoners stood in rags and silently screamed obscenities. The guards took their time, making certain everyone was present and accounted for. The only consolation for Janek was that he'd made it through another night and that he'd be fed in another few hours. Satisfied that all the men were punished sufficiently for being Poles, the guards ended their charade and ordered the men back inside.

Once back in the barracks, Janek lay down for a little more sleep, but others gathered around the lone heating stove at the far end of the room and reminisced, as they always did, about Poland and their families. Some of the newer men wept, consoled by the veterans, who knew that in a few weeks it would all seem like a dream: the arrests, the journey to the gulag, the ceaseless hunger and endless suffering. Nothing in the world would matter, only survival or the hope that God was real and would one day embrace their withering bodies in His arms.

Unlike Janek, who prayed each morning and each night, a handful of the men had given up on their faith, no longer believing that a merciful God would allow such pain and suffering. For them, it was at that moment that fear of death was most palpable. If there *was* no afterlife, they thought, then all that horror would eventually end with nothing to show for it but skin and bone, forever left behind as part of Siberia's unforgiving landscape. But all the men, Janek included, regardless of their beliefs, feared one thing more than anything else: that eventually no one would know they'd ever existed; that they were like ghosts, living in the shadows of human history, doomed to a life as meaningless as that of a lowly insect. The thought of that made the strongest among them toss and whimper in his sleep, woken through the night by cold sweat and the sound of his own screams.

Janek tried to sleep but could not. He stood almost lifelessly by a small window and peered through the metal bars at the blackness outside. Despite its merciless cold and desolation, the Siberian sky, with stars so numerous they seemed to dance from one end of the horizon to the other, was almost magical. But as a million stars were ready to disappear into the morning sky, Janek's stomach told him it was nearly time for a breakfast not fit for pigs. It would make no difference to him. He would have eaten dirt if there were bugs in it and it satisfied his constant hunger.

Janek spent whatever free moments he had, before the guards came back, tying together his tattered clothes and making sure his shoes had some cloth inside to keep his toes from getting frostbite, although a good case of frostbite, which meant a missing toe or two, would get him a few days of welcomed rest in the hospital. He lay back down and tried to rest, but his body sensed it was almost time to spend another punishing twelve hours in the brutal cold. "Dear God, watch over me," he prayed. "Keep me safe and let me live another day."

Chapter 10

Sandusky, Ohio
August 15, 2004

"I know her," Wanda said under her breath, her soft brown eyes lighting up, and then beamed with delight when Sophie walked into the room. Fewer and fewer things would trigger Wanda's memory these days, but just seeing her daughter's face was enough to jar her back into reality.

"Sophie," she mouthed. "Come here next to me, my love."

"Hello, Mama." Sophie, whose frequent visits brought so much joy to Wanda, had come this morning to attend Sunday mass with her mother. "Sister Regina says you're doing well, and you've been remembering things."

"Is that good?" Wanda asked.

"Of course it is," Sophie replied, then bent and kissed her. "Isn't it?"

"Depends on what you remember," Wanda said. "Sometimes I try not to, but it comes to me anyway."

"Hello, ladies." Sister Regina strode in with a pitcher of fresh flowers. "These will make your room smell like our lovely garden." She set the pitcher down on the windowsill.

Sophie settled into a chair next to Wanda and took

hold of her mother's frail hand. "Sister Regina tells me you two have been talking about Poland and the war. Are you okay with that?"

Wanda sank back in her chair and shrugged. "It's part of our history," she whispered, her lips turned down into a frown. "It'll be part of me till I die. And I suppose the more people who know about it the better."

Surprised to hear that coming from her mother, Sophie turned to Sister Regina and said, "She never wanted to talk about it when we were younger. Too many bad memories. Too much pain. My parents would send letters and medicine to our families, but we hadn't spoken to anyone in years. Whenever my father even mentioned anything about Russia, you'd think the sky was about to crash down on us. It was very painful for her to hear it." She turned to her mother and said, "I'm surprised you'd even bring it up."

Sophie thought back to the stories her aging father would begin to tell until Wanda overheard him, rushed into the room, threw up her hands, and ordered him to stop. "*Nie tatuś, nie mow*: No, Daddy, don't talk," she'd say, her thin finger wagging, a look of fright spreading across her face as if what he was saying had happened to her yesterday.

As Sophie had once explained to Sister Regina, Wanda would always call Janek '*tatuś*'—'Daddy' in Polish—because she'd become almost childlike after the war, the years in Siberian labor camps with a young daughter scarring her beyond measure. Experiencing it herself, Sophie knew all too well that her mother had been through a living hell, and she understood how such horrors could change a woman to the point that a single word about Russia would bring her to tears.

Looking somewhat sheepish, Sister Regina said apologetically, "It's my fault. I thought it would help with her memory…and it was so interesting coming from someone who actually lived it. I'm sorry if I dredged up things I shouldn't have."

"You didn't," Wanda interjected. "After so many years keeping it in, I wanted to."

Sister Regina turned to Sophie with a puzzled look. "How does a child live through something like that?" she asked. "It was bad enough for Wanda and your father, but you were only six when they took you away to the camps."

"It was a horror at first. Brutish men rushing into our home, ordering us to pack only what we could carry with us. I remember screaming and watching my mother panic, grabbing coats and a blanket, some food, and a small bag. We were pushed through the door and stood there in the freezing cold with other families. If I didn't know better, I would have thought it was a nightmare I was having." Sophie glanced over at Wanda, whose teary eyes were fixated on the window as if reliving that moment along with her daughter.

"I can't even imagine going through that," Sister Regina said. "You must have been scared out of your mind."

Sophie nodded. "At first, yes. By the time we got on the train, it was more of a shock than anything else. I didn't know what was happening. I think Mom probably did. People were crying. There were other children, but mostly it was women because a lot of the men had been captured or arrested, or they were dead or still fighting, if not in prisons."

"And your father?"

"We had no idea where he was. He'd been called up by the army in the summer of thirty-nine, and we never heard from him after that."

"So you didn't even know if he was alive."

"No one knew who was alive or where they were. After the Soviets invaded, Poland surrendered on October sixth, and everyone captured was taken prisoner."

"When did you find out he was alive?"

"Not until later, in 1941. We eventually got word he'd been taken to a prison in Smolensk after being captured by the Soviets and then shipped off to a gulag somewhere in Siberia. But it would be another five years before we saw him. That's a whole other story."

"Are you okay, Wanda?" Sister Regina asked, seeing that Wanda had turned from the window and gone into an expressionless stare. She did that frequently these days, animated and talkative one minute, quiet and melancholy the next. Sometimes it would last only a few seconds before she'd snap out of it and continue as if nothing happened. Sister Regina had noticed it occurred more often when she reminisced about Poland, but especially when she remembered and spoke of Janek.

Wanda sat quietly, gathering her thoughts, then said, "He almost died in that place. A few more months and we would have never seen him again. I prayed to Jesus and Mary every day, thinking that it couldn't hurt to ask them both to watch over Janek. Two for one, I guess."

Sister Regina chuckled that Wanda still had her sense of humor. "I do the same," she said. "Mary has been a comfort and an inspiration to me all my life."

"That's especially true in Poland," Sophie added. "Mary's had a special place there for centuries and is considered the Queen of Poland."

"That's beautiful," Sister Regina said. "I didn't know that."

Sophie then explained how Mary had become one of the most important religious figures in Polish culture. She was crowned Queen of Poland in 1655 when Swedish invaders overran the country but couldn't defeat the monastery at Jasna Gora, which houses the famous painting of Our Lady of Czestochowa. According to historical accounts, seventy monks and a handful of supporters held off nearly four thousand Swedish soldiers for forty days and nights. After the Swedes withdrew, the Polish Army eventually drove them from Poland. King Casimir declared the victory a miracle and dedicated Poland to the protection of Mary. On April 1, 1656, he issued an official proclamation:

"Great Mother of God, Most Blessed Virgin, I, John Casimir, by the grace of your Son, King of kings and my Lord, and by your mercy, King, falling at your most holy feet, choose you for my Patroness and Queen of our country. I entrust to your admirable care and protection my own self with my Kingdom of Poland."

As Poland and its culture were systematically erased from history, Poland's faith only strengthened, kept alive by its citizens' love of and devotion to Mary. During the four partitions of Poland from 1772 to 1939, that love and devotion was the binding force that sustained it through some of the darkest periods in history, when the Polish State could not be found on any map of Europe. In 1923, Pope Pius XI designated May 3 as the feast of Our Lady, Queen of Poland, which also happens to be the day that 123 years earlier Poland created its nation's first constitution. But more than anything else, the people of Poland looked to Mary as not only the mother of Jesus but as the mother of their nation, embracing it during the darkest moments in human history and, most recently, delivering its people from the cruelty and horrors of Adolph Hitler and Joseph Stalin.

"People are surprised when they read about Polish history how much devotion to the Blessed Mother there still is today," Sophie continued. "We're a very Catholic nation, and we pass it down from generation to generation. It was faith that sustained us as we watched our country torn to bits by savages who considered any kind of devotion, other than to the system they'd created, a dangerous form of insanity."

"Speaking of Mary, I guess you both know that today is the feast day of the Assumption of Mary," Sister Regina said. "A holy day of obligation—and it's time for mass." She saw no reason to remind Wanda and Sophie that the feast day celebrated Mary's assumption of both body and soul into heaven.

As the three made their way to the residence chapel, Wanda's mind kept drifting back to 1941. She never had the heart to say it, even when her mind was right, but every time she looked at Sophie, watched her eat or walk, or observed her smallest movements, she'd be reminded of the labor camps. Why did she feel so guilty, she thought? So ashamed? What had she done? What was it that held her memories hostage and would not let go? She did everything she could to keep her daughter safe, after all, and here they both were, in Sandusky, Ohio, alive more than sixty years later; and instead of feeling despondent, she should be happy that she was sitting in a chapel with her precious daughter.

"Here we are," Sister Regina said. "And there's your

favorite pew." She wheeled Wanda to her usual spot, and they all sat and waited for Father Michael to begin mass.

On the far wall of the chapel hung a glass mural of Saint Augustine, one of the most important church fathers, and whose writings had influenced the early development of Christianity. Wanda's eyes wandered from Augustine to Saint Francis on the opposite wall and then to the front altar where Father Michael had arrived to celebrate the feast day of the Assumption. She didn't know why she was there among all those people looking down at red books she didn't recognize and saying words she couldn't understand.

"Where am I?" she whispered. "What is this?"

Sophie leaned over toward her mother and said, "We're in the chapel, at Sunday mass, Mama," then she took hold of her mother's frail hand.

The sound of Sophie's reassuring voice consoled her, and she bobbed her head as the rhythm of an opening hymn echoed through the chapel. When she looked down at the hand that was holding hers, feeling its warmth and its softness as it gently stroked her fingers, she thought of the countless times she'd done the same for Sophie. "My poor baby," she whispered. "How you suffered with me. I'm so sorry."

Sophie ignored what she thought were ramblings her mother would often mutter whenever she'd visit and sit with her. Sometimes Wanda would make no sense, and Sophie would just smile and nod as if she understood every word. What is she thinking, Sophie always wondered. Who is she with, in that secret place of hers? Janek? Her? It was as if Wanda would curl up and withdraw into a world to which no one else could go.

After mass and back in her room, Wanda lay down

and closed her eyes. Exhausted, she fell asleep. Sophie touched her hand and felt it turn ice cold.

"That happens," Sister Regina said, seeing the concern on Sophie's face. "She'll be fine."

"Thank you," Sophie said. "I think she just misses it so much."

"Misses what?"

"Poland. I always had a feeling, whenever she spoke of her life in Poland, that she and my father would have gone back in a heartbeat if they could. But for soldiers like my father, part of a Polish Army created by the government-in-exile, returning to Poland would have meant certain death. The Soviets believed that Polish soldiers, especially officers who fought with the British Army, were potential spies—or worse, revolutionaries. So, after leaving us behind in Lwow while he was a captain with the Second Polish Artillery Unit and then fighting with the British army, he knew he could never set foot on Polish soil as long as it remained in Russian hands."

"Tell me about that," Sister Regina said.

"Before the dual invasions," Sophie began, "my parents were living a pretty comfortable life. As an engineer with the national railroad company, Dad supervised a section of track in and around the city. Polish State Railways had given us a house and a piece of land, and everything seemed perfect—until September of that year, when Germany invaded Poland from the west and reached the suburbs of Lwow eleven days later. By then, most of the men in the city, including my father, had been called up and sent to the front lines and had no idea what the fate of their families was."

Sophie stopped and took a deep breath, looking over

at Wanda and seeing through her mother's eyes the torment inflicted on every man, woman, and child in Lwow. From everything Sophie had learned and all she'd experienced during World War II, she knew that, for its size, no country on earth had suffered more than Poland. It was, after all, the place where Auschwitz, Treblinka, and Birkenau still stand as ghastly reminders of what hell on earth was like. Isn't it something, she thought, how an average man could create such hell and fury; how the very name—Adolf Hitler—could trigger the most visceral feelings of hatred and loathing? Not surprised that nature and nurture had converged so cruelly to shape a leader who nearly destroyed the whole of Europe, she pictured the man's face and shuddered.

He had dark brown hair, parted almost pageboy-like to one side, a small mustache barely spanning his nose, and thin lips that pursed angrily as he shouted vitriol to throngs of admirers who viewed him as a Germanic savior. Always a poor student, frail and sickly much of his young life, never athletic or particularly adept at manual work, Hitler suffered from feelings of inferiority so pathologic that he grew to worship strength and power. He loved his mother, but hatred for his father, who ruled the family with a brutal and tyrannical fist, had transformed young Adolf into a sadistic rogue incapable of normal sexual relations, abusing all those he loved. A set of grayish blue eyes, hypnotic, large, slightly bulging, bordered underneath by semicircular pouches, appeared dead and impersonal until—as was his custom—they would stare at someone he'd meet for the first time with a penetrating glare meant not to greet but to intimidate. And on those rare occasions when he'd reach out with a weak and clammy hand, those who reached back knew at once they were in the presence of evil.

Wanda had always lamented that when Germany launched its invasion, Poland was the first to live under Hitler's tyrannical rule; when Russia invaded seventeen days later, the Poles fell to a different but equally brutal tyranny of mass executions and deportations to arctic Russia and Siberia. So, while the Nazis simply murdered, the Soviets condemned Poles to a slow and agonizing death by freezing and starvation until, by the fall of 1940, half of all men, women, and children deported to labor camps were dead.

Even before the Nazi invasion, the Soviets and Germans had signed an economic and non-aggression pact on August 29, 1939 so Russia would not intervene as Germany plundered its way east and made Poland theirs for the taking. It was perfect, as far as Russia was concerned: the Germans march in, overwhelm the Polish army, and the Soviets simply watch on the sidelines as World War II unfolds. A few weeks later, it would be their turn to kill and plunder and take over Lwow. Janek had already been gone for months, fighting in western Poland, when Soviet soldiers marched in with lists of names and selected families to deport.

Although Germany and Russia each had their own murderous styles, both were clearly executing, imprisoning, or deporting civilians as a method of cleansing the ethnic population. Sophie knew that all too well from photographs of women and older men, some holding suitcases, others with small packs on their backs and carrying children, their faces twisted in agony as though the world they knew had suddenly come to an end. She remembered looking into her father's eyes a few years back, seeing the same indescribable pain she'd seen in the faces of those poor souls in the photographs; pain that most people couldn't imagine and never knew existed outside of books and news clippings and movies.

As Sister Regina sat spellbound at Sophie's story, she wondered what evil could conjure up such things. What kind of person could rip a baby from its mother's arms and toss it like garbage into a pit of fire before her eyes? What sort of men could send entire families to their death while theirs fed like gluttons on borscht and sausage in the comfort and warmth of their own homes? If it didn't make sense to her, how could it possibly make sense to anyone who'd spent a lifetime not knowing the horrors of war and what real hunger or homelessness were?

"Thank you for taking such good care of my mother," Sophie told Sister Regina. "She seems to like you very much."

"Believe me when I say that everyone loves Wanda. She never complains, even when she's not having her best day."

"They're getting more frequent, aren't they? The bad days."

"They are, but we're managing. She's very talkative on her good days, though."

"She used to be, about most things, but like I said, she never liked to bring up her life in Poland. My father knew when to stop by just looking into her eyes. Those five months we spent in Lwow under Soviet occupation and then the labor camps were enough to change her forever."

Sister Regina paused, not sure if what she was about to say was appropriate. "There's something I wanted to mention but I wasn't sure if I should."

"What's that?"

"The other day, when your mother was taking a nap, she was tossing in her bed and I overheard her say, 'I should have told him. I kept it hidden from him all those years.'"

Sophie eyebrows raised. "I'm not sure what she could have meant by that, but it was probably just something she had on her mind. Who knows what she's thinking these days?"

But as soon as she said it, Sophie considered another possibility; one she had never allowed to enter into her mind, until now. As she pulled the blanket over Wanda's chest, images of their life in labor camps flashed before her eyes. What could her mother have done that she kept secret all those years? What mystery had plagued her life that she lived with it alone ever since they left Kazakhstan? Was the "him" she was talking about even her father? The secret, she concluded, must have been something that happened when her mother first arrived in Kazakhstan. And the more she thought of it, the more she remembered how her mother would seem to go into a trance, staring off into the distance as if the room surrounding her was their beloved Poland and that she was remembering a time and a place she could only go back to in her dreams.

It was at that moment that Sophie's imagination ran wild. Men and women, toiling day and night alongside each other, surely must have grown tolerant of the filth and stench that clung to their withering flesh, eventually giving in to their lust, if for nothing else than for the comfort and companionship of another human being of the opposite sex. It was a desperate and primeval urge, no doubt; for in any other situation, at any other time, those poor, filthy, smelly creatures would have been repulsed by one another. Instead, they probably shed their clothes, wrapped themselves in each other's arms and legs and, for a brief moment, could forget the cruelty of a world they would wake up to the next morning.

As young as Sophie was at the time, she no doubt figured that things were happening during the war that no one wanted to remember or talk about. She'd seen how Polish women in Kazakhstan labor camps were singled out only because they were Polish. Survival often depended on who the women knew, who they could make friends with, and who had wanted something from them. They were the most vulnerable of all, and they would do anything they could to save themselves and their children.

Sophie looked down at her mother and said to Sister Regina, "How peaceful she looks. Almost like an angel." And then she remembered how her mother would shuffle as she walked, then try to rub the pain from her legs whenever she sat. It was the long and frigid Siberian winters in labor camps that had left her legs permanently damaged, one day burning as if on fire, another feeling like pieces of dead wood with little sensation. She remembered listening to her poor mother groan, tears in her eyes, scratching at her legs to bring a few minutes of relief from the pain. Only when she got older did it occur to Sophie that her mother had been suffering that way from the moment they left the frozen taiga of Kazakhstan, where no amount of clothing would keep them warm, and the bone-chilling cold could eat a person's flesh in minutes.

Now that her mind was preoccupied with Kazakhstan, Sophie recalled spending their first winter fighting the bitter cold, doing whatever they could to survive until the spring. Conditions for men were brutal; for women, especially those with children, they were even worse. Women, even the frailest, were expected to do the same physical work as men twice their size. Guards routinely assaulted them. In some camps, where guards couldn't care less what happened, gangs of criminals roamed freely, preying on anyone they saw as weak and vulnerable.

Sophie thought back to how women would arrive so frightened and desperate they took camp husbands who were nothing more than rapists that protected their human property in exchange for an extra piece of bread and the promise they would not be beaten and raped by other men.

For Polish women, it was an unspeakable and unimaginable existence. At home, in Krakow and Warsaw and Lwow, they were loved and respected. Their role as wife, mother, and the heart of the family had elevated them to an honored place in Polish society. Only in their worst nightmares did they ever think such brutal things would happen to them. But they did. Every day. And some, rather than return to Poland shamed and disgraced at what they had done—often just to save themselves or their children from starvation—committed suicide, their numbers never to be known since the dead were dead regardless of how and why they died.

Sophie was content that at this point in her life it wasn't necessary to know what had happened to her mother or what she may or may not have done in Kazakhstan.

But her instincts, as much as she hated to admit it, told her the reason Wanda had grown so angry at any mention of Russia and hated talking about her past was a fear of Janek's reaction and her wish to never reopen a wound that had festered and never quite healed.

Chapter 11

Yakutsk, Siberia
February 1941

"Time to get up!" a snarling guard called out as two others banged iron pipes together. "Ten minutes to roll call."

Like zombies come to life, Janek and the other men leapt from their beds, forcing themselves into consciousness as they scurried to dress and prepare themselves for the horrors to come. The men had learned to arrange everything the night before so that no detail was left to chance. A mistake such as a missing glove or too little cloth in a torn shoe or not enough string to bind together a tattered coat with missing buttons would make the day even more miserable than it would already be. An engineer by trade, Janek would calculate every last detail to ensure his brigade came back in one piece.

In a wild frenzy, a wave of tired men rushed into the bathroom to relieve themselves. Washing would have to wait until later. For now, the most important thing was emptying one's bladder, dressing warmly, and getting ready for roll call and a meager breakfast that would leave everyone hungry for more.

"Line up outside for roll call and work assignments," one of the guards shouted, then turned on his heels and went outside.

"Make sure nothing is exposed," Janek told the new prisoners in his brigade. "And wear two pair of socks. We can't afford to lose anyone to frostbite."

Bogdan, one of the other men from Lwow, his cheeks sunken, his eyes protruding from their sockets, said, "I don't know if I can make it another day. I can hardly breathe, and it was hard to drag my body out of bed." Tall and gaunt, he had thinning hair and a flat nose that looked as if it had been beaten repeatedly. Three of his front teeth were missing. The rest were brown pegs.

"We'll help you," Janek said. "Don't give up. If we see that you're about to collapse, we'll take some of the burden off you. Just try to make it to the worksite."

"If I don't survive and you do, tell my wife that I thought of her every day."

"I will, but you'll survive as well. We'll make sure you do."

As they had on every morning since arriving, the men gathered in the middle of the dimly lit room. Janek then led them in the same ritualistic prayer from Joshua: "Be strong and courageous. Do not be afraid; do not be discouraged, for the Lord will be with you wherever you go. May God be with us."

"May God be with us," all the men repeated, then made the sign of the cross before dispersing and walking out the door.

The men went out in the darkness and lined up. Janek stood shivering in the snow, already feeling the cold air seep up through the bottom of his coat and into his bones. He wanted to move but was forced to remain in place until the guards were satisfied that all men were accounted for. The thirty-minute march to his worksite would help generate some heat, even make him sweat beneath his coat, but until then there was nothing he could do to keep his body from feeling as if it were about to freeze solid.

"Good. Everyone is accounted for," the guard announced, checking names off his list and surprised that no one had died during the night.

That particular morning, the camp guards were less generous. Winter supplies were becoming scarce, and another shipment of what they called food wasn't due for another few days.

"Line up for your rations," a guard ordered. "There's less this morning, so it shouldn't take you as long to eat. Move now."

After spending the night dreaming of breakfast, Janek got to the cauldron and nearly cried when he received some watered-down cabbage soup and a piece of bread half the normal size. How am I to work, he thought to himself, when I'm being starved? And then, as he sat and looked at the man across from him, whose bones protruded from his chest like thin sticks, he knew for certain that he'd not see the poor soul in another week. When he turned away and finished off what meager rations he'd been given, he could still feel the pain deep in his stomach. It wanted more than he'd given it, and it would continue burning for another eight hours until the next meal. But of course, that was how prisoners were controlled: kept hungry on purpose, given just enough food to be thankful for the little they received. Janek was luckier than most. He felt well enough that he was certain he'd survive the remaining winter months, and then in the spring and summer he would ease his suffering and hunger pains by chewing on a handful of grass or some leaves and insects.

Breakfast came and went too quickly. A fight erupted in one of the lines when angry men with nothing to lose and who would rather die anyway pleaded for an extra drop of soup. They were usually on the second line. The first line, always the shortest, served the fittest men who'd exceeded their daily work quotas, rewarded with a piece of black bread, a large ladleful of thick soup, and a chunk of salted fish. On the third line, always the longest, the weakest and sickest men stood huddled against each other, barely able to grip their tin bowls with fingers that resembled broken twigs, their sunken eyes dazed, nearly convulsing as they looked over at the other cauldrons. Those were the underperformers. When they finally staggered to their cauldron, they begged for an extra dribble, but no amount of whining softened the hearts of the guards who threw a spoonful of thin soup and a small piece of bread into their bowls and nothing else, not even a scrap of spoiled fish.

The middle or second cauldron was reserved for prisoners who had reached their daily work quotas. Janek often found himself on that line, his ration barely more than the third cauldron—a ladleful of thicker soup and a medium piece of bread. It seemed to him that he and his men were working themselves to death for not much more than the poor wretches in the third line, so eventually he and the men decided that twice a week it would be better to conserve their energy, work a little less, and eat a little less than to work as hard as they could and die from exhaustion.

"Let's go, let's go! You've wasted enough time!" Like a bolt out of nowhere, the shouts forced everyone's spindly legs to prop them up and get ready for the three-mile trek across the tundra to an area where Janek's brigade had been building bridges and roads that would link a southern route to the Trans-Siberian Railroad.

At 5,700 miles and spanning eight time zones, the Trans-Siberian Railroad connects Moscow with the Russian Far East along a vast and open stretch of southern Siberia. Because economic development and colonization of Siberia was hampered by poor transport links, the Russian government had begun construction of the railroad on May 19, 1891. Eventually, the monumental project brought millions of peasants and migrants from Russia and Ukraine who'd started construction at both ends and worked their way to the center through Siberia's frigid and unspoiled wilderness. During World War II, the Trans-Siberian Railroad had served an essential role in supplying the powers fighting in Europe with materials such as metals and natural rubber. After the German invasion of the Soviet Union, the railroad was used to relocate industries from European Russia to Siberia. Since the NKVD learned during its many interrogations that Janek had worked as an engineer in Poland, he was assigned to a prison camp responsible for bridge repair and road construction along a two-hundred-mile stretch just north of Yakutsk.

The gulag was located near Kolyma, a region in the Russian Far East bounded by the Siberian Sea on the east and the Arctic Ocean to the north where average temperatures during a six-month winter reached forty below zero and a three-foot layer of permafrost covered much of the soil. Even Janek, accustomed to snow and ice in the Polish mountains, never imagined such frigid and desolate regions existed on earth. It was a place of death, where work, rather than setting men free, brought them that much closer to withering away until there was nothing left. So why such a godforsaken swath of land such as Kolyma? One word: gold. When the precious metal was discovered in the region during the early twentieth century, it solved the dilemma of how Stalin would finance his ambitious industrialization and economic development plan. The problem: manpower. The solution: a vast penal system that would supply, in limitless numbers, however many workers it took to do whatever Stalin wanted done.

Under Stalin's cruel leadership, as many as 12,000 Poles, including Polish officers like Janek, were sentenced to hard labor and a grueling train ride to what Aleksandr Solzhenitsyn called the "pole of cold and cruelty" in the gulag system. Cutting trees was typically the hardest job, and prisoners only lasted a short time before dying of exhaustion. Altogether, 160 separate camps dotted the uninhabited landscape, each one accessible only by ship across the freezing waters and ice floats of the Sea of Okhotsk, or by the Kolyma Highway, known as the Road of Bones because thousands of gulag prisoners had died during its construction and still lay buried beneath it.

In Kolyma, only the most foolhardy, desperate, or suicidal even thought of escape, for if one didn't succumb to cold or starvation within the first few days, he would surely be devoured by packs of wolves or bears that scoured the countryside and made no distinction between foolish men and other prey. But even those odds were tempting, knowing from day one that men sentenced to the most notorious of all gulags stood little chance of seeing the morning sun three months from the day of their arrival. That was the design and the expectation; because as Naftaly Frenkel, camp commander of Kolyma at the height of Stalin's great purge, was quoted as saying, "We have to squeeze everything out of a prisoner in the first three months—after that we don't need him anymore." Therefore, it mattered little that a civilian was convicted for being an hour late for work or given a five-year sentence for stealing a bottle of milk. There was an endless one-way journey of prisoners who came and went like moths to a flame.

Janek and his men had been growing increasingly weak and exhausted, partly from hunger but mostly from the backbreaking work of logging trees in temperatures that often approached thirty below zero. Their coats were heavy but often worn; some had ill-fitted boots but no socks, only cloth they would wrap around their feet, and they were forced to march into driving winds and snow to get to the work zone. Every morning, the escorting guard, rifle and bayonet raised and pointing at them, issued the same warning: "A single step to the right or to the left and you'll be shot in the head." They were five abreast, marching in fear for their lives because they'd seen a prisoner stumble out of line from exhaustion and, without warning, drop to the ground, a pool of blood spreading from his body. Janek thanked God each time his fellow prisoners marched on either side of him.

Sometimes a man didn't need a bullet to the head. One day, shortly before reaching his work zone, an exhausted and starved prisoner dropped to his knees, closed his eyes, and slumped face first to the ground like a bird falling dead from its perch. The guards, with no hint of emotion or concern, ordered the brigade to keep moving. The next day, the men passed his frozen corpse, half eaten by wolves, wondering if tomorrow one of *them*, especially those who routinely ate from the third cauldron, would become food for whatever was lurking in the dense forest around them.

"Keep up. You can do it," Janek urged his friend. "And don't drag your feet through the snow. It wastes energy. Try to pick them up."

"I feel like I'm about to fall over," Bogdan said.

"Take deep breaths. We're almost there. Another ten minutes and they'll let us rest before we start work. If we exceed our quota today, I'll slip you a little piece of my bread."

"God bless you," Bogdan wheezed, his face twisted in pain. "I remember what you said about eating any little thing we can find. If I make it to spring, I'll look forward to that."

"Until then, chew on a little piece of bark—not too much or it'll make you sick, just enough to ease your hunger until they feed us at noon. And don't swallow your food all at once. Eat slowly. It'll trick your mind into thinking you're getting more than you are."

Bogdan nodded and plowed straight ahead alongside Janek, who feared that his friend was worse off than most of the men in the brigade. "Thank you for everything," he said, then lowered his head to keep the snow from blowing against his face and tried hard to keep himself upright.

The thirty-minute march to his work zone was bad enough, but at least it had given Janek time to stretch his legs and ease the constant ache in his joints from the previous day's work and the wooden bunks that pressed into his bones each night and by morning caused them to stiffen like pieces of cadaver. By the time he reached the work zone, the pain and stiffness had subsided, but just the sight of the place brought a different kind of pain, as it reminded him there were twelve more hours of brutal work to be done that day.

By the time Janek's brigade arrived, six inches of snow had fallen, but daybreak brought with it a few more welcomed degrees of warmth. The air, damp and heavy, felt to him as if a cold blanket had added an extra layer of weight to his already wet coat. Gray skies loomed above and threatened even more snow. Janek knew from experience that work would be especially difficult in those conditions, with the guards angrier than usual for having to be there with the prisoners despite not needing to lift a finger or do anything other than smoke cigarettes, drink vodka, and bark orders the entire day.

"See, you made it," Janek told Bogdan. "You can look at another sunrise."

With a weak smile, Bogdan breathed a sigh of relief. "Yes, thank God, today I made it," he groaned and hoped that in ten more hours he would watch another sunset.

"Fifteen minutes rest!" the lead guard announced, then lit a cigarette and stared up at what appeared to be a gathering storm.

At the camp guard's command, the men broke ranks and walked single file into a makeshift building to gather their tools, a sad collection of axes, saws, picks, and shovels that looked for all practical purposes to be worthless yet would have to do the impossible. Starvation was a great motivator for prisoners on the verge of death. And since the guards, suspecting that some men were purposely working less than they were capable of, pitted them one against the other, organizing them into groups that had to work together in order to meet their daily quota. It usually worked. No one was tempted to rest more than anyone else, and no man risked the wrath of a hungry group just to save himself a little extra pain and suffering and then eat from cauldron number three. What was a broken finger, after all, if it meant licking an extra spoonful of soup?

On that day, sometime in February of 1941—no one really kept up with what day of the month it was—Janek worked all day in a blinding snowstorm. Because the road was still covered in a foot of ice and frozen mud, he and the men spent the morning felling trees and moving them by sled across snow that blew up and clung to their coats. The harder and faster they worked, the less they felt the burning of cold against their skin. A small comfort. But the minute they stopped to breathe, the frigid wind would whip up through their coats and nearly eat them alive. So they worked nonstop, if for no other reason than to keep from freezing to death.

Hour after hour Janek worked, hungry to the point of near delirium, thinking of nothing but the sun setting in the west so he could march back to camp, eat what little they'd give him, and collapse like a dead man on his bunk. And as he watched the sun gradually fall from the sky and looked at the band of ragged men around him, he realized that one of the saddest things in life would be to die in that faraway land and eventually be forgotten. Nothing he'd ever done would matter, he thought, because generations after he was gone the only thing left of him would be distant memories and dusty photographs. A tear rolled down Janek's cheek at the very thought of it. He rubbed it away before anyone could see it, then willed himself to finish pushing a ten-foot log from the road.

The walk back was a hundred times worse than the

walk twelve hours earlier. But before Janek could eat, there was roll call. Another excruciating hour passed as he stood in the bitter cold, waiting for the camp guards to smoke their cigarettes and make sure everyone was present and accounted for.

That day was a good one—Janek's brigade ate from cauldron number two. They were now free, if one could call it that—free from the torment of endless work, free from the cruel abuse, and free from the cold that would take another two hours to seep from their bones. Strange as it seemed, Janek took solace in those precious few moments—talking, praying, and hoping to God that the war would soon be over. Then, exhausted, still hungry, and barely able to walk, he fell onto his bunk like a piece of dead wood and prayed desperately that he would get through the night.

Chapter 12

Northern Kazakhstan
May 1941

As Wanda soon learned, Kazakhstan was a place of violent extremes, where six months of blinding snow and freezing temperatures melted into the unbearable heat of summer, and the blazing sun would fry one's skin into a tan leather. Had she not been there a slave, forced to till the earth until her fingers bled and her spine warped from stooping twelve hours a day, she would have seen beauty in the land. Instead she cursed it, hatred seeping through every bone in her body. And all she could see through her anger and despair were endless rows of dirt where women next to her dropped as they plowed and left orphans behind to become wards of the State.

Life in Kazakhstan labor camps had become worse than anything Wanda could have imagined. She knew from history that Poles had been deported to northern Russia and Siberia since the first partition of Poland in 1772, an effective way of eliminating segments of Polish society and weakening the Catholic population. But this was the twentieth century, after all; and men were supposed to be more civilized than they were two hundred years ago. She'd learned quickly enough that time and progress do not necessarily make the world a more humane place.

The four major deportations following the Soviet invasion of Poland in 1939 were chilling reminders that history is often unkind to people naïve enough to think that aggressive neighbors are ever satisfied living behind their own borders. Between 1939 and 1941, nearly two million Poles were deported to Siberian Russia, from Kolyma to Kazakhstan, where many of them were swallowed into oblivion by the land they were forced to till. The extreme conditions were especially brutal for people too genteel to believe they'd be treated worse than farm animals. In Kazakhstan, pigs grew fat while people starved. It was a bizarre and cruel existence, Wanda would often think, where one's past and social status meant nothing and one's life could be extinguished as easily as a flame in a cold wind.

No one escaped the abject cruelty: women with small children, the elderly who barely survived the two- or three-week train rides, helpless men tormented at the sight of their wives and children suffering and dying before their eyes. Arrival at each labor camp would bring the same misery to Wanda: little food, filthy conditions, families exhausted and sleeping side by side with other families in stark barracks or on mud floors covered with straw. By the third morning, everyone would find themselves infested with lice, and if lucky enough to have blankets, they'd also be covered with bedbugs that spent the night feeding on their victims. Along with lice and bedbugs, poverty in Kazakhstan was a way of life, and the only way for Wanda to keep from falling into a spiral of despair was to delude herself into thinking that America would soon join the war and become part of the solution. In the meantime, she'd spend each day working until every bone in her body ached, collapsing from exhaustion, and dreaming of a freedom that seemed too far away to be real.

By the time Wanda had been assigned to a third labor camp, her body had become a shell of what it was in Poland. Her hair thinning, her teeth loosened in receding gums, she could see and feel bones protruding from places where she'd not felt bones before. Perhaps that's what the Soviets had intended, she'd think, a way of breaking everyone down so they'd become nothing more than mindless slaves. It worked, as far as she was concerned, because every minute of every day, food was on everyone's mind. And everyone was hungry. All the time. Within a few months, no one even noticed that everyone around them had become skin and bone. Winter in Kazakhstan's labor camps was especially harsh since the ground lay frozen solid and stealing an extra potato or piece of cabbage would have to wait until the spring.

But arrival at new labor camps was always a mixed blessing. A torturous, week-long train ride would thankfully come to an end, and the prisoners would either drop to their knees and thank God they'd survived or curse Him for once again delivering them to such an evil place. And then the backbreaking work and fight for survival would begin, no sooner than the sun had set on the western edge of what for many would be their final resting place. Some fully expected to be buried where they worked, giving up any hope of ever seeing Poland again. Their past was nothing but a dream, their present a nightmare, their future so bleak and uncertain that some prayed death would come quickly and end their misery. For many, though, the belief that the war could not go on much longer was enough to keep them fighting for life one more day.

By the spring of 1941, Wanda and Sophie had been ordered to pack up and travel to yet another labor camp, this one even farther north. Along the way, as the train weaved past mixed forests of pine, birch, and fir, Wanda would stare through the wooden slats and see abandoned orchards, untilled fields, and settlements of scattered, dilapidated huts that looked as though they'd blow away in the next storm. If there were workers in the fields, they appeared pitiful, their cracked and weathered faces showing what years of living in the steppe could do to a person. By the next morning, the landscape was so flat that one could see clear to the horizon and nothing else: an endless swath where squalid mud buildings with thatched roofs provided the only protection against the harsh elements.

"Where are we going now?" Sophie asked her mother, saddened that she'd left another set of friends behind and once again finding herself homeless and riding in a filthy boxcar to God only knew where.

"I don't know, sweetheart. Another camp, I suppose."

"Will there be other children?"

"Yes, I'm sure. You'll make friends, just as you did at the last camp."

Sophie began to weep and drew closer to her mother. "When are we going home?"

Wanda pressed Sophie tightly against her and began weeping herself. "Soon, I hope," she whispered.

"Do you think Daddy is okay?"

"Your father is very strong and brave." Wanda choked on her words. "I know he's going to be with us very soon."

A young woman who'd been picked up at the last stop overheard the conversation and chimed in. "Was your husband fighting in the war?" she asked. "I'm Eva, by the way."

"Yes," Wanda answered, then introduced herself. "First against the Germans and then the Soviets. He was captured back in October and is probably somewhere in Russia right now. And yours?"

Eva paused, then said, "He died soon after Germany invaded. We were only married a few months."

Wanda reached out and took Eva's hand. "I'm so sorry," she said. "If you'd like, you could stay with us when we arrive at the new camp."

"Thank you," Eva said. "That would be nice, since I don't have anyone else."

"I'm not sure exactly where we're going, but I hope we get there soon."

"How many camps have you worked?"

"This will be my fourth. At the first one, we planted and harvested winter wheat. After that, they moved us farther east to plant spring wheat and barley. Then it was sugar beets at the next. I can't imagine what kind of crops would be grown this far north, if that's what they have planned for us. Who knows? Maybe more wheat."

"How was your last camp?" Eva asked, suddenly trembling, the fear in her voice palpable.

"How is any camp? We work and then we sleep and hope we don't die. This one will be no different."

Eva wrapped her arms around her chest and asked, "Were there many men in your last camp? Did they do things to the women?"

Wanda nodded. "Yes, a few, and some were disgusting brutes. Maybe this camp will be better."

"I hope so," Eva whispered. "I'm not sure I can go through that again."

Wanda wasn't sure what Eva meant by that and didn't ask, but she suspected that such a lovely young woman was easy prey for men who didn't think twice about using their power and their positions to use women in whatever way they saw fit. "As soon as we get there, it's best the women stick together," she said. "Safety in numbers."

The farther north the train journeyed, the more remote and Siberian the steppes became—cold and damp, with misty coniferous forests, peat bogs, and pristine glacier lakes dotting the landscape. It was a mysterious world of natural beauty, its lakes teaming with migrating flamingos and its rugged mountains rising high above lush green valleys. But it was also the most Russian part of Kazakhstan, where two of the most brutal Soviet gulags were built to house and punish thousands of criminals and political prisoners during Stalin's reign of terror. Wanda prayed that where they were being taken was a farm labor camp and not a gulag where the odds of survival would be a thousand times worse.

Along the way, Wanda could see pockets of civilization and what looked like a mix of ethnic Russians and typical Kazakhs, historically a nomadic people predominantly Asian by race and Muslim by religion. Beginning in 1890, large numbers of Russian settlers had moved south and colonized that area of Kazakhstan, bringing with them a Russian presence that would sow the seeds for a future communist takeover. By the 1930s, Kazakhstan had become a principal destination for deportees and home to some of the largest

Soviet labor camps in the world.

Another day and night passed before the train finally ended its trek north. Wanda thanked God when she saw they had arrived at a labor camp just south of Ekibastuz, less than a hundred miles from the Russian border. As she stepped down from the boxcar with Sophie in her arms, what she saw was a different land, wilder and more desolate than their last camp.

"Is this our new home?" Sophie asked, her tiny hand squeezed tightly onto Wanda's fingers, her eyes welling with tears as she saw nothing but a desolate village with stark buildings.

"It is," Wanda said, pulling Sophie closer to her side, hoping they'd not have to fashion their own homes at this camp.

"Gather your things and move this way," a guard ordered. He pointed a finger toward an expansive camp with five rectangular buildings. "Your living quarters will be in building number three. When you get there, you'll be given instructions on where to go and what you need to do."

"Thank God," Wanda exclaimed, almost overjoyed that she'd not have to construct a mud hut from the earth.

Eva pressed up against Wanda, thankful she'd found a companion she could at least talk to and take solace with. "What do you think they'll have us do here?"

Wanda examined the area as they walked and saw nothing that resembled a farm. "I would have guessed wheat, but now I have no idea," she said. "I don't think it's farming."

"How do you know?" Eva's eyes widened.

"Look at it." Wanda pointed her chin at the expanse of barren land in front of them. "There are no fertile fields for crops, no farm equipment, not even any animals. Just land."

"What then?"

Wanda shook her head, puzzled at what it could be they'd been sent there to do. "I suppose we'll know soon enough."

"This way!" a female guard yelled as Wanda, Sophie, and Eva made their way to building number three. "Go inside and settle in. Bathrooms with soap are at the end. Wash thoroughly and dress. In one hour someone will be there with your work assignments."

"Work assignments already?" Eva exclaimed. "Not even a day to rest?"

Sophie let go of Wanda's hand and ran to one of the unoccupied sleeping bunks. "I like this one," she said. "Can this one be mine?"

Wanda nodded. "I'll take the bunk next to yours. When it's cold, we can sleep together and keep each other warm. How's that sound?"

Sophie smiled enthusiastically. Wanda's heart sank at the idea that her precious little girl was actually happy she'd found a roof over her head and a bare wooden pallet to sleep on. How cruel it was for a child to be thrown into such a brutal and depraved life, she thought. What evil could possibly have invaded men's hearts that, for them, human beings had become nothing more than expendable livestock?

For the next hour, Wanda and thirty other women scrubbed the stench from their bodies and made their new barracks home. Sophie tucked a little doll she'd fashioned out of rags beneath her blanket and kissed it. "Go to sleep now," she whispered, then kissed it again before pressing it against her cheek.

Everyone was apprehensive about work assignments because they'd all seen what Wanda had— a place with nothing farm-like and suspiciously devoid of activity. The work area must be somewhere else, Wanda assumed, fearful of what that could be. No sooner had she lain down to rest than a large, uniformed woman carrying a clipboard walked through the door and stationed herself in the center of the room.

Without as much as a greeting, Colonel Natalia Koshenko began. "This is not a farm, in case anyone is wondering. It's a labor camp. Your job here is to make peat bricks for fuel."

The women all looked at one another. One asked, "How would we know to do that? We've been farming for the past two years. We know nothing else."

"It doesn't take much of a brain," Koshenko sneered. "Only a strong back. Don't you Poles have strong backs? Tomorrow morning, you'll be taken to the peat bogs and given instructions on how and where to dig."

Wanda closed her eyes and sighed. "Dig?" she scoffed. It was hard enough for her small body to plant and till. Now she would have to spend her days digging peat so that she and Sophie could eat.

"On some days, you'll also make kiziak," Koshenko added.

"And what's that?" Eva asked.

"A fuel made from dung," Koshenko said. "You'll see. And as always, your rations will depend on work. You'll be given a daily quota of bricks or kiziak for a given ration of food. Make your quota and you'll eat. Refuse to work and you'll starve. Today you'll rest and eat because tomorrow work begins."

"What about the children?" Wanda asked. "Is there a place for them?"

"They'll remain behind and be taught to make themselves good Soviet citizens."

"You mean good communist atheists," Wanda said to herself. This is what she'd feared most—that while she toiled in the fields, her daughter would be brainwashed into believing that what they were doing was necessary for the good of the State; that it was the Soviet Union and not Poland that would care for their needs and offer the world a system of government that promised everyone a utopian society in which all would share in the benefits of their labor.

"God help my child," Wanda cried. "God help us all." She lay back on her bunk when Koshenko finished and stared at the ceiling, grief stricken at the notion of Sophie actually becoming one of them.

At five a.m. the next morning, Wanda rose from her bed at the sound of sticks banging against the bunks. "Everyone up!" A guard yelled, then watched as a flurry of women raced to the bathroom to relieve and to clean themselves. "After breakfast, you'll line up outside. The children will be taken to the school building. No exceptions."

Following a meager breakfast of soup and bread, Sophie was escorted away as Wanda looked on with tears in her eyes. She and thirty others then lined up and walked like zombies through fields and forests for what seemed like miles, passing groups of Kazakh families who looked at them with a mix of suspicion and sadness. Many of the locals appeared afflicted with disease— disfigured women, men in rags and turbans with few teeth, and children with bone-thin legs and swollen bellies from malnourishment. Here and there, a cow was seen grazing, so sickly-looking it was a wonder it could provide enough milk for a single person, much less an entire family.

Wanda's weary mind wandered as she and the group marched on, not knowing if she still had a husband, her legs burning with pain as she tried to keep up, each labor camp she'd called home worse than the last. When the work had entailed farming and harvesting crops, it was at least doable. On most days, she seemed to work harder than most other women yet barely met her quota, so every now and then she'd steal a little extra to make life more bearable. At her last labor camp, she'd pilfer a little sugar every so often, tucking it inside her sock so she could smuggle it back to Sophie, not giving any thought to the harsh punishment she'd receive for such a lowly infraction.

"It's so good!" Sophie would squeal as she licked the rare treat from her fingers, her face lighting up and warming Wanda's heart.

"Don't tell anyone," Wanda would admonish. "It's a secret we need to keep to ourselves, okay?"

"Okay," Sophie had agreed, then hungrily finished the last of the granules.

Wanda would nearly cry at the thought that for Sophie a teaspoon of sugar was the highlight of her week, and it would never cross her mind that what she was doing could cost her everything.

This last journey had taken her and Sophie to a camp deep into northeastern Kazakhstan, where the work involved mining enormous fields of peat, an important source of fuel for the Soviet empire. The region they now called home was a vast and sparsely populated lowland of boreal forest, bogs, and wetlands where continually damp and decaying vegetation captured CO_2 that, over thousands of years, formed six-foot deposits of sphagnum moss, the main component of peat.

By six a.m., Wanda had managed to endure the two-mile trek and arrive at the worksite. She stopped to suck in the crisp air and gaze out at a land so unfamiliar she may as well have entered a different world. Nothing she'd ever seen compared to what stretched before her in every direction: a flat and featureless terrain with few trees and vast areas of swamp, floodplains, and peat bogs. It was the Western Siberian Plain, something she'd only read about in school but which was now seeping into her boots.

The Western Siberian Plain or Zapadno-Sibirskaya Ravnina, as it was called, occupied the westernmost portion of Siberia between the Ural Mountains in the west and the Yenisei River in the east. What she didn't know was that it was home to the world's largest high-latitude wetland, where immense fields of oil and natural gas deposits lay hidden beneath its crust. It was also an ideal environment for peat, a naturally existing sedimentary material that developed wherever the remains of plants, animals, and microbes exceeded the ecosystem's ability to decompose it. With its cold, damp climate, northern Kazakhstan was in one of the most favorable locations on planet earth for peat deposits to grow and accumulate. But to Wanda, whose body had slowly withered away from exhausting work and malnutrition, the richness beneath Kazakhstan's soil was nothing more than a toxin that would seep through her skin and lungs and bring her that much closer to death.

For the next hour, experienced workers, under the

watchful eyes of ten burly guards, explained and demonstrated the process of harvesting and preparing the peat, a job that would go on six days a week for twelve hours a day or until the blazing sun had set in the western sky.

Wanda stood beside Eva and said, "This work is going to kill me. I don't know how much longer I can do this."

The last thing Eva wanted to do was agree, but seeing how small and fragile Wanda was, feared she was right. "Don't worry, Wanda," she said, putting a reassuring hand on her back. "We'll help you if it comes to that."

Wanda smiled weakly but she knew, from watching the experienced workers, that what she was expected to do would be backbreaking. First, the top layer of soil had to be shoveled off, so the underlying peat was exposed. Next, heavy slabs of peat would be cut with a long, wood-handled tool, removed, and set out to dry in the sun. To make sure that slabs were cut properly, the tool's cutting edge had to be pushed with great force down into the dense peat and then, with a backward pull of the angled blade, the brick would be dislodged from the bank and tossed to the side for drying. Once dried, anywhere from days to weeks, the bricks of peat would be stacked onto carts and hauled away to waiting trains that would transport them to Russian factories and farms for heat and energy production. The physical labor alone, Wanda shuddered to think, would require far more strength than she could muster.

By month's end, Wanda had learned her job as well as workers half her age and settled into a routine that kept her from expending too much precious energy. She had calculated how much soil she needed to dig and how many bricks of peat she could get away with making before exhaustion took over and wore her down. She learned to pace herself, to balance her meager food intake with the number of calories she was burning by feeling the bones protruding from different parts of her body—clavicles that began to look like thin sticks beneath her skin, a hip joint that moved more freely than it had before, an elbow or a knee that creaked whenever it bent. It was as if her weakened skeleton was speaking to her, telling her how much it could endure before the body covering it disappeared forever.

But at least Wanda could still work. Some of the women suffered with urinary tract infections, others with lice-infected typhus and diarrhea so severe that all they could manage was to curl up and lie in their own bloody waste. Scrapes and open wounds festered, and two days later oozed noxious pus. Within days, an overpowering stench had seeped into every plank of wood in the barracks, every blanket, fiber of hair, and shred of clothing.

"It hurts so much," a young girl cried, clawing at her groin with both hands to ease the pain.

"Rub it with piss," an older woman shouted. "It'll help the healing."

"Don't listen to that fool," another shouted back. "Piss only makes it burn more. Just put up with it until they give you some soap."

As the women argued with one another, Wanda would hold Sophie's head against her breast, trying to keep her from hearing the wails of women around them. But as the days grew longer and the work more difficult, cries turned into faint whimpers, and even the whimpers eventually faded. Before long, everyone had settled into a quiet, collective stupor, and the constant burning, the cramps, and wet feces that soaked through their undergarments and covered their legs like thin bark had become almost bearable.

Most of the women, Wanda included, no longer menstruated, a sure sign that their frail bodies had been reduced to less than ten percent fat. For Wanda, it was a blessing, since not having a period became one less thing in her miserable life she had to worry about. But the loss of so much body fat also decreased hormones like estrogen; and lower estrogen levels meant weaker and more brittle bones that could break under the withering stress of digging for peat twelve hours a day. It seemed that no matter how much she did, Wanda would take two steps back for every step forward, and what she'd feared at the end of each day was that no amount of calculating or balancing or pacing herself would be enough to survive another six months.

"The day will end soon," Eva said, seeing how Wanda had been struggling to push her shovel even a few inches into the ground.

Wanda reached down and tried to massage the pain from her legs, nearly brought to tears by the thought that she'd have to walk two miles back to their camp. "I pray this ends soon," she sighed. "My legs feel like stone."

"Don't crouch so much," Eva said. "And try to rest a bit before we have to go back."

The minute Wanda saw that the guards had wandered off to smoke, she stopped what she was doing and allowed her lungs to recover from the torture she'd put them through. The endless, grueling work of digging peat sapped not only Wanda's strength but her psyche as well. Every waking moment was dominated by thoughts of food, and that was exactly what Soviet leaders intended. Man or woman, big or small, strong or weak made no difference. Whoever worked ate. Whoever did not, dropped dead. A piece of bread and a portion of soup versus punishment and starvation. Those were the only choices.

For Wanda, as it was for all Polish women, this atrocity went against the very laws of nature. From the moment she arrived, Wanda had become a genderless animal with no regard for her physical being. The Soviet ideology that sought to erase any distinction between male and female labor had become apparent each time she stood next to a hulking man and was expected to perform exactly as he did. She held out hope that tomorrow the work assignment would be to make kiziak, a brick-like fuel made from animal dung. At least that would not be as backbreaking as digging for peat. From a pile of dry manure, Wanda would have to combine a portion with water and straw, load the mix into wooden forms, then pile it up to dry in the sun. Each dung brick would be molded by hand, so by the end of the day, her fingers would be cracked and so filthy that no amount of washing would remove the brown stain. But brown fingers and the smell of dung was heaven compared to wielding a shovel all day.

"Everyone stop!" a guard yelled. "Line up!"

Wanda thanked God the workday was over but cursed the fact that she now had to march through miles of open swamp and peat bogs on legs that felt as if they'd caught fire. The walk back was always exhausting, especially when driving winds blew clouds of stone and twigs against her uncovered legs and face. On that day it rained, so the earth turned into sticky clay, but somehow she willed herself to make it, not by physical stamina, because she had little of that, but because her mind kept telling her that Sophie was back at camp waiting for her to return.

"Mama!" Sophie called out when she saw her mother walk through the door, then ran to her and wrapped her arms tightly around her.

"I missed you, my love," Wanda said, kissing her daughter repeatedly on the top of her head. "Let me clean up and we can eat."

The food that evening was not much better than it had been the day before. Wanda never quite made her quota, thereby suffering from constant hunger, growing weaker and thinner with each passing day. Even stealing and scavenging had become impossible, with no crops to harvest or fields to search in for roots and wild mushrooms. All seemed lost. The harder she worked, the weaker she became.

Poor Sophie had turned eight years old that year, old enough to suffer alongside her mother and certainly old enough to think that the world she barely remembered would never exist again. What a terrible thing for a young child to endure, Wanda lamented: fearing that her mother might die before she reached her ninth birthday, that her father was probably dead, and that today, as unimaginable as it was, might be the best day of her life.

But at least they ate, and they were still alive. Wanda would try that night to erase the Soviet ideas from Sophie's head and hope that eight hours of brainwashing had not taken hold.

Chapter 13

Sandusky, Ohio
August 21, 2004

This day promised to be a good one. It was Saturday, which meant that, after finishing a breakfast of oatmeal and toast by eight a.m., Wanda would be back in her room and would stare at the clock until Sophie walked through the door and brightened her world. Alert and attentive, she was chattier and more convivial than usual because she knew that in another hour Sophie would be wheeling her out to the garden and reminiscing about anything that brought joy into her life. Little else mattered—not friends who'd peek into her room nor custodians or nurses making their morning rounds, not even Sister Regina, who Wanda loved almost as much as she did her own daughter.

"Sophie should be here soon," Sister Regina said with a wide smile. She brushed Wanda's hair from her face. "You're blessed to have such a good daughter."

By nine a.m., Wanda turned her attention from the clock to the door, then beamed with delight when Sophie walked in.

"Hello, Mama," Sophie said. "You look good. How are you feeling?"

Wanda stretched out her arms like a child. "Wonderful," she purred.

They embraced for a minute, and then Sophie pulled away. "You feel thinner. Are you not eating?"

Sister Regina, on her way out the door, turned back to Sophie and said, "Not as much lately. Your mother's lost her taste for food, so she puts sugar on everything. Even *that* doesn't help very much."

"What do you mean, you have no taste for food?" Sophie asked her mother. "What's going on?"

Wanda frowned. "Everything I eat is like putting paper in my mouth. Nothing tastes like food."

That was not a good sign, thought Sophie, knowing from conversations with Wanda's doctor that as dementia progresses, the brain produces less insulin, resulting in sudden changes in appetite or increased cravings for sugary foods. Worse, the drop in brain insulin leads to death of nerve cells, especially in parts of the brain responsible for memory.

"I'll talk to your doctor about that," Sophie said, though she feared the inevitable: that her mother had reached the point when the few good days would begin to fade and eventually disappear forever. Tears formed in her eyes as she stroked her mother's head.

Sister Regina lowered her voice so Wanda couldn't hear. "It's been that way for the past few weeks. The doctor says it's not uncommon when the brain starts to deteriorate. All we can do is flavor her food as best we can so that she eats *something*." She turned back to Wanda and leaned forward to give her a hug.

Wanda pointed a finger at Sophie. "Sophie is here," she said.

"I know, honey. And I'm sure you'll both have a lovely day."

"She's my daughter, you know."

"Yes; a very good daughter."

"Her name is Sophie. She's my daughter." Wanda's eyes searched the room as if everything familiar a minute ago had suddenly become new and different. And then, as if a light switch were turned off, Wanda fell into a trance and withdrew from the world.

Sophie slumped into a chair and wiped tears from her eyes. "I know it's getting worse," she said, "but it's so hard to see her this way."

Sister Regina slid her hand on Sophie's shoulder and said, "It's hard for me as well. Your mother has been so kind to me, and it makes me sad to think that soon she won't know me."

"How much does she talk to you?" Sophie asked. "About Poland? About the camps?"

"Depends. Sometimes she's very talkative. Other times, not that much. When she does, it's bits and pieces...until she remembers something that either makes her cry or makes her angry; and then she tells me it's enough and shuts down."

"I can understand that. She went through more in a few years than most people go through in a lifetime."

"Tell me about that," Sister Regina said. "About you. What was it like for such a young child?"

Sophie looked over at Wanda, who didn't look back but instead fell lifelessly back in her chair, mumbling something in Polish that even Sophie could not understand. There'd be no hair brushing or walks in the garden or lunch that day, only a brief visit Sophie hoped had given her mother at least a few moments of joy.

"Mom suffered so much," Sophie began. "We had a wonderful life in Lwow, from what I remember. I was only six at the time...when Germany and Russia invaded and destroyed our lives."

"What was Lwow like?"

"Before the war, it was one of the most beautiful cities in Poland...the first European city to have streetlights, powered by kerosene. By the twentieth century, it became one of the most important centers for culture and science in all of Poland. But once the Nazis and Soviets divided Poland, Lwow was taken over by Russia and eventually became part of Ukraine, where it remains to this day. Whenever my parents thought about their home no longer being a Polish city, it was like a festering wound that never healed. I hated even bringing it up."

"And the camps? Were they as bad as your mother described?"

"It was much worse for her than for me. Children are more resilient, but it was still bad. The lack of food was often worse than the bitter cold. Not a day went by that we weren't in constant pain from hunger. On some days, when the guards were too drunk to make their way to the food lines, women would faint from weakness. Food was all anyone could think about. It consumed us. For my mother, from the moment she woke up until she went to bed at night she thought about food and how hungry she was. At least in the spring we could keep our eyes open for anything we could eat to give us a little relief. It was a daily struggle for survival, and too many to even count lost the battle."

"What did you do while your mother worked?"

"I remember at one camp, for much of the day, the children's job was to run through the fields of crops and chase birds away. Because we were children, we made a game of it. While we chased birds, the women worked the fields."

As she described to Sister Regina what life in the camps was like, Sophie remembered how her mother tried as best she could that Sophie not go hungry, giving up some of her own food so her daughter would have just a little more. Now that Sophie thought about it, she recalled how no one in the camps was ever satisfied, walking about in a constant state of near starvation that wore on them like a growing cancer.

"You didn't know where your father was at the time?" Sister Regina asked.

Sophie shook her head. "No one knew where their husbands, sons, or brothers were. Once captured or arrested, they could have been taken anywhere. Mom tried to be positive about it, but in reality all she could do was hold out hope that Dad was still alive. We'd heard rumors and horror stories about Soviet prisons and gulags, so after a few years of not knowing, it was hard for us to imagine he survived."

"Would he have known about you and Wanda? Where you were and what you were doing?"

"No. He had no idea where we were, or even if we were alive, because Soviet authorities would move workers from camp to camp depending on where labor was needed. Someone could be harvesting cabbage or beets one day then told to pack up everything and be ready to leave by the next morning for another camp hundreds of miles away. In some ways, that may have been a blessing."

"How so?"

"Polish officers were sometimes allowed to write to their families, not out of compassion but so the secret police could gather names and addresses of family members. Had my father known where to write, God knows what would have happened when the authorities tracked down who he was writing to."

"Your mother must have thought of him every day...every minute."

"Every Polish wife hoped she'd see her loved one again. But they all resigned themselves, especially if they were married to Polish officers, to the reality they might never hear from their husbands again. That became a part of life they were forced to accept. Husbands left and disappeared as if the cold earth swallowed them up—no records of their deaths, no bodies to bring back home, no graves to mark where they drew their last breath, just the memory of their faces as they said their final goodbyes and then faded into oblivion."

As Sophie thought back to a time more than sixty years ago, a chill ran through her bones as though still there, watching her mother weep from the pain in her legs and moan from hunger in the middle of the night as she slept. She remembered the anguish her mother felt each time she couldn't meet her quota because it meant less food for herself but also less for her daughter. It was one of the cruelest things the camp guards could do, Wanda had said, to starve innocent children so that desperate parents would work themselves to death. But small and frail as she was, Wanda, as Sophie recalled, had worked harder than anyone else just to keep up, and harder still so that Sophie would have a piece of bread each night before bed. And as those painful memories flashed before her eyes, Sophie looked over at her poor mother and began to cry.

"Are you okay?" Sister Regina asked.

Sophie shook her head. "You can't imagine what

she went through unless you were there. We're both lucky to be alive."

Sophie recalled being tossed from her home in the middle of a cold night and deported a thousand miles away. As a child, she couldn't understand why her mother was being treated as though she were less than human. But she did now. She'd learned that one of the first things the communists had done was set up a system where men and women were made equal in every way. According to Marxism, women could never be free unless they first rid themselves from the yoke of family, and so government became family. That was so alien and unnatural to the Poles, whose culture dictated that men and women, though equal in many ways, were still different and played different roles in society. In Russia, women dressed like and worked alongside men, and so they'd become used to hard, physical labor. Polish women had not, so within a few months of their imprisonment, many grew so weak they could do only half of what was expected of them. The less they produced, the less they ate and the weaker they became, until they withered away into skeletons and dropped dead in the fields.

During one of her last visits with her father, Sophie remembered him saying that history had forgotten the plight of Polish deportees like Wanda. Textbooks and movies had usually depicted the horrors of Nazi atrocities, and rightfully so. Jews, after all, were singled out in the most vile and brutal way possible. But the more people learned of what Poland had gone through following its invasion by both Russia and Germany, Janek said, the more they'd be convinced that historians got it right—that its people had suffered more than any other nation on earth during and after the war.

As Sophie got older, something would gnaw at her from time to time, something she couldn't reconcile. Her mother had arrived in Kazakhstan a small and frail woman, yet she survived years of brutality and hunger while so many others had succumbed to exhaustion and starvation. How was it that such a woman had beaten the odds when others she'd worked alongside had not? She tried to put any suspicions out of her mind, but they would surface nonetheless and leave her wondering, even now, more than sixty years later, as she remembered what Sister Regina had said about Wanda muttering in her sleep. She began to think the worst about what a mother would do in that situation and what *she* would do if she had watched her only child suffer or slowly die of starvation. And suddenly Sophie thought what she had thought a thousand times before: that she couldn't imagine her and her frail mother surviving on their own.

"What's wrong?" Sister Regina asked, puzzled at the expression on Sophie's face.

Sophie hesitated as their eyes met. "Nothing. I was just thinking how difficult it was for a mother and young child in that harsh environment, with so little food and so much hard labor."

Sophie then wondered, as she had so often over the years, if her mother had ever told Janek that something *did* happen, or if he just suspected that it must have but never wanted to know or simply didn't have it in his heart to ask. Let the past be forgotten, he'd probably told himself, so the two of them could erase the years and live their lives as if back in their beautiful city of Lwow.

"Most deportations to labor camps were often death

sentences," Sophie said, "especially for families whose only crime was being related to someone. Disease and starvation killed thousands, their bodies buried in the fields they worked, never returned to Poland. It's so sad for relatives who never knew what happened to them."

Sister Regina fell silent, lamenting the fact that so little was known about the millions of Poles like Wanda and Sophie who'd suffered and died in Siberian Russia simply because they were Poles. She asked herself how *she* would react, how *she* would feel being woken in the dead of night by a sudden knock on the door, marched lockstep to a frozen boxcar, and taken 2,500 miles from the comfort of her home to a foreign land where she probably would starve or work herself to death. The images of that had her thanking God how lucky she was to be born in a different world at a different time.

Is that how we live our lives, she thought, slogging through life not caring about things that don't affect us, choosing the paths we take in life based only on how important they are to us. Everything else is a distraction. An annoyance. A world in which we see people live and die around us and not even realize who they are and what they've done. She suddenly realized who Wanda and Janek really were, what they'd been through, and how their generation had changed the world.

"Your parents were heroes," she said. "Not like pampered athletes or celebrities or politicians, but real heroes who lived like ordinary people and never knew how much they affected the rest of us."

"They *were* ordinary people. And they never talked about what happened to them. All they ever wanted was for their children to be happy and have good lives."

"Your mother told me the story of how your dad

escaped the Katyn Massacre when he was first captured. I'd only read about that, but to think that your father may have been one of only a few who survived is incredible."

Over the years, Sophie had overheard the tragic story of the Katyn Massacre on several occasions—that is, whenever her normally docile mother was not in the room to put an angry and abrupt end to it. But it wasn't until she was much older that she sat alone with her father during one of her visits, his deep blue eyes looking straight into hers, welling up as if what he was about to tell her was still haunting him, that it hit her as if nothing else he'd ever said to her mattered. There she was—a daughter, a wife, a mother, a grandmother—alive and enjoying her life because of her father's incredible act of sacrifice and bravery. And on that day it suddenly dawned on her that maybe she'd never given her father's stories much thought because not until then did she realize what it took for him to do what he did.

Sophie closed her eyes and remembered seeing a copy of Stalin's top-secret memo ordering the execution of more than twenty-thousand prisoners of war. She thought back to her father's anguished account of his capture and escape while his fellow prisoners walked to their death, and as she pictured the memo in her mind, there in front of her, a chill ran through her body:

LAVRENTII BERIA, TOP SECRET.
MARCH 5, 1940
Top Secret
5 March 1940
USSR People's Commissariat for Internal Affairs
Moscow
A large number of former officers of the Polish Army, employees of the Polish Police and Intelligence

services, members of Polish nationalist, counter-revolutionary parties, members of exposed counter-revolutionary resistance groups, escapees and others, all of them sworn enemies of Soviet authority full of hatred for the Soviet system, are currently being held in prisoner-of-war camps of the USSR NKVD and in prisons in the western provinces of Ukraine and Belarus.

The military and police officers in the camps are attempting to continue their counter-revolutionary activities and are carrying out anti-Soviet agitation. Each of them is waiting only for his release in order to start actively struggling against Soviet authority.

The organs of the NKVD in the western provinces of the Ukraine and Belarus have uncovered a number of counter-revolutionary rebel organizations.

Former officers of the Polish Army and police as well as gendarmes have played an active role in all these organizations.

Amongst the detained escapees and violators of the state borders a considerable number of people have been identified as belonging to counter-revolutionary espionage and resistance organizations.

14,736 former officers, government officials, landowners, police, gendarmes, prison guards, settlers in the border regions and intelligence officers [more than 97% are Poles] are being held in prisoner-of-war camps. This number incudes soldiers and junior officers.

Included are:

Generals, colonels and lieutenant colonels—295
Majors and captains—2080

Lieutenants, second lieutenants and ensigns—6049

Officers and juniors of the police, gendarmes, prison guards and intelligence officers—1030

Rank and file police officers, prison guards and intelligence personnel—5138

Government officials, landowners, priests, settlers in border regions—144

18,632 detained people are being kept in the western region of the Ukraine and Belarus [10,685 are Poles]

They include:

Former officers—1207

Former intelligence officers of the police and gendarmerie—5141

Spies and saboteurs—347

Former landowners, factory workers and government officials—465

Members of various counter-revolutionary and resistance organizations and other counter-revolutionary enemies—5345

Escapees—6127

In view of the fact that all are hardened and uncompromising enemies of Soviet authority, the USSR NKVD considers it necessary:

[1] To instruct the USSR NKVD that it should try before special tribunals:

[a] the cases of the 14,700 former Polish officers, government officials, landowners, police officers, intelligence officers, gendarmes, settlers in the border regions and prison guards being held in prisoner-of-war camps;

]b] together with the cases of 11,000 members of various counter-revolutionary organizations of spies and saboteurs, former landowners, factory workers, former Polish officers, government officials, and escapees who have been arrested and are being held in the western provinces of the Ukraine and Belarus and

*apply to them the supreme penalty: **shooting**.*

[2] Examination of the cases is to be carried out without summoning those detained and without bringing charges, the statements concerning the conclusion of the investigation and the final verdict should be as follows:

[a] for persons being held in prisoner-of-war camps, in the form of certificates issued by the NKVD of the USSR NKVD;

[b] for arrested personnel in the form of certificates issued by the NKVD of the Ukrainian SSR and the NKVD of the Belarus SSR.

[3] The cases should be examined and the verdict pronounced by a three-person tribunal consisting of comrades Merkulov, Kobulov and Bashtakov.

People's Commissar for the Internal Affairs of the USSR

L Bergia

[Signed by Stalin, Voroshilov, Molotov, Mikoyan, Kalinin and Kaganovich]

Since that visit, Sophie had welcomed her father's heart-wrenching stories of war and suffering every chance she could, but it pained her that it wasn't until his final years on earth that they'd taken such a hold of her soul. She figured it was because, like most everyone, her own world and her place in it left little room for anything else, including her family's history. It didn't help that her mother, who'd suffered more than most women suffer in a lifetime, prohibited even a mention of anything Russian. And so, whenever she could, Sophie would sneak away with her father and listen in rapt disbelief as he poured out his heart and described a time in history when hell had descended upon the earth.

"You okay, Sophie?" Sister Regina took hold of

Sophie's hand.

"Not many people know, because he wanted to forget," Sophie said, "to put it behind him, since so many of his friends died while he lived. Sometimes he'd bring it up, but my mother would quickly put an end to it. She, more than him, never wanted to talk about Russia or anything Russian."

"I get it," Sister Regina said. "Too much pain to think about."

"And now she probably wishes she could bring back even her bad memories. Who knows how much time she has before she forgets everything?"

"You know I'll do whatever I can to make her last days comfortable."

Sophie reached out and took hold of Sister Regina's other hand. "I know you will. You've been a godsend to both of us."

Sophie and Sister Regina spent the next few minutes with Wanda, who dozed on and off and occasionally mumbled something incoherent. Sophie urged her mother to speak, but it was futile. It seemed as though Wanda's lucid moments were becoming less frequent, her episodes of withdrawal noticeably longer and deeper. The doctor had told Sophie it would be that way from now on, and there was no way of knowing when or even if her mother would remember her recent visits. One day soon, she would withdraw completely and not come back.

Though she knew it was inevitable, Sophie found it hard to accept that Wanda would no longer recognize her own daughter's face. After all, they'd lived through bombings and mass deportations together, travelled in cramped and filthy boxcars to labor camps where they struggled to keep from starving to death, and survived one of the most brutal episodes in Poland's history. Soon it would be over, and Wanda, like so many others who'd survived while millions perished, would quietly fall into a deep sleep and vanish from this earth.

Chapter 14

Yakutsk, Siberia
August 25, 1941

Every night, as his weakening body tried to recover from the brutal punishment of work, Janek would dream of Wanda and Sophie, his eyes welling up with tears in his sleep. It was the only thing that kept the horrors of each day from killing him, the one hope he had that the madness of war would soon be over and he could see them again. Many of the other men had given up hope long ago; and so they'd fall asleep, half dead, their bones so thin and brittle they ached whenever they moved, begging God to take them from the cruelty of life and praying that at least their families would somehow go on without them.

That morning, Janek opened his eyes and looked around the barracks. Something was different. No banging of pipes, no screaming at prisoners, no beatings of men who walked too slowly. At breakfast, he noticed a palpable silence from the usually brutal guards, and it made him fear the worst. He looked over at Bogdan, sitting across from him, and asked, "You feel as if something's going on?"

"What do you mean?"

"Look over there." Janek pointed a chin at two guards standing in the corner. "They're not even looking at us. The one in the doorway has his rifle propped against the wall. That never happens. Something's going on."

Janek and the men stiffened at the sight of an NKVD officer striding into the room and positioning himself before them. He held in his hand a paper he quickly unfolded and brought up to his face.

"What the hell is this?" Janek whispered, suddenly frightened at the prospect that an execution was imminent. He watched the officer grimace, almost hesitant to read what was there in front of him. "Some sort of official order?"

"Maybe we're being moved," Bogdan suggested, "or worse."

"Attention!" The officer looked out at a hundred men, all anxious to hear what he was about to say. "I have received a directive from General Secretary Joseph Stalin. On Sunday, June 22, Germany invaded the Soviet Union. As of this day, amnesty is given to all Polish citizens deported to the Soviet Union, as agreed upon on August 14, 1941."

As they stared in disbelief, what Janek and his men didn't know was that a month earlier, Germany and its allies had ended the Nazi-Soviet Pact by launching a massive invasion of the Soviet Union. After defeating Europe in less time than he'd anticipated, Hitler decided that the Soviet Union would be his next conquest. Operation Barbarossa became the largest military operation in history, opening the eastern front of World War II. Its purpose: for Nazi Germany to conquer western Russia, repopulate it with Germans, and seize the oil reserves and farmlands of the Soviet territories, which meant they would have to go through Poland once again.

Despite warning signs leading up to it—intelligence reports had shown that Germany was mobilizing forces along Russia's western front—Stalin refused to believe that Hitler would break their pact and invade an ally. But Hitler, cunning as he was, knew about the purges and about Stalin executing hundreds of his own generals. The Soviet Army, he concluded, had become so depleted by that fool it would take years before the military could reverse its dysfunction. It was the perfect opportunity to seize the moment and invade Russia.

So, as the Soviet Union focused on spreading its barbaric ideology, not thinking for a moment that anyone would dare cross its borders, four million German troops drove the Soviets from eastern Poland and slaughtered their way into the very depths of the Russian empire. With lightning speed and precision, the Nazi blitzkrieg had killed over four million Russian soldiers as it took over every Soviet republic along Russia's western front. And like a stunned child, shocked at his miscalculation and Hitler's treachery, Stalin had retreated to his office and sat paralyzed while Hitler's army stormed into the Ukraine and Belarus and did not stop until it surrounded Leningrad itself. Within a month, the man of steel, desperate, reeling from Soviet casualties, and seeing that the Germans were only weeks from driving into Moscow, turned to Poland, a nation he'd ruthlessly subjugated, for an alliance, agreeing to a one-time amnesty in return for a much-needed Polish Army.

When the NKVD officer finished his sentence, a chorus of cheers filled the room. Some of the men cried. Others fell to their knees and thanked God their prayers had finally been answered. Janek sat in stunned silence, too weak and shocked to even move.

The officer continued. "All soldiers and officers who have served in the Polish Army and who agree to the terms of the directive, which is recruitment into three infantry divisions, will immediately be released to find transportation to Buzuluk. There you will join forces with newly formed military units under the command of Wladyslaw Anders and prepare to fight against Adolf Hitler who has broken his alliance and invaded the Soviet Union. This one-time amnesty is offered only to those willing to ally with the government of Russia and sign papers to that effect. If so, your names and ranks at the time of your arrest will be given to the camp commanding officer who will provide each of you with temporary documents that will be replaced later with Polish passports." And with that, the officer turned on his heels and marched from the room, seemingly disgusted at the position his nation had been put in, even more disgusted that he had just begged imprisoned Polish soldiers to come to its rescue.

Bogdan leaned over and laughed, saying, "Stalin must be desperate if he's willing to join forces with the West and asks us for help."

Janek shook his head. "It makes no sense. Why would he do that? He committed mass murder against people who want freedom and democracy, and now he wants to fight with them? I thought capitalists were the enemy."

"Survival always trumps ideology. He needs us if he's going to survive."

And that was exactly what had occurred on August 14, 1941—a signed military convention between Stalin and the British government in which a military force would be formed, subordinate to the Polish government-in-exile stationed in London.

"After all we've been through," Bogdan said, "we're actually going to fight for the Soviet Union."

With a pronounced scowl, Janek shot back, "No. If we fight, it'll be for Poland."

Janek's eyes reddened with tears. His body had become no more than skin and bones, and he'd resigned himself to the probability that Yakutsk would be his final resting place. "Thank you, Lord, for keeping me alive," he prayed, then spent the next few minutes watching his fellow prisoners eat and drink more than they'd had in the past month.

"Come join us," Bogdan urged, wrapping his arm around Janek's shoulder.

"You go," Janek said. "I just want to close my eyes and rest." He leaned back against a wall and pictured how Wanda and Sophie would look, had they also survived. And though he would have liked nothing more than to celebrate his newfound freedom, he also knew that war was still raging throughout Europe and that he and his men would now become a part of it. How many will die after surviving the hell they'd just endured, he wondered. The thought of seeing even more of his friends die in battle left him shaking and weeping where he sat.

The next day, what happened following the amnesty order would become the single greatest odyssey in military history. In one fell swoop, survivors of arctic gulags and deportees to labor camps throughout Russia and Kazakhstan following the Soviet invasion of Poland in 1939 packed what little belongings they had and began their long-awaited journey out of hell and into the promise of a new life. Janek, who saw no end to the war anytime soon, feared it would be years before he set eyes on Wanda and Sophie again. For them, the torturous ordeal of labor camps may finally have been over, but for Janek the horror of prisons and gulags was suddenly replaced with the even greater horrors of an ongoing war. And after narrowly escaping the atrocity of Katyn, then barely surviving the cruelty of Stalin's prisons and gulags, Janek was ready to fight and risk death for the slim chance of one day being a husband and a father again.

For Janek, the joy of freedom that day was akin to a drowning man taking a final, desperate gulp of air—he believes he's about to die, his entire life passes before his eyes, and suddenly an arm reaches down and pulls him up seconds before he takes that last swallow of water. That's what Janek felt when the NKVD official entered his barracks and, to everyone's disbelief, announced that the Polish government-in-exile—which none of the prisoners even knew existed—and the Soviet Union had agreed to a one-time amnesty for all Polish soldiers in return for their allegiance to Russia against the German forces.

At most gulags throughout Russia, news of the amnesty trickled in slowly, partly because communications were so unreliable, but mainly because authorities feared the gulags and labor camps would be unable to fulfill their quotas without much needed Polish slave labor. Release of prisoners was often at the whim of camp commanders, who then withheld freedom for months. But eventually, the stunning news reached even the most remote camp: Hitler had invaded Mother Russia. Even then, the fate of prisoners freed from bondage was left to Stalin, who felt little mercy for those who despised everything Russian. So, as if the plight of innocent Poles was not heinous enough, the NKVD, to ensure that as many prisoners as possible perished so as not to reveal the cruelty of their captors, left them stranded on the Russian steppes without food or water.

When the mass exodus began in earnest, the journey from the frozen north to the south was no more humane, and often worse, than the nightmarish train rides the hordes of people had already experienced. Some had no idea where they were. Most left the camps and gulags not even knowing where the Polish Army was being formed. They didn't care. All they knew was that they could finally leave hell and hopefully find heaven. For many, however, the promise of heaven might as well have been a road back to hell. Rampant disease, as well as shortages of food and water, made what should have been a joyous migration back to their homeland a final and tragic end. Along the way, thousands of men, women, and children perished, many from typhus, their fear of never seeing Poland again sadly realized.

Every man, including Janek, had gladly signed his name across the bottom of the recruitment paper. Holding it in their hands was like feeling gold against their bony fingers—priceless, but almost too good to be true. No one trusted the Soviet Union, especially the NKVD, so given the opportunity to walk away from starvation and certain death, even if it meant fighting a bloody war with Russia against Hitler, every last skeptical soldier took it before Stalin could change his mind.

Bogdan, who'd been Janek's closest friend since arriving at the gulag, had watched him slowly wither away before his eyes. Janek's muscles were gone, and what little protein was left in them barely kept his body alive. Before they set out on their journey out of Yakutsk, Bogdan looked at Janek's thin frame and held out little hope his friend would make it.

"How are you doing?" he asked.

"Not good," Janek said, "but the more I eat, the better off I'll be."

Bogdan smiled and tried to be positive. "Isn't amnesty wonderful?"

"Don't tell me about amnesty," Janek snapped back, hating that term because it implied the Soviet Union had a legal basis for arresting Polish citizens. Everyone knew it didn't. Poland's only crime had been resisting a Russian invasion and not accepting Russian authority. "Stalin's directive should have said *released* instead of amnesty, since we're innocent, and our only crime was to defend our homeland." But then he calmed himself down and thought better of it. Who was he to quibble over a word, he thought. He was free and he was eating, and that was all that mattered.

"Sorry, my friend, I just…"

"I know," Janek said. "I'm just angry that Stalin thinks he's doing us a favor by not killing us." He laid down on his bunk and closed his eyes, too weary to think any more about it.

The next day, Janek and the rest of the freed prisoners, with little more than the clothes on their backs and whatever food they'd managed to hoard before they left camp, headed south to find an army they were not even sure existed. Along the way, villagers took pity on men who only yesterday were on the verge of starvation, offering them raw potatoes and water, enough to sustain even the most wretched among them until they could find more food or more kind villagers. September's crisp air and cool nights had become a blessing, allowing the men to walk farther each day without collapsing from heat and exhaustion. Janek couldn't have weighed more than ninety pounds when he left Yakutsk, but had since gained weight each day, thanks to the rations he was fed daily.

In less than three weeks, the men had arrived at a railway station where they congregated for three more days before boarding a train heading south to Buzuluk. Praise God, Janek thought for the first time in weeks, believing he'd left the worst behind him and in a few short days would become a part of Anders' Army. He leaned back and felt a sharp pain as the wood pressed against the bones protruding from his skin, but nothing in the last year had felt better than sitting with his men and knowing they were free.

It had taken over a month for Janek and more than a hundred men to arrive in Buzuluk, an area of Southern Russia situated near Kazakhstan along the western Ural Mountains. Founded in 1736 as a Russian fortress, it now served as the gathering point for 40,000 thankful Polish soldiers who had been weeks, if not days, from starving to death. Janek himself could barely muster the strength to walk, so he knew it would take many more months before he was ready and able to take command of an artillery unit.

"You know who this Wladyslaw Anders is?" Bogdan asked Janek as they felt the train slow and screech to a stop.

"I do. He was commanding Polish forces against both the Germans and Soviets when he was captured and eventually sent to Lubyanka prison in Moscow. I heard he was released by Stalin last month to form a Polish Army. So here we are."

Commander Wladyslaw Anders, a thin but imposing figure with piercing dark eyes and a bald head, was captured near Janek's hometown of Lwow on September 29, 1939 after being wounded twice in battle. He'd been jailed in Lwow but then transferred to Lubyanka, where Soviet authorities could interrogate him more effectively. After surviving torture and deprivation for nearly two years, Wladyslaw Anders, tasked with forming an army in exile like no other in military history, was now welcoming tens of thousands of refugees and prisoners of war from every corner of Russia. Nothing in modern times compared. Like Moses who led his people from bondage out of Egypt, Anders had been gathering soldiers, husbands, wives, and thousands of children and preparing them for a mass exodus from the scourge of Soviet domination to the Soviet Union's southern frontier. From all corners of Siberia they came, in rags, mainly by foot and by train, hungry and exhausted, and many, tasting freedom for the first time in years, had died tragically from disease and malnutrition within days of their arrival. According to some accounts, as many as fifty were dying every day.

No sooner had Janek climbed down from the train than he was rushed to a mobile hospital for treatment and recovery. Four days of rest and food kept him alive and at last he felt as if he'd been pulled from death's door. The camp tent to which he was assigned was palatial, he thought, compared to where he'd come from. It was like a dream, and he feared that he'd be woken in the middle of the night and be back in the gulag. During those first few days, he suffered with nightmares, at times screaming as if Ivan were beating him to death. But over the next few days, a hint of a smile would actually cross his face whenever he looked out of his tent and gazed at the Russian landscape through much different eyes.

"You're looking better, my friend," Bogdan said, then sat at the edge of Janek's cot.

"I'm feeling better," Janek said. "How are the others?"

"Recovering. But it'll be a while before they're ready to go anywhere."

"They told me I wouldn't be ready to do very much until early next year."

Bogdan shrugged. "Better than Yakutsk." And then he leaned forward with a puzzled look and said, "Everyone's wondering where all the Polish officers are. I was wondering that myself, seeing that you're one of only a few."

In fact, so few Polish officers had arrived in Buzuluk that Commander Anders had questioned Stalin repeatedly about their status, only to be told that most had deserted or escaped and fled to Manchuria. But Janek knew better. He had been there with them, and he suspected that every one of them had marched to their deaths. Though he didn't tell Bogdan the tale of what had happened to him that day, he spent the rest of the evening thinking of those fellow officers and friends who would haunt him for the rest of his life. Wiping a tear from his eye, Janek tried to convince himself that anyone, if he could, would have done the same, but he kept those thoughts and the secret of Katyn close to his heart.

By October, British uniforms for the Polish troops had finally arrived. Janek had gained thirty pounds since leaving the gulag, and as he buttoned his new uniform and brushed it clean with his fingers, he felt like a real soldier once again.

"They actually fit!" Bogdan exclaimed, seeing how nicely he and Janek had filled out their uniforms. "And they're not rags."

"We got these just in time," Janek said. "I heard that in a few months we're being moved farther south, near Tashkent."

"Where it's warmer, I hope."

It was mid-September when Janek and his men arrived in Buzuluk. But each day after that brought with it colder weather, and by January, new arrivals were being greeted by harsh and extreme conditions—living quarters were no more than flimsy tents, which only added to the misery when temperatures fell and men would go to sleep and be found the next morning frozen to death. Even in the middle of a brutal winter, many soldiers were still without good shoes and heavy coats. But despite their suffering, each soldier had willingly given up one daily ration of food a week to help feed the civilians arriving at the camp each day.

Meanwhile, halfway across the Siberian Plain, Wanda and Sophie had also been granted amnesty and had begun their own long and arduous journey back to Poland. Kazakhstan, at the time they were there, was a nation divided, part of it populated with hospitable people who hated Russia as fervently as did Poles. And why wouldn't they? Following Russian occupation of Kazakhstan, repression and forced collectivization brought poverty, mass hunger, and unrest. Soviet domination took root, Stalin's communist ideology spread to every corner of the land, and whether they wanted it or not, Kazakhstan had been fully integrated into the Soviet empire. Wanda took advantage of that hatred and was able to spend a night with Sophie here and there on a farm or in a settlement along the way. But the other Kazakhstan was a wild and dangerous place, with perils around each bend and thieves and rapists lurking in the icy darkness of its lawless frontier. Searching for food and shelter between their trips on railway cars had become a constant struggle to stay alive long enough to reach the Polish border. What Wanda hoped would be days or weeks had turned into agonizing months before she and Sophie finally crossed into what they thought was heaven on earth.

Janek, a dead man walking from his year in the gulag, had been rehabilitating, eating, exercising, and writing to anyone in Wanda's family who would have known her whereabouts. As it turned out, workers in the labor camps of Kazakhstan and Siberia were left to make their own way home with little food and no money. Typhoid, cholera, and scarlet fever, rampant among the local populations, had sent many evacuees to their graves before they could set foot back on Polish soil. Janek, racked with grief and suffering from malnourishment himself, sought desperately to learn if Wanda and Sophie had met a similar fate. But just when the anguish of not knowing had become as painful as his suffering in the gulag, he'd gotten word that his wife and daughter had made their way back to Poland with nothing but the clothes on their backs.

Janek cried like a child that day, then cried again with his comrades as he retold the story of Wanda's arrest and how it had been three years since he last saw his wife and daughter. Most soldiers had similar stories, but some sat by silently, expressionless and somber, because their stories were ones of wives and children missing, tortured, or dead.

As the Russian winter eased slowly into spring, Janek, along with tens of thousands, was moved nearly 1,400 miles to the southern border town of Tashkent. There, for the next four months, Janek would regain the strength he'd lost over the past two years and prepare for whatever it would take to defeat Hitler. Finally, in August 1942, a meeting between Wladyslaw Anders and Winston Churchill led to an agreement that the Polish armed forces, along with some civilians, were to be transferred to Iran to serve under the British Command of General Wilson. Stalin reluctantly agreed, mainly because the ongoing war with Germany had led to greatly diminished food supplies and other provisions needed by the Polish Army.

Within days, the floodgates had opened. Thousands upon thousands of former POWs evacuated and took flight toward Russian borders. Through Central Asia and Siberia to the Caspian Sea they went—on trains and ox carts, by foot, and finally on ships and barges—until they reached Iran, where the British allied forces met them at the port of Pahlavi. What the British found shocked them to their core. For along the way, the humanitarian boats that ferried sick and starving Poles across the Caspian Sea—overloaded, unsanitary, with little food and un-boiled water—had turned into a fleet of death traps. So, halfway to Iran, the sea had become a mass graveyard for the souls of men, women, and children who'd survived the torture of camps and gulags only to die below decks from typhoid and dehydration. Those who staggered ashore and kissed the ground were unlike any humans the British had ever seen.

Thousands more, with no resources other than the clothes on their backs, had dragged their haggard bodies in a months-long trek from the southern border of the Soviet Union by foot, and many of those, existing only on raw potatoes and filthy water, had also died from disease and starvation. For the emaciated and lice-infested survivors who lived through hell and teetered on the verge of death, it seemed like paradise found.

Meanwhile, Stalin had demanded that Anders deploy whatever men he had to the front lines, where they would surely be used as cannon fodder for German troops. Anders refused, citing the men's poor condition and the need for more training and additional supplies. Incensed, Stalin cut supplies even further, which led Anders to order the remainder of his Army still in Russia to evacuate. In all, nearly 120,000 soldiers and civilians moved out of the Soviet Union and were placed under the British Middle East Command. The majority had become a part of Anders Army; the rest were eventually taken to refugee camps in Tehran and Isfahan to begin their new lives. Not all the poor souls were allowed to leave the Soviet Union, however. And those that remained behind would live out the rest of their days on Russian soil because Stalin had declared that all Poles still in the Soviet Union would forever be Soviet citizens.

What the survivors who had finally made it to Iran didn't know was that their latest destination from exile, the hospital at Pahlavi, rather than welcoming them as a place of healing and recovery had become the epicenter of mass death from an epidemic of typhus. Tragically, thousands of broken and emaciated patients, too weak to stand or even feed themselves, had reached the nation of

Iran only to die within hours or days of coming ashore. Even in freedom, short-lived as it was, the scourge of Stalin's purges and deportations had followed them from the gates of hell in Russia all the way to their graves in Iran.

Janek was luckier than most. He was alive, and he had learned that Wanda and Sophie had also survived their ordeal in the brutal labor camps of Kazakhstan. He wasn't sure, though, where or even when the Polish army would be assigned to fight, but fight he would, and after everything he and his nation had endured, the risk of death on the battlefield in return for peace and freedom was a price he was willing to pay.

Chapter 15

Port of Pahlavi, Iran
July 5, 1942

"It's a beautiful sight, isn't it?" Janek looked on as the transport ship overflowing with Polish soldiers and civilians eased gently against a dock in the principal port city of northern Iran. "I had doubts we'd ever make it."

"You almost didn't," Bogdan said. "Another week and you'd have been buried in that filthy place."

Janek nodded. "You're probably right," he agreed, then put his arm around Bogdan's shoulders. "Thanks for looking out for me."

"You would've done the same, my friend."

The men lining the starboard side could not find words to describe the feeling of having left Russia behind. "I'm happy for us," one of the men said, "but I pray for those still there." Each man then bowed, made the sign of the cross, and thanked God for delivering them from an evil they'd never before known in their lives.

Janek stared at the bustling port and squinted into the morning sun, his eyes tearing up as gaunt faces flashed before him. Some had died only days before the amnesty, tortured and abused by maniacal guards whose only thoughts were of the cruelty they could inflict on men they hated for no other reason than that they were

Polish prisoners.

Once the ship had docked and been cleared, an announcement rang out from several speakers: "All civilians will disembark aft and gather in Building C for processing and transport to Tehran. When all civilians have deboarded, soldiers will disembark at midship. Once ashore, soldiers report to Building A for further orders."

Throngs of refugees suddenly rushed to shore, beside themselves, almost delirious, having tasted freedom for the first time in years. Pahlavi was receiving over 2,500 refugees per day, all so desperate for food that many, not knowing or caring how their bodies would react, ate as much as their stomachs could hold. Malnourished to the point of near hysteria, they hadn't realized how much their starvation had changed the way they metabolized nutrients. In the absence of carbohydrates, insulin production had gradually decreased while their bodies used fat and muscle as a source of energy. That, in turn, depleted life-saving electrolytes. When too much food was reintroduced too quickly, sudden and extreme shifts in electrolyte balance led to seizures and coma. So, ironically, while many victims left behind had died in gulags and labor camps from too little food, some of the newly freed were literally eating themselves to death.

"Let's go," Janek told his men as soon as the last civilian stepped foot off the ship. He then faced them and said, "None of us will ever forget what we've been through, but I couldn't have done it without all of you. Together we survived hell, and we'll survive again, no matter where we go."

One by one, the men stepped off the ship and onto

Iranian soil. Janek was well aware of Persian history, so he found comfort in knowing that it would be there that he'd begin the final stages of his recovery and training for the battles to come. As he walked along the dock and looked out at the Caspian Sea, the largest inland body of water in the world, he reflected on what he'd learned about the nation of Iran, which until 1935 was called Persia.

In 1828, Russia had conquered the weaker northern region of Persia in the second Russo-Persian War, and thereafter sought to subjugate the population. For the next century, hatred toward its invader festered, becoming as deep-rooted as hatred toward any occupying country could be. The southern region, rich with vast fields of oil beneath its sand, was dominated by the British, who occupied the land during World War I and whose petroleum companies built massive refineries, extracted the liquid gold, and kept the lion's share of profits for themselves. Powerless to resist, the Persians, looking north saw Russia, looking south saw Britain, and looking inward saw a nation whose fate and future was being dictated, not by them but by infidels and foreign powers that cared more about themselves and geopolitical outcomes than about their impoverished subjects. In fact, control of Persia between Russia and the United Kingdom had become known as the "Great Game," in which both saw the oil-rich nation as a strategic island in the middle of an otherwise barren sea.

By 1919, the dual spheres of Russian and British influence had become a way of life. To poor civilians, many living in squalor next to wealthy neighborhoods lined with colorful English gardens and lavish British homes, this shameful state of conquest and occupation was a cancer they prayed would one day be excised. Their prayers were finally answered. Following the Russian Revolution that same year, and the country's withdrawal from the region, Persia had finally been freed of Russian domination, for the time being. As for the British, after unsuccessful attempts at establishing a protectorate in Persia, Reza Shah Pahlavi had risen to power and established instead a dynasty that lasted until 1941, at which time he was forced to abdicate when Russia once again invaded his nation. And yet again, Iran, thinking foolishly that it had rid itself of Soviet tyranny, was pulled back into Russia's sphere of influence.

Along came Germany. The Iranians had genuinely believed that, with so much success against Russian forces, Germany would certainly win the war and thus establish a powerful bulwark against further aggression toward Iran. That miscalculation cost them dearly. Because the Iranians rejected demands to expel the Germans from their territory, the Allies invaded in August 1941, overwhelmed the weak Iranian Army, secured the Iranian oil fields, and established a conduit that ensured a steady stream of troops and supplies to North Africa and Italy.

Since Iranians held such deep hostilities toward Russia, it was natural for them to invite Poles into their country despite the newcomers being members of the British Army. Besides, they saw Polish refugees as victims of Russia as they themselves had been and, therefore, were sympathetic to their plight. As for Polish soldiers, the Iranians figured the poor wretches were simply passing through on their way to Iraq and the battlefields of Italy where they'd probably be slaughtered anyway. For both the soldiers and the civilians, Iran may have been a temporary layover, but after years of torment in the vilest places on earth, many saw it as a desert paradise.

Others, however, had not been so lucky, as Janek later discovered when he strolled along Khalat Street in the eastern suburbs of Tehran and came across something out of the ordinary: a walled-in Roman Catholic cemetery in the midst of a predominantly Muslim nation. And upon entering the rusted gates of that cemetery, he meandered through perfectly straight lines of teetering and faded gravestones until he came to the Polish section tucked inconspicuously away in the farthest corner. There he stopped and noticed something unusual: almost two thousand newly erected gravestones in all, most with 1942 engraved as the year of death. In the center stood a beautiful stone memorial, a reminder to the few visitors who trickled in and lit candles to the dead, that read:

In Commemoration of Thousands of Poles
The Soldiers of the Polish Army
of General Wladyslaw Anders
Former Prisoners of War and the Civilian Captives
of the Soviet Union
Who Died in 1942 on the Way to their Homeland
Peace to their Memory

Janek stood silently before one of the gravestones and whispered reverently, "Rest in peace, my friends. Poland will remember you, no matter where you lie." He turned and began to walk away, thankful that his countrymen were being so generously welcomed, and grateful that the dead among them at least had a decent and proper burial. Tehran, which had been receiving the flood of refugees that disembarked in Pahlavi, could not save the worst of the sick and dying, and those were the bodies that Janek knew would forever lie beneath gravesites in a foreign land.

By the next month, Janek and his men had recovered enough that they were ready to begin actual combat training. So off they went to Iraq, where the blistering summer heat could overwhelm and kill a man if he were not careful—one hundred twenty degrees at times, with the men living in tents that trapped the air and baked whoever lay inside. Of course, after what Janek had gone through in the last year, nothing fazed him, not heat, not cold, not eating enough, not sleeping enough. It was a blessing he'd survived and was standing there in one piece. Everything else, as far as he was concerned, was a miracle.

Once established, the Polish Army, scattered by divisions across the vast Iraqi desert, helped organize training camps and hospitals. Some divisions spent their days guarding Iraqi oil fields against Nazi attacks while preparing for upcoming war in North Africa and Italy. A number of the men could not go on because of illness or grave injuries, and so, as others had done in Iran, they chose to stay behind and live out the rest of their days in Iraq.

That summer in the Iraqi desert was brutal. Janek and his men spent nights resting and days preparing for an all-out offensive that would be taking them through Egypt, North Africa, and finally to Italy, where they'd be fighting in the fiercest battles of the war. The allies needed Polish fighters ready to die if it meant ridding the world of evil such as Hitler and Mussolini. Everyone felt the same way. To the last man, they vowed to fight until the end because they'd seen it with their own eyes. Those who hadn't, like the Americans, could not fully understand what they were fighting against. Yes, they had a grand notion of standing up for freedom and democracy, but had no idea what was happening to millions of innocent people in countries most of them could not locate on a map. Janek and his men did. They'd lived it. They'd seen the concentration camps. They'd survived the gulags. Their families had died by the hundreds of thousands from cold and starvation and were left to rot thousands of miles from home. For them, it was not some distant struggle. It was at their doorstep.

When the time came, Janek and his men deployed from the tranquil deserts of Iraq to the bloody and violent deserts of North Africa, where allied forces had been fighting since Italy declared war on June 10, 1940. For years before Janek joined the fight, battles had raged from Egypt to Libya, with offensives and counteroffensives pummeling each side in some of the crucial turning points of the war. Back in December 1941, British forces, in Operation Compass, had destroyed the Italian Tenth Army and the German African Corps led by Commander Erwin Rommel, later known as the "Desert Fox." That was followed in October 1942 by a decisive victory over Rommel in Libya, who was forced to retreat into Tunisia. Six months later, the advancing British Eighth Army had encircled the German and Italian army in northern Tunisia and forced their surrender in May 1943.

At the time, much of Germany's communications had been intercepted by allied codebreakers using a modified Enigma, an electro-mechanical cipher machine developed and used in the early to mid-twentieth century to protect sensitive information. For the Nazis, the German Enigma machine had become their principle ciphering system, producing a polyalphabetic substitution cipher consisting of purely random key sequences with no repetitive patterns. Each character was altered by means of a scrambler comprised of rotors that changed the electrical path from character to character, which produced an alphabet sequence much longer than any message. By the time Hitler had set his sights on Europe, Enigma had become one of the most important developments in his army's arsenal.

Unfortunately for Hitler, the Polish Cipher Bureau, realizing that mathematicians would make excellent codebreakers, had recruited Marian Rejewski, a twenty-seven-year-old Polish mathematician, to help break Enigma. After numerous failures, Rejewski used the theory of permutations, and flaws in the German enciphering procedures, to break the message keys of the Enigma machine. Had the Germans enforced good operating protocols, Enigma would have been unbreakable. Fortunately for the Allies, they had not, which allowed the Enigma machine to be reverse-engineered and the ciphers read. When the Germans added more rotors to Enigma, making it ten times as complex, the Poles recruited British and French intelligence operatives to assist in deciphering encrypted messages. The intelligence gathered, codenamed "Ultra" by the British, resulted in a string of German defeats and helped turn the tide in the Allied war effort.

By June of 1943, the British agreed that the Polish Second Corps was fully combat ready. Janek and his men joined the battle-hardened Third Carpathian Division, ordered deployed to Egypt. Stalin immediately ordered the border sealed. No more refugees were to be allowed to leave because Russia was losing too much valuable labor. But the real reason was that Joseph Stalin had broken off relations with the Polish government over its investigation of the Katyn massacre, to which he refused to admit. As the convoy of military trucks drove south from Iraq, Janek looked north at the horizon and thought about those left behind. This is why we must go to war, he told himself, because at least we're free, and it's our sacred duty to help bring the rest back.

The road to Cairo was almost surreal. After looking at frozen tundra and wilderness, marching through blinding snowstorms and drifts waist deep, Janek and his men were crossing a strange and unique sight—the desert. Vast swaths of fine sand, shimmering in the sun like a sea of tiny jewels, surrounded them, some of the men having never walked on desert sand in their lives. The air could be at one moment so still Janek could hear camels bellowing in the distance, yet in the next came swirling, violent windstorms that bit into his flesh like shards of glass.

Nothing in this country, thought Janek, was the least bit familiar. Not the landscape nor the religion, the cities, or the people. It was something out of a storybook; something most people only saw on television or read about in textbooks. And the first time he laid eyes on the ancient pyramids, the world suddenly grew bigger and infinitely more diverse. "One doesn't look at the pyramids and not be awed at the sight of them," he said, staring in wonder and forgetting for the moment why he was there and where he was going.

Janek knew every soldier with him felt the same way as they set off to war, hoping to live through it but expecting the worst. He looked at men around him who could not have been more than eighteen, their entire lives ahead of them and probably wondering if they'd have limbs to walk on or hands to eat with when they got back.

It was almost eight months before Janek's division had finished training in the desert before readying to move on to Palestine and then to Italy in March of 1944. Janek had tried to familiarize himself with Palestine, what it was and who those people living there were, because until then he couldn't even remember anyone using the word Palestine in normal conversation. All he knew of it was what he'd read in the Bible, an ancient land where Arabs roamed and no one in their right mind would ever call home. But Janek, who'd spent a month there, living in tents and lying beneath stars that seemed to go on forever, had taught himself things he never knew.

Palestine, he learned, was not a single country but a region in the Middle East between the Jordan River and the Mediterranean Sea. From 1920 to 1948, it was governed by Great Britain, but to Arabs who lived there it was their homeland. They'd fought and died for it against the Ottoman Empire despite being outgunned and outmanned by a superior and well-equipped Turkish army. But in 1916, Captain T.E. Lawrence, a British liaison officer, had come forward with new tactics, fresh ideas, and much needed supplies to fight a guerrilla war that eventually defeated the much stronger Turkish military. What Lawrence of Arabia, as he'd become known, did was to convince the Arabs to put aside their independence and tribal quarrels and fight as one nation in order to vanquish the fourth largest army in the world.

But during that time, in 1917, the land had been

promised to the Jews in the Balfour Declaration, a public statement issued by the British government announcing support for the establishment of a national home for the Jewish people in Palestine. Anxious for their own homeland after so many years without one, Jews had begun migrating to Palestine and living in harmony with their Arab neighbors. Following the war, however, a collective clash of cultures, beliefs, and religions had reared its ugly head, and both Jews and Arabs found it more difficult to share land that each thought did not belong to the other. The Arabs, who'd joined the Allies in their fight against the Turks, believed the land was theirs to begin with. The Jews, on the other hand, insisted that Palestine had been their historic homeland since biblical times and was promised to them by the Balfour Declaration.

There would be no compromise, and in August 1929, anger and hatred boiled over with the massive influx of new Jews, which the Mufti of Jerusalem, Haji Amin al-Hussein, feared would result in more Jews in Palestine than Arabs. By 1936, violence had reached a breaking point, so much so that the British felt compelled to restore law and order through military intervention. That, in turn, spurred more violence and further military intervention. For the Arabs, the Jews were the enemy, along with the British, who they believed had betrayed them. For the Jews, the Arabs and the British, who they hated because they'd instituted a quota on Jewish immigration, were the enemy. There were no winners in this tug-of-war between two great cultures.

Following World War II, the British still controlled Palestine but looked for a way to relinquish its grip and allow Palestine to forge its own destiny. Along came the

United Nations in 1947, seeking a solution acceptable to both Jews and Arabs: two separate states—Israel and Palestine. By May 14, 1948, the British withdrew, and within weeks the newly formed state of Israel was attacked by surrounding Arab nations in a war that lasted eight months. Refusal to recognize Israel and the creation of the Palestinian Liberation Organization (PLO) had made peace impossible because for Arabs, Israel would always be Palestine. And looking forward a thousand years, some say, a strip of desert, 270 miles long and 85 miles wide, ten miles at its narrowest, will forever be fought over as the rightful homeland to both Jews and Arabs.

Janek was thankful to God he was finally in condition to fight against what he considered a scourge upon the earth, the Nazis. The first six months following his release, he and his men were walking skeletons, each one barely a hundred pounds. Not until they had all gained weight and become more fit did they spend the next year in serious training. By then—March 1944—the Second Polish Corps had been transferred to Italy where Janek and his men became an independent unit of the British Eighth Army under General Oliver Lee. Two months later, they were joining the Americans, Brits, French, Indians, Australians, New Zealanders, South Africans, and Canadians at Monte Cassino, where allied forces had already fought three bloody and losing battles. At the time, Monte Cassino had stood as the strongest line of defense in German-occupied Italy, so the allies, in four months of constant assaults, had suffered some of the greatest casualties of the war. For Janek, who'd escaped death not once but many times over, in the past three years, the thought of not risking his life in this epic struggle had not even crossed his mind.

Chapter 16

Sandusky, Ohio
September 11, 2004

The TV was tuned to CNN when Sister Regina stepped into Wanda's room and looked up at a somber news anchor, microphone up to his lips, reporting from ground zero, where three years earlier two planes had flown into New York's twin towers and erased the lives of almost three thousand innocent people. Ignoring Sister Regina's presence, Wanda sat fixated, hanging on every word, seeming to understand the gravity of what she was watching.

"This morning we remember the lives lost three years ago today, and the lives forever changed by what happened on that day," the news anchor reported, microphone visibly shaking in his hand. "Leaders from around the world have been expressing sympathy and vowing to fight the scourge of terrorism that threatens the very fabric of their societies."

A minute later, Wanda's eyes widened as Iran's president, Mohammad Khatami, appeared on the screen. A CNN interpreter, voicing over Khatami, repeated his words: "We believe the world...more than ever...needs peace. The United States was punished for imposing its will. We sympathize with the people of America...and we hope that the United States government will act realistically and rationally in the long-term interest of other nations."

"It's a sad day." Sister Regina sat next to Wanda and stared up at the TV. "I remember exactly where I was. I think everyone does."

Wanda nodded, her memories triggered by images of Khatami, thinking how tragic it was that the story of civilians and soldiers buried under Iranian soil was completely unknown to most people. Equally tragic, she lamented, were the untold stories of Polish women who'd remained behind after losing husbands and children, rebuilding their shattered lives by marrying Iranians, then spending the next five decades trying to erase the past. But, of course, there was no way they could. Their past would continue to haunt them until the day they died, at which time their bodies were laid to rest in the Polish cemetery while those of their Muslim husbands were buried elsewhere. And despite so much suffering and loss, not even in death could they lie in peace alongside the ones they loved.

"Janek spent time in Iran," Wanda said, turning from the TV. "The Iranian people were so kind and hospitable. Not like now."

Sister Regina finished watching Khatami's fiery speech and said, "I didn't know very much about Iran until the revolution, when it took those American hostages."

"It was different during the war," Wanda said. "All those starving refugees were coming to Iran; but despite widespread famine in their own country, they accepted Poles with open arms, feeding them, offering them work, and setting up orphanages for thousands of children who'd lost their parents in the camps and gulags throughout Russia."

"What happened to the children?"

"Most were sent to Isfahan, a city about three hundred miles south of Tehran where the climate was warmer and better for their recovery. So many—over two thousand, they say—that Isfahan became known as the city of Polish children. By the summer of 1942, the influx to Iran was so great that other nations—India, South Africa, and New Zealand—agreed to accept the wave of refugees. Today, any sign of Polish life in Iran has vanished." Wanda stopped to take a deep breath, tears welling in her eyes, dismayed that the only reminder of Poland's struggle against the Soviet Union lay hidden behind cemetery walls and buried beneath Iran's once welcoming soil.

"What did Janek think of the Iranians, especially after the American hostage situation?"

"He loved them. From the moment he got off the ship to the bus ride into his camp, they were offering him food and water and showering him with candy. After how he was treated in the gulag, it shocked him. He wasn't prepared for such kindness."

"When did he find out about you and Sophie?"

"While still in Iraq. He got word that once we were granted amnesty, we traveled for over a month through Kazakhstan. Sometimes we'd walk for hours to train stations scattered across the countryside, where groups of Poles boarded trains and rode to other train stations. On one of those train rides, Sophie came down with chickenpox. I was desperate, so we found a local hospital where Sophie could stay and recover from her illness. Days went by before we could leave and find another train heading west to Poland. When we did, it routed us in the wrong direction. So, back and forth we traveled, east then west, for almost a week before someone finally gave us the correct instructions and directed us to a train station a few miles away. By the time we arrived, the train had already left. We'd missed it by minutes."

Wanda suddenly ended her story and leaned back in her chair. Her eyes glistened as if remembering something she would sooner forget.

"What's wrong?" Sister Regina asked.

"We later discovered that the train we were supposed to be on and barely missed by minutes—filled with hundreds of Polish refugees, mostly women and children—had been diverted to a mountainous region in Russia, all the passengers ordered off, and shot to death."

"My God," Sister Regina gasped. "After what you'd gone through…to think you and Sophie could have been on that train."

All Wanda could do was weep at the thought of it. Surviving the brutal labor camps was a miracle in itself, but missing the train and avoiding execution had to be, in her mind, divine intervention.

"I don't care if you're an atheist or not," Wanda said. "How else would you explain it unless God answered our prayers. I can't accept that it was all some coincidence; that the two of us survived when we should be dead."

"Most people have no idea…"

"That's why I've never talked about it," Wanda interrupted. "The few times I did, people stared in disbelief…thought I was making up stories…figured things like that couldn't possibly be true. Anyway, I never wanted to bring it up because I'd get nightmares. So I spoke of it less and less over the years unless someone really cared and wanted to hear."

Sister Regina reached over and grabbed Wanda's bony hand. It felt cold and withered to the touch, like a thin sheet of parchment. But it was the hand of a labor camp survivor, she thought; frail but surprisingly strong for a woman who'd lived a full ninety-two years. What those hands must have been through, Sister Regina wondered, imagining at that moment how or whether she herself would have survived if history were different and she were the one who'd lived in Poland in 1939 when life for everyone had changed forever.

"I'm so glad you came into my life," Sister Regina said, still clinging to Wanda's hand, believing that most people were inherently good and, if they could, would never allow such evil to happen. But lately, the more she thought about it, the more she'd become convinced that most people seemed to care little about what happens half a world away, because if they did, they'd never sleep. "I guess the world will always have evil men who do evil things."

Wanda shook her head and scowled. "Evil is too kind a word."

"How did you manage without Janek, not having any contact at all until after the war?"

Wanda wiped tears from her eyes and took a deep breath, searching her mind for the right words. "I had Sophie. I had to manage…for her."

"It must have been difficult with such a young child."

"It was," Wanda said, her voice trembling. "The children didn't suffer as much as we did. They played with each other, chased birds, and ran in the fields while we worked. I don't think they really knew what their parents were going through, mostly because we tried to make the best of it for them. If we didn't have enough food, we gave it to them and went hungry ourselves. But I think as they got older they saw what was going on."

For the most part, Wanda had avoided bringing up the worst of it, but not all, and judging by her body language and the sorrow Sister Regina saw in her eyes, nothing about her life after Poland had ever filled the void she felt. It was as if she'd existed in two disparate worlds—the one in Lwow as a doting mother and a young wife to a handsome officer, and the one following their arrest by the Soviets, when the heavens above their peaceful city darkened and hell devoured them. That was how it felt, Wanda had said. "No one really knows what hell is like," she told Sister Regina, "but ask any Pole who lived through that, and they'll tell you."

Sister Regina could have listened for hours, spellbound at the things Wanda was telling her. Her entire being, she told Sister Regina, was dominated by backbreaking labor and constant thoughts of food. But though the camp guards worked the women like animals from morning till night, what had agonized Wanda most was the Soviet attempt at breaking the bond between parent and child. It was a Bolshevik thing, she said—eat away at the family and the State will take over the role of mother and father. Nothing, according to Wanda, was as cruel as that, especially when she'd hold her precious Sophie tightly against her and cry at hearing her daughter moan and whimper each night.

In Poland, Wanda had devoted herself completely to Sophie from the moment of her daughter's birth. But in the camps, children were denied that presence and spent their days alone or with strangers or in Soviet classrooms, forced to learn Russian songs and be drilled on Russian history. In some camps, women locked their young children in huts with little food and water and returned twelve hours later to find them huddled in a corner, staring vapidly as though nothing in the world mattered any longer. It was like torture, Wanda said, to know that children were denied everything they needed for their development and would never be the same again.

Some mothers, she said, wracked with the guilt of watching their children slowly die from hunger and disease, had chosen to send them to Russian orphanages rather than see them suffer. As one woman had told Wanda, "I'd rather never see my child again than see him suffer the worst death I could imagine." Each day, countless children withered away and died from malnutrition and disease, and each night mothers anguished over having to leave their beloved sons and daughters buried in a land they despised so much. In the worst cases, mothers so distraught at losing their children—either because the little ones died in their arms or were taken to Russian institutions to become new little Russians—had taken their own lives rather than return to Poland and have to live with that for the rest of their days.

The one saving grace, Wanda explained, was that Poles stuck together. "We all hated Russians," she told Sister Regina, "so everyone was like one big sad family, helping each other as much as we could, and talking every day of Poland." That was the difference between the Poles and the Russians, she said. The Russians thought like Russians—they were part of the State, not members of a family, and according to Wanda they were disgusting, primitive people in constant fear of their government and what it would do to them. The Russian women, Wanda recalled, were equally as barbaric as the men, vulgar, crude, dirty, aggressive, violent. "Living among them was like living with a pack of jackals," she said. "The Poles, on the other hand, thought like Poles." As devout Catholics, they considered themselves part of the western civilized world, and they held family and their faith as the central pillars of society. Even in the worst conditions, they felt compelled to maintain a sense of dignity and order in their lives. Family, to Polish women, was everything, Wanda told Sister Regina with anger swelling in her voice. "Losing it to a nation like Russia was like losing your virginity to a rapist who then demands gratitude for offering himself and for not killing you."

Sister Regina knew how much Wanda hated what the Soviets had done to her and Sophie, but she'd had no idea until then that Poles felt such visceral animosity toward everything Russian. But she understood why. How do people lose everything, she thought—homes, country, spouses, children, dignity, freedom—and not be forever scarred by such evil and brutality. Not for a second would she have felt differently, she told herself as she looked at Wanda's face and saw pain looking back.

Hoping that Wanda had one final answer left in her, Sister Regina asked, "After you and Sophie got back to Poland, how did you manage to get out of the country? Wasn't it controlled by the Soviet Union after the war?"

Wanda froze as though the question had touched on something she'd tried to block from her memory but now was forced to relive. If Sister Regina could have taken it back, she would have.

"No more talk," Wanda demanded, her face flushed

as she turned away.

At that moment, Sister Regina suspected something traumatic had happened to Wanda when she returned from Kazakhstan and tried to reunite with Janek. Thinking back to her discussion about Polish history, she remembered reading how Poland was the only Allied nation that fought the entire war beginning to end, victorious against all odds, yet losing its freedom in the outcome. In an ironic twist, the liberation of Eastern Europe from the tyranny of Nazi and Soviet occupation had been turned on its head, and it was the reason Janek could never again set foot on Polish soil, and how Wanda and Sophie became trapped in a country that no longer belonged to them.

Wanda closed her eyes and tried to rid those thoughts from her mind. "I want to sleep," she said.

"Of course." Sister Regina let go of Wanda's hand and helped her into bed. "I'll be back to check on you later." She figured that what Wanda had told her was enough, but something stirred her to wrap her arm around Wanda's thin shoulder and press it into hers. Maybe it was the thought of how Wanda had held Sophie tightly against her on those cold nights in Siberia, and Sister Regina wanted to do the same for her. She noticed that it was the first time in a while that Wanda had not fought or labored to catch her breath. Thank God, Sister Regina thought, because if anyone deserved a good night's rest and a little peace, surely it was Wanda.

"Sleep well," Sister Regina said. "We'll talk more tomorrow." What she couldn't get her head around, much as she tried, was how two simple people, separated in 1939 at a time when so many millions had perished, were able to survive. How could anyone, she wondered, have gone through arrests, brutal interrogations, torture, deportations, forced labor camps, gulags, Siberian winters, starvation, disease, mass killings, and the abject brutality of Stalin's purges and murderous regime? It was like a fairytale, she thought, or more like a nightmare, but as unlikely as it seemed each time she'd hear one of Wanda's stories, she knew they were all true, every one of them. And as she stared into Wanda's eyes and watched her chest rise and fall beneath her blanket, she saw a woman who lived a life few people, unless they'd lived through it themselves, could even imagine.

After Sister Regina left, Wanda tried to sleep but could not, images of her and Janek dancing in her head. "I wish you were still here," she whispered, "beside me." And as she did each day and each night, she filled her mind with thoughts of her past life and eventually fell asleep in Janek's arms.

Chapter 17

Taranto, Italy
December 1943

As temperatures dropped and falling snow appeared along the coast of southern Italy, the allies were preparing for the Italian Campaign. Mussolini, a brutal dictator who rose to power in 1922, had established a fascist government that sought three things: to restore and expand Italian territories, create an Italian Empire for colonization by Italian settlers, and establish control over the Mediterranean Sea. While Italy did not espouse the same genocidal ideology as Nazi Germany, the two nations had grown politically closer until 1938 when Mussolini and Hitler, a staunch admirer of the Italian dictator, formed the Rome-Berlin Axis, an agreement linking the two countries. For the next four years, this gathering storm had simmered and brewed like a witch's cauldron, then spread like wildfire across two continents. And together the two rulers began ripping North Africa and Europe apart in their obscene quest for land, power, and the minds and hearts of everyone they conquered.

But the Fall of 1940 proved to be the beginning of the end for Mussolini. Wanting desperately for his new alliance with Germany to succeed, and with a fanatical desire to expand his African Empire and take over the Suez Canal, he had declared war on Britain, which held territory in both Egypt and Libya. With help from Hitler's armed forces, fighting had intensified and reached its climax with the defeat of Rommel and Italy's surrender of Tunisia in May 1943. Once the Allied forces, including the Polish Carpathian Brigade, had conquered the battlefields of North Africa—from Egypt to Libya and Tunisia—the stage was set for them to abandon the desert and begin plans to move on to Italy where the real fighting would begin.

By the time Janek arrived in Italy with the Second Corps, Mussolini's onslaught had devastated his nation. German troops, spread across the country like vile locusts, had established strongholds they hoped would stop the Allied wave in its tracks. The most prized stronghold, ninety miles from the gates of Rome, was Monte Cassino, where Hitler's troops would try to keep his dream of world domination alive. But before the Allies could even think about Monte Cassino, they desperately needed Sicily.

The Allied invasion of Sicily was code-named Operation Husky. It was July 1943. Germany's forces numbered more than fifty thousand alongside Italian troops, so to counter such superior forces, something out of the ordinary had to be done. A briefcase with fake secret documents containing plans for an invasion of Greece, not Sicily, was planted on a corpse disguised as a British marine officer and allowed to drift ashore in Spain. The hope was that Germany, believing the documents to be authentic, would divert many of their troops to the western Mediterranean.

It worked. While Hitler pulled troops from Sicily and into Greece, General Dwight D. Eisenhour was massing air, land, and naval forces in preparation for an assault. On the night of July 9th, it began. After just thirty-eight days, the Allies drove the Nazis and the Italian army from the island and, for the first time since 1941, the sea lanes were cleared in the Mediterranean. The collapse of southern Italy had opened the way for the Italian Campaign.

In January 1944, Janek and the Second Corps landed at the Port of Taranto, a coastal city in the heel of Italy's boot. The German Army had already set up a main line of defense—the Gustav Line—with Monte Cassino at its center.

The world knew that Germany was on the verge of losing the war. Battles had been raging in Italy for the past year. And a meeting was convened in Yalta, a city on the southern coast of the Crimean Peninsula, surrounded by the Black Sea, to discuss the reestablishment and organization of nations decimated by war over the past six years. Present at the conference were President Franklin D. Roosevelt, Prime Minister Winston Churchill, and Premier Josef Stalin, collectively known as the "Big Three." Each had his own agenda for post-war Germany and Europe. Roosevelt needed the Soviet Union's support against Japan in the Pacific. Churchill wanted free elections and democratic governments, specifically in Poland, which had suffered the brunt of Nazi and Soviet aggression. Stalin demanded influence over Eastern and Central Europe for security reasons, but especially over Poland, since Poland had historically been an easy access route through which enemies would invade Russian territory. In fact, Poland was the first item on Stalin's agenda.

Naively, both Roosevelt and Churchill believed Stalin when he said, "Poland must be strong. The Soviet

225

Union is interested in the creation of a mighty, free, and independent Poland." But to assuage that view with Soviet interests and security, he also demanded that all Polish territory annexed in the 1939 invasion be kept under Soviet control in return for free elections in Poland. Stalin's demands went counter to the "Declaration of Liberated Europe," created by the Big Three as a promise to the people of Europe that they would create democratic institutions of their own choosing. The Soviet Union, however, had no intention of granting freedom or accepting free democratic governments to exist in its sphere of influence. Instead, Stalin used every tactic at his disposal to undermine fledgling democracies and install communist governments in every nation he dominated, including Poland, Romania, Bulgaria, and Hungary, which collectively became known as Soviet satellite nations.

To Janek and his fellow Poles, President Roosevelt, a charming and gregarious man with deep blue eyes, dark wavy hair, and chiseled features that enhanced his charisma, was, as they'd said, a goddam traitor. The Great Depression, the war, and polio had taken a heavy toll on his physical appearance and his health, but despite all that, he was running for a fourth term, and he needed every Polish American vote. To get them, he'd convinced Stalin to delay his occupation of Poland until after the election. Once in the White House again, Roosevelt figured that Uncle Joe could do as he pleased with his Slavic neighbor.

As a result of Stalin's lies and the Allied powers' betrayal, Poland ceased to exist, a communist government was installed, and Soviet repression of Polish citizens began anew. Tens of thousands of Polish troops who had fought with honor and valor alongside the British and Americans to defeat the Germans in North Africa and Italy lost their homes to the Soviet Union and would never return to their homeland. Janek knew he'd be one of them.

While in Palestine, most of the Jewish soldiers under British command had deserted—some 3,000 of them—so they could join the underground forces seeking to create a Jewish state. Menachem Begin, future prime minister of Israel, was one of the soldiers Janek had served with in Anders Army. To bolster his forces, Anders had a plan—he'd conscript prisoners rescued from the Germans, including Polish citizens being used as slave labor in Italy. By the time Italy had surrendered to the Allies, those numbers had grown significantly. A month later, Italy declared war against Germany. Three months after that, Janek had arrived in Italy as part of the British Eighth Army.

Janek and the Second Corps were well aware of how important Italy would be in the war effort. Capturing Rome and gaining Italian territory would force Germany to send reinforcements and weaken their stronghold on France. But the Allied long-range plan for ultimate victory was Operation Overlord, the D-Day invasion of Normandy that, if successful, would be key to winning the war.

Wanda and Sophie, meanwhile, had returned to a country they no longer recognized. People had grown fearful. Food, at one time plentiful, had become as valuable as gold. Lives once content and prosperous were shattered. And returning Poles, with no families or jobs and little prospects for the future, wondered if the world they left was better than the world they now found themselves living in. To make matters worse, following the defeat of Nazi Germany, Poland's borders had shifted indiscriminately based on decisions made by the Allies, who ceded to Stalin's ultimatums. Lwow, where Wanda and Janek had settled into a life they hoped would last forever, was permanently annexed into a borderland region called Kresy, which comprised twenty percent of its prewar borders. Most of the Polish inhabitants were expelled, and the territories became part of Ukraine, Lithuania, and Belarus. To the south, regions of Poland were given to Czechoslovakia. And for Wanda, her beloved Poland had suddenly become a Soviet puppet state in which she could no longer bear to live.

Wanda's eagerness to escape her wretched existence intensified at hearing that the Polish Second Corps, fighting under British command and refusing to pledge allegiance to Russia, were deemed traitors to the Soviet Union and no longer welcomed in Poland. Since many in the Second Corps had come from the annexed Kresy region, they no longer had homes to return to and would have to become Soviet citizens—or worse, be arrested and sent back to their gulags and be worked to death.

That fear was realized when Soviet-picked officials won the rigged Polish elections in July 1945. General Anders was stripped of Polish citizenship by the newly formed government, and Poland's government-in-exile, which at one time worked hand in glove with Stalin to form the army that helped save him, was delegitimized for anti-Polish activities. So, for Wanda, what began as a chance at freedom after nearly dying in the fields of Kazakhstan would soon become one of the most terrifying and life-changing chapters of her life.

Chapter 18

Sandusky, Ohio
September 12, 2004

There was nothing Sister Regina loved more than listening to Wanda recount stories of her life, bringing history alive and painting a vivid but dark picture of a world Regina knew little about. And for the last few days, whenever Wanda's mind allowed her to remember the past, she'd guided Sister Regina from Russia to Iran, through Iraq and Palestine, and finally to Italy, where Janek's journey with the Polish Second Corps would nearly cost him his life.

"Where were you when Janek was in Italy?" she asked, pulling up a chair, hoping Wanda was lucid enough to continue.

"I couldn't go back to Lwow," Wanda began, "because there was nothing left. We lost everything we had to the Soviets. Besides, Germany had established ghettos in Lwow, so the area was in chaos and too dangerous."

"Where did you go?"

"I had family outside of Warsaw, so we went there. The city itself was a Nazi stronghold. The northern part was turned into the largest Jewish ghetto in all of Europe, about one square mile in size with ten-foot walls and guard towers. Jews living there were being shipped off to Nazi death camps; and by the following spring, after an uprising, the Germans completely destroyed the ghetto and sent whoever was left to Auschwitz."

"What about the rest of Warsaw?"

Wanda explained how for the next two years, life for Poles, who'd found themselves existing in an alternate world, had become impossible, with Nazi Germany transforming the beautiful city of Warsaw into a place of darkness where people feared for their lives every minute of every day. No one knew when a knock on their door would bring accusations of hiding Jews or treason against Hitler's Third Reich. By then, everyone had heard of concentration camps spreading across Poland, and each day witnessed women and children murdered in their homes as they slept. So, out of desperation, an underground Polish Army had formed and foolishly believed they could overthrow their Nazi occupiers because they'd been promised support from Russia. A violent uprising erupted, German soldiers slaughtered. And Hitler, furious at the insurgents and determined to make an example of Warsaw, gave the order to destroy one of the most beautiful cities in all of Europe because Russia, which had pushed Germany back to Poland's western border, had inexplicably stopped and made no attempt to move.

"Why would Germany destroy an entire city they controlled?" Sister Regina asked.

"Because the destruction of Warsaw was planned even before World War II," Wanda said. "Hitler wanted it as the future site of a Germanic city with the Royal Castle—one of a few historic landmarks to be saved—as his state residence. The architect of the plan was Fredrich Pabst, who argued that destroying a nation's physical and architectural places would destroy its morale and culture."

According to historians, since Hitler wanted the city destroyed and replaced with his own, what better time than after the uprising? So the order was given: not a single stone should remain standing, every building razed. And for sixty-three days and nights, Warsaw was pounded by Nazi artillery and air power until it lay in smoldering ruins, annihilated, sixty percent of its population killed, whatever remained standing burned to the ground to deprive insurgents of hiding places.

Wanda described Warsaw in one word: rubble. The few who remained behind, scurrying and hiding in the ruins, were called Robinson Crusoes of Warsaw, likened to rats by the Germans, who killed anyone they found still alive and living beneath the piles of cement and stone.

"What's it like now?" Sister Regina asked.

"It's beautiful." Wanda's face beamed as she spoke of the city, though she'd only seen it in photographs since leaving Poland. "If you go to Warsaw today, you see a modern city, but the oldest section, which looks several hundred years old, is less than fifty. The Poles wanted to remember it exactly as it was before the war, so they reconstructed it brick by brick from old photographs, eighteenth-century paintings, architectural drawings, and building plans."

"How far from all that were you?"

"Close enough to know what was happening. Terror ate at us every second because we didn't know if Hitler, at any moment, would do to us what he'd done to Warsaw. Our only consolation was news about Allied victories and how Poland would soon fall into Allied hands. Day and night we prayed it was true. And in January 1945, our prayers were answered."

Wanda grew more animated as she told Sister Regina what life had been like for her and Sophie, this time under Nazi occupation. They'd gone from one hell to another, and they couldn't decide which was worse: Soviet death from cold, hard labor, and starvation or Nazi death from a bullet to the head. Either way, the entire country seemed frozen in fear and suspicion they could see in the eyes of everyone they'd meet.

"I remember people walking as if already dead," Wanda said. "One woman, holding a child in her arms, shuffled past me and stared ahead as though in a daze, the child so thin and frail I was surprised it was even alive."

Following Operation Barbarossa in 1941, Nazi Germany had spread its terror across all of Poland, becoming the epicenter of Hitler's final solution. What it had done in the west, it hoped to do in the east—enslave and exterminate local Polish populations and gradually replace them with German settlers. Hitler's grand scheme, according to Wanda, was to transform the nation of Poland and incorporate all Polish territory into the Third Reich.

The term "Reich enemies," as Wanda explained, described anyone with a higher education or who'd shown any signs of Polish patriotism. They were the first to be expelled and never heard from again. The remaining population, by design, were to be deported to Siberia and replaced by deserving Germans who passed strict racial evaluation. Heinrich Himmler himself had declared that "no drop of German blood would be lost or left behind for an alien race." The Nazi racial theory, after all, was to wipe from the face of the earth any inferior mixed or non-German blood. So, from the moment Germany set foot on Polish soil, it looked upon its conquered citizens as subhuman. Within months of its invasion, Germany had begun a reign of terror largely ignored by a world at war but whose goals were threefold: biological eradication of the Polish nation, replacement of Poles from annexed areas with Germans, and use of Poles as low-skilled slave labor.

The first goal was accomplished through a deliberate and systematic increase in mortality. Married couples were separated in forced labor camps, infants left without care, children denied enough food, pregnant women ordered to perform backbreaking work until childbirth, and mass sterilization programs initiated to ensure that so called "primitives" would not breed.

The second goal was even simpler: remove Poles from their homes and deport them. Germans had the right to enter any Polish home at will and take whatever possession they wanted. In fact, they could request the home itself from the government, even if Poles were still living in it. Hitler's Youth, established in 1922 to recruit and train future members of the Nazi Party, were assigned the task of ensuring that everything Poles left behind was given to new German settlers.

The third goal, at the outset, was all too real for most Poles. All property, including buildings, furniture, jewelry, money, and clothing, was subject to confiscation. All executive positions held by Poles were given to Germans. No shop, enterprise, and firm could be owned by Poles. All holidays and leave from work were banned. And all Polish workers from the age of fourteen were given the lowest pay for the lowliest work.

As though a magic wand was brushed over their homeland, every Pole had become a slave and every German the rightful heir to everything Polish.

For Jews, Poland from east to west had become a Nazi killing field. For ordinary citizens, it was paradise lost. From the lush meadows and fertile valleys to the rugged mountains, Hitler tore at Poland's roots and stopped at nothing to cleanse from all records its history and culture. Polish as a language was banned at all institutions and offices. Education standards were lowered so that future Poles would become ignorant workers. Teaching of history, literature, and geography was prohibited. Libraries went up in flames, millions of books burned, and distribution of Polish literature forbidden. Polish children were ripped from their families and forced into labor or used for medical experiments. Legal protection was nonexistent. In fact, public beatings of Poles by Germans had become legal so long as the beatings didn't lower the victim's productivity. Such was the life of an average Polish citizen.

And then, when all seemed lost, the Soviet Army began its push into Poland to retake territory mile by bloody mile. When it finally reached Warsaw, soldiers found nothing left but burned-out shells where grand buildings once stood and mounds of twisted debris and rubble thirty feet high. Meanwhile, in Auschwitz, just 200 miles south, the Nazis, in a final, desperate attempt to massacre as many Jews as they could before the Soviets arrived, gassed thousands in just a few days before abandoning the remaining prisoners and corpses. Before they retreated, however, the Nazi guards, desperate to hide evidence of genocide, destroyed four large gas chambers where over a million people had been murdered, along with camp records, barracks, and clothing warehouses. What they failed to destroy were the freight cars that had transported the poor souls into the camp. When the liberators arrived and forced open the train doors, emaciated bodies, stacked on top of one another like cords of firewood, fell out like broken sticks. As one soldier described it, "The bodies didn't even look human. They were ghastly, like pieces of dried wood, and only resembled bones. If you didn't know they were people, you'd think they were just part of the trash that surrounded us."

Wanda told Sister Regina that news of the German Army being driven from Poland had created such euphoria that every Polish soldier was ready to give his blood for his country. Sadly, many would, because as the Polish Second Corps packed up and headed north toward Monte Cassino, the Germans, 50,000 strong, were also ready and willing to give their last drop of blood for Hitler, who knew that Italy would be his final stand.

Chapter 19

Monte Cassino, Italy
January 1944

After months of delays, equipment and supplies arrived from the warm deserts of Egypt to Taranto, Italy in preparation for an assault on a historic hilltop monastery founded in the sixth century by Saint Benedict of Norcia. The Germans had chosen the monastery, adjacent to the town of Cassino, as a main line of defense because it lay strategically on a hill along deep valleys created by three rivers. Surrounding peaks and jagged ridges guarded the entrance to the valleys, some of which had been flooded by the Germans. Fast-flowing waters made crossing especially dangerous, so an assault on Monte Cassino from any direction seemed nearly impossible.

The road from Taranto to Monte Cassino took Janek and the Second Corps along the eastern coast of Italy where they fought against sheets of heavy snow, at times blinding and pummeling them in what seemed like a frenzy of white cotton. As they marched forward, small white crosses dotted their route, a constant reminder that death for soldiers can come in an instant. Janek knew that Hitler's objective was to bog the Allies down in Italy and prevent their march through Rome and across the Alps into Austria. The defeat of Sicily was the first step in breaking his hold on Italian territory. The next step would be to sweep north with the British Eighth Army and march on to victory through the ancient cobbled streets of Italy's most holy city.

It had been two long years since Janek's miraculous release from Stalin's gulag in Siberia, and despite months of intense training in Iraq and Palestine, and his itch to use that training in real battle, he shuddered in fear at what lay ahead. In the past months, the Allies had attempted three times to storm Monte Cassino, and three times they'd been repelled. Casualties mounted, men sent home in pieces or not at all because nothing of them was left. The Germans had held the high ground and fought viciously to keep their main line of defense from being breached. As the Polish Second Corps moved closer to the front lines, all Janek could think of was surviving the fight and returning to Wanda with his limbs intact.

Well aware that the battle for Monte Cassino had been raging for months, Janek knew the difficulty lay in the unique geography, with the mountain rising majestically seventeen thousand feet above its valleys, giving the enormous fortress a perfect position from which to look out and repel invading armies. So long as the Germans held the abbey and its surrounding towns, they'd kept the Allies from seizing the central Apennine Mountains and driving on to Rome. But for Benedict of Norcia, who'd built the abbey, it was a place between heaven and earth, perched high enough to receive the light of God and far enough from Rome to keep the darkness of paganism from its doors. Who would have imagined in AD 500, when Benedict strained under flickering candlelight to write his monastic rules for the

Benedictine Order, that hell would be unleashed on such a sacred site?

From everywhere across Europe they'd come, monks to breathe the spiritual air of what had become the capital of western monasticism, and ordinary people who sought the purity and richness of its burgeoning tradition as the cultural center of all Christendom. By the twelfth century, the abbey had acquired large tracts of land surrounding it and was heavily fortified with castles. That was its golden age. Artisans and fine craftsmen had made it a destination, monks rose from their simple lives to become bishops and princes of the church, and three had eventually become popes.

But all that disappeared as the centuries passed and wars between Italy and its enemies transformed Monte Cassino into a battleground. First it was Frederick II of Germany, whose troops had occupied the abbey during his war with the Papacy in the thirteenth century. Then it was the French who sacked it during the French Revolutionary Wars. Along came the Italian government in 1866, dissolved the abbey, and made it a national monument, with the monks as custodians. And then, with German troops stomping their boots past Saint Benedict's tomb, the abbey had once again grown dark as the evil of Hitler's regime turned Monte Cassino into Europe's last hope for salvation.

Several months before the first Allied assault, the winds of war had already shifted south and become palpable in the usually still air. An influx of German troops to the picturesque streets of Cassino had sent alarm bells throughout the city. Distant artillery fire had grown more frequent and was inching closer. Allied air strikes had come with more urgency. Terrified citizens, fearing the onslaught, sought refuge in the monastery despite no electricity or public services because they were certain no one would dare bomb such a holy site. But when the abbot learned of Hitler's order to stop the Allies at Monte Cassino at any cost before they could reach Rome, he knew what he had to do. So, on October 17, 1943, the first caravan of refugees and private property had evacuated and headed for Rome. By January, the abbey and every surrounding town, including Cassino, had been mostly abandoned. Monte Cassino, at one time brimming with over a thousand monks, nuns, orphans, and refugees, was now in the hands of the Nazis and isolated from the rest of the world. Only a handful of souls had chosen to stay, praying that God would come to their rescue and deliver them from Allied bombs.

And then it began. On January 11th, the first artillery shells fell from the sky near the monastery grounds. In the following days, the main assault took the Polish Second Corps across the swollen Gari river five miles downstream from Cassino while the French, in an attempt to draw Nazi troops away from their positions, moved in from the right. An amphibious landing by the Allies at Anzio had failed to loosen Germany's firm grip along the Gustav line. And the U.S. Fifth Army, fighting their way seven miles toward the abbey, sustained 16,000 casualties before reaching Germany's main line of defense.

Within weeks, bombardment had grown more violent, shaking the abbey's thick walls like thunder as countless explosions ripped the land around it to pieces. Whoever remained behind took refuge in cellars and underground bunkers while German troops above them fought to the death and repelled any advancing forces. When the dust settled, the Allies offered a ceasefire so that refugees could be moved to safer ground. One by one, terrified and injured civilians emerged from hiding and were loaded onto trucks and ambulances and driven from Monte Cassino, where the Allies were already preparing their next assault.

Janek, meanwhile, had been moving slowly through wet and freezing cold from Bari, Italy in a line of artillery that would join the fight in less than two months. The soldiers of the Second Corps had been told that assaults on Monte Cassino had so far failed and that crossing the swelling rivers and ravines had led to massive casualties. Weather conditions, with heavy snow blanketing the peaks and valleys, favored the German Army. For three months, the Germans had prepared their defensive positions, sowing mines, planting hidden barbed wire, stockpiling munitions, and establishing an impenetrable line between them and Rome. And then, on February 11th, after a disastrous three-day assault, the Americans withdrew from their positions. A fear like they'd never known swept over the troops of the Second Corps. If the American Army was unsuccessful, they thought, what chance did *they* have? It would be a suicide mission, they all suspected, with Polish troops used as disposable fodder to wear down the German forces.

The Second Corps did not arrive until the spring of 1944, traveling over 250 miles from where they'd landed in Taranto to the front lines. Winter that year was brutal. Camps had been established along the way so equipment could be refueled and soldiers readied for battle. The move had been slow and exhausting, with heavy rains eating into the earth and turning mud into a thick goo that gripped the men and equipment like quicksand. The troops had slept in flimsy tents, praying each night that the fighting would be over by the time they arrived. Of course, no one had admitted that, but every soldier in his right mind would rather not fight and not be added to the white crosses they'd seen along the way.

By the time Janek arrived, the British Eighth Army had recruited Algerians, Moroccans, French, New Zealanders, and even Polynesians. It was a multi-ethnic group that spoke at least four different languages, but it worked because the only words that counted were "kill Germans." The Polish Second Corps, led by General Anders, consisted of the Third Carpathian Infantry Division, the Fifth Kresowa Infantry Division, and Janek's, the Second Armored Brigade. In all, the Poles were three of the twenty Allied divisions ordered to make the final assault on Monte Cassino.

After the first three assaults, all unsuccessful, the Allies had spent the next two months preparing the fourth and what they hoped would be the final battle. That was where Janek and his men would come in. The Polish Second Corps and the British Eighth Corps, in an elaborate secret plan, had been moved to the center of the front lines. Operation Diadem, as it was called, would be a deadly assault along the twenty-mile German front.

"Have you seen the reports?" Janek asked one of the commanders on the ground. "You must have heard what I have. It's not been successful so far."

The commander nodded, his face grim. "The second assault was an attack from the north along the mountains...and from the south, where the Allies tried to capture the railway station near the town of Cassino."

"And the German intercepts?"

"Intercepted communications convinced the Allied forces that the abbey's being used as an enemy observation point, which is preventing its breach. They had to do *something.*"

Janek and his men had learned that on the morning of February 15, despite outcries and objections that the historic site not be touched, 230 heavy and medium bombers had dropped nearly 1,200 tons of explosives and incendiary bombs on top of the monastery while artillery units pounded the mountain mercilessly. Six hours later, another round of air strikes and artillery had torn through the landscape but left German positions above and behind the abbey unscathed. Once destruction of the abbey was complete, German troops had moved in and were using the ruins to store ammunition and quarter troops. By the end of the second assault, Monte Cassino's rubble had been transformed into a Nazi fortress.

Meanwhile, winter's frigid weather had persisted well into March. Freezing rain had kept heavy bombers grounded, while along the valleys and ridgelines it had pelted troops praying for less miserable conditions. After two costly assaults, the Allies hope was that a third would bring the Germans to their senses. On March 15th, it began. A four-hour bombardment with 1,000-pound bombs had shaken the land in every direction. Even the mountains around Monte Cassino groaned under the withering attack. The New Zealand Division, despite a steady and harrowing barrage of artillery fire, had advanced through rubble and rain-flooded bomb craters and captured strategic positions along the front. In nearby towns, success was measured by house-to-house combat, where soldiers slashed each other to pieces with knives and bayonets. In the end, German defenders had held their ground while Allied forces paid a heavy price in killed, wounded, and missing. It seemed that no matter what the Allies had thrown at enemy forces, they emerged broken but not beaten and ready to fight on until no soldier was left standing.

As the third assault came to an unsuccessful end, the Polish Second Corps was arriving in full force. In the past week, Janek and his men had passed groups of exhausted and bloodied men who stared ahead as if shell shocked, with little emotion on their faces and only sadness and fear in their eyes. Once they crossed the river and approached the front lines, the men looked out at complete devastation. Instead of a beautiful and serene Italy, they looked out at once lush valleys where nothing was left but twisted remnants of trees and hills blackened from the constant shelling. In the distance, Janek spotted the ruins of Monte Cassino. A light drizzle had begun to fall and gave what was left of the abbey an almost peaceful appearance.

How could this once beautiful monastery have brought such misery and suffering, Janek thought. And how many more young men would die or go home with no arms or legs to keep one man from spreading such evil on the world? As he stared up at Monte Cassino, none of it made sense, but there he was, ready to help launch a final assault and praying to God that Poland's Second Corps would make a difference.

Days went by. Artillery units positioned themselves strategically along the front lines. As an officer in charge of men who'd face death in less than twenty-four hours, Janek gathered his troops and prayed. Between them and the abbey stood fields where tens of thousands before them had gone and now lay dead. Would it be the same for them? What irony it would be, Janek lamented, if six years after first being captured by the Soviets his life would come to end on a scorched battlefield in Italy.

It had taken two months from the third assault to position troops along the forward areas. To maintain secrecy and give the impression that a seaborne landing north of Rome was imminent, the Allies had broadcast false radio signals they hoped the Nazis would intercept and act on. Movements between the camps and front lines had taken place in the dead of night. As armored units moved, they were replaced by dummy tanks, vehicles, and artillery units to give German reconnaissance flights the appearance that nothing out of the ordinary was being planned. By May 10th, thirteen Allied divisions had been positioned, ready for the signal to unleash hell. The Germans, fooled by the clever deception, had allowed the Allied forces to double their offensive capabilities.

Janek and the Polish Second Corps were assigned the mountain ridges above Cassino and the Liri Valley several miles west of the abbey. Janek had no idea they were being positioned to take Monastery Hill in a frontal attack where they'd be under constant and withering artillery and mortar fire. All they knew was that if this final assault failed, the Germans would most likely drive the Allies from Monte Cassino, secure the Gustav Line, and maintain their hold on Rome and Austria. Janek and his men, ready for the most difficult assault of the battle, had no intention of allowing that to happen.

Janek knew from reports that the Germans had spent months laying mines across the three-mile valley leading up to Cassino, so a single white line had been drawn along a path where the mines would have to be cleared. Still, soldiers in the dead of night would step outside the safety zone and be blown to bits, blood and limbs flying through the smoke. From above the valley, the Germans, using machine guns, mortars, and infantry fire, overwhelmed whoever was advancing. Shrapnel mixed with rocks flew nonstop through the air like deadly missiles. If the shrapnel didn't rip through flesh and bone, the rocks did.

Then, on May 11th, one hour before midnight, the signal was given. Black skies above Monte Cassino lit up in a blaze of fire as more than 1,000 guns rained death upon the abbey in a relentless onslaught that went unabated until the sun rose the following morning. Daylight was the enemy. Therefore much of the fighting was to take place in the dead of night, although that mattered little because the constant barrage of artillery fire turned night into day anyway. The Germans counted on that as they picked men off one by one from vantage points above the valley. Janek would turn to his right and his left and see faces glowing in the darkness from the shelling, and when he blinked, the faces would disappear, replaced by pieces of a body lying there on the ground.

As he moved forward, Janek stepped through bomb craters filled with rainwater, some red from blood, fingers and hands floating and bobbing like stew. Everywhere he looked, smoke lifted into the sky as if the earth were set on fire. Even the mud smelled of death whenever he dropped to his stomach and pressed his face into it to keep from getting shot—an acrid, rotten smell from corpses and body parts dragged through it before being dumped onto stretchers.

For two days, Polish attacks from surrounding valleys had heavy losses, with nearly 4,000 soldiers dead in one valley section alone. German artillery and mortar fire from above the clouds atop the abbey had nearly wiped out every Polish infantry division positioned along the mountains. When the fury stopped for a moment, Janek looked out at the sea of death and wept for the families who'd never see their brave soldiers again.

Minutes later, Janek heard a loud explosion and felt burning through his entire body as shrapnel ripped open his chest near his heart and sent him reeling to the ground. Soldiers immediately surrounded his body, tending to a gaping wound spewing blood across his torso. For two hours, Janek lay dying as his unit, their artillery destroyed by German mortars, waited for medics to arrive and carry their leading officer away. When they did, a lull in the action allowed them to transport Janek from the front line to a mobile hospital unit where once again his life was miraculously spared.

As one medic pumped morphine into Janek's vein, another sewed up his chest. Barely awake, he could hear bombers overhead and the distant screams of battle from where he lay. For three days, Janek slipped in and out of consciousness while war raged a mile away.

"What's happening?" Janek asked one of the medics, barely able to keep his eyes open.

"The Second Corps just launched another assault on Monte Cassino…along the northern hills."

"Dear God, that's where the strongest German fortifications are located," Janek mouthed, knowing that he'd not be with his men during what he feared would be their fiercest battles. "I heard some of the fighting has been hand-to-hand...soldiers so battered they could barely stand their ground."

But stand their ground they did. By the next day, Janek was told that, somehow, whoever survived had reached deep inside and found the strength to scale the mountain crags, climb the last few hundred yards to the summit, and take the abbey from the few wounded Germans remaining. Behind them, almost 300 officers and more than 3,500 men had given their lives for freedom.

By dawn on May18th, the last shell had fallen. Following a nonstop barrage that had reduced the abbey to shapeless debris and ash, not a tree or blade of grass was left alive. Smoke drifted from the ruins like ghostly mist. German and Allied uniforms clung to twisted and shredded bodies that lay scattered along the abbey's periphery. As far as the eye could see, carnage filled the once lush and fertile landscape. And Janek, lying in his mobile hospital bed a mile away, thanked God that it was only a six-inch piece of his chest he'd left behind at Monte Cassino.

General Wladyslaw Anders, stepping over limbs and corpses strewn in every direction, raised the Polish flag above the ruins of Monte Cassino as a lone Polish bugler played Saint Mary's Trumpet Call, a five-note Polish anthem bound to the history and traditions of Krakow. The stench of rotting bodies and smoldering rubble filled the air. Men too shaken and exhausted from battle to celebrate their victory looked grimly over the landscape and wept for the brave soldiers of the Second Corps who'd given their last drop of blood for Poland. Many raised their eyes to heaven and thanked God. Some fell to their knees and prayed. But most, knowing that history would remember what they'd done that day, simply stood and bowed their heads in silence.

Janek, his eyes closed, his hands clenched as if still looking out at the battlefield, knew that Monte Cassino was one of the most important battles of the war because it had kept German troops bogged down and unable to go on and fight. The allies, he'd later learned, lost 55,000 men in four months but had killed 35,000 German soldiers.

Shortly after the battle, a Polish war cemetery was built at Monte Cassino to hold more than a thousand Poles who'd died storming the Benedictine abbey, and as a reminder that it was at that place that Polish soldiers had helped change the course of World War II. A memorial bears the inscription:

For our freedom and yours
We soldiers of Poland gave
Our souls to God
Our life to the soil of Italy
Our hearts to Poland

Chapter 20

Sandusky, Ohio
September 16, 2004

In the few lucid moments she had these days, Wanda would slump in her chair, stare out at the garden, and accept the reality that she was dying. Sometimes she would beg God to just take her memory away and block out the world around her. But whenever she caught glimpses of Janek in her mind, she prayed the opposite: "Please, dear Jesus, give me a few more days with my beloved Janek before I go."

On this day, Wanda's mind had been drifting back to the war and the stories Janek had told her when they'd finally reunited. Sister Regina sat by Wanda's side, waiting for her to waken enough to talk.

"Are you okay, Wanda?" Sister Regina asked when she saw her stirring.

Wanda nodded weakly. "I was remembering what Janek told me about the end of the war."

"What did he tell you?"

Her eyes glistening, Wanda whispered, "He would always say that life goes by so quickly." A tear formed in her eye. "It's hard to believe that all of it happened in what seems like the blink of an eye. There he was, fighting at Monte Cassino and here I am now, alone and sitting in a chair waiting to die. Where did it all go?"

Wanda dabbed her eyes with a tissue as she thought about her life and how it was all finally coming to an end.

"Did Janek talk much about Monte Cassino?" Sister Regina asked.

"It was Monte Cassino that defined him as a soldier," Wanda said proudly. "The worst battle he'd been in during the war. At times the artillery never stopped, he told me. Not for a second. Sometimes he'd think about it, then reach up and feel his chest where the wound he suffered took him back to the battlefield where so many of his friends died around him."

Wanda clenched her teeth and took a deep breath, remembering the one thing Janek regretted was rotting away in the gulag instead of fighting the war against Hitler. Poland, after all, was at the heart of that regret—its invasion triggered World War II, it had more Nazi death camps than any other country in Europe, and it was the only Allied nation that fought from the moment German boots first hit its ground to the last day of the war. So, when he finally arrived on the shores of Italy in the winter of 1944, Janek felt a sense of pride swelling inside him. Italy, he'd bragged, his chest puffed out at least six inches, was where Poland showed the world what brave men did when all seemed lost.

Sister Regina reached out and clutched Wanda's bony hand. When she looked into her sad eyes, they revealed the torment that stemmed from her forced exile to a place that had changed her life forever. How could they do that to her, Sister Regina thought, take everything she loved and held dear, then tell her she'd never be welcomed back in her country again. But before she could offer her a little comfort, Wanda braced herself and finished describing what happened once Monte

Cassino fell into Allied hands.

With Monte Cassino behind them, the Polish Second Corps had reorganized and broken through the Gustav Line with 20,000 vehicles and more than 2,000 tanks. On May 23rd, they attacked Piedimonte San Germano, a province seventy miles southeast of Rome, where they met heavy Nazi resistance. Two days later, the Gustav Line collapsed and the way was cleared for the Allies to move north to Rome. Although the Germans had several lines of defense between Monte Cassino and Rome, the Allies battled their way to Rome and captured the city on June 4th. Two days later, Allied forces stormed the beaches of Normandy, with Polish forces joining in the ground campaign that lasted well into mid-July.

"Where was Janek when all this was happening?" Sister Regina asked.

"Still recovering from the wound that nearly killed him. They transported him to a hospital back in Taranto where he stayed for two months. Once they knew he was fully recovered, it was back to the front lines."

"With the Second Corps?"

"Yes. They saved his life...and he owed them his." And then Wanda's smile disappeared. "While recovering, he couldn't communicate with me and tell me he was fine, since all correspondence to Poland was cut off by the Germans. Maybe it was better I didn't know he'd been wounded so badly."

"What happened when he got back to his unit?"

"It was like a reunion. They'd just fought in the bloodiest battle of the war together, so they loved each other like brothers. Some of the men cried when they saw my Janek. I can't imagine any soldier under his command not loving him or risking their lives to save his."

"Did he join up with them in Rome?"

Wanda shook her head. "By the time he was transported out, it was the middle of July. The Allies had taken Rome a month earlier and were fighting along Italy's east coast on their way to Bologna. When Janek arrived, they'd just won the battle for Ancona on the Adriatic Sea."

Wanda's face suddenly twisted into a scowl, the exuberance she'd shown as she spoke of Polish victories vanishing as quickly as it had come.

"Not three days after they took Ancona," Wanda went on, "the Soviets announced they were no longer negotiating with the Polish government-in-exile, and were beginning long-range plans for control of Poland. Janek's heart sank. Victory after victory and thousands of men lost, and even America and Britain, allies they fought with and died alongside of, were unwilling to face Stalin and demand that Poland be set free."

"Wasn't that right before the Warsaw uprising?" Sister Regina asked, remembering what she'd read about the reaction General Anders had at the time when he said, 'We have our wives and children in Warsaw, but we would rather they perish than have to live under the Bolsheviks.'

"It was," Wanda said. "Two weeks after Ancona, the Polish underground army was ordered to launch the uprising. And as you know, it failed...and Warsaw was destroyed."

Wanda drifted back into herself, remembering what Janek had described about his time with the Second Corps. At first, they were hopeful. During the uprising, they'd taken Gabrielle, Mondolfo, Poggio, and Orciano from the Nazis. A week later, they crossed the Metauro River and reached what the Germans called the Gothic Line, the last major line of defense along the Apennine Mountains. By the end of August, the Second Corps had captured Pesaro and broken through the eastern flank of the line. For the next month, they stood their ground, and then they heard that the Germans had taken Warsaw. The Soviets had broken their promise and never helped. Troop morale sank as low as it had ever been, but they kept fighting because there was always hope that after the war this would all change. At the end of October, with that in their hearts, they captured Preddapio, the birthplace of Mussolini and a major symbolic victory for the Polish Army.

"Did Janek get word how you and Sophie were doing?" Sister Regina asked.

"All he knew was that the Germans were clearing Warsaw out."

"What about Lwow?"

With deep sadness in her voice, Wanda whispered, "One of Stalin's greatest resentments was Poland's claim to disputed Russian territory, which included our hometown of Lwow. I suspected that, even after the war, Lwow would never be the same. I was right, because Lwow is no longer part of Poland. It's now Lviv, in Ukraine."

As Wanda spoke of the anguish they all felt at Soviet betrayal, she remembered how terrifying those final few months in Warsaw had been. The tide was finally turning against Germany following the invasion of Normandy in June 1944. And for nearly four years, the Nazis had occupied Warsaw with little to no resistance. So it was a shock when a force of 50,000 soldiers had taken up arms and began their assault on strategic positions throughout the city. The initial short-lived skirmishes and victories were meant only to hold the city until the Soviets joined their ranks and helped finish the job. But rather than rescuing Warsaw from destruction, Stalin, who hated the Poles and wanted nothing better than to reduce their numbers so he would have free reign over the remains of their nation, had ordered the Red Army to halt their advance. The struggling resistance fighters, exhausted and disheartened, were left to orchestrate hit-and-miss attacks from sewers beneath Warsaw. It was only a matter of time before their bodies and spirits were crushed.

While the Polish Home Army fought as valiantly as they could despite tens of thousands of dead and wounded, the Germans were rounding up and butchering the civilian population. It was all part of Hitler's grand plan: commit genocide on the people of Poland and wipe Warsaw from the face of the earth. No one was spared. Even small children and infants were taken from their homes and shot in front of their parents. In the end, a quarter million Polish citizens had been executed as retribution for the uprising. Finally, sixty-three days after it began, the insurgents, seeing that not a soul outside Poland cared that Warsaw and its people were being extinguished, had surrendered.

"Luckily for us," Wanda continued, "we were spared the genocide because we stayed with family a few miles outside the city."

"Still, Janek must have had little comfort, not knowing your whereabouts or whether you were even alive," Sister Regina said.

"That's true." Wanda nodded. "Especially when he learned that Hitler had ordered the complete annihilation of Warsaw. It wasn't until Poland was out of German hands that I was able to smuggle letters across the border to the Second Corps in Italy saying that we were alive and well."

Wanda fell silent and remembered Janek telling her how his heart was filled with joy one minute then nearly broke the next as he thought about the upcoming Battle for Bologna and the possibility that after all he'd been through, she and Sophie could lose him to a single German bullet. And as she sank back in her chair, in her mind she could see and almost touch his face as she recalled the final days of the war.

Janek had arrived a week before the Second Corps' planned assault of Bologna, which lay sixty-five miles north of Florence on the outskirts of Tuscany. On the road through central Italy, all thoughts of war and death had vanished, such was the beauty of its countryside. As he passed through what at one time had been the breadbasket of Rome, it was as if conflicts between nations had not ever touched that part of Italy.

Bologna, once a part of the Etruscan world, had been a powerful and wealthy civilization of ancient Italy that fell to Rome and faded from history. When Rome itself fell, the region known as Emilia-Romagna saw a millennium of war and conquest until the Dark Ages gave way to the light of the Renaissance, which spread across the whole of Europe. Monasteries dotted the landscape. Christian trade and religion dominated the region for centuries. And a rebirth of art, literature, and science had transformed Italy into the greatest civilization the world at the time had ever seen.

Wanda would think of that as she pictured Janek and the Second Corps moving through the beauty of Emilia-Romagna, its rich earth eaten up by the treads of rumbling tanks heading toward German-held Bologna. It was March 1945. The Allies were reinforcing and preparing for the spring offensive in northern Italy. But whatever morale the Second Corps' victory had brought was lost when they got word that the Americans and British, at the Yalta Conference, had negotiated away Polish territory to the Soviet Union. In a way, Janek had said, it was like fighting for Stalin's Russia. The thought of winning the war and returning to a Poland still enslaved was incomprehensible. No matter. On April 9th, the Polish Second Corps, their hearts broken yet again, roared into battle as they fought, not for themselves but for their beloved homeland.

"It was 4 a.m. April 9th," Wanda said, suddenly more animated. "I remember that because it was the final battle of the war. Janek told me that for two weeks they pushed the Germans back from the rivers around Bologna and finally broke through to the city on April 21st. Polish flags went up on the town hall and the towers around the square. As Polish troops marched through the city, the entire population had come out to welcome their liberators, kissing them and giving them flowers and candy."

And then, as if none of that mattered, Wanda grew angry, clenching her teeth.

"What's wrong?" Sister Regina asked.

"It didn't matter," Wanda scoffed. "Because no matter how victorious they were, the homes they left behind in Poland were now Russian. The day after they took Bologna, the Second Corps was disbanded. It was as though all those brave men sacrificed their lives for their nation, did everything they were ordered to do, and then were told they were no longer needed. I guess it didn't matter, since Germany surrendered two weeks later."

Wanda's eyes turned to glass, and she began to weep. "So many Polish soldiers dead," she said, her voice trembling. "So much pain and suffering. And then, after successful campaigns that drove Hitler from Africa and Italy, the Poles, unlike the rest of the Allies, wouldn't taste freedom for another fifty years."

"What happened after Bologna?" Sister Regina asked.

Wanda, barely audible as she wiped tears from her eyes, said, "The Americans wanted Russian support against Japan more than they wanted to meddle in Poland's affairs. What Roosevelt and Churchill did was inexcusable...allowing Stalin to install a communist government in Warsaw and turn Poland over from one vicious dictator to another."

"After the war was over, why did no one give a second thought about Poland?"

"Because history is written by those in charge," Wanda sneered. "Churchill convinced everyone they could trust him...that he would never abandon Poland, where any mention of the Warsaw uprising was forbidden. And when it *did* come up, the Polish resistance fighters were criminals and fascists rather than heroic soldiers who died to rid their city of Nazi tyranny."

Wanda's voice trailed off as she recounted how the Second Corps' final days in Italy had come to a bitter and heart-wrenching end. As the Allies fought on without their Polish brethren, Poland was swept up and delivered like a sacrificial lamb into the Soviet sphere of domination. Remnants of the Home Army were arrested, put on trial, imprisoned, many of them deported to gulags where they'd spend the rest of their lives. Janek and the Second Corps had been given a choice: return to Poland and face imprisonment as fascist collaborators and imperialist agents or resettle in the United Kingdom, never to see their homeland again. Torn at the very thought of it, Janek would choose the latter, and after risking his life across Africa and Italy so the world could once again live in freedom, he would now have to risk Wanda's and Sophie's lives by smuggling them out of Poland.

"Where did Janek go after they disbanded the Second Corps?" Sister Regina asked.

"They couldn't go back to their homes like the Polish soldiers who fought alongside the Soviets. *They* were welcomed as heroes while Janek and his men were outcasts. Even schoolchildren were taught that the war was won by the Soviet Union while the Western Powers, including Poland, simply stood by. All their victories were erased from history in their own country. All records of what Russia did to Poland were stricken from public record. Every Polish soldier who died in battle never even existed. If you went to the Soviet Union right after the war, you'd think it was Russia that saved the world and that Poland should be grateful that it could become part of Stalin's great new empire."

Wanda's voice grew weak, her eyes searching for lost memories. As she rocked back and forth, she remembered the story of Janek's voyage from Naples, Italy as bittersweet. Some of his fellow soldiers stood by his side, watching the rugged coastline of Italy disappear on the horizon. But others stayed behind and chose to settle half a world away—in Australia, New Zealand, India, South Africa—where they hoped the horrors of war would gradually fade from their lives and become a distant memory. But Janek, as many did, felt a special bond with Britain, a country they'd fought with and then welcomed the Poles with open arms despite cultural, religious, and language barriers.

As the ship passed the Isle of Capri, it was the first time in years that Janek noticed the beauty of nature. "It's difficult to see anything," he said, "when bombs are exploding around you and all of God's creation is being obliterated." And so, as he gazed out at the azure sea and the white limestone peaks of Capri against a backdrop of the bluest sky he'd ever seen, it was as if the world was at its beginning. It was hard for Janek to hold back tears at the thought that this was what it should be like always: peaceful, beautiful, tranquil, with no Hitlers or Stalins or Mussolinis to destroy all that was good.

The turquoise waters off Capri soon gave way to the deep black of the Mediterranean Sea as Janek's ship continued past Algeria and the rocky shores of Spain. By the time they reached the Strait of Gibraltar three days later, a sense of peace had overcome the men because they knew that in a few hours they'd be steaming north across the Atlantic toward their destination in Scotland.

Janek was surprised that most people didn't know about Poland's deep roots and connection with Scotland. But war has a way of bonding nations more than anything else. After the fall of France in 1940, Scotland was completely vulnerable to a German invasion, and according to intelligence, it was how Hitler planned to launch a surprise attack from Norway. Seeing Polish boots on Scottish ground was a welcome sight, especially since the Poles had a reputation for being brave and fearless soldiers, fighting everywhere and with everyone in Europe during the war.

Two months after the first troops arrived, Polish destroyers moved to Scotland and fought in the Battle of the Atlantic. The *ORP Blyskawica* was the longest-serving ship of the Allied fleet. Much of the Polish Air Force was stationed in Britain, flying alongside the Royal Air Force, and according to eyewitnesses, some of the best fighter pilots were Poles. By February 1942, they'd created the First Armored Division, which trained in Scotland and then transferred to Normandy to participate in the D-Day invasion as part of the British command. They fought from England to the Middle East and into Africa and Italy. They died on ships, in the air, and on the ground, all with the Brits. Even after the war, Polish warships delivered Red Cross supplies and participated in mercy missions. They did it all. So it was not unusual to see Poles welcomed in England as much as the British soldiers were.

Despite the fact that German and Soviet invasions of Poland set all of Europe on fire, and that Poland had been decimated and suffered more than any other allied nation, the Polish Armed Forces were the fourth largest after the Soviet Union, United States, and Britain. It was no wonder that Poland felt betrayed. They helped win the war, liberated millions, were the first to die on the front lines, and were rewarded for their loyalty and service by having their country taken and their soldiers sent into exile. Nothing in modern history compared to what Poles had seen as treachery by allies who didn't even invite

Polish troops to march in their victory parades. That shameless act alone, Janek had always thought, was enough for Poles to weep at how the world stood by while the light of freedom had once again been extinguished across their own nation.

Once Janek's ship sailed into the Royal Naval Base at Faslane, the soldiers had already been assigned where they'd go. Janek spent several weeks in the Scottish Highlands, which reminded him so much of Poland that it would break his heart every time he'd think of it. "It was so beautiful," he said, remembering the lush green mountains and valleys, dotted with white specks of sheep grazing on clover and grass. And then there were the lochs, so deep and black they looked as if they could swallow ships. When he stared at them long enough, he reminisced, imagining how one could believe there were monsters beneath the surface. And as the sun began to set, shadows stretched their fingers along the shore, melting into the still water and spreading dark gloom across the landscape.

"Did Janek find comfort in Scotland?" Sister Regina asked. "It must have been so different from what he knew."

"In a way, it was." Wanda nodded. "He'd walk with his friends for miles sometimes, bundled against the cold and the rain, reminiscing about his life and wondering what was happening back home. And then he and his friends would stop and just stare, not saying a word because they all knew what the other was thinking...that Poland was no longer Poland, and that life would never be the same again. As much as they all knew they'd never see Poland again, none of them thought of themselves as Brits. They were Poles in their hearts, and they'd be Poles till the day they died."

"Was he bitter…about what happened, despite all his sacrifices?"

Wanda shook her head and said, "No. But though no longer bitter about how Poles were treated after the war, he still held in his heart the sorrow a man feels when losing something he loves. At least that's what I sensed whenever he'd speak of Poland and a palpable sadness would suddenly fill his voice. When the war finally ended, everyone was so happy they'd almost forgotten the pain of what they did to us. But then, as everyone else began making plans to return to their homelands and go on with their lives, we realized that we were the only ones who couldn't."

Wanda paused to take a long breath, and for a moment seemed to relive the pain before exhaling and coming back to the present. "It made no sense. At first it filled us with rage, but by the time Janek left Italy and arrived in Scotland, we accepted our fate. It's what we Poles have done for centuries. And though it didn't make it any easier, it's what we had to do again…for us…for our families."

Sister Regina's evening with Wanda was ending as it began: with Wanda whispering over and over again how much Janek had loved her, to do what he did to bring her and Sophie to England. To leave his precious wife and daughter in Soviet hands, he'd said, would have killed him. And to remain in Poland, a nation they loved with every fiber of their being, was impossible. Not only had the Allies given the Soviet Union the right to administer elections in Poland, it had accepted Stalin's ultimatum that eastern Poland be his for the taking. So, when he finally arrived in England, Janek had immediately set into motion an elaborate scheme to smuggle Wanda and Sophie through Russian-held territory and into Allied-controlled Germany. That, he knew, would be no small feat. For Wanda and Sophie, it would prove to be their most dangerous journey since being set free in Kazakhstan.

Chapter 21

Sister Regina sensed in Wanda's voice that what happened next in Poland was what changed their lives forever. Sophie had already disclosed that her mother was never the same, that she was almost like a child when she and Janek finally reunited. But it wasn't until Wanda continued her story that Sister Regina understood why.

"So what happened when Janek tried to get you out of Poland?"

"He managed to save enough money by winter to pay a foreign agent—someone who helped family members behind Polish borders—to smuggle us into Germany and on to freedom in England. The risk was great. Fleeing Polish citizens were arrested or worse. But the risk was better than the alternative...a life of misery and despair. Besides, as family members of a Polish officer who'd served with the British Allies, we'd be deported once again. For Janek it was unthinkable. The gulags or labor camps would have killed us. And so we waited, spending our final moments with family we knew would never see us again."

Sister Regina sat spellbound, staring into Wanda's eyes as she listened to a story that seemed too improbable

264

to be true...

In the early morning hours, somewhere on the outskirts of Warsaw, a knock on the door had sent everyone's heart racing. All of Poland was on edge. Stalin, no longer satisfied with Russian obedience alone, had demanded Polish loyalty as well. Wanda feared the worst as she approached the door and cracked it open, a strange face peering in and announcing that a man named Janek had sent him all the way from England. Wanda nearly collapsed with relief as she pulled the man in and looked out to make certain no one else had seen him. Finally, the moment she'd been waiting for had come, but at what cost?

While her sister stood guard at the window, Wanda sat across the table from the stranger and examined the fake documents and passports she hoped would look authentic enough to fool Soviet authorities. In her mind, they did. But were they good enough to risk their lives? At that point, they had little choice. Because the Soviets had been cracking down on smugglers, the window for escape was closing fast. And Wanda, desperate to see her husband for the first time in seven years, would forever be trapped behind the Iron Curtain, a thousand miles from the man who risked everything to save her. In her mind, it might as well have been a million. She nodded and said, "Yes, we go."

What Wanda did not anticipate was that five other people were to join them: three more adults and two children, making escape that much riskier. The smuggler, knowing his trade well, waited until the dead of night before giving the signal that it was time. With tears in her eyes, Wanda embraced family members staying behind. Sophie couldn't tear herself away from her little cousin, who promised to think of her every day and write as often as she could. The smuggler's patience wearing thin, he yelled, "Move! We have to go now!" Turning away and sobbing, Wanda grabbed Sophie and rushed through the door as it closed behind her, realizing that her life in Poland would soon be over.

Along abandoned streets they walked, each with a single bag across their backs, until they reached another home with no lights or any activity. The smuggler knocked twice, then three more times. A door opened and five people emerged, so frightened they shook visibly. The seven then moved stealthily behind the smuggler through a dark neighborhood, their lips closed tightly to keep from uttering a sound. A light snow began to fall. Cold winds whipped around dark buildings and pierced their exposed skin. Sophie, shivering from cold, pressed up against Wanda, who wrapped her arm around her daughter and grimaced as pain shot through her legs, a constant reminder of the ravages that freezing Siberian winters had wrought on her body.

By morning, hungry and exhausted, they watched the sun rise as they reached a small town and stopped to catch their breath. The plan, so far, was working as they'd hoped, the food they brought enough to sustain them another week until they reached Germany. But as they sat on some logs and began to eat, Wanda sensed something was not right—she heard a sickening sound in the distance that had become all too familiar. Panicked, she threw down her piece of bread and shouted for everyone to move on. And then, as if their world had suddenly come to an end, a group of soldiers, with snarling German Shepherds straining on their leashes, descended upon them and ordered the group to follow them into town. For Wanda, who understood that it was Russian the soldiers were speaking, it was the end of everything.

No sooner had the group been marched to the outskirts of town than the unimaginable happened. Parents, separated from screaming children, watched as their little ones were torn from their arms and told they'd be transported to an orphanage across the Czechoslovakian border. All Wanda could do was look on in horror as Sophie, her arms raised helplessly toward her mother, disappeared. The adults, crammed into an army truck, were driven to a local prison once used as a labor camp.

Once in the prison grounds, and fearing that Sophie would be lost forever, Wanda's only hope was to make her way out where guards had left a door open and unattended. "If I die," Wanda said to the others, "then I die, but I'm getting my child back." So without a word and without looking back, much as Janek had done to escape the Katyn massacre, Wanda and the others, more terrified than they'd ever been in their lives, walked quietly across the grounds, through the open door, and on to freedom.

From that moment on, the group traveled only at night, retracing their march, and returning to where they'd begun. Wanda, barely able to walk and fearing the Soviets would most likely be looking for them, split from the others and made her way to Lodz, knowing that once there, her older brother would shelter her while she tried desperately to find a way to get Sophie back.

Meanwhile, Janek had gotten word of the foiled plan and now hatched his own. Another smuggler was paid. But this time, the fake documents and passports were for two, not seven, and the risk of detection and arrest far less. The plan, however, included something new and equally as dangerous—freeing Sophie from the orphanage in eastern Czechoslovakia, which had been annexed by the Soviet Union shortly after its liberation from Nazi Germany.

Weeks went by until Wanda found her way back to Lodz and finally heard from Janek about their latest plan of escape. Everyone in Poland knew that if fugitives were found, they and whoever helped them would be arrested and likely sent to Siberia for God only knew how long. The sooner Wanda could leave, though it would break her heart to do so, the safer her brother would be. As much as she tried to keep thoughts of failure out of her head, she had doubts that Janek's plan, daring as it was, could work. But what choice would she have? To even consider leaving Poland and going to England without Sophie was as unlikely as her not breathing. She would rather have died.

And so they waited. A familiar two knocks followed by three more knocks on the door brought both a sense of relief that it was really happening and dread that once again Wanda would be risking her life to bring Sophie home. A different smuggler appeared through the crack in the door this time. His grim face sent a chill through Wanda's bones as she remembered her last arrest and the sight of children screaming for their parents.

There was no waiting this time. And as before, Wanda embraced her family with a tearful goodbye, knowing that, whatever happened, she would not be returning, either from her new life in a new land or from the gulag she and Sophie would most likely be buried in. Stepping onto a layer of fresh snow, Wanda shuddered as the door behind her closed. Her only thought now was of Sophie and whether their plan to get her out of the orphanage would be good enough.

Days passed before Wanda and the smuggler reached the Czech border 180 miles away and were met by armed guards who stopped them and asked for documents, their voices stern, their stares suspicious. Russian cigarettes dangled from their lips. The smuggler reached into his pocket and hoped the counterfeiter had done his job well.

"My wife and I need to get our daughter out of the orphanage in Ostrava," the smuggler said, then handed both sets of papers to one of the guards. "She was mistakenly taken there, but here are *her* papers." He then handed Sophie's documents over as well.

The guard studied the papers carefully, then looked up at them, staring intently into their eyes, looking for signs of deception, and waved them through. Wanda, finally able to breathe, staggered arm in arm with her smuggler husband, who smiled at the guard as though he'd done this a hundred times before.

Sister Regina poured Wanda a cup of tea and sat beside her, hoping Wanda's memory would not drift away before finishing her story. "How did you manage to get Sophie out?" she asked.

"After crossing the border, it took another day to reach Ostrava," Wanda began. "I was nearly delirious when I set my eyes on the orphanage, a massive stone-gray building that looked more like a prison. It probably was. What I did then terrified me more than anything I'd been through, because if I failed, I knew I'd never see Janek or Sophie again." Wanda took a sip of tea and relived the rest of the story...

Visibly trembling, her heart pounding, Wanda walked into the orphanage with the smuggler, announcing to a menacing guard that she was there to claim her daughter, who was mistakenly taken from her family.

"And who are you?" the guard demanded, skeptical of this strange couple, since children in those days were being claimed—some for prostitution or farm labor—by people not their parents. The guard and several administrators huddled together and studied the documents, especially Sophie's, to make sure they were genuine. Wanda held her breath as she watched the group whispering, looking over at her and the smuggler and then down at the fake papers. Fear swept over her. Each time the brutish guard looked her way, her heart nearly stopped. Desperate to keep from falling to her knees and vomiting, Wanda tried as best she could to stand confidently next to the smugger and wait.

And then, just when it seemed as though their fake documents would be exposed, the guard handed them back and ordered Sophie be brought down to the receiving area. Luckily, because the orphanage was overcrowded, the administrators were more than happy to make another bed available for someone else, though it didn't hurt that the smuggler slipped one of the attendants an envelope with enough money to make him think twice about keeping a girl worth half that.

The minute she saw her mother, Sophie ran into Wanda's arms and wouldn't let go. Wanda, crying with joy, clung tightly to Sophie until the orphanage was out of sight and the three were well on their way back to Poland. The next step, Wanda feared, was to try once again to cross the border into Germany.

Desperate to leave her beloved Poland, Wanda returned to her brother's house in Lodz. He was shocked to see her again, this time with Sophie by her side. As the three fell into each other's arms, weeping at the thought of what they'd all just gone through, Wanda recoiled at seeing that her brother had no teeth and a broken nose—because soldiers had come in the middle of the night for a routine security check and used the butt of a rifle to pummel his face.

"What will you do?" Wanda's brother asked, barely able to move his jaw.

"We'll travel by foot through the countryside until we reach Germany. It's the only way out of Poland."

"Be careful. You know what the Russians will do if they catch you."

Wanda nodded, well aware of how barbaric the Soviets could be, especially to innocent civilians trying to escape. By the next morning, and with bitter sadness, they were gone, with 250 miles to go before they reached the border.

It took days. For Wanda, it seemed like an eternity. After their last arrest, they made sure to avoid larger towns and cities, but fortunately only three of them would be escaping this time, looking, they hoped, like an ordinary family traveling through the country on their way to visit other family members in Gorzow, just east of the German border.

As night fell, they snuck across the border on foot and, once on German soil, knelt and thanked God it was finally over. Poland and the Soviet Union were now behind them. The next problem, however, was finding their way to Berlin. To do that, they'd have to cross sixty miles of Soviet-controlled eastern Germany. But at least they were out of Poland.

As part of the surrender agreement, the United States, Great Britain, and France controlled the western part of Germany and East Berlin. Once they reached Berlin, they could seek asylum—being family members of the Polish Second Corps—and then arrange passage to England through the west, which was controlled entirely by the British.

Meanwhile, life in England for Janek was far different than he'd expected. Fighting and nearly dying alongside the British, he assumed, should have given Polish soldiers special rights. In fact, he'd been promised—by people who had no authority to promise anything to anyone—a job and riches in this new land of opportunity. Instead he found himself competing with returning British soldiers who expected favoritism and demanded that foreigners only be given whatever economic crumbs were left. Engineers were now janitors, doctors served meals in corner cafes, and intellectuals spent their days debating science and philosophy between shifts in sweltering textile factories. But at least it was not the Soviet Union—or Poland, which may as well have been the Soviet Union once Stalin reached in and crushed the soul of a once-proud nation.

For Wanda and Sophie, sneaking across the Polish border was one thing, but reaching East Berlin was another. That would take another two days. The Soviets had been stopping anyone who tried to get through. Wanda's smuggler had arranged with a worker in Germany to take them only so far. So, hiding in a work truck, they drove at night until they got closer to Berlin. A few miles away, they were ordered out to walk the rest of the way, through fields and forests, until they peered over the bushes and saw in the distance a checkpoint into the city. The moment they thought it was safe, they made a dash for it and reached four American guards who let them through.

At that moment, it seemed to Wanda as if she were stepping from darkness into light, as though she could once again breathe the clean and vibrant air of freedom. Still, she instinctively looked back each time she heard footsteps or someone talking behind her. A glance here, a whisper there sent shivers through Wanda's body. Fear and suspicion had become a part of her life ever since the secret police tossed her and Sophie from their home, and it had not yet left her, at least not until they were taken safely to an American command post several blocks away. The smuggler, satisfied he'd done his job, wished her well and went on his way. Wanda, throwing her arms around his neck, kissed him goodbye and, with tears in her eyes, thanked him for giving them back their lives. The rest was now up to her.

The Jeep carrying Wanda and Sophie from the American checkpoint sped past craters and along cobbled streets lined with shops and storefronts long closed or destroyed in the bombings that had killed nearly 50,000 citizens in the city alone. Berlin, once the capital of Nazi Germany and seat of Hitler's power, had been the focus of intense bombing following the fall of France in 1940. Prior to that, both Britain and France had agreed to limit air raids to military targets, provided the enemy did as well. However, with Germany's air attack on Rotterdam, all bets were off, and Britain had conceded that its only option for bringing the war to Germany and opening a second European front was to abandon its humane policy and unleash hell on Hitler's Third Reich. So, between 1940 and 1945, the British, American, and French Air Force had dropped over 80,000 tons of explosives on the people of Berlin.

As bombing continued and grew more intense, nearly forty percent of the population had abandoned their city. Hitler, naively believing he could indiscriminately bomb whoever he wished without fear of reprisal, learned how delusional that belief was. The Allied campaign of aerial bombing shocked him to his core once Berlin was in its crosshairs. But precision bombing, a new technology at the time, was erratic at best and possible only in daylight, which led to unacceptably high Allied casualties. Thus, night bombings brought fewer pilot losses, but many more innocents killed and wounded. Neither worked. Hitler remained defiant. So, in November 1943, the Allies launched the Battle of Berlin, a campaign designed to bring Germany to its knees.

It worked. As Wanda looked out at the city rushing past her, it appeared gloomy and bleak, like some tragic 1940s black-and-white movie. Buildings, all uniformly gray as though all other colors in the world had disappeared, stood empty, riddled with gaping holes and brick walls torn open by bombs and tank shells. Debris lay scattered everywhere, ruins piled on top of ruins. People stared past them, their eyes dull and sunken yet expressing a glimmer of hope that better days were ahead. How could they not be, Wanda thought. Hitler was gone, Germany had sought to rule the world and found itself defeated and broken, a lifeless shell of what it had been, and the Allies were there to pick up the pieces. Shaken by the amount of destruction she was witnessing, Wanda looked at the streets of Berlin through the eyes of a Pole. "This is for Warsaw," she whispered. "For Poland."

As the Jeep swerved to avoid a large section of rubble, it turned the corner and pulled up next to an official-looking building draped in a British flag unfurled in all its glory. Wanda clutched her chest and wept. Sophie gasped at the sight of British soldiers standing guard at the wooden barracks and large metal doors. Nothing they'd experienced in the last few years compared to the flag of the United Kingdom flapping in the breeze where once a Nazi emblem had looked out over Berlin. Wanda closed her eyes and prayed that what she was feeling at that moment was not another dream. She drew a deep breath and stopped, thanking God that the rotten stench of communism was gone from her life. When she opened her eyes, the flag was still waving, the British soldiers still standing at attention before her, the air around her seeming to wrap her in its invisible arms and embrace her. It was not a dream, she realized—it was all real. "*This*, my love," she said, as she pulled Sophie close to her and kissed her repeatedly, "is why your father sacrificed so much and why we risked our lives."

Inside the consulate, Wanda was not only a free woman, she was the wife of a Polish officer who fought with the Second Corps under British command. And that had given her special status to emigrate to Great Britain. She felt reborn, as if the years she'd spent in hopeless despair, though seared forever into her memory, no longer mattered. And then she thought of her beloved Poland and the family she'd left behind, her beautiful city of Lwow, now in Soviet hands and part of Ukraine, and her new life in England, which she had longed for ever since her escape from Poland.

As the flood of emotions swirled inside her, fear bubbled to the surface and made Wanda question whether to sign the document that would send them across the English Channel to a new homeland. But the second she looked at Sophie and thought of Janek waiting for them, she picked up the pen and signed her name. There was no turning back. Poland had been her homeland, but England, as strange and unfamiliar as though a million miles from everything she had ever known, would now be her home.

Wanda and Sophie spent the next few days resting in the barracks and waiting for word on transportation out of Germany. There were many other families— Poles, Jews, Hungarians—also seeking asylum and waiting as well. Some were sent to Australia, Canada, France, and other places that agreed to take them. The families bound for England were housed in a common holding facility and given word that trains would take them from Berlin to Belgium where they would board ships, cross the English Channel, and sail on to Liverpool.

Seeing the English Channel for the first time was euphoric, like a dream come true. After what they'd been through, those last few miles at sea before they reached England were torture. If Wanda could have jumped from the ship and swum to get there faster, she would have. Inside the cabin of the ship, Wanda was tormented by the feeling that once Janek saw how she looked, things between them would not be as they were seven years earlier. The vision looking back at her in the mirror didn't reflect the woman he'd left behind in Lwow. She'd become gaunt, almost stoop-shouldered from slave labor, her legs damaged by frigid Siberian winters, her teeth crooked from starvation and malnourishment. What had once been a lovely face and svelte body had aged and weathered more than ten years. Will he still love me, she wondered, the way I am now?

Meanwhile, Janek, who caught sight of the ship in the distance, wept uncontrollably. He'd not seen Wanda and Sophie for seven years and was also apprehensive about their reunion. Sophie, six years old when he went off to war, was now thirteen and nearly a woman. Wanda had been through hell, and he knew she'd be scarred from her days in Soviet labor camps. None of that mattered, though, as the ship drew closer and he realized that in a few hours they would all be together again.

As Wanda and Sophie gathered their belongings, Janek paced back and forth on the dock, watching the ship ease slowly against the pier, straining to see into the dense crowd of strangers and passengers waving enthusiastically to waiting relatives below. And then, as if the sky above the ship opened, he caught a glimpse of Wanda walking between the crowds and positioning herself against the railing. For a moment, Janek stood in disbelief that it was really her. He yelled her name and lifted his arm, waving frantically so she could see he was there. When she did, Wanda screamed his name as tears poured from her eyes. Sophie clung to her mother's arm and waved to her father, a man she barely remembered but a man she knew had spent every waking hour for the past year trying to bring her and her mother home. *That* she would remember for the rest of her life.

Once the ship docked, it seemed like hours before the first ecstatic passengers were allowed off. One by one they disembarked until a small woman, her daughter latched onto her arm, stepped onto the gangplank and shuffled down toward a man who looked as different to her as she did to him. At first it was a shock. Wanda was terrified, self-conscious of her appearance. The labor camps had not been kind to her body, and she wanted so much for Janek to have her the way she was seven years ago. But the brutality of war and gulags had taken a heavy toll on Janek as well. Neither was the same, physically or emotionally. But the minute they set eyes on one another, they were taken instantly back to Lwow. Wanda tried to run, but her legs screamed no. So Janek ran to her and Sophie, and with an embrace that seemed to last forever, the three held each other and wept uncontrollably.

"It must have been an emotional roller coaster," Sister Regina whispered, her eyes welling with tears. "After seven years, suddenly Janek sees you and a teenage daughter who was just a child when he left. I can't even imagine what it was like."

"Especially since we all survived when so many others we knew died," Wanda said.

Sister Regina thought about that for a moment and realized how unlikely that was, how the three of them survived years of terror and brutal conditions that had extinguished millions of other lives. Why were *they* spared, she wondered. What was it about *them* that fought through the horrors of those seven years only to be reunited once again? There *was* no explanation, she concluded. It was meant to be, and she left it at that. Some things, she always believed, just couldn't be explained.

Wanda looked out her window and seemed to drift away. A hint of a smile crossed her face. "When I kissed

Janek that day, I knew at once that nothing else mattered," she said. "I no longer worried about what I looked like, and it really *was* like being back in Lwow. We walked arm in arm away from the ship and into the receiving and immigration station where the three of us were welcomed by the British authorities to our new home."

Sister Regina stroked Wanda's head and smiled. There was something remarkably special about the love that Wanda and Janek had for one another, she thought, believing that some love transcends the horrors of war, making one look at life in a new and different way. But more often, the battles waged did not end on bloody battlefields or in the gulags, and the withering experience of constant torture and cruelty had a way of transforming even the most hopeless romantic. That, she was certain from how Wanda had described her reunion with Janek, was not the case. Theirs was a love that embraced everything new and different, scarred and broken, fragile and disfigured. To Janek, Wanda was as beautiful as the day he'd left. It didn't matter how much she'd changed, how *they* had changed. In his eyes, she was perfect in every way.

When Sister Regina reflected on that, it took her breath away. Love stories were a dime a dozen, she thought, and people tell each other all the time how much in love they are and how they would do anything for the other.

But she also knew that as memories fade and years soften the glow of physical attraction, only the deepest of loves last. At least that's what she always believed. And that's how she imagined it was with Wanda and Janek.

More than just love, it was a deep and everlasting bond, forged by the ravages of war and separation, unbreakable even to the end.

Chapter 22

Sandusky, Ohio
September 18, 2004

Wanda had opened her eyes more than an hour ago, lying motionless in bed and staring at the gathering clouds outside her window. Her mind, thankfully, had allowed her to delight in the rising sun and the beauty of the dawn sky. For much of the morning, she pictured Janek's rugged face, heard his soft voice whispering in her ear, and prayed to God that whatever memories she had of him would not disappear that day. "You were so brave, my love," she mumbled to herself, then began to remember what happened once the horrors of Stalin's gulags were behind him.

Sadly, the soldiers of the Polish Second Corps, despite risking everything for their country, found themselves on the wrong side of the Iron Curtain. Rescued by what they believed was divine intervention from the hell of Siberia's worst gulags, fighting their way to victories in North Africa and Italy, their ranks swelling to over 100,000 by the end of the war, they were suddenly without a home. Kresy, the eastern region that included Lwow and other towns from which the soldiers had come, vanished from Polish maps as if it had never existed. So distraught were some of the soldiers at losing their families, their homes, and now their country, that some had committed suicide. Wanda remembered hearing the sadness in Janek's voice at describing how abandoning Poland was akin to ripping out a piece of his body, and how he'd spend the rest of his life imagining what it would be like to have it back but knowing he never could.

Most Poles, however, accepted the fact that their beloved nation, as though history had not taught the world anything, had once again been torn apart and devoured. What hurt most was that it had been Poland's allies who watched their brethren fight and die and still allowed it to happen. And so, with heavy hearts, the soldiers of the Second Corps had left the beauty of Italy and, like the pioneers who'd settled America, traveled west to England where at least there was hope for a better future.

But England, despite its vow to welcome new immigrants, was not all it promised to be. Once Janek and the Second Corps arrived in Scotland, soldiers were separated by a lottery system and sent where needed, typically coal mines, textile factories, and farms. The more highly educated Poles found it difficult to use their skills and ended up buried in lower-paying work. The more fortunate went on to London where jobs were more plentiful. Janek was transferred to Liverpool, where he was processed, placed in government housing, and offered a menial job as a maintenance worker for the railroad, since his records showed he'd worked for the railroad back in Poland.

Barely adjusting to his new life, Janek turned moody and depressed, especially when he remembered the friends he'd lost and would never see again. And every day, as he reflected on the wasted years spent fighting and surviving, he'd think how true the old saying was that a soldier dies twice: once on the battlefield and then again when he's forgotten and his name never spoken again.

Soldier or not, Janek wanted desperately to be remembered as he pictured himself lying in a bed at Monte Cassino, expecting to die. Was that what he feared most, he wondered. That he and all those Polish soldiers would be forgotten, their graves honored, then quickly abandoned, their names never spoken again?

"Good morning, Wanda," Sister Regina sang out as she bounced into her room with a tray of tea and biscuits. "I have a special treat for you."

Wanda turned from the window and smiled. "You're an angel," she said. "Is that what I think it is?"

"Your favorite." Sister Regina placed the tray on the table next to Wanda and helped her out of bed and into her chair. "How are you feeling?"

Wanda turned back to the window. "I was remembering some of the things Janek told me when he first arrived in England."

"You want to talk?" Sister Regina asked, trying to encourage a conversation.

"Janek told me something interesting one day…that after the war ended, we had no idea who was coming to America and living among us. When I asked him what he meant, he described something called Operation Paperclip."

"What's that?"

Wanda described what Janek had told her was a top-secret order signed by President Truman in 1946 allowing as many as 1,600 German scientists, many of them Nazis, to emigrate to the United States and help develop America's rocket program. Because Janek had kept up with news from the Soviet Union, and because he was an engineer, he knew all about America's race to stay ahead of Russia's missile program. Eventually, rumors of Operation Paperclip leaked out because Albert Einstein and Eleanor Roosevelt went public and opposed it, infuriated that these monsters, people who tortured and murdered innocent women and children, were allowed to settle like normal immigrants in the United States.

Sister Regina shook her head and asked, "Is that what it was all about? Keeping up with Russia no matter who helped us do it, even Nazis?"

Wanda nodded. "Once the war was over, and Stalin showed himself for who he truly was, everyone agreed that the new global threat was communism and the Soviet Union. That's when Truman signed off on the operation. Just like he did with the atom bomb, he felt he had no choice. It was a matter of national security and survival. At least that's what everyone behind the operation thought."

Wanda went on to tell Sister Regina that the plan had previously been rejected by President Roosevelt but at the time was the only viable way to keep Josef Stalin from spreading his monstrous revolution across the globe. Knowing that thousands of Nazi scientists and doctors had scattered like vermin across Europe, the heads of U.S. intelligence proposed bringing all that brain power to America rather than see it go to other countries such as the Soviet Union. A memo initially released by the War Department never mentioned that some of the scientists were the world's most wanted Nazis who'd be given immunity from war crimes and employed in government and civilian facilities.

The project's code name, initially known as Project Overcast, was changed to Project Paperclip because files of those selected to be brought into the United States had paperclips attached to them as a clandestine signal to those familiar with the selection process. Many of the paperclips were attached to war criminals, their backgrounds expunged so they could be exploited in the West's struggle against communism. Researchers who used prisoners as lab rats, scientists working on biological warfare agents, and doctors who'd performed human medical experiments were actively sought and given refuge. Two of the prime recruits, because of their work on human physiology, were Sigmund Rascher and Herman Becker-Freysendg, whose experiments at Dachau were among the most gruesome.

Entry into the United States was facilitated by the CIA Act of 1949, which allowed U.S. entry "without regard to admissibility under any other laws" if the entry advanced national security. Many of the criminals were first sent to Canada or Mexico, after which they reentered the United States and were placed at research facilities and major universities. If security was ever breached, or if any of the war criminals were in danger of being discovered or arrested, he'd be smuggled to a South American country such as Brazil or Argentina.

By 1973, Project Paperclip had ended. In all, almost two thousand scientists and doctors, some living out their lives in comfort and security, continued their work in the United States. The ultimate goal was to keep these men out of Soviet hands. To that end, the project proved a success. But the price Americans paid to fight the new communist threat was to have the worst Nazi scientists living among them and not even know it.

"I guess I'm not surprised that sort of thing happened after the war," Sister Regina said. "But what about your life in England with Janek?"

"Janek and I spent that first year in England trying to adjust to our new life together. I suffered with nightmares, screamed in my sleep, sometimes woke up crying, thinking I was back in the labor camps. But the worst nightmares were of my escape from Poland, and when Sophie was taken from me. It changed me…and I was never the same…never looked at people in the same way."

"Losing a child must be the most traumatic event that could happen to a parent," Sister Regina said, clasping Wanda's hand and rubbing it between hers. "You didn't know if you'd ever see your daughter again. I could see why you'd have nightmares."

Though Sister Regina had never experienced having children of her own, she understood what it must have been like; what a mother must experience watching the person she loves most in the world ripped from her arms and taken away. And as she thought that, she remembered watching the movie *Sophie's Choice* ten years earlier, and how she sat there stunned and traumatized by scenes of Auschwitz and the main character's choice of which of her two children would live and which would die in a gas chamber.

From what little Soviet history Sister Regina had read about, she knew that Wanda must have saved her daughter's life ten times over, and she was certain *that* was part of the reason Wanda had been forever changed after the war. She'd learned that Polish women in labor camps, especially those with children, did unnatural, sometimes monstrous things to save them. More than stealing. More than going without food so their children wouldn't starve. Things like prostitution, submitting to gang rapes, taking on camp husbands for food and protection, even murder. What Wanda had done or not done was something Sister Regina did not want to think about. But whatever it was, she figured Wanda had done it so her daughter would survive the brutality of Soviet labor camps, and so in Sister Regina's mind it was right, no matter what it was.

"What's wrong?" Sister Regina asked, seeing that Wanda was beginning to stare into her glass.

"Living in England…it wasn't exactly the best five years."

"How so?"

"Life was hard. There was no way we could go back to Poland after Stalin's decree that Polish soldiers that fought under British command were enemies of the people and not welcome back home. So we made a life for ourselves in Liverpool and got by as best we could."

"What kind of life was it for Polish exiles?"

"Soldiers of the Second Corps, though anxious about an uncertain future, settled into their new assignments and their new lives. It wasn't easy, but then we thought about those poor souls back in the countries Russia defeated and was controlling. We thought fascists were bad, but the communists were as bad or worse. Yes, sometimes they were far worse."

Sister Regina could see the pain on Wanda's face. From what she'd read of Soviet history since caring for Wanda, she knew that the Third Reich's defeat gave Stalin an opening to impose his will on a beaten and broken Italy. And General Wladyslaw Anders, who denounced the Soviet leader as a vicious thug, was eventually accused and found guilty of planning an assault on Soviet-controlled Poland. Tensions rose and steamed to a boil until the Spring of 1946 when Janek and the Second Corps had finally learned their fate: a mass repatriation from the splendors of Tuscany to the shores of Britain where Stalin and his secret police could never set their claws into them again. So, in a matter of months, over 100,000 Poles set sail on a one-way voyage that began September 1st and continued until year's end.

"All those years apart," Sister Regina said, her voice cracking. "It's almost like a dream."

"Yes, all those wasted years," Wanda uttered. "But seven years after he held me and Sophie in his arms and kissed us goodbye, we gathered what little we had, reflected on what happened to us and what could have been, and never looked back."

Wanda stopped and stared out the window, remembering those years as if they'd come and gone in the blink of an eye. There was Janek, one minute crying and holding her in his arms, the next vanishing into the blackness of war for seven years. She suddenly pictured his handsome face and heard his voice, thinking back to the emptiness and pain she felt, despite having Sophie by her side. England had changed all that. Though Poland would be in her heart forever, she'd found a new home in a place where she could look out at the stars and feel freedom in the air.

Thanks to Poland's contribution to World War II, not a single Allied nation blinked at the request to accept Polish exiles, and none better than Great Britain. It was Poland, after all, that had broken the early version of the Enigma machine, which led to British cryptographic breakthroughs that helped win the war. Poles fought alongside British Forces from North Africa to Italy and comprised the greatest number of non-British troops in the Royal Air Force during the Battle of Britain. And since 1940, following the Nazi-Soviet Pact, the Polish government-in-exile, which launched the ill-fated Warsaw Uprising and orchestrated the creation of Anders' Army and the Second Corps, had made London its official home base. By the time Janek made his decision to set sail for a new homeland, there was no question in his mind that England would be it.

Sister Regina reached over and took hold of Wanda's hand, caressing it as she would a child's. She knew that it wasn't possible to understand, but she could see Wanda's pain as she looked into her sad eyes and watched her lie back in her bed. She'd heard that patients close to death have an innate ability to reach deep inside of themselves and pull their most suppressed memories from their subconscious. Some memories, they say, are so vivid it's as if the person is living them at the moment. No one knows why that happens. Perhaps chemicals in an aging brain trigger some physiological reaction, or because memories are forever, as they say, and when life is about to end, they pass before us like a movie.

One theory of memory Sister Regina had learned as a young nursing student is that everything we see and hear is embedded forever in our brains, much like a computer file. Sometimes we lose the password and can no longer access that file. Memory experts have learned that the secret to accessing those files is by using tricks and techniques that force open the memory bank. Sister Regina often wondered if, as our brains begin to age or we're on our deathbeds, those memory banks naturally unlock and flood our neurons with all things past and present.

Is that what was happening to Wanda? Was she suddenly remembering an entire lifetime of pain and joy and wanted to replay it like some movie passing before her eyes? Or was she simply responding to a physiological and uncontrollable drive to purge her memory bank before she died? Sister Regina had no idea why Wanda had chosen to unburden herself as she did, but she promised herself that if by doing so it would make Wanda's last days on earth a little better, she would gladly listen to it a hundred times over.

Chapter 23

Sandusky, Ohio
September 18, 2004

As her eyes darted back and forth, nothing in Wanda's room looked the least bit familiar except for a photograph that sat inches from the side of her bed, the edges of the silver frame dulled smooth by the touch of her fingers. Even the sound of Sister Regina's voice could not stir Wanda from thoughts of her beloved Janek.

"Wanda, can you hear me?" Sister Regina draped a blanket across Wanda's lap and left her to her thoughts.

Sitting motionless in her chair, Wanda's mind suddenly drifted back more than fifty years, when her only thoughts of war were how miraculous it was that they had all survived and were reunited in England. Those initial days in Liverpool were magical, as if time stood still and the war, with all its ugliness and despair, had never happened. But as days drifted into weeks and then months, and the reality of a new home in a foreign land crept into their day-to-day lives, little things would bubble up and emerge from their emotional hiding places.

Sophie, six years old when Janek had last seen her, was thirteen and struggling with changes to her body, as any teenager would, and suddenly confronted with having two parents after knowing only one. She'd matured beyond measure, having seen what no child should ever see. Wanda, having barely survived the torment and horrors of Siberian labor camps and the trauma of nearly losing her only child, was stricken with fear and nightmares and had become childlike herself. And Janek, a gulag prisoner who'd seen the very worst of humanity and then the very worst of war, could never again look at life in the same way. All three had been shattered, physically and emotionally, by the brutality of their circumstances and the cruelty of a world they felt had all but abandoned them.

But shattered as he was, Janek was determined to erase his past, settling down in Liverpool where he and his small family were accepted as perfect immigrants: white, Christian, and willing to do whatever their new country asked of them. For most, this would have been enough. But for Janek, who had grander dreams, Liverpool felt more and more like a respite, a place to gird one's loins before moving on to bigger and better things.

Following the devastation of war, England, though basking in its victory over Nazi Germany, stood battered and broken. In some cities, it looked more like a third-world country than an empire where the sun never set. Where once there was abundance, there was now widespread misery and scarcity. Rationing had become a daily struggle. Shelves lay bare. Shops, at one time bulging with goods, had been emptied of even the most basic and vital necessities. Janek and Wanda, who'd barely escaped the hunger and tyranny of Russia and Kazakhstan, had at first ignored their poverty and tolerated the Brits, who demonstrated to the world the meaning of keeping one's upper lip stiff and one's resolve even stiffer. But as the nation pulled itself out of malaise, nationalizing industries, instituting a socialized medical system, and rebuilding tattered infrastructure, Janek felt as though he and his fellow Poles were being left behind, abandoned orphans, unfortunate casualties of a once-grateful nation that desperately wanted to begin anew and sweep its past away.

Thankfully for Wanda and Janek, Liverpool was one of many cities and towns across the United Kingdom where Polish refugees were embraced because of Poland's contribution to the war effort. But as they'd soon learn, being welcomed as refugees often meant being treated as second-class citizens—second in line for housing, second in line for jobs, second in line for everything that mattered. And as the ravages of war faded slowly from everyone's memories, attitudes changed. An aloofness permeated society that Wanda could sense and see beneath her neighbors' smiles, as though they pitied the unfortunate Poles who had no other place to go and nothing to offer anyone else. Being welcomed with open arms, Janek would say, doesn't mean being treated equally. Even so, Janek, after what he'd lived through, was thankful that the city had become their home.

Unlike Lwow, Liverpool had the look and feel of a typical industrial town, a major port city with a large and important manufacturing base. But sections had been heavily bombed during World War II because Hitler considered it a strategic military target. Only London had been bombed more. The Battle of the Atlantic, the longest battle of World War II, lasting from September 1939 until May 1945, had been fought and won from Liverpool. But despite the bombings, much of Liverpool retained its charm as England's finest Victorian city, and Wanda and Janek would often stroll past sixteenth-century Tudors and along the ancient roads that still followed their medieval twists and turns.

Because the city's history, culture, and economy had attracted such a diverse population, as early as the nineteenth century it was described as "the New York of Europe." Even today, it is home to Britain's oldest Black community, as well as the oldest Chinese community in Europe. It has a rich tradition of religious diversity and is known as "the most Catholic city in all of England. For centuries it was the destination for migrants from across Europe, Africa, and Asia, and because of its reputation as a vital port city, Liverpool expanded its economy and remains one of the most important ports in the United Kingdom.

Eight hundred years old, the city's name originated from the Old English "lifer" meaning muddy water and "pol" meaning creek, the tidal creek which filled up when two converging streams drained into it. The Industrial Revolution, starting in 1760, triggered the city's rapid growth as a manufacturing center and a major port, becoming the port of registry for the ill-fated ocean liner *Titanic*, as well as the *Queen Mary*, the ship that Wanda and her family boarded when they set sail for America. But Liverpool had a dark side as well, serving as a hub for merchants involved in the Atlantic slave trade, with cotton, critical for Britain's textile industry, being shipped to England each day from America's Deep South after passing through the bloodied fingers of American slaves. It wasn't as if the British were ignorant of what was happening in the New World. They'd simply turned a blind eye for the same reason every rich cotton farmer in the South had. In fact, the historian Sven Beckert, during the American Civil War, had called Liverpool "the most pro-Confederate place in the world outside the Confederacy itself."

Whenever Janek spoke of his life in England, he'd do so with mixed emotions, one minute beaming with delight that such good fortune, after so much pain and suffering, had blessed his family, the next minute scowling as he'd lament his plight as a second-class immigrant who found it impossible to get ahead, no matter how much he tried. But with the war behind him and thoughts of gulags less frequent, Janek, at least for the time being, had seemed content to live his life in Britain's shadows.

It was there in those shadows that Janek had felt the first twinges of pain in the middle of his chest. At first, flinching and rubbing the depression where the old wound from Monte Cassino had often taunted him, he tried to assure himself that it was nothing more than that, because the pains would accompany screams of soldiers in his mind and images of men fighting valiantly while five thousand miles away those left behind lay dying and disappearing without a trace in the fields and forests of Russian Siberia.

As the pain grew sharper and more frequent, Janek knew it was not the shrapnel that ripped off a piece of his flesh that day but the strains of war, heavy smoking, and starvation in the gulag that had eaten away at his heart to the point that he would eventually need surgery. More angry than concerned, Janek had resigned himself to the fact that he'd become yet another casualty of war, not on the battlefield but years afterwards when it was all supposed to be over. And so, because the army, if anything, had taught him discipline, Janek replaced his unfiltered cigarettes with medication that would at least give his heart a chance at a longer life, and for the next fifty years, he'd not hold another cigarette in his fingers again.

By March 1948, Wanda was pregnant with their second child. The elation they both felt at another baby fifteen years after their first was quickly tempered by Janek's desperate itch to give his family a better life. Two children would only make that itch grow more unbearable. And so, wrestling with conflicting feelings and sadness that their lives would have to change, Janek and Wanda made the decision to once again bid their homeland farewell.

At week's end, after hearing that the United States had announced a new refugee quota, Janek applied to the immigration lottery system for entrance to America, where he could make the kind of life for his wife and children he'd dreamed of ever since the final shots of World War II were fired. There was no guarantee, as he would learn. The waiting list was long. Sponsors in the United States were required to ensure that immigrants had American families to guide them through the nuances of the system and help them with jobs and housing. And so, they waited.

Meanwhile, Elizabeth, their second child, was born on a cold winter morning, December 28, 1948. And once again, Janek and Wanda ignored the poverty that surrounded them, and instead basked in the joy of a new life. But happiness went only so far. Janek's eagerness to leave England consumed his days and tormented him at night. Wanda, whose new child filled her life like a breath of fresh air, was at least given some solace and comfort. The nightmares, however, returned. Little things—the burning pain in her legs, the bitter cold of Liverpool's winter, the rationing of food—would bring her back to the camps in Siberia, and she would sit and rub her legs and begin to cry.

Janek, whose own health had suffered from the brutality of prisons and gulags, could not decide if Wanda's was a simple case of postpartum depression or the subtle effects of long-term hunger. And hunger, from what Janek knew all too well, was too mild a word for the cruelty of what they had both experienced. Could starvation have somehow affected her brain, he wondered. Was the woman who stepped off the gangplank in England with Sophie and had embraced him in her arms with such joy not the same woman he'd left behind in 1939?

Janek would spend nights staring into the darkness, praying to God that Wanda could forget the years of torment she'd suffered, but he also knew in his heart that she'd probably been changed forever. If there was one thing about gulags and labor camps that affected their victims more than anything else, it was how hunger had overpowered everything else, the poor victims so overcome with the constant gnawing pain that every waking moment was consumed with thoughts of food and how they could snatch an extra morsel of bread or a spoonful of soup. Nothing else mattered. Because, according to experts, there is no greater driving force in human physiology than hunger. Not thirst, not fear, not safety, not sex, not even social bonds with other human beings. It is, in fact, the most viscerally primeval of all senses, and it was the reason that keeping slave labor in a constant state of hunger was at the core of behavioral control, as the Soviets discovered when establishing their maleficent system of gulags. Food, or the lack of it, they'd learned, was the greatest of all human motivators.

But what of starvation? Hunger was one thing, but starvation a different phenomenon altogether. During starvation, the body's only job is to do one thing: to preserve the brain at the expense of itself. Because of the blood-brain barrier, a system of capillaries that prevents most things from getting through to the brain, feeding those billions of neurons begins with the breakdown of fats and proteins into glucose, the principle nutrient that nourishes the brain.

Fat stores are the first to go, along with muscle. Once fat is gone, the body wastes away because muscle becomes the primary source of fuel for brain tissue. Within days, cells break down critical molecules and proteins, which release amino acids that are then converted into glucose. Prolonged starvation invariably leads to some degree of organ damage. The main cause of death from starvation, in fact, is cardiac arrest due to electrolyte imbalance, and because cells in the heart are literally being eaten alive.

But even though the brain does everything it can to maintain cognitive function, it eventually begins to metabolize itself in order to get the nutrients that will keep it alive. When that happens, the brain shrinks. But something even more sinister occurs. Starvation—and even hunger, for that matter—alters the brain's neural pathways and leads to marked changes in behavior. Hungry people, scientists had found, have different brains. They become more hostile. They make poor decisions. And they take risks they normally would not, which explains prisoners stealing from camp guards, despite the risks, or their willingness to have indiscriminate sex or even to kill.

Victims of starvation, because they lose muscle and nerve tissue, eventually become lethargic and apathetic, too weak to even sense thirst. They quickly dehydrate. Loss of fluids leads to dry and cracked skin, allowing microbes and fungi to invade the body. The fungi often settle beneath the cells of the esophagus, making swallowing painful while microbes attack vital organs and trigger a host of diseases.

Scientists don't really know the long-term psychological effects of hunger and starvation. What they do know is that the emotional effects can be more devastating and longer lasting than even physical disabilities. In the labor camps, prisoners were in constant fear that food would be used as a form of torture, withheld for even the smallest infractions. In both Nazi concentration and Soviet labor camps, prisoners were deliberately malnourished and starved. "Watery soup and a crust of bread were never enough to provide nourishment for hard labor," Janek would say. But that was the point. Fresh bodies worked harder and faster, and there was a seemingly endless supply. So why keep worn-out slaves when you could work them and starve them to death and simply replace the dead with new arrivals who'd start the cycle all over again? The Soviets, in particular, believed it was the most effective way to keep the camps and gulags running.

After Elizabeth was born, not much had changed. No matter what Janek did, he couldn't make his family's life much better. They were assigned to a makeshift refugee village constructed during the war, with small homes that each housed two families. Janek took any job he could—in factories or restaurants—while he waited for word about their immigration status. While they survived on meager wages and struggled to make ends meet, Wanda became pregnant for the third time. Three children with mouths to feed would make life in England even more difficult, and by the time Andrew was born, Janek felt a sense of hopelessness, especially since the U.S. Immigration Service moved at a snail's pace, making sure that whoever entered the country would not become a ward of the state.

But the summer of 1951 brought with it a joy that Wanda and Janek could not even imagine. Their immigration status was approved. Six months would be enough time to get their affairs in order, save a little more money, and arrange for passage across the Atlantic on the *Queen Mary*, which was sailing to New York in November. As Janek had described, for the next six months, whatever life they had in England did not much matter. They were going to America, though they would think of their beloved Poland every day—listening to national radio, trying to catch news clips of events happening in Eastern Europe—and when they did, they would say a prayer thanking God for delivering them from such evil. But sometimes they'd sit by the radio and begin to weep at what had happened to their nation and how it had been so easily swallowed up by evil men who thought the lives of ordinary people meant nothing.

It seemed almost surreal, Janek would say, that they'd lost everything, but at least they had their lives and they had each other, and when he thought of that, the world did not seem so bad after all. So, for Janek and Wanda, Poland was gone. England would soon be a memory. And America, though they had no idea what to expect from this new land an ocean away, was the place they could finally realize their lost hopes and dreams.

Chapter 24

Sandusky, Ohio
September 19, 2004

Her mind blank one minute then alert and lucid the next, Wanda had slept on and off throughout the day, wanting desperately to remember the joyous moments in her life and discard the rest. But to her misfortune, a brain in the fickle stages of dementia does not allow such capricious things. Her eyes filling with tears, Wanda remembered being alone and fearful as she called her son to tell him that his father was in the hospital awaiting surgery.

"Andrej, your father was sent to the hospital with terrible chest pains," Wanda had told her son. "He's having surgery to fix his bypass."

Andrew, the youngest of Wanda's three children, was not surprised by the call that morning, since his father had suffered with heart problems ever since he could remember. He was also not surprised that Janek would not tell his children about the surgery, insisting they not disrupt their busy lives until after he'd recovered. Andrew expected no less from someone who'd always calculated how his actions would affect others. It was how he served in the Polish Army and commanded his men, and he'd not changed one bit in the sixty-three years he and Wanda had been married. So, even though he knew it could be his last day on earth, he looked at Wanda and said, "Who am I to have everyone stop what they're doing just to see me lying in a bed? They can come once this is over."

"Is that you?" Wanda whispered beneath her breath as she reached out from her bed and tried to touch the image of Andrew's face in front of her. "Come in and see me, my son. I miss you." When she felt only air, she pulled back and closed her eyes, remembering the unusually blustery morning the day everyone had left her small apartment nestled along Scenic Highway in a quiet section of Pensacola. It was the last time she remembered seeing icicles dangle from porch banisters or slivers of frost lacing the dormant azaleas that lined the elegant homes along Escambia Bay. She suddenly pictured herself ten years younger, fighting back tears and watching tall pines whiz past their car on the way to the hospital, thinking at the time how quickly time had passed and how they'd both grown old before their eyes.

In the hallway outside Wanda's room, Sophie had just arrived for a visit, but stopped when Sister Regina took her by the arm and led her to two chairs.

"Is Mom okay?" Sophie asked, puzzled at Sister Regina's abrupt action.

"Today was not a good day, I'm afraid," Sister Regina warned. "Your mother's been going in and out for most of it. She even missed dinner."

"Progressively worse?"

Sister Regina nodded. "I'm not sure if she would even recognize you right now. She's been mumbling things about Poland and the war. Listening to her, I can't imagine what all of you must have gone through."

"Theirs was a hard life," Sophie said. "I've watched

my mother struggle to walk even a few steps, from her time in the labor camps, and my father taking labored breathes the last few years. Every time I've seen them, especially as they got older, I thanked God they had each other because they had no one else."

Sophie and Sister Regina turned in unison at the sound of Wanda's voice.

"Hurry to the hospital," Wanda shouted, her eyes widening, thinking back to a cold December drizzle that left everything in Pensacola glistening like jewels beneath the soft glow of streetlights. "Your father is very sick and…" Wanda suddenly fell silent, her eyes focused on the blackness outside her window as she thought back to the day when her life had changed forever:

On that frigid December morning, the thirty-minute drive to Sacred Heart Hospital had given Wanda a chance to accept the fact that Janek, after all he'd lived and gone through, might not make it through surgery. As they pulled into the parking deck and headed for the elevators, Wanda turned and fell into Andrew's arms, hoping for one more miracle. "I can't believe this is happening," she whispered into his chest. "It can't be real."

"There's always hope," Andrew tried assuring her. "He'll make it through surgery. I know it. He's a strong man."

Of course, she knew he wasn't. At least he hadn't been for a long time. And at his age, any operation, much less heart surgery, was complicated and more than risky. "Yes, there's always hope," Wanda answered, sounding more convincing than she really felt as they ascended to the fifth floor and were met by a flurry of nurses flying past them like flocks of white doves. Then, for whatever reason, perhaps because she was sensing the end of her own life, the minute she turned and began walking toward his room, visions of the past forty years suddenly flashed before her eyes.

Wanda shuffled one foot in front of the other, holding tightly onto Andrew's arm as her mind whirled nonstop through scenes of earlier years—emigrating to New York from England when Andrew was only a year old, settling down in the Bronx, and then spending beautiful summers in the Pocono Mountains where her children could swim in fresh water and feel grass beneath their feet. It was on those vacations that Wanda would listen to Janek tell stories to his children about life in their beloved Poland, then reminisce about the old country as frogs croaked and crickets chirped around them. By the end of the evening, they would all crawl into bed and gaze through their windows at a black sky dotted with endless stars, imagining what life would be like anywhere but the Bronx.

Their little cabin, the paint on its wraparound porch and white clapboards peeling like newly tanned skin, stood no more than fifty feet from the railroad tracks. So at least twice a week, when trains rumbled like thunder in the middle of the night, Wanda would force open her eyes and lie motionless, listening to the screech of a hundred wheels that instantly reminded her of the filthy trains that transported her and Sophie to the labor camps of Kazakhstan. Not until they had faded into the distance, and the images of torture and hunger and hard labor had seeped from her dreams, could she feel herself stop shaking, her deep breaths lulling her slowly back to sleep. So, for the next five years, Warsaw Village had become a summer refuge from the stifling heat and filthy streets of New York, a place where Janek's stories would come alive and take his children into a different world, but also a place where constant reminders of Poland and Russia would haunt her.

But as the years passed, Warsaw Village seemed to age along with everything else, though not in a graceful way. Nothing was the same—not the streets nor the little shops, not even the tiny Catholic church that drew fewer and fewer worshippers. The community simply grew sad, like a lovely garden that blooms with flowers and manicured bushes and then turns brown and lifeless from years of neglect. Wanda would often think, when she remembered those wonderful years, that life was like a movie with scenes you replay in your mind over and over again. Sometimes she'd catch glimpses of her past flashing before her eyes, making her smile, but mostly it left her melancholy and wishing she could do much of it all over again, differently this time. But what she remembered most fondly of all were those five summers she'd spent in that little cabin, watching Janek's face light up and then looking into his sad eyes whenever he began to speak of Poland.

By the spring of 1975, Wanda and Janek had finally packed up and headed for the sugar white beaches of Pensacola, Florida. By then, Janek was sixty-three and suffering with a heart condition he suspected began the day he left Wanda and Sophie behind in Lwow and headed west to fight a madman about to devour their nation. As one year melted into the next, his health grew progressively worse, but at least in Pensacola he could look out at the ocean, breathe in a lungful of salt air, and for a moment forget the pain in his chest.

Summers in Pensacola were sometimes mild but

often so hot and humid that clothes became a second skin. Winter, with its leaden skies and cold winds that blew sheets of mist from the south, gave way to the sweet smell of lilacs in the spring and an explosion of colors from azaleas and gardenias that lined every street. The scent of new rain and warm dew—crisp, fresh, and musty—was like walking into an outdoor bakery. Wanda had never forgotten that smell. Even as she grew old, at the first hint of a springtime drizzle, she'd close her eyes, take a deep breath, and go back to a time when her son and grandchildren would drive to her apartment along Scenic Highway for a Polish dinner and one more story to bring back home.

"How are you feeling, Mom?" Sophie asked as she walked into her mother's room, kissed her on the cheek, and wakened her from her memories.

"Who are…" Wanda thought for a second and smiled, and then turned sad. "Isn't that something?"

"What is?" Sophie asked.

"That we can so easily go back to a time and a place we've all but forgotten."

"What were you thinking about?" Sister Regina asked.

"It's been a long time since I've thought about those years in Pensacola…the giant oaks lining the dark waters of Escambia Bay. It's as if everything is merging into a second in time."

"Mom?" Sophie looked into Wanda's eyes and saw a tear run down her cheek. "What's wrong?"

Wanda didn't answer. She turned from Sophie and was back at Sacred Heart Hospital. By the time she arrived on Janek's floor, she was clutching onto Andrew's arm, about to see Janek for what she feared would be the last time.

Janek's nurse, a tall woman in her thirties named Kate, whose family had moved to Pensacola from Defuniak Springs when she was a teenager, had been assigned to his care. When Wanda walked into Janek's room that morning, she was hovering above him, taking his temperature and blood pressure. "This must be your family," she said, then turned to them with a broad smile. "I'm almost finished with my best patient, and then he's all yours."

Kate turned out to be a godsend, a wonderful and compassionate nurse who loved old vets and cared for them as if they were family. She'd later told Andrew that it wasn't until she spent her first night with Janek that she realized who this ordinary man was and how men like him had immeasurably transformed the course of history. And for three days and three nights, she learned how Jan—as she would affectionately call him—had defied all odds and left his family a tale of extraordinary valor. He convinced her that few really know these kinds of men, brave souls who were vanishing each day like ghosts, haunted by a past they rarely talked about, forgotten by friends and neighbors and even family, then lost to the obscure scribblings and footnotes of history. When Andrew sat with her one day, Kate revealed to him the incredible details of his father's life that Janek had shared with her. Because of those details, Janek and Kate and Andrew would never be the same again. Spellbound by what he was hearing, Andrew sat mesmerized, listening to his father's nurse as she described her first night with him.

As fate would have it, Kate, because of an especially virulent flu season, had been assigned work on her scheduled weekend off. Her shift that Saturday morning had begun uneventfully for a late December weekend. But as she pulled out a metal clipboard with the health chart of a male patient who'd just been admitted for surgery to repair an old bypass, she caught sight of a thin, elderly woman hovering next to the bed in his room.

"How are we doing today?" Kate asked as she walked in and put on her usually positive nurse face. She knew by the chart in her hand that it wasn't good.

"Okay, I guess," Janek answered. Wanda turned and acknowledged Kate's presence but didn't smile, her demeanor telling Kate at once that this was not the first time those two had been through something like this together.

"Your vitals look good," Kate reported matter-of-factly. "The doctor will be in shortly to discuss the procedure. And you are?" she asked Wanda, who was smartly dressed, though her clothes were simple, and Kate could see by her manicured nails, neatly coiffed hair, and perfectly applied makeup that age had not stopped her from proudly displaying an appearance that was simply beautiful for a woman she took to be at least eighty.

"Wanda," she whispered. She pronounced the W like a V, which indicated to Kate, from having visited Eastern Europe some years ago, that she spoke with a Slavic accent.

"We'll take good care of him," Kate said, noticing that Wanda could not have been more than five feet tall, with pale thin arms, her fragile fingers stroking Janek's head as if caressing a child. Stooped over him, she looked even smaller. Large, framed glasses that sat halfway down the bridge of her nose couldn't hide the visible anguish in her eyes.

"Wanda," she repeated, as though Kate didn't hear it the first time, then pursed her lips and continued brushing the few thin hairs on the side of Janek's head before falling into a chair beside him.

"Are you okay, Wanda?" Kate asked.

A tear ran down Wanda's cheek. She said nothing, just nodded once again.

"Are you sure?" Kate asked again.

"She's worried about me," Janek interjected half-jokingly, though there was obvious worry on his own face despite a facade of strength Kate had only seen on men—old vets, mostly, in her experience—who'd been through hell and lived to tell of it.

It seemed to Kate, from what she saw that first night, that Janek's failing heart could no longer keep up with his spirit; the frail body, which hinted of a once muscular physique, had long since given up whatever strength it had left. But each time she looked into his eyes, they'd draw her in, and, without a word spoken otherwise, he would begin to tell her stories.

The night Andrew arrived at the hospital, Kate took him off to the side and told him his father was very fragile but had an amazing spirit. "He's a strong man for his age," she assured him.

Andrew nodded and said, "We haven't spoken to his surgeon yet, but we're hoping for the best. He's been through this before."

"You okay?" Kate asked.

Andrew smiled and nodded weakly. "Thanks for what you're doing for him."

"I take care of old vets all the time here in Pensacola," she said, whose job it was to prep her patients for surgery. Most days were routine, she explained, often mundane, never boring. But there were days, she said, when she wished Pensacola wasn't such a navy town, or such a popular resting stop for old sailors and soldiers waging their final battles.

"Whoever said that old soldiers never die, they just fade away—I think it was General MacArthur—was wrong," she said. "For us, they never fade away."

And the more of those men she took care of, Kate said, the more wrong she thought that was, because she'd seen her fair share of old vets who never made it through surgery or who simply died waiting. It never got easier to let them go, their craggy faces rattling around in her mind for days until the next round of surgeries or the next time she'd have to unplug monitors and tell families there was nothing more anyone could do. So to make it more bearable, she said, nurses tried never to get close to their patients, never to look too deeply into their eyes or allow feelings to creep into their hearts; to simply accept the reality that once they were gone, it was on to the next patient.

But it wasn't that way with Janek, Kate had to admit. She told Andrew that after spending three days with him, she would see his face in every vet that looked her way, and there were moments, as she listened to the soft wind sweep past the oak trees in her backyard, that she could hear his gentle voice with its Polish accent, and it was like a song stuck in her head and wouldn't let go.

Pensacola would become Janek's final home, a typical navy town flanked on the east by Escambia Bay and on the south by the turquoise waters of the Gulf of Mexico that wash over the whitest beaches anywhere in the world. His street, along the other bay—Pensacola

Bay—was lined with crimson azaleas and giant gnarled oaks weeping with Spanish moss and spreading their arms to entangle their neighbors on either side. It was a quiet street, an even quieter neighborhood, with history behind it. Names like Cervantes, Tarragonia, Zaragoza, and Cevallos reminded one that ours were not the first ancestors to step foot on Florida's panhandle.

Originally settled by the Spaniards, who'd displaced a tribe of Native Americans called the Muscogee or Creek people, Pensacola—nicknamed the "City of Five Flags"—was later ruled by France, Great Britain, the Confederacy, and finally the United States. A thriving seaport, it's home to the first commissioned Naval Air Station in the United States and the base of the Blue Angels. Tourism and aerospace attract waves of northerners who feel the white sand between their toes, then pack their bags to come south where they knew they belonged all along.

But for Kate, Pensacola had always been a military town, a place where John Glenn and Neil Armstrong called home before reaching the stars; where the Southern Vietnam Veterans' Wall reminds visitors of fallen heroes; and where Civil War remnants like Fort Pickens stand like monuments to tell us, whenever the marsh winds blow past the turrets and stone towers, that on those hallowed grounds a generation of men lived and fought and died. She couldn't help thinking that perhaps this place, Pensacola, was an appropriate final resting stop for Janek. He was a military man, after all, and she'd known enough vets in her life to know that military men feel a bond with others who've seen the worst of war and the very worst of humanity.

The last time Kate sat by Janek's bed, he seemed

eager to tell her part of his story as if time were running out and no one else in the world would listen. Perhaps no one would, or perhaps he never had it in his weak heart to bring back so much pain. Whatever it was, Kate figured, he probably decided that life was too short, and getting shorter, and that his was a story that needed to be heard.

Chapter 25

Sandusky, Ohio
September 20, 2004

When Sophie looked over and watched her mother open her eyes, she saw no hint of a smile or emotion on her face. Sister Regina had spent much of the morning checking for any change in Wanda's condition. At ten o'clock, she swooped in and gave Sophie a grim look.

"Looked like you needed some coffee," Sister Regina said, placing two cups on the table next to Wanda.

"Thanks," Sophie said, then asked, "It's getting worse, isn't it?" She could see that it was by just looking at Sister Regina's face.

"I'm afraid so." Sister Regina nearly choked on her words. "The last few days have been bad. She hardly recognizes anyone. Last night she was mumbling something about England and Poland and their trip across the Atlantic on the *Queen Mary*. Those memories must be some of the few she has left. How were those final days in England? Did she have any regrets about leaving?"

"Some," Sophie answered softly, then thought back to their life in the refugee village that reminded them so much of a small Polish town, where they'd speak freely with Polish neighbors and lean on one another when life was almost too tough to get through and never seemed to be getting better; and though they knew it would be difficult to leave people they'd grown to love since the war ended, they were ready to move on. When they finally did, knowing they would likely never return, it was as if they'd once again lost everything they had.

Then, as if more than fifty years had passed in a second, Sophie thought back to the morning they all had tears in their eyes as they left their home for the last time and boarded a train to Southampton, where the *Queen Mary* was docked. It was such a grand ship, she remembered thinking. Not quite the *Titanic*, but with history behind it, and like nothing she'd ever seen. As they approached the enormous ship, the finality of her parents' decision had sunk in. She looked into her father's eyes and saw doubt and anguish. Was he making the right move? Would it have been easier to remain in a country they knew so well, that had welcomed them at a time when their own had rejected them? Not since that morning in Liverpool, she recalled, when she and Wanda had first set foot on English soil, had her father's heart ached with fear and apprehension. But once through immigration and on board the flagship of the British Cunard Line, their fears melted quickly into the mahogany and Art Deco that took them all to a world they never knew existed.

The *Queen Mary*, along with *RMS Queen Elizabeth*, was built to sail primarily over the North Atlantic Ocean, between Southampton and New York. Though her interior was more conservative than her French counterpart, the *Normandie*, the *Queen Mary* featured two swimming pools, beauty parlors, libraries, lecture halls, tennis courts, and even children's nurseries for all passenger classes. The main dining room, spanning a full three stories and lined with columns and wood-paneled walls, was the largest and grandest room on board. Of course, Janek and Wanda never saw it since it was reserved for first class passengers. Tourist class, 577 cabins of it, was confined to the regular dining room, which to them seemed luxurious compared to where they'd eaten their last meal.

Splendor exuded from every square inch of every wall and ceiling. From gilded entranceways to teak decks to bathrooms with Florentine tile and bronze faucets, it was as though they'd fallen asleep and entered a dream. They had just come from a place where refugees thanked God for hot water and leftovers to a place where people gorged themselves like pigs and threw out more food than Wanda would cook in a month. That first night, they strolled the decks and stopped every few minutes to marvel at it all. Nothing they'd ever seen compared. If this was what a ship carrying them to America was like, they wondered, what was America itself like? They weren't naïve enough to think that its streets were paved with gold, but surrounded by this kind of luxury, they started to believe they had made the right decision.

Influenced by the Art Deco movement of the 1930s, the *Queen Mary* would visually stun passengers as they boarded the ocean liner for the first time and drifted in awe past some of the most beautiful interior designs they'd ever seen. Elegant curves mixed with geometric forms enhanced the fifty species of luxurious wood culled from every corner of the world, some of which had gone extinct and could only be found lining the ship's passageways. For the "Ship of Woods," as the *Queen Mary* was called, nothing was too fine, inside or out. Every ballroom, every salon, every hallway screamed grandeur. As the ship rocked, it groaned under the weight of intricately decorative carvings, sculptures, exquisite paintings, and marble-accented murals so grand that passengers thought they'd boarded a museum in Paris and not an ocean liner. What a shockingly different life Janek and Wanda had suddenly found themselves in, along with the thousand other poor refugees who gazed in awe at the decadence that enveloped every square inch of the ship.

Janek and Wanda had learned that four years after its maiden voyage, the *Queen Mary* sat idle in the port of Southampton until plans were set into motion to convert her into an Allied troopship. Leaving from New York in March 1940, it had sailed to Sydney, Australia, where the conversion began. Like a dazzling butterfly turning back into its cocoon, the majestic liner had slowly morphed into a "Gray Ghost" as she'd become known. Navy gray replaced her brilliant black and white colors. Stateroom furniture and artwork were removed to make space for three-tiered bunks that housed thousands of troops ferried across the Atlantic. Every exposed piece of fine wood was covered with leather, while miles of carpet was ripped from stateroom floors. Finally, her entire hull was wrapped in a special degaussing coil to protect against German mines the Nazis had laid as close as a hundred miles offshore.

When all was said and done, in a single five-day voyage as many as 15,000 men would sail across the Atlantic to join the Allied Forces in Europe. It had seemed like a miracle, but because of her great speed—the *Queen Mary* was capable of speeds up to thirty-five miles per hour—and her ability to set a course in zigzag patterns, not a single German U-boat was capable of keeping up with and catching her as she roared through waves sometimes fifty feet high. Following the war, the *Queen Mary* retreated into her cocoon, was refitted for passenger use, and once again emerged as the elegant butterfly she'd always been. What Janek and Wanda saw as they first stepped aboard her freshly painted decks and railings was a ship even grander and more glamorous than what had sailed before the war.

Sister Regina, pouring Sophie another cup of coffee, asked, "Was sailing on the *Queen Mary* everything people say it was?"

Sophie nodded, a smile crossing her face as she remembered the grand ship as it set sail in November of 1951, when the north seas turned unusually frigid and violent, tossing her back and forth in her cabin for days. Once they arrived in New York, the immigration service had changed their strict immigration policy, and Janek had unexpectedly been given a choice to either go on to meet their sponsor in Buffalo or to remain behind in New York City. Wanda and Janek didn't hesitate for a moment to make New York their new home.

"Like most immigrants," Sophie explained, "we arrived with nothing but a few suitcases of clothing and the little money my parents had saved to get by until my father found work. The city put us up in a rotting three-room Manhattan apartment building converted for refugees. It got so hot in the summer we could hardly breathe, but it was cheap, and it was a place to lay our heads and dream of better days. My father took whatever work he could, in restaurants and factories mostly, and when he finally landed a decent paying job, we left the roaches behind and moved to a better place in the Bronx.

With a few more dollars to spend, my father was able to attend night school and eventually get a job as an engineer. With his first decent paycheck, we began to see the fruits of his labor pay off, so we moved again to a better place and a better neighborhood."

Sophie stopped to reflect, with a mix of sadness and fondness, how Janek would often say that the time he spent in the Bronx was wonderful, despite their living conditions. "If you drive through that part of the Bronx now," Sophie said, "you'd never know how good a neighborhood it was back then. Yes, the five-story apartments were old, there was no air-conditioning, no elevators, only two bedrooms, but it was the first time since leaving Poland that my parents felt at home. The entire neighborhood was built around Saint Adalbert church, a parish devoted to serving Polish immigrants in the area. Times were different. It was the Bronx, but you could send children out to play and tell them to be back by suppertime. No one even thought about what could happen because nothing ever did. By the time they moved there, I'd already met someone, got married, and moved to Greenpoint in Brooklyn."

"Saint Adalbert," Wanda suddenly whispered, turning to Sophie and breaking into a broad smile at hearing her daughter's voice. "I remember that old apartment building across the street from Saint Adalbert's school. It was a godsend."

Wanda's eye's sparkled as if back in the Bronx, remembering the aging and dilapidated buildings lining 155th Street. Tucked so closely together one could almost jump from one rooftop to the next, their better days had come and gone, but they sat directly across from the Catholic grammar school, where Wanda could look down from her fifth floor window and watch the children scurry at hearing the school bell ring, march in rows past the convent steps, and disappear through a set of large double doors for the next six hours.

But it was also painful for her to see the little ones running around on dirty asphalt streets instead of the emerald, green fields she loved so much in Poland. Sometimes Wanda cried like a child, wishing it were all a dream and she could just open her eyes and be back in Lwow. Christmas was especially difficult. But making pierogi, borscht, babka, and cookies like she did back in Poland occupied her mind and at least made her sorrow a little more bearable.

Despite their poverty, it was a joy having her children attend a Polish Catholic school, go to mass and listen to a homily in Polish, mingle with parishioners who'd reminisce about the old country, and go back in time whenever she stepped foot inside the corner bakery on Sunday morning to buy babka and paczki. But she'd also turn melancholy whenever she watched Janek grimace at the pain in his chest, not because she knew that heart surgery was not far off but because each twinge of pain reminded her of Poland and that what she smelled in that bakery each Sunday morning would be the closest she would ever come to the real thing.

"What are you thinking, Mom?" Sophie asked, seeing her mother's face turn pale.

"Janek," Wanda mouthed, recalling how difficult it had been for him. "We had no air-conditioning...no elevators. I don't know how he managed climbing five flights of stairs every day...I don't..."

Sister Regina took Wanda's hand and stroked it gently, watching the expression on her face wash away into a blank stare once again. "You get some rest now, love," she said.

"Mom worried all the time about my father's heart condition," Sophie said. "It was only medication at first. He got his first real job, a good one, and he didn't want to do anything to jeopardize it."

"Like having heart surgery," Sister Regina said.

"He delayed it as long as he could. Back then, it was a big deal. It was the fifties. You didn't know if you'd even survive the operation. So he decided to wait."

And then, as Sophie's eyes welled up, she remembered how her father would take the younger children to a park and play with them, all the while taking nitroglycerine pills to ease the sharp daggers in his chest. "It would have been more painful not playing with them, he once said, so he took his pills and fought through the agony as best he could."

By the time Janek turned fifty, the daggers had grown into what he described as unbearable suffering. Pills were no longer enough. The walk up five fights might as well have been five times that. He'd stop at each flight and rest until the pain subsided and he could once again breathe the hot, stale air between floors. But the final straw had come when he took his son, Andrew, out to play catch and felt himself grow so weak and out of breath—even after putting two nitros beneath his tongue—that to do nothing was to commit suicide in front of his own child's eyes. The next day, Janek's doctor, telling him that he was lucky to be alive, had scheduled immediate surgery.

For a while, Janek was fine. No pain. No other symptoms. But a few years after that first surgery, he felt discomfort in his chest while working on a project at work, and he knew at that moment that it would be a lifetime struggle. And though he'd changed his lifestyle, the stress of living in New York only worsened the heart problems he would suffer with the rest of his life.

"Your history," as Janek would often say, "catches up with you." Unfortunately, Janek had too hard and too much of a history to overcome. As the years passed, those wonderful and intimate experiences with friends and neighbors on 155th Street in the Bronx had begun to fade. The neighborhood's face was changing, buildings and streets decaying, crime, at one time an afterthought, gradually seeping in like a cancer from surrounding areas. When Polish families moved on to better lives, they left behind a void impossible to fill by new immigrants with different customs and foreign views of history and culture. And like sand that swirls and shifts in a constant and imperceptible wind, the streets around Saint Adalbert's sadly but inexorably changed before his very eyes.

Janek knew it was time to leave when his walk between home and the closest subway station—some eight long blocks—would leave him exhausted by the time he arrived at work or came home at night. The sweltering heat of long New York summers followed by cold damp winters did little to improve his health and, in fact, exacerbated the pains that grew more frequent and increasingly more severe. So, by 1964, Janek and Wanda, with heavy hearts and fond memories of Saint Adalbert's, had reluctantly joined the migration away from their neighborhood. After several more moves, they found themselves in the heart of Pelham Bay.

It was the first time since their exile from England that Wanda and Janek did not have to brush cockroaches from their breakfast plates each morning. Wanda found work as a seamstress, which helped pay for their newfound lifestyle and brought some much-needed comfort and purpose to her life. The pain in her legs, though, and the constant thoughts of Poland, continued to haunt her, but their home in Pelham Bay, with clean sidewalks and flowering trees outside their windows, was like a little bit of heaven.

Janek, despite taking pride in his work and their new home, found life in New York harsh and unbearable. He'd sit alone in his living room, listening to Chopin and questioning how they had survived the war and the gulags and the labor camps and were now living in comfort while so many others remained behind, buried in the frozen tundra, forgotten by friends and family, never thought of again. "Why did God choose to spare us but not others?" he'd often ask himself, and then realize that God, despite His infinite goodness, does not control the actions of mankind.

Sister Regina pulled a blanket across Wanda's chest. She turned back to Sophie and asked, "Did your father talk to you much about the war?"

"Only when Mom was not around," Sophie said. "She hated talking about it. They say people can sense the end coming, maybe not like a flash but in more subtle ways. Maybe that's why Dad was so anxious to tell the stories he did, and why it seemed so urgent for him to gather his memories and relish them one more time before taking them to his grave."

"He almost died at Monte Cassino, from what I hear."

"He told me that story many times," Sophie said. "Monte Cassino was the defining moment of his life during the war. He was so proud of being a part of it, but he was never the same after that."

Sophie fell silent as she remembered listening to her father recount the legend of the red poppies that grew wild in the fields surrounding Monte Cassino. They grew redder over the years because of the blood shed by Polish soldiers who'd crossed the fields and died as they bravely stormed the abbey. That legend, Janek had told her, was memorialized by an anthem, *The Red Poppies on Monte Cassino*, composed on the eve of the Polish army storming the monastery and is familiar to most Poles. When she looked it up one day, Sophie thought of what her father had gone through and cried.

> *The red poppies on Monte Cassino*
> *Drank Polish blood instead of dew*
> *O'er the poppies the soldiers did go*
> *Amid death, and to their anger stayed true!*
> *Years will come, and ages will go*
> *Enshrining their strivings and their toil!*
> *And the poppies on Monte Cassino*
> *Will be redder for Poles' blood in their soil.*

"Are you okay?" Sister Regina asked.

Sophie wiped her eyes and said, "I'm fine, just tired. I'll be back tomorrow." She bent over and kissed Wanda on her forehead, hoping to have just one more day like this one.

Chapter 26

Sandusky, Ohio
September 21, 2004

Wanda could barely open her eyes, lying motionless, her gaze fixated on the open window next to her bed. The moonlit sky illuminated the trees above the garden, triggering faint memories from a time when she thought her fragile world would come crashing to an end. Her breathing erratic and shallow, Wanda's mind seemed to clear as she pictured her life in New York, her pain and suffering, her joys and sorrows, good memories and bad. What sort of cruelty is this, she remembered thinking, that after finally realizing their own American dream, their lives would once again be devastated by crushing news that Sophie's oldest son—her first grandchild—had committed suicide. Whatever she and Janek had gone through, she thought at the time, could not compare to the sorrow and despair at hearing those words from her daughter: "Paul died from a gunshot wound to the head."

For the next few heart-wrenching years, she, but especially Janek, would not be the same. Though his other grandchildren had brought immeasurable joy to his life, nothing could ever fill the void of losing his first grandchild, and Janek would spend the rest of his life partly blaming himself and wondering if there was anything he could have done to prevent his precious grandson's death. Wanda often thought that it wasn't the war that had permanently broken Janek's heart but the misery and despair of such a senseless death.

Tears suddenly formed in Wanda's eyes as her memory turned from her grandson to the hospital where Janek had been scheduled for emergency surgery. She remembered thinking how senseless it all was, why some died in the blink of an eye while others like her and Janek were spared and survived to live long and beautiful lives. What was so special about *us*, thought Wanda, that we'd be chosen to live through such evil while so many perished and were never heard from again? Her heart ached at the possibility of her beloved Janek dying, at the thought of this wonderful and unlikely survivor closing his eyes to the world for the last time and having so few people who had heard and knew his incredible story.

Wanda remembered her chest feeling as if it were being crushed as she shuffled from the parking deck to the main lobby and into the elevator. When she'd left Janek the night before, he looked much frailer than she'd ever seen him, a ghost of a soldier in the twilight of his life. What would she do if the man who'd taken such loving care of her did not make it through surgery, she'd questioned. How could she go on without him? She recalled the hospital elevator doors opening, being overcome with a feeling she'd not experienced since her grandson's death, and a quiet, palpable gloom filling the air.

"Good morning," said Janek's nurse, who'd come in early for her shift, no trace of a smile on her face.

"I thought we'd drive in and check on Dad before he went in for surgery," Andrew had said, looking anxiously at the nurse and then toward his father's room.

The nurse gave Wanda a sorrowful look and said, "I'm sorry, but your husband was having such bad chest pains last night they took him in for surgery early this morning."

"How is he?" Wanda's heart, feeling as if in her throat, was racing. "Is he okay?"

Just as the nurse was about to answer, the surgeon appeared and stood next to her. Wanda could still hear the words in her mind: "I'm sorry," she remembered him saying. "Your husband had a massive stroke during surgery. They've got him on a ventilator until the rest of your family arrives. We're so sorry for your loss."

Wanda's room seemed to go black as she wrapped her fingers around both arms, thinking back to the words she knew she would remember until her last breath: "I and the staff did everything we could."

Andrew had steadied her as she buckled and nearly collapsed but then staggered down the hall toward Janek's room. When they turned and walked in, what they saw was not Janek but the shell of the man they'd spoken to not twelve hours earlier.

"Is there any hope?" Wanda asked the nurse who'd been there all morning with him. She feared what she would hear next.

The nurse shook her head. "I'm afraid there's no brain activity. The neurologist who examined him confirmed it. Once we take him off the ventilator, everything will stop."

And then, as Wanda stared down at the lifeless fingers she'd held every time she sat with him, she thought of all those years that Janek had suffered but, despite that, how he'd done everything for her, from the moment he held her in his arms when she walked off the ship in Liverpool until the day he was admitted to the hospital. What would she do now, she wondered. How would she go on without the man she adored and who'd sacrificed every day of his life to make up for what she and Sophie had been through. She spent the next two hours in Janek's room, anticipating how family members would react after getting word that their father and grandfather was now on life support.

By eight o'clock, the rest of the family had arrived and gathered by Janek's bedside, all feeling in their hearts the kind of sadness one feels at only a few moments in life. Crying softly into a handkerchief, Wanda sat hunched in the chair she'd made her own for the past three days. Her three children stood by her side. The grandchildren wiped tears from their eyes and watched silently at the foot of Janek's bed as his chest artificially rose and fell with the rhythm of his ventilator.

When Andrew spotted Janek's nurse, Kate, in the hallway, he went to her and extended his hand. "Thank you for being there for my father," he said. "I'm sure he appreciated everything you did for him."

"He did," Kate answered. The words barely came out. "I knew him as Janek, you know."

Andrew looked at his father's nurse with surprise. "No one's called him that in years. Not even my mother." He smiled at that, though it made him a little sad that his father wanted Kate to call him by the name he'd left behind in Poland.

"He was such a wonderful man," Kate said. "We talked every day whenever your mother wasn't with him, and he told me some incredible stories about Poland and the war."

Andrew's face stiffened, his eyes growing moist. "Thank you for that," he said. "My father didn't talk that much about his past, especially when my mother was around. I knew his story but always assumed he wanted to put that part of his life behind him. You're very fortunate he shared some of them with you. And I'm sure it was good for him to tell someone other than his family." Wiping tears from his eyes, Andrew reached out and hugged Kate. "Thanks again for being there for Dad when he needed it most."

"How's your mom doing?" Kate asked.

"Going back to North Carolina with us," Andrew said, "where she'll be with family who love her as much as my father did."

"You know, I've never met anyone quite like him," Kate said. "He was a true hero, and there aren't too many of them left. You should be proud."

Andrew nodded and thanked her again, though her kind words were not enough. When he headed back into Janek's room, he took hold of Wanda's frail hand as she leaned over and rested her head against his arm. Seeing her in such sorrow broke his heart, and all he could think of at that moment were the stories his father had told him about her life in Poland and Kazakhstan, which he knew could not compare to the pain she was feeling as she stared almost lifelessly at Janek's body, as she must have watched her entire life flash before her eyes.

"Your dad was special," Kate had said as she walked with Andrew outside Janek's room. "He really got to me."

"Tell me," Andrew said, curious to know why she thought his father was any more special than her other patients.

Of course Andrew knew the answer before Kate could say another word, because Janek was not like most people who simply meandered through life as if not much else in the world mattered, people who wake up, go to work, come home, bitch about their day, watch TV, climb into bed, and start the routine all over as soon as the alarm brings them back to reality. Kate had to admit that much of her own life was like that, and on most days she thought herself lucky in her ignorance and bliss, confined to a little corner of her world, oblivious to the pain and suffering she couldn't see. But since meeting Janek, the world for Kate had become a smaller place. She no longer thought of Poland or Russia or the Middle East as far away destinations one reads about in travel brochures, but real places where people like Wanda and Janek had lived and worked, made love, got married, sang and danced at weddings, had children and grandchildren, grew old together, and cried at funerals.

"When your dad talked to me, I really felt like I was a part of his story," Kate told Andrew, "because up until now, I never met anyone quite like him, and I never knew people like your dad outside the pages of history books. He was the first person I ever met who was in a gulag."

Andrew nodded and smiled. He walked back into his father's room, sat by Wanda, and reflected on the stories he'd heard over the past thirty years. He'd never thought about it that way, never really appreciated what his parents had gone through…because it was simply part of their history. At least Wanda, whom Janek had cared for, especially as she grew older and knew her days were coming to an end, would not have to anguish over what she'd do or where she would go. North Carolina, a place that Janek had once said reminded him so much of the

Polish mountains, would be the place she'd call home.

Taking a few labored breaths, Wanda stared out her window and pictured her family, who had all travelled from three states, walking into and out of Janek's room, milling about, visiting with one another, exchanging pleasantries, finding solace in each other's arms, sometimes laughing, but mostly crying. She thought how sad it was that people became so preoccupied with their own lives that they could find little time for each other except at weddings and funerals. Not that she blamed them. She just wished at that moment they could all hold each other more often before they passed from this life.

And then she remembered the shudder that ran through her body as Kate said, "As soon as everyone's done, the doctor thinks it's time to disconnect everything. I have the papers here for you to sign." Wanda could still see the pen shaking in her fingers, and how, as soon as she finished signing her name, everyone had stepped out of the room and waited for Janek's nurse to unhook his life support and announce to her that it was done.

"My darling," Wanda whispered in the quiet solitude of her room, picturing Andrew taking her hand and walking back into Janek's room. She remembered barely standing upright, tears in her eyes, looking on as each of Janek's grandchildren took turns stroking his head and kissing him goodbye as his breath slowed and finally stopped. As much as she wanted to keep him breathing, at least for a few more minutes, she'd accepted that he was finally gone. The man who'd suffered and sacrificed so much, the father and husband who'd lived a life that few people could even comprehend, would soon be just a memory.

And now, almost ten years later, she could still see his face, still remember not a war hero but a loving and decent man, so unassuming that to work with him, meet him on the street, or sit next to him in a coffee shop where he'd eat his favorite cherry pie you would never know who he was or what he had done. And other than his children and grandchildren, not even his closest neighbors really knew his story.

Wanda spent her next four years in North Carolina before deciding she wanted to live out her remaining days with Sophie. Her health deteriorating, her legs barely able to hold her upright, she relocated to Sandusky, Ohio where she could look at her daughter's face and remember the years they'd spent together in labor camps and lived to tell of it. But more than that, she needed a soulmate, someone who understood the pain and horrors of war and all its tragic consequences. The little time she'd spent with Sophie before having to move into a nursing home because of progressive dementia were some of the best years of her life. But sometimes, despite the joy of having her precious daughter by her side again, memories of war would surface and take hold of her as though she'd suddenly been transported back to Lwow. As Wanda would often say to her daughter, as she'd sit in their garden and stare blissfully off into the distance, "I'll take care of you, my love. We'll get through this together and we'll be home soon. Your father will be waiting for us."

Sister Regina had gone home early for the evening, hoping to see signs of improvement when she returned the next morning. The nursing home grew quiet soon after, its residents having finished dinner and settling in for the night. For hours, Wanda lay in her bed, confused and disoriented, but at times remembering bits and pieces of her life that brought her both joy and sorrow. Afraid to fall asleep, it terrified her that each breath might be her last, and though she believed with all her heart that she'd be in a better place, all she wanted was one more day to live her life.

Finally, as Wanda closed her eyes and took a few labored breaths, her mind drifted back again to that hospital room in Pensacola, where her beloved Janek had spent the last three days of his life. "My love," she said, raising her arm toward him, seeing his face as clearly as if he were there with her. She held her breath for a second. Then, with all the energy she could gather, she whispered, "After all we've been through…all we've suffered…we're finally together again."

And with those words, Wanda slipped away, leaving her precious children and grandchildren with stories of love and sacrifice and the unspeakable horrors of war that made ordinary people like her and Janek shine brilliantly in the darkest moments of history, like embers in the night, living lives that most could not even imagine, lying forgotten in obscure and unmarked graves, fading bit by bit from each generation's memories like the fleeting and cold winter mists of Pensacola Bay.

A word about the author...

Andrew Goliszek received a Ph.D. in Physiology from Utah State University. He was a research associate at Wake Forest University School of Medicine in both the department of Physiology and Pharmacology and the department of Medicine.

Following that, he was Associate Professor of Biology and Human Anatomy & Physiology at North Carolina A&T State University, received several NIH research grants, and was the recipient of the prestigious College of Arts & Sciences Faculty of the Year Award for excellence in teaching, research, and student advising.

He has written numerous articles and books and currently lives on the coast of North Carolina with his wife.

For photos and Polish documents and other items of interest regarding this book and its author, please go to the author's website:

www.andrewgoliszek.com

Thank you for purchasing
this publication of The Wild Rose Press, Inc.

For questions or more information
contact us at
info@thewildrosepress.com.

The Wild Rose Press, Inc.